Praise for *New York Times* bestselling author Tanya Michaels

"Michaels...gives a familiar plot an interesting and fantastic twist—one that's laden with terrific charm and sexy sparks."

—*RT Book Reviews* on *Mistletoe Cinderella*, 4.5 stars, Top Pick

"*His Valentine Surprise* is a delight and I hope the beginning of another one of [her] series."

—*Dear Author* on *His Valentine Surprise*

"A sweet, heartwarming, fun and steamy story that you will not be able to put down."

—*Harlequin Junkie* on *Her Secret, His Baby*

Praise for *New York Times* bestselling author Virna DePaul

"Tender scenes...leading to a dramatic ending, will touch readers' hearts."

—*RT Book Reviews* on *Texas Stakeout*

"Lots of tension and thick suspense lead to a fast-paced story. Add to that a complex, vulnerable hero, and you're left with a great read."

—*RT Book Reviews* on *Deadly Charade*

"Plenty of chemistry between the leads—along with edge-of-your-seat suspense—will keep you riveted."

—*RT Book Reviews* on *Shades of Passion*

HOME ON THE RANCH:
THE TEXAS COWBOY WAY

———— ⚒ ————

New York Times **Bestselling Authors**
TANYA MICHAELS
VIRNA DePAUL

**Previously published as *Claimed by a Cowboy*
and *Texas Stakeout***

H HARLEQUIN® HOME ON THE RANCH
TM

ISBN-13: 978-1-335-50713-6

Home on the Ranch: The Texas Cowboy Way
Copyright © 2018 by Harlequin Books S.A.

First published as Claimed by a Cowboy by Harlequin Books in 2012 and Texas Stakeout by Harlequin Books in 2014.

The publisher acknowledges the copyright holders of the individual works as follows:

Claimed by a Cowboy
Copyright © 2012 by Tanya Michna

Texas Stakeout
Copyright © 2014 by Virna DePaul

Recycling programs for this product may not exist in your area.

HARLEQUIN®

Printed in U.S.A.

™www.Harlequin.com

CONTENTS

Eight-time RITA® Award finalist **Tanya Michaels** is the *New York Times* bestselling author of more than forty books and novellas. Her stories, praised for their poignancy and humor, have received awards from readers and reviewers alike. Tanya lives outside Atlanta with her two teenage children. Together, the three of them watch way too much TV, which Tanya happily justifies as the study of plot arcs and characterization.

Books by Tanya Michaels

Harlequin Western Romance

Cupid's Bow, Texas

Falling for the Sheriff
Falling for the Rancher
The Christmas Triplets
The Cowboy Upstairs

Harlequin American Romance

Hill Country Heroes

Claimed by a Cowboy
Tamed by a Texan
Rescued by a Ranger

The Colorado Cades

Her Secret, His Baby
Second Chance Christmas
Her Cowboy Hero

Visit the Author Profile page at Harlequin.com for more titles.

CLAIMED BY A COWBOY

TANYA MICHAELS

This book is dedicated to Jane Mims (what would I do without you?), who graciously chauffeured me around the hill country in spite of the world's most diabolically uncooperative GPS.

Chapter 1

The fifth floor of the insurance company was impressively quiet. Nothing so crass as *noise* leaked from the opulent and distinguished conference rooms at the end of the long corridor—which made junior actuary Lorelei Keller want to cringe at the staccato echo of her navy pumps against the marble tile. She preferred to stand out in meetings because she possessed a lightning-quick mind, not because everyone could hear her coming from a mile away.

As if her footfalls weren't making her self-conscious enough, the cell phone in her jacket pocket suddenly buzzed. Even with the ringer turned off, the vibration seemed loud in the empty hall. She fished the phone out to check the display screen and scowled. Though no name showed, the 830 area code meant Fredericksburg, Texas. More specifically, her mother. Again.

Exhaling an impatient breath, Lorelei turned the phone off completely and repocketed it. Wanda Keller was her only immediate family and Lorelei loved the woman. But mother and daughter were painfully dissimilar. Graduating from an Ivy League university had been easier for Lorelei than getting through to her mom. *Not that I'm deliberately avoiding her.* She fully intended to call Wanda back later, after business hours. Headed into a meeting with one of the company's top executives was not the time to rehash their argument about Lorelei's refusal to visit at the end of the month.

"You loved Frederick-Fest as a child," Wanda had burbled just two days ago, sounding as enthusiastic as a child herself. She claimed the timing of the week-long March event would be extra festive this year, since its dates fell over St. Patrick's Day—never mind that their ancestry was German, not Irish—and the spring equinox.

"But I'm not a kid anymore," Lorelei had pointed out as gently as possible. "I have adult responsibilities, like a job I worked hard to get."

"They have to give you vacation time, don't they?" Wanda had persisted.

Lorelei had bit her tongue to keep from saying anything cruel. Like, *I'm not about to use up vacation to come help sell crystals and hand out bookmarks on the protocol for "What to Do if You Encounter a Hill Country Ghost."* "I've got a really busy month ahead of me, Mom."

Wanda's voice, which had been by turns cheerfully cajoling and stubbornly challenging, fell to a barely audible level. "You haven't been home in over a year."

Home. How could Lorelei explain that Texas hadn't felt like home since her father had died twenty years ago? Her freshman year of college, Lorelei had joked with her roommate about "Philadelphia freedom" because moving to Pennsylvania truly had liberated her. She'd been free of living in a house that was a shrine to her dad, free of her mother's increasingly bizarre beliefs. Lorelei had soothed her frazzled nerves with the orderly logic of numbers and let her first snowy Pennsylvania winter numb a decade of tangled emotions.

"You know I had to cancel at Christmas because I had the flu," Lorelei had defended herself. "I'll come down for a visit this year. I promise."

"When?"

"I don't know, Mom. Soon." Soonish, anyway. "But not this month, okay? I'll look at my calendar, talk to my boss and get back to you."

Her mother had sighed, clearly skeptical. "Sure. I'll be here."

Reaching for the door to the conference room, Lorelei gave a quick shake of her head, her long dark hair swirling about her shoulders, and banished the memory of her impulsive promise. Now was the time to focus on the more pressing topic of risk management. One of the few women in her department, she was determined to distinguish herself among her colleagues. She straightened her spine and stepped into the office, her footsteps now swallowed by the plush carpet. But a last lingering stab of guilt pierced her. *I'll talk to my supervisor tomorrow about vacation time.* Conscience appeased, Lorelei lost herself in the two-hour meeting, all thoughts of Texas and her mother pushed aside.

Lorelei was seated at her desk, immersed in notes for a liability audit, when a male voice said, "Knock

knock," from the doorway. She glanced up to see Rick Caulden.

He flashed a knowing smile. "You forget about me again? Reservations? Tuesday night? Any of this ringing a bell?"

"Of course I remember. I've been looking forward to our dinner. I just thought you were going to call when you got here." She enjoyed her periodic dates with the handsome attorney.

Employed by a law firm several blocks away, Rick worked as hard as she did. He was charming but refreshingly unsentimental. They shared the same pragmatic streak and career drive.

"Tried calling," he said. "Kept going straight to voice mail, so I decided I should come up, find out if your meeting ran long and if I was on my own for dinner."

"Oh, right—I turned my phone off before the meeting and totally forgot to turn it back on." A mistake, or a Freudian slip? Had she deliberately left it off because she suspected Wanda would call back? Maybe Lorelei had been trying to avoid the guilt trip of feeling like an ungrateful daughter yet again.

As soon as Lorelei repowered the phone, a message bubble appeared. She frowned. "Wow, that's a *lot* of missed calls."

"At least three of them are me," Rick said.

And the other six? "Hang on a sec." She stood, gathering her purse and coat. "I just want to check voice mail before we go."

"Sure." He smirked. "I always make our reservations for fifteen minutes later than I tell you. I know how difficult it is to drag you out of the office."

Under different circumstances, she might have

pointed out that she spent an equal amount of time waiting on him or assuring him she didn't mind canceling because he needed the extra time to prepare a motion or speak with a client. Right now, she was more concerned with her messages than Rick's unexpected double standard.

Because of the 830 area code on the missed calls, Lorelei assumed her mother was phoning from one of the hotel lines instead of her private number. But it wasn't Wanda's voice that greeted her.

"Lorelei? I don't know if you remember me, but this is Ava Hirsch."

As if Lorelei had been gone so long she wouldn't recall her mom's best friend? Though Ava's husband was of the vocal opinion that Wanda was "a gallon shy of a keg," the two women had always been inseparable.

"I'm calling…" Ava stopped, sniffed and tried again. "I'm calling about your mother, dear."

At the end of the sentence, Ava's voice broke and the world tilted beneath Lorelei's feet. She groped blindly for her chair.

"Lorelei? What is it?" Rick's concern sounded miles away; Ava's condolences were even more distant, fading beneath the pounding in Lorelei's ears.

But Lorelei didn't need to hear the rest of the message to know. She was going home to Fredericksburg, after all.

Chapter 2

Sam Travis was well-versed in the ghosts of Texas lore—he'd shared many a local legend with tourists around the campfire—but he'd never felt haunted until now.

No matter which room he moved to in the bed-and-breakfast, he still saw his landlady, eccentric Wanda Keller, who had been mothering him on and off for the past three years. *Maybe I should have left with the others.* As of this morning, there had been two other guests staying at the inn. Another proprietor in town had promptly offered them free rooms in light of the tragedy. Wanda had been well-liked in town, even by loners like Sam.

Sam worked multiple seasonal jobs that kept him in motion, but he always circled back to Wanda's, helping her with minor repairs and enjoying her cooking for a week or so before leaving again. It had taken him over a year of just being able to show up, his usual room always vacant, before he'd realized that she held it perpetually open for him. When he'd insisted she shouldn't do that, she'd called him *dummkopf* and responded that it was her inn and she'd do whatever she liked. This B and B, now painfully devoid of her presence, was the closest thing he'd had to a home since the dusty bunkhouse where his uncle had raised him.

But not close enough that he wanted to own the place. He recalled the shock on Ava Hirsch's tear-streaked face that afternoon—it had mirrored his own.

"What do you mean, she *left it to me?*" Too flabbergasted to keep his voice down, Sam had earned angry glares from all the nearby nurses.

Behind her wire-rimmed glasses Ava's eyes had been the size of poker chips. "You didn't know? I never would have said anything. I thought…"

Sitting alone in the dimly lit kitchen hours later, Sam raised his half-finished beer in an affectionate toast. "Still meddling from the great beyond, Wanda?" She'd always nagged him to settle down. If Ava were right about the change to her friend's will—something Sam still didn't quite believe—then maybe it was Wanda's gentle way of coercing him into putting down roots.

He shook his head at the asinine idea of him as a hotel manager. Granted, this was a very small hotel, but that made it worse. Guests expected a personal touch, that extra dose of folksy hospitality. On the trail, in his element, Sam did just fine with tourists as long as they followed his rules about the horses. Most clients who wanted to rough it had a certain expectation of what their guide would be like. His occasionally gruff demeanor fit the part. He didn't have Wanda's gracious nature. The first time some the-customer-is-always-right twit complained about sheet thread count or something equally ridiculous... Well, being raised by a cantankerous bachelor uncle was not the same as attending charm school.

Even though he wouldn't be staying, he was touched by the gesture. If she had bequeathed him the inn, her intentions were good. Wanda may have been trying to give him a home—which was more than his actual mother had ever done—but she seemed to have overlooked that what he'd loved most about the inn was gone. He'd once got jalapeño juice in his eye, and it had burned like hellfire. His dry, unblinking eyes stung far worse now.

"Place won't be the same without her," Sam declared aloud.

A plaintive, otherworldly yowl of agreement came from the floor. Sam nearly jumped until he realized that the reclusive white cat had finally made an appearance—his first all night, although he'd halfheartedly eaten the small plate of food Sam pushed under the bed.

"You miss her, too, don't you?" Sam reached down to scratch Oberon's head, which the cat tolerated for a millisecond before scooting back, his ears flat and his yellow gaze suspicious. The feline had worshipped and adored Wanda Keller, but regarded all other human beings with contempt.

Sam might have made a sarcastic comment, such as telling the cat to have fun opening its own damn can of tuna tomorrow, except he couldn't forget the pet's distress earlier. It had been Oberon who had found Sam in the kitchen and let him know something was wrong, meowing anxiously, tail twitching, constantly glancing back over his shoulder, as if he wanted Sam to follow. Although Wanda normally rose at sunrise to roll out dough for breakfast, Sam had assumed she was sleeping in because of the bad headache she'd mentioned last night. He'd tried to help out by brewing coffee for everyone and putting boxes of cereal around the bowl of fresh fruit on the dining room table.

Sam had followed the cat to her room, but there was nothing to be done. She'd gone in her sleep; the doctors diagnosed a ruptured brain aneurysm. When the paramedics had tried to take the body, Oberon had launched himself at them in hissing attack. Attempts to get hold of the cat had proven futile, and the feline disappeared under Wanda's bed, where he'd begun a low, spine-tingling wail. When Sam had returned from the hospital, Oberon had still been there, his cry hoarser than it had been hours before but just as heartfelt. Sam believed the cat was ornery enough to have tried stalking the ambulance, if Wanda had ever installed a cat door. She worried about him ending up in traffic and getting hit by a tourist watching for street signs.

Now, Oberon sat back on his haunches and studied Sam as if assessing him. The uneven triangle of black fur around the cat's left eye added to his sinister expression. When his slim body tensed to pounce, Sam wondered if he was about to get lacerated for letting them take Wanda away. Instead, the animal shot into Sam's denim-covered lap and circled twice before curling into a warm ball. Sam was shocked, but assumed this was a temporary truce. They were each saying goodbye to the only family they'd had.

We weren't her *only family.* Wanda might have been

"like a mom" to him, but she was a real mother to some-one else. If there was one thing Wanda had talked about more than her legends, herbs and woo-woo philoso-phies, it was Lorelei. Sam's jaw tightened. He'd heard dozens of stories about Lorelei, who'd pretended at five that her bicycle was a horse named Spokes and, at ten, had been the first in her class to memorize all the state capitals. Wanda always bragged that Lorelei was as "smart as a whip," which would explain the extra cords and whatnot draped over the young woman's gown in graduation pictures.

Most of the family photos Wanda liked to show off were from back when her husband was alive and Lo-relei had been a chubby-cheeked little girl. The most recent portrait he'd seen was from several years ago: a flinty-eyed, unsmiling college grad who looked just a bit too smug beneath her mortarboard. Wanda had al-ways made excuses for why her pride-and-joy didn't visit. Sam was less inclined to do so.

"Things were hard for her after her dad died," Wanda had said once, looking faraway and sad.

Not wanting to upset his friend, Sam had held his tongue. But he had trouble sympathizing. As a child, he, too, had lost a father. What he'd needed most was comfort from his mother. Instead…

Sam didn't realize he'd been absently petting the cat until he stopped and Oberon butted his head into Sam's arm, protesting.

"Enough of this," Sam told the cat. "You want me to pet you, you have to come with me into the den. No more sitting in the dark, crying into our beer. Metaphor-ically speaking. Let's see what's on the tube."

He gently set the cat on the floor, and, sure enough,

Oberon followed him down the hallway. They passed by a framed picture of Lorelei as a teenager and Sam shook his head. If the woman was so damn smart, why hadn't she known how lucky she was to have Wanda?

Lorelei was a little surprised that the man behind the counter handed over keys to the rental car. After her sleepless night and turbulent flight into San Antonio this morning, she had deep bags beneath her bloodshot eyes. She probably looked strung out and wouldn't have blamed the guy if he'd insisted on some kind of drug test before letting her drive a car off the lot. Then again, he was already a little scared of her from when she'd growled, "Trust me, I *understand* the optional insurance policy, you can stop overexplaining!" So maybe his thrusting the keys at her was less about customer service and more about getting rid of her.

"Your luggage is already in the trunk," he informed her. "You have a nice day."

Not a chance in hell. "Thank you," she said tightly. She'd been speaking through clenched lips all day; now she gripped the keys so hard they dug into her palm.

It was as if she were trying to hold herself together through sheer physical force because if she didn't, Lorelei might fly apart. She stalked across the lot toward her assigned car, barely giving herself a moment to buckle in and adjust the seat and mirrors before heading for the exit. If she paused to consult a map, paused to find a radio station, paused for one second to think...

Although it had been a while since her last trip here—*I'm sorry, Mom. I will always be sorry*—she knew the I-10 route by heart. There were no surprise detours this Wednesday afternoon. The city gave way to unmanicured vistas, tree-studded hills and pastures that looked furry due to bunches of some tawny untamed grass.

About fifteen minutes from Fredericksburg, she stopped at a filling station to use their restroom even though it wasn't really necessary. Maybe she was just stalling because she couldn't face what awaited her.

It was surprisingly warm outside—she'd dressed that morning for March in Philly, not March in Texas. On her drive, she'd already seen a few patches of bluebonnets in bloom. Wanda had loved plants of all kinds. Lorelei had a stray memory of a picnic with her parents, long ago, in a field of wildflowers. Her mother had told her a Native American legend about how flowers had become fragrant. Wanda had grown plants both decorative and functional in window boxes and pots all through their house and yard. She and her husband had turned to medicinal herbs and holistic treatments when he was diagnosed with liver cancer, rather than to oncologists.

With a hard swallow, Lorelei climbed back into the rental car, annoyed with herself for postponing the inevitable. She could stop every mile between here and the bed-and-breakfast and it wouldn't change anything. *I've lost them both.*

When she'd called Ava last night with her flight details, Ava had volunteered her husband, Clinton, to come pick up Lorelei in San Antonio. "If you insist on driving yourself, at least call us when you get close. We'll meet you at the B and B."

Lorelei had thanked the woman sincerely for the offer but had said she'd call them later because she might want a nap before seeing anyone. It had been a half truth. There was no way she'd be able to sleep, but she needed to be alone in her mother's inn. Being there would solidify the loss and Lorelei wasn't sure how much longer she could keep from detonating. The last thing she wanted was a witness.

Though she had to slow down temporarily for a stretch of road where signs warned Loose Livestock, she didn't encounter traffic. Judging from the wry sign on a dilapidated diner—Over a Dozen Served!—she was officially on the road less traveled. All too soon, she was turning onto the street where the Haunted Hill Country Bed-and-Breakfast sat.

Lorelei parked the car in front of the stone-faced two-story building, bracing herself for not hearing her mother's voice when she walked inside. Would she still smell the uniquely familiar blend of lemon, lavender and nutmeg from the incenses and oils Wanda had favored? Those aromatherapy scents had permeated the entire inn. Except during Christmas seasons when the bed-and-breakfast was filled with fresh pine and baking gingerbread.

"Get out of the car," Lorelei muttered. If she sat in the driveway much longer, some kind passerby would stop to tell her that the B and B wasn't currently open for business, that the owner had…

She wrenched open the door, then crossed the short sidewalk leading to the porch. The front steps creaked softly beneath her weight, and she was attempting to fish the key from her purse when the door swung open.

A tall man in a plaid button-down shirt and a cowboy hat greeted her. "Sorry, we're not— Ah. It's you."

She drew herself up straighter, the involuntary reflex making her feel a touch juvenile. Even if she stood on tippy-toe, she wouldn't be level with him. He was at least six feet. "I'm L—"

"Oh, I know who you are," he interrupted in a lazy drawl. He rocked back on his heels, seemingly in no hurry to move the hell out of her way so she could lock herself in a bedroom and have a private breakdown. Not that indulging in an emotional fit would bring her mother back.

"You're little Lori," he continued, thumbs hooked in the front pockets of his jeans. "Wanda's girl, all grown up."

She almost snapped that she wasn't anyone's "little" anything. She was five foot eight for crying out loud! And what was with the *all-grown-up* condescension? He looked three or four years older, tops. "I go by Lorelei. No one's ever called me Lori, particularly not total strangers who block doorways." She glared meaningfully.

He glared back.

"So who are you?" she demanded. "An employee?"

"Not exactly." Hardly an informative answer, but at least he stepped to the side.

"Ava told me all the guests were relocated," she said as she crossed the threshold into the foyer. A cursory glance at the adjacent dining room and den showed that everything was as she remembered—except for her mom's absence and this annoying man's presence. "I had expected to be alone."

The man shrugged. "Someone had to take care of Oberon."

How could she have forgotten the maniacal cat? As a scraggly kitten, Oberon had shown up on the front porch while Wanda and the real estate agent had been doing a walk-through of the inn.

"He was a sign," Wanda had told her daughter over the phone. "I was meant to buy this place, and he was meant to keep me company. It's been so lonely with your father gone and you at college."

"Ow!" A sudden scratch to the ankle jolted Lorelei back to the present, and she bumped the *willkommen* table. Brochures detailing area activities sat alongside the guestbook and one pamphlet fell to the floor. A tell-tale white paw jutted out from beneath the tablecloth. *Speak of the freaking devil.*

Grimacing, she took a large step away from the table and, more importantly, the extended claws. "I see Oberon hasn't mellowed with age."

"Nope."

She suppressed a sigh at the man's flat tone. Good thing he was attractive; he'd be doomed if all he had going for him was personality. *Attractive?* That must be the sleep deprivation talking. While she couldn't find fault with the cowboy's well-muscled body—and his green eyes were admittedly arresting—he was a bit scruffy with his too-long dark golden hair and the stubble dotting his jawline. Not her type at all.

"I assume you have a name?" she prompted.

He flashed a mocking smile that lasted just long enough to reveal deep dimples. "Good assumption. Now, if you'll excuse me, Miz Keller, I was on my way out. Help yourself to any room except the Faust suite. That's mine."

As in, he would be sleeping there? She'd hoped he was only dropping by to feed the cat. "You'll be back tonight?"

"Yes, ma'am." He must have caught the dismay in her expression because his eyes narrowed. "Don't worry, this place is plenty big enough for both of us."

Despite the multiple bedrooms in the two-floor structure, she didn't believe him. And she couldn't help noticing he didn't seem convinced, either.

The door banged shut in Sam's wake as he strode toward the truck parked behind the inn. He wanted to leave quickly, before the B and B's omnipresent reminders of Wanda nettled his conscience like the spines of a prickly pear cactus. She would have wanted him to be more welcoming to her daughter. *Hard to believe they're related.*

He'd known from pictures that Lorelei was dark-haired and striking. He just hadn't realized she was so tall; her mama had been a round little dumpling of a woman. Other than her height, though, Lorelei Keller had been pretty much what he'd expected. Purse-lipped and haughty, with no mention of her mother. Granted, Lorelei's dark eyes had been puffy, but no more than most tourists' in pollen season.

He could almost hear his former landlady's chiding voice. *Oh, and you were a real charmer during that encounter? You didn't even give her a chance.* With a sigh, he glanced back over his shoulder, then retraced his steps.

Through the window in the door, he could see the brunette slumped in a chair at the kitchen table, much the same way he'd been last night. As soon as he turned the knob, her backbone went ramrod straight. Her expensive-looking cinnamon-colored sweater dress was probably hot and itchy on a day like this. Over it, she wore some kind of full-body vest in an even darker brown. In contrast, he couldn't help recalling the way Wanda had cheerfully embraced colors—the brighter, the better.

"Forget something?" Lorelei asked without turning to look at him.

"Just wanted to say, name's Sam Travis. I was a good friend of your mother's. Damn fine woman." He paused a beat, to see if Lorelei recognized his name or had any comment. Did she know what Ava suspected, that Wanda had altered her will in the past year? "I'm the one who found her. Yesterday."

Red-rimmed eyes met his, and Lorelei swallowed, struggling to speak. "Do you think she was in pain?"

"She complained of a headache when she went to bed the night before, but no, I don't think she suffered. Doc Singer made it sound as if it was about as peaceful as passing can be."

Lorelei drew in a shaky breath. "Thank you, Sam."

He nodded uncomfortably. "I won't be back for a couple of hours, but is there anything I can bring you from town? Anything you need?"

Her gaze clashed with his, naked and vulnerable. For a split second, all he saw was need. Then she blinked, eradicating the defenselessness so fast he could pretend he'd imagined it.

"That won't be necessary," she said. "But I appreciate the offer. By the way, I've decided to take the wolf suite."

The one farthest in the house from his.

Good. Maybe they would only bump into each other a minimum of times before the memorial service on Saturday.

He knew from Wanda's lawyer that the reading of the will would follow—Wanda's way of making sure that on the same day her loved ones were honoring her, she'd get to express her love for them—and Sam's attendance was requested. Considering how much Wanda had adored her prodigal daughter, would she really have left Sam the inn?

And what the hell was he going to do with it if she had?

Chapter 3

Lorelei hung up the phone with a sigh and glanced across the kitchen. Ava was stocking the refrigerator with all manner of casseroles and comfort foods. Judging by the dozens of containers she'd arrived with an hour ago, she'd been cooking nonstop since yesterday.

"That was the last one," Lorelei said wearily. She'd gone through her mom's reservation file at the computer and called to cancel all the guests scheduled for the following week. After that... Well, surviving this week was the first step.

Lorelei didn't really know what she would do about the inn. She supposed hiring someone to manage it for her was a possibility, but she'd never really warmed to this place. When her mother—who'd worked previous jobs as a cook in another hotel and an administrative assistant in the town tourism bureau—first said she wanted to open her own inn, Lorelei had thought it would be a good fit for her, assuming Wanda could get the necessary loans. Ever since her husband's death, Wanda had slipped into more and more elaborate flights of fancy. She used to wake Lorelei up in the middle of the night to excitedly tell her, "Your daddy visited me again. He's watching over us, honey, and he's real proud of you." Lorelei had wanted to shake her, had wanted to yell at her mother to stop it. It was so hard to let go and heal when Wanda kept his specter alive and well in their home. Lorelei had foolishly presumed that running a business would keep Wanda more grounded.

Should've known better. There were lots of bed-and-breakfasts and guest ranches dotting the Hill Country. Wanda had tried to set hers apart with its theme. Her place served as sort of a museum for Hill Country folklore and ghost stories. Each guest room was based on some local legend.

For instance, Lorelei's room, from the comforter printed with running wolves to the hand-carved figures on the wooden vanity, centered on the wolf spirit that "haunted" nearby Devil's Backbone, an area also rumored to host the apparitions of monks, Native Americans and Confederate soldiers. Sam's suite was based on the famed Faust Hotel, a historic haunted site, and Wanda had decorated it based on old photos she'd seen of the establishment. The only creepy room was the one based on a cave, in which Wanda had blacked out the windows and bat noises played periodically through a hidden speaker. In addition to the themed decorating, Wanda had also arranged tours that took visitors through the region from one "unexplained phenomenon" to another. And Wanda had always been a hell of a storyteller, probably because she believed the outlandish tales she shared.

"She'll be missed," one of the scheduled guests had told Lorelei, choked up by the news that the inn's proprietor had died. "My husband and I came to the Haunted Hill Country every year for our anniversary, and we just loved Wanda. Your mother was a special woman."

Ava came toward her with two cups of coffee. "You look like you could use some." Then she reached into a cabinet beneath the counter and procured a bottle of whiskey. "And maybe a shot of this with it."

Lorelei gave a dry laugh. She wasn't much of a drinker, but she appreciated the thought. "Thanks, Ava."

"Least I can do." Ava slid her glasses up on her nose with a finger. "I wish you had let me help with those calls. You didn't have to take care of them alone. Can't be easy to tell people over and over that your mama's gone."

"I wanted to." Saying it forced her to accept it. Running from the truth wouldn't change it. "I needed to be doing something, keeping busy."

Ava cast a sheepish look over her shoulder, at the crammed full refrigerator. "Guess I can understand that."

Lorelei poured a modest token shot into her coffee and raised her eyebrows questioningly at Ava, who nodded and pushed her own mug across the counter.

"Hit me, barkeep." Ava waited for her own more generous slug, then stirred cream into both mugs with a cinnamon stick.

Lorelei inhaled deeply. Her mug smelled like heaven. "Ava, can I ask you a…delicate question?"

The older woman nodded, her faded grey eyes earnest. "I know we haven't seen much of each other in the years since you got your degree, but Wanda was the closest thing I ever had to a sister. I'd be honored if you thought of me as kin."

"Was there something romantic going on between Mom and Sam Travis?"

Ava spluttered, choking on coffee.

"Sorry." Lorelei handed her a couple of napkins, feeling guilty as Ava continued to cough.

"What a thing to suggest!" Ava finally managed to say, cream dotting her upper lip. "Of course there wasn't anything romantic. Thank God you asked me and not Sam. He'd be horrified."

Lorelei's face grew hot. Now that she'd voiced the question, it did sound absurd—especially given how devoted Wanda had remained to her late husband. "Well, I didn't think so, but I wanted to be sure. It's not like she was always conventional with her beliefs, so she might have overlooked the age difference. He was cryptic and grudging. All he told me was that they were 'good friends.' But he'd obviously talked to her right before she went to sleep and he was the one who found her in her bed."

Had Sam Travis been the person to hear her mother's final words?

Lorelei couldn't help flinching, recalling her mom's last words the last time they'd spoken. *I'll be here.* The mug trembled in Lorelei's hands. She'd taken for granted that her mother would, indeed, always be here.

She cleared her throat. "The biggest reason I wondered about their relationship is because of you."

"Me?" Ava squeaked.

"Well, you didn't mention him to me when we spoke

on the phone and you said all the guests had gone." A heads-up that someone else was going to be under the same roof with her would have been nice. "But every time he's come up in conversation this afternoon, you've…"

Ava turned away, busying herself with a rag and wiping down the long expanse of already clean counter.

"You're acting weird about Sam." Almost guilty, which had made Lorelei speculate that maybe Ava harbored a secret about her mom and the cowboy. *Something* was clearly bothering Ava.

"Is there anything you want to tell me?" Lorelei prodded.

"Only that it's wonderful to see you again." Ava put the rag down and smiled sadly. "I just wish you could have come home before this." There was no accusation in her voice, but that made it even worse somehow.

Lorelei was tempted to agree with Ava, to say *I wish I had, too,* but Lorelei had given up wishing a long time ago. When her dad died, she'd wised up—no wishing wells or "first star I see tonight" or fairy stories for her. Those were all just pretty guises for denial. Lorelei needed to live in cold, hard reality. And that meant she knew what to do with the inn.

She'd sell the property and use the money to help with her staggering college loans. Wanda would approve. Her mother had been proud that Lorelei got into such a prestigious school and she'd always fretted that she couldn't do more to take care of her daughter from so far away. The woman who'd once given her crystals and dream catchers for protection would be assisting in protection from debt, a far more useful security. It was something tangible and *parental* Wanda could do for her, which made Lorelei feel, for a moment, closer to the mother she'd lost.

Lorelei bit her lip, wondering if she should tell Ava what she intended to do. But it seemed cruel just now, with the inn being the most visible reminder of Wanda. Lorelei didn't want the kind-hearted woman to feel as if she was losing her friend twice in one week. *I'll tell her after the memorial service Saturday.*

With the decision made to sell, Lorelei felt as if she could breathe easier. As an adolescent, grieving for her father, she'd hoped that they could move away, start fresh somewhere his memory wasn't so potent. At the very least, she'd wanted Wanda to date, to set the example that it wasn't a betrayal to move on with life. Instead, Wanda had continued to talk about him as if he were a member of their household. On holidays and special occasions, she set a place for him at the table. She talked about having spirit conversations with him in her dreams and seeing his ghost in his favorite recliner. The lack of closure had ripped at Lorelei.

Not this time. After the service and the will-reading, when she officially inherited the inn, she'd call the would-be guests in her mom's files and break the news to them. She'd sell the B and B to someone who could create their own niche here, and she'd return to her life in Philly, her ties to Fredericksburg severed. Lorelei would have the closure she so desperately needed.

Sitting in the middle of a semi-circle of pictures, Lorelei debated opening a window. *It's stuffy in here.* Given the high ceiling of the great room and the dropping evening temperatures, she knew the stifling sensation was in her imagination. Raising a window would be yielding to her sudden illogical claustrophobia. Lorelei was a pragmatic woman. She refused to start acting squirrelly just because it was late and she was all alone in the inn.

Sam's estimated "couple of hours" of being gone had turned into all afternoon and evening. Ava had insisted on staying long enough to have dinner with Lorelei but then had returned home to her husband. Both women had listlessly pushed their food around on Wanda's sunset-colored ceramic plates. During the meal, Ava had tentatively broached the subject of the eulogy Lorelei needed to write for Saturday's memorial. There was also the task of selecting pictures for display at the funeral home. A salon decorated with mementos of Wanda Keller's life would open an hour prior to the formal service so that loved ones could gather to share their recollections. And their grief.

The service would take place there at the funeral home. Wanda, never really a churchgoing woman, had decided against having her final farewell at one of the local chapels. Since she was being cremated, like her husband before her, there would be no graveyard burial, either.

Lorelei shoved her hands through her hair. Her first attempt at drafting a eulogy had been disastrous. She'd thought that pulling out all these old photos, conjuring the memories, would help organize her thoughts. Sort of like an outline for a college paper. But seeing her mother's life, now ended, spread out on the carpet around her...

A jagged keening broke the silence, and she pressed her fist against her mouth, trying to stem the dark wave of despair. Though she was usually comfortable with

solitude, right now the overpowering sense of alone-
ness choked her. She gripped her cell phone, wanting
to escape by talking to someone outside of Fredericksburg. But it was too late to call any of her work friends
back in Philly, especially given the time difference.
Rick, maybe?

No. She recalled with a grimace his distant response
when she'd learned of her mother's death. He'd said he
was sorry, naturally, had even offered the rote "if there's
anything I can do…" But he'd sounded more like a lawyer giving a client bad news than a potential lover. "Can
I send flowers?" he'd asked. "Or was she one of those
people who'd prefer a donation to charity, in lieu of?"

A metallic jiggling cut through Lorelei's thoughts
and she stiffened. The B and B had never seemed creep-
ier than it did at that moment.

Once she realized that what she'd heard was the back
door being unlocked, she expelled a shaky breath. *Sam.*
When they'd met earlier today, all she'd wanted was for
him to get the hell out. Tonight, though, she was grateful for his presence. She almost called out to him but
bit her lip, embarrassed by her neediness. He'd come
through here anyway to get to his suite.

Sure enough, a moment later, booted footsteps
sounded in the short, hardwood hallway leading from
the kitchen. Then Sam appeared at the edge of the spacious living room, his face shadowed by his cowboy
hat and the dark hall. It probably would have been better for her nerves if she'd turned on more lights than
the standing fixture in the corner and a stained-glass
antique table lamp.

She felt exposed in her circle of photos and muted

light. The fact that she was wearing a tank top and flannel pajama bottoms didn't help. "Hi."

He leaned against the wall, seeming caught by all the images of Wanda. "Can't believe she's gone." His quiet murmur didn't completely mask the emotion in his voice. Once again, Lorelei wondered how Sam and her mother had met and what their relationship had been. It was easy to picture Wanda and Ava as best friends, laughing over botched recipes and antiquing together on the weekend. But what had Sam and Wanda shared?

"I'm supposed to pick photos for the funeral home," she told him, her voice cracking only the slightest bit when she said *funeral*.

"Would you like to know which ones were her favorites?" Sam offered.

Her erstwhile relief at his company crisped and blackened to irritation. "I'm her daughter," she said defensively. "You don't think I can figure that out for myself?"

He tipped his hat back with a finger, staring her down with those green eyes.

"You think you knew her better than I did," Lorelei said.

He somehow shrugged without ever moving his shoulders. "Even when we suppose we know someone, we can be surprised. But I did spend some time with her."

And I didn't spend nearly enough. Guilt clogged Lorelei's windpipe, making it impossible to speak.

"She dragged out her box of photos plenty," he said. "Made me look at them so she could talk about her husband. Or brag about you."

Lorelei wanted so badly to ask what her mother

had said. How had she described the brainy, estranged daughter who had so little in common with her?

Sam straightened slowly, awkwardly, and it was only as he moved away from the wall that she realized he was unsteady. Come to think of it, was his drawl more pronounced than it had been that afternoon?

"You've been drinking!"

"Not uncommon in these parts to honor a person's memory by hoisting a glass." He paused. "Can't say I recall the exact number of glasses, but that's why I walked. Left my truck at the bar."

A strange shiver pulsed through her. She was alone in this large house with a broad-shouldered cowboy she barely knew and he might be inebriated. Should she be concerned for her welfare? Wanda had apparently believed in him, but then Wanda had believed a lot of things.

Sam approached, and Lorelei felt the instinct to scoot back, except there wasn't much room behind her. She was between the ring of pictures and the bottom edge of the sofa. When he crouched down, Lorelei breathed in a subtle blend of denim, soap, beer and the crisp March night. It was unexpected. Rick always smelled like designer cologne—appealing, in a manufactured way, but indistinct from dozens of other successful men.

Sam Travis was distinct.

Looking into his eyes, she couldn't remember having ever seen a pair like them. "Wh-what are you doing?"

"Helping."

"I didn't ask for your help." It felt invasive, having him loom over these snapshots of her life. The too-short era when her mother and father were both alive, the later pictures of a smiling Wanda and tense adolescent Lorelei.

Sam's jaw clenched. "Maybe I'm helping *her*. You'll probably pick out the most formal portraits in the bunch, regardless of how Wanda would want to be remembered."

"That's not true. I'm aware of how different my mother and I are. Were."

A fuzzy photo that predated the age of clear digital prints caught her eye, this one of a blurry Wanda laughing with tourists at a festival booth. She had thrived on the conversation and merriment around her. At the edge of the picture was a dark-haired smudge. *Me.* Though it was difficult to tell from the shot, Lorelei had been huddled in a lawn chair with her nose in a book. For all that Lorelei had excelled in school, she'd always had the feeling that her free-spirited mother, who held no degree of her own, would have been more proud if her daughter had put the books down and just enjoyed the sunshine and crowds more.

Sam rocked back on his heels. "Sorry. You're right, this isn't my place." He stood, exiting the room with efficient speed and purpose despite however many glasses he'd drunk in Wanda's memory.

Lorelei bit her bottom lip hard, staring at the mix of antiques and fanciful touches in this central Texas bed-and-breakfast, none of which spoke to Lorelei or resembled her life in Philly. An all too familiar bubble of alienation surrounded her. *It's not my place, either.*

Thursday night, Sam stepped into the kitchen as gingerly as a prowler trying to pass through the house unnoticed. He'd grabbed a burger in town a couple of hours ago, but judging by the angry meow that had greeted Sam as soon as he set foot inside, Oberon had not yet eaten dinner. *At least he has his appetite back.*

Now that Sam was moving in the direction of the cat food, Oberon trilled his approval and wound figure eights between Sam's cowboy boots, nearly tripping him. "You know," he whispered, "you'll get fed a lot faster if you don't knock me on my ass."

The tiptoeing and whispering was embarrassing—but preferable to another charged encounter with Lorelei Keller. Last night, a number of folks in town had been commiserating over Wanda's death; though Sam wasn't usually much of a joiner, he'd ended up drinking with them before walking back to the inn. The sight of Lorelei in the middle of the living room had surprised him. She'd looked like a completely different woman with her arms and shoulders bared in a thin tank top, her long dark hair cascading over her skin.

Or maybe it was the play of vulnerability across her face that had changed her appearance. At any rate, it hadn't taken him long to realize he was intruding on her grief. He didn't want to make the same mistake twice, especially on a night when he was bone sore and smelled like horse. He'd spent the day several towns over, helping a friend train an Arabian.

Suddenly a woman's agitated voice cut through the silence. "Yes, but I'm telling you, that's not necessary!" After that brief outburst, her voice trailed off some—he could only make out the words *information* and *tomorrow*. Whatever Lorelei was feeling in the wake of her mom's death, he'd been wrong to imagine she was fragile and weepy. Even through a closed door, Sam could hear the steel in her voice.

"She's about as warm and fuzzy as you are," he told the cat, scooping canned food onto a small mound of kibble. Sam was just placing the plastic bowl in the floor when light flooded the kitchen. He blinked at the sudden illumination.

Lorelei gasped in the doorway, one hand flattened over her chest. Along with a pair of jeans, she was wearing another sweater that seemed too thick for Texas. "Jeez. What are you doing skulking in the dark? You scared the hell out of me."

Sam glared. No way was he admitting he'd been sneaking around, trying to make himself as invisible as possible, out of respect to her. "I just came in to feed the cat. Someone should," he said pointedly.

Her lip curled. "I don't think vamp-cat wants pet store food. He's after fresh blood. After trying to take a chunk from my leg yesterday, he lacerated my arm this afternoon when I stopped him from running out the front door."

"Starving an animal does tend to make it mean." He didn't share that he himself had once suggested that Lucifer would be a more appropriate name for the animal.

Lorelei sighed. "You're probably right. Not that he wasn't mean to begin with, but I was negligent, forgetting to feed him. I suppose there's a litter box around here somewhere, too?" She made a face. "I'm not used to taking care of anything."

"Yeah, you don't seem like the pet-owner type."

She narrowed her eyes but didn't argue. Instead, she sidestepped him. "I just came in here to get a drink. I'll be out of your way in no time." When she opened the fridge to retrieve a gallon of lemonade, he saw the mountain of food Ava had stocked was virtually untouched.

"You eat any dinner?" he heard himself ask awkwardly. Stupid question. *She's a grown woman, not the cat. She can feed herself when she chooses.*

"Actually, no." Lorelei sounded bemused by the realization. "Guess I forgot. I've been working all evening."

"Working? Surely your bosses don't expect you to be on call two days before your mother's memorial service?" Sam had worked for a few hard-hearted SOBs in his time, but they'd all understood stopping to remember the dead.

"It was my choice. And my business."

Right—so butt out, cowboy. Message received loud and clear.

He tipped his hat to her. "Good night then, Miss Keller. Oh, but before I forget." Bending to the cabinet beneath the sink, he retrieved a small trash bag and a slotted plastic scooper. "Here. Cat box is in the sunroom."

Lorelei's fingers shook as she unlocked the back door on Friday morning. In order to pull out her keys, she'd had to set down the cardboard flat she'd carried. The thought of picking it back up didn't help her trembling. What she wouldn't give to be in her office right now.

The desperate thought conjured an image of Sam's disapproving expression last night. No doubt he considered her an unfeeling ice-queen for obsessing over work at a time like this. Not that she gave a damn about his opinion.

Her job was soothing. Numbers and facts and statistics—they'd always lulled her out of anxiety. Wasn't that why people were supposed to count sheep? Unfortunately, being an actuary wasn't really a work-from-home kind of career. She'd prevaricated yesterday. Her hours spent on the phone hadn't been so much working as turning her projects over to two other junior actuaries at the company. Her supervisor had insisted.

"Take a couple of weeks off," he'd told her. "You haven't used a single vacation day in what, over a year? You need it. And we need you at one hundred percent. You're officially on sabbatical."

Tears stung her eyes. What her boss saw as sabbatical, she saw as exile from the only thing that might keep her sane through the next few days. Today had been awful, and she still had the memorial service and an obligatory meeting with her mom's lawyer tomorrow.

Maybe I should have let Ava come with me this morning. The older woman had offered, but Lorelei had suspected her mother's friend would dissolve into tears, threatening Lorelei's own composure. Taking a deep breath, she carried the open-topped box inside and set it gingerly on the counter. The green-and-azure urn that rose from within was porcelain, decorated with bluebonnets and Indian paintbrush. Objectively, Lorelei had to admit it was a lovely container. Wanda had selected it to coordinate with her late husband's urn, which bore a picture of a pecan tree.

Hysteria rose inside of Lorelei and erupted as a horrified giggle. *Oh, God. This is all that's left of my family—matching vases.*

Reflexively, she reached into her pocket for her cell phone. She could call Celia, see how the policy presentation—which had been Lorelei's and had now changed hands—was going. Part of Lorelei acknowledged that she was micromanaging a peer and that she was undoubtedly annoying Celia with her offers to answer questions or to email additional background information. As she dialed, she promised herself she'd do something to make it up to the other woman when she returned to Philadelphia. For now, Lorelei just needed to survive the next forty-eight hours.

Chapter 4

Picturesque clouds dotted an impossibly blue sky, un-interrupted by air traffic or hazy pollution—only the occasional songbird in flight. The sun shone, but gently enough that no one broke a sweat, even in black mourning attire or a suit jacket. It was the afternoon every bride would want for her wedding.

Well, except for Wanda, who'd once claimed that she'd been "delighted" it rained during her long-ago September wedding and had in fact been hoping for a downpour. She held with the superstition that rain on a wedding day meant good luck. Another tradition she'd embraced was the prewedding *Polterabend*. Many dishes had been broken in hopes of bringing luck to the happy couple.

Lorelei's throat tightened as she thought of pictures she'd seen of her parents' wedding day. They'd been so young and in love! Neither of them had been old enough to die. Yet here Lorelei was once again at a family-owned funeral home that had been part of the community for a hundred years, entering through the same white columns she'd passed through on the day of her father's memorial service.

One of the brothers who ran the place was at her side immediately, murmuring his condolences and ushering her to the salon where her mother was being honored today. They'd done a lovely job displaying portraits amid floral arrangements, but the overpowering scent of so many competing flowers in a closed space made Lorelei's nose twitch and irritated her eyes.

Ava and her husband arrived first, immediately followed by other people who had adored Wanda. A crowd gathered around Lorelei, men and women anxious to share their memories of her mother. All around her, the town's citizens regaled each other with stories. The room took on a buzz that made her feel as if she were trapped in a beehive. Lorelei knew her mom had been a very gracious person, could remember the comfort Wanda had taken in those close to her when her husband had passed. Wanda had laughed with them, cried with them and hugged everyone.

In contrast, Lorelei seemed to stiffen at contact. After thirty minutes, her head throbbed. She kept eyeing the door, wanting to escape and steal a few moments of peace for herself before the official service began.

Halfway through yet another recollection from the head librarian, a woman who had helped Wanda do folklore research for the B and B, Lorelei finally interrupted. "I'm sorry," she said, placing a conciliatory hand on the woman's arm. "If you'll please excuse me for a moment, I just need…" *To get the hell out of here.* Luckily, the circumstances didn't require an excuse. The small circle of people who'd gathered around her nodded sympathetically and immediately broke formation so she could pass.

Lorelei went as quickly as decorum allowed toward a side door that led into the employee parking lot. She figured there was less risk that way for running into anyone. The service started in fifteen minutes, and there might still be mourners arriving through the front door.

She stepped outside, lifted her face to the breeze and inhaled deeply when the door shut, muffling the conversations she'd left behind.

"How're you holding up?"

Whipping her head around, she spotted Sam Travis. He was perched on the ramp railing that ran the length of the building. She'd seen him earlier—without his cowboy hat, for once—talking to Clinton and Ava Hirsch, and she'd been relieved when he didn't approach her. Sam made her…uneasy, a sensation she hadn't experienced in a long time.

By the end of elementary school, she'd known she didn't fit in with other kids. They labeled her a math geek and didn't invite her to the giggly slumber parties her female classmates later rehashed in the cafeteria. She'd told herself it didn't matter. At thirteen, she'd decided she was getting out of town as soon as possible. In college, she'd bonded with students similar to her and had been comfortable in her own skin ever since. She knew who she was and what she wanted out of life. She made sensible decisions, such as dating eminently compatible men and not wearing ridiculously high-heeled shoes that could injure her joints or back.

But something about Sam made her feel as if she were teetering even in her practical pumps. She swallowed. "Wh-what are you doing out here?"

"Same thing as you. Hiding."

She bristled at the implied cowardice. "I'm not 'hiding,' Mr. Travis. I just—"

"Easy, darlin'. I wasn't criticizing. There are a lot of very emotional, very *talkative* people in that building. Enough to make anyone skittish." He shook his head. "Not that Wanda would have bolted. She was damn good at listening to everyone, making them feel welcome. Special."

Lorelei was torn. She knew what he meant, yet how many times growing up had she tried to explain to her mother how she felt? How often had Lorelei retreated to her room, frustrated that her mother *wouldn't* listen?

"I've always felt so removed from her," Lorelei heard herself admit. She wasn't sure why she was confiding in him, but she'd be gone soon—back to her real life—so what did it matter? "I tried telling myself I take after Dad, but I don't think it's true. He and Mom were like two peas in a pod, and I was, I don't know, some kind of changeling baby." Of all the crazy legends her mom had ever voiced, that one Lorelei could have believed.

Sam squinted at her from his spot in the shade. "You were how old when you lost your dad?"

"Six when he was diagnosed, seven when he died."

"I was nine when I lost my father. I don't know about you, but a lot of the memories I have are hazy. Maybe you're more like him than you recall."

There he went again, knocking her off balance. She hadn't expected him to try to comfort her. Nor had she expected them to have anything in common. She wondered how he'd lost his own father, if the tragedy had brought Sam and his mother closer.

"I should go back inside," she said, unenthusiastic about the prospect. "The service will be starting soon." The hours she'd spent working on the eulogy had been grueling, but she didn't back down from a challenge.

Sam nodded. "I'll be along in a minute. You look real nice, by the way."

Could he guess how many times she'd changed, trying to decide the right thing to wear? The navy-and-yellow print sheath dress allowed her to wear the big bright yellow earrings her mom had sent for her birthday; the cropped navy blazer helped subdue the outfit enough for the occasion.

Wanting to downplay the way she'd overanalyzed her decision, she made light of Sam's compliment, keeping her voice wry enough that he wouldn't take her seriously. "I don't think it's appropriate to flirt with the deceased's daughter."

He rolled his eyes. "I just meant it's good to see you wearing some color. She would have liked that."

"Says the man in head-to-toe black?" She doubted Sam owned a suit. Today he was showing respect in black boots, crisp jeans that looked starched to within an inch of their life and a black button-down shirt that was a dramatic foil to his light hair and eyes.

"Well." His expression didn't change, but there was a grin in his voice. "I had planned to accessorize with yellow, too, but I couldn't find my headband."

Lorelei laughed before she could stop herself. "I'll see you inside. And thank you."

He inclined his head in a silent "you're welcome," and she turned to go. When she'd fled the guests in the building, her body had been rigid with tension. Now, though far from relaxed, she felt calm enough to deliver her mother's eulogy. How had a virtual stranger Lorelei didn't especially like known what to say? He'd even made her laugh, which was a hell of a feat on this particular occasion.

Lorelei still didn't have the whole story on how Sam and Wanda had become friends, but she understood how much her flamboyant mother had appreciated people who were unpredictable. And Sam Travis was full of surprises.

The barrage of mourners and conversation didn't stop after the memorial service; it followed Lorelei back to the inn. She would forever be grateful to local B and B owners Clare Theo and Bertha Hoffman—women who'd respected Wanda enough to want to honor her without being so close to her that they were overcome with their own grief. They took point on making gallons of coffee and splitting hostess duties, managing the flow of traffic through the downstairs rooms.

Though his truck was in its customary spot out back, Lorelei hadn't spotted Sam in the throng. Was he avoiding the crowd, sequestered away in his room, or was he in this crush somewhere? People kept coming up to hug her and present her with foil-covered dishes. She had enough king ranch casseroles and pecan pies to last until summer. Thank God her mother had purchased a deep freeze, because the refrigerator was long past full.

"Lorelei?" Ava's voice broke through the hum of surrounding conversations. "Lorelei, dear?"

Lorelei glanced over a petite blonde who'd been extolling the virtues of cheddar mashed potatoes as comfort food and saw Ava totter into the formal dining room, wobbling on fancy shoes and too little sleep. Lorelei thanked the guest whose name she'd never quite caught and met Ava in the center of the room.

"I'm glad to see a friendly face," Lorelei said. "This is all a bit...overwhelming."

"Let's go upstairs," Ava suggested. She hesitated before adding, "The lawyer's ready for us."

Lorelei had met Robert Stork earlier in the week when he'd come by with a fruit basket to offer his condolences. He was a sandy-haired man with a round face that made him look barely old enough to drive. She'd been startled when he first introduced himself.

"But Mr. Stork is a white-haired man shorter than I am," she'd blurted, remembering the attorney from her dad's death.

"You're thinking of my father, for whom I'm named," Robert the younger had said. "He's retired and plays a lot of golf now. I took over the family business."

And part of Stork Jr.'s business was to go over Wanda's last wishes with Lorelei and Ava.

Lorelei took a deep breath, steadying herself. "Lead the way."

Instead of going up the steps at the front of the house where all the guests were, the two women detoured to the laundry room and took the narrow spiral of back stairs. *Library* was a rather pretentious term for what Lorelei suspected had once been a generously sized walk-in closet. The cramped area was furnished with four chairs too close together for personal space and built-in shelves, probably meant for linens but now filled with books. Still, the tiny room had the advantage of being removed from the nonstop conversation and parade of food on the first floor.

Just before they reached the room, Ava paused, twisting the slim gold bracelets on her wrist.

"What is it?" Lorelei asked. For obvious reasons, Ava hadn't been very jovial today. Yet now her expression seemed particularly troubled.

"I...nothing, dear. We should probably get this over with."

Lorelei offered a nod of encouragement and they proceeded. Surprisingly, two of the four chairs were already filled. In addition to the lawyer, Sam Travis was also present. Lorelei's eyebrows rose. Then again, maybe she shouldn't be so surprised to see him. He'd obviously cared enough about Wanda to brave her demon cat; it would be like Lorelei's mother to leave him something to remember her by, something of sentimental value. Lorelei studied the tall man, hunched in his chair and staring intently at his folded hands. Sam Travis didn't seem like a man who was easily sentimental.

Ava slid into the chair next to Mr. Stork. That left Lorelei with the seat closest to Sam, a rather pointless distinction since all four chairs were so close their occupants could practically bump knees. With Sam's kindness to her earlier still fresh in mind, she tried exchanging smiles with the man but he wouldn't meet her gaze. The expression froze awkwardly on her face as she took her seat. This wasn't an appropriate time to be grinning at cowboys, anyway. She adopted the air of solemn reserve she used to get through difficult meetings, the ones where she had to tell people things they didn't want to hear, and looked expectantly at the attorney.

Robert's ruddy complexion flushed an ever deeper red as he sorted through pages. "As all three of Wanda Keller's beneficiaries are now present, I shall begin?" In contrast to the words, his tone was pure halting question, as if he were a timid boy asking a parent's permission to stay up past his bed time.

Ava patted his hand. "You're doing fine."

Just how recently had his father retired? Lorelei wondered. He gave the impression this was his first day on the job.

"Thank you, Mrs. Hirsch. We'll start with you, with a message from Wanda." He shuffled his papers some more, stopping a moment later and clearing his throat. "'To my friend Ava, thank you for always being there. I can't express my gratitude for your support over the years. You are such a special, generous soul that even Oberon likes you.'"

Stiffening in her chair, Ava muttered, "The hell he does."

Robert ignored the aside and kept reading. "'I even thought of asking you to be his guardian once I've passed, but ultimately decided that he should stay with the inn. After all, it's his home.'"

Stay with the inn? Lorelei managed not to grimace. How was she going to make that a condition of sale? *Beautiful, well-kept bed-and-breakfast...plus, one evil-tempered feline with possible Satanic affiliations.* Her attention divided, Lorelei listened absently as Robert detailed the personal possessions Wanda had wanted her best friend to have. Among the keepsakes were an antique tea set, a fluted stoneware pie plate, a silver pig charm bracelet and Wanda's dragonfly wind chimes. It was difficult to imagine standing downstairs in the kitchen and not hearing their music tinkling through the window.

Not that she would be standing in the B-and-B kitchen after this trip, she reminded herself. It was right that Ava should take the chimes. They should go to someone who'd known how much Wanda loved them. She'd believed they brought a bit of good luck each time they rang.

Robert turned to Lorelei, his expression apologetic. "You're listed next, Miss Keller. Do you…need a moment? Before we continue?"

And drag out what had already been one of the longest, most difficult days of her life? "No. Let's keep this moving along," she suggested, her voice tense.

Her tone must have been sharper than intended because Robert flinched. For his sake, she hoped he never saw the inside of a courtroom because opposing counsel would eat him alive. Poor man looked afraid of his own shadow.

"First, there's the matter of your parents' ashes. Wanda Keller asked that her remains and her late husbands' be eventually combined and sprinkled somewhere in the Hill Country, as this was their home. The exact place is to be determined by you, but I can assist you in matters of state law and regulations." He withdrew a thick folder from his briefcase and handed it to Lorelei. "Inside that is a specific itemization and financial statements, but, to summarize, 'I leave my strong, independent daughter, Lorelei, my remaining personal effects, all belongings not specifically tied to the decoration and running of the bed-and-breakfast. I hope she will use my things and remember her mother, who loved her. I also leave her the balance of my checking and savings accounts. To Samuel…'"

Lorelei blinked, confused. She hadn't been aware that Stork had already moved on to the next person. A number of questions churned in her mind. Was the deed to the inn one of the things listed in the hefty folder she'd been given? She tried to process what her mother had meant by "not tied to the bed-and-breakfast." Did that mean the décor in the themed rooms and equipment like the bread machine and coffeemaker were to be sold along with the B and B?

Robert coughed and started again. "'T-to Samuel Travis, I leave all the money in my business account, which he will need to manage the inn as I am leaving him the Haunted Hill Country Bed-and-Breakfast.'"

Chapter 5

Even though Sam had been warned this was a possibility, he could not believe what the lawyer had just said. And he wasn't the only one.

"What?" Lorelei's body tensed, muscles bunched, as if she was going to leap from her seat. Instead she leaned forward, pinning Robert with her gaze. "That can't be right. I think we need a…" She looked blank for second. "A second opinion! I'm dating an attorney back in Philly."

She was? Sam frowned. He couldn't recall Wanda mentioning a boyfriend. Although Sam steered clear of romantic entanglement, if he ever *did* get into a relationship, he'd for damn sure be there for her if she experienced something as devastating as the loss of a parent. Where exactly was Lorelei's legal eagle this weekend?

Sounding more in control of her emotions, Lorelei continued, "I'm sure Rick would be happy to—"

"Are you saying that you want to contest the will?" Robert blanched. "The court doesn't entertain those cases lightly. It requires citing specific grounds that—"

"Why don't we all stop and take a deep breath?" Ava interjected nervously. "Robert, calm down. I don't think Lorelei plans to run out and file a suit. She's just surprised, is all. Give her a minute to adjust."

"That might take more than a 'minute,'" Lorelei muttered. "But thank you, Ava." She was in the process of relaxing back into her chair when she froze, eyes widening. "Ava, you don't seem all that surprised. Did you know about this? That Mom left the B and B to *him?*"

Sam's jaw clenched at her tone. "Excuse me?" He hadn't asked for Wanda to do this! He didn't deserve to be discussed with the same kind of loathing historically reserved for rattlesnakes and horse thieves.

"Well, I'm sorry," Lorelei grumbled, clearly not sorry at all. Her gaze was as sharp as a bowie knife. "But you can't just turn over an established business to someone because you...what? Liked the color of his aura? How did you get her to do this?"

"What do you mean 'get her' to do it?" he growled. As if he were some con artist who looked for opportunities to swindle kind-hearted ladies out of their property?

Lorelei looked momentarily abashed. "I just don't understand. *I'm* her only living family."

Sam saw red. Even though he consciously tried not to dwell on the past, he could still hear his mother's oh-so-sincere tone when she'd dropped him off with his uncle. *Just because I won't be here every day doesn't mean we aren't still family. I'll be back for you, Sammy.* He had no patience for people who were related only when it was convenient.

"Do you think family is just genetics?" he challenged Lorelei. "Because it meant a lot more than that to Wanda. You say you're confused—well, so am I. And what I want to know is, just where the hell have you been for the past two years?"

With that, he got up and stormed out, so ticked off that he temporarily forgot he didn't even *want* the inn.

There was a shocked silence following Sam's departure. No one was more shocked than Lorelei. She kept trying to reconcile the righteously indignant man who'd just given her an earful with the taciturn cowboy she'd first met. *I think I liked him better when he was monosyllabic and uncooperative.*

She turned to Ava and Robert, Sam's parting shot still ringing in her ears. "It hasn't been two whole years," she said. Immediately, she was annoyed both by the sudden need to justify her actions and how lame her attempt had been.

Ava was far too gracious to roll her eyes. "We know, dear. Sam's just…"

"Just what?" Lorelei demanded in frustration. "I don't even understand who he was to Mom."

"Maybe I should give you ladies a chance to talk privately," Robert suggested. Beneath his suit jacket, his shirt clung to him in damp patches. Beads of sweat dotted his forehead, and he eyed the doorway like a hostage evaluating his chance for escape.

Lorelei sighed. "I'm sure you can understand that it's been a difficult day for all of us. Maybe we could talk next week, after I've had a chance to read through this folder you gave me?"

"Yes, ma'am. Absolutely," he said as he stood. "Call me anytime."

"Thank you. There's coffee and lemonade and lots of delicious-looking cakes downstairs. You should try some before you go."

Nodding, he clutched his briefcase close and disappeared down the hall.

Ava shook her head. "Five bucks says he clears the staircase and bolts out the front door in under thirty seconds."

Lorelei chuckled, and the other woman leaned forward to pat her cheek.

"There's the smile that reminds me of your mom," Ava said approvingly.

"I don't look anything like her," Lorelei said, too practical to pretend otherwise, even on a day like today, when she might take comfort in thinking she did.

"Maybe not, but Wanda was all about looking at a person's spirit, not just their face. I'd like to think some of her spirit lives on in you."

Lorelei expelled a puff of air. At least Ava wasn't planning to have tea with her mother's ghost. "You were pretty evasive the other day when I tried to ask you about Sam. Was that because you didn't know how to tell me about Mom's will?"

Ava raised an eyebrow. "The only specific question I remember you asking was if they were romantically involved, which I believe I answered."

"Fair enough. I'll try to be more specific this time. Who is he and why is he here?"

"Sam was working on a nearby ranch during a real dry summer, helping with the horses, and a fire broke out. They got all the animals safely out of the barn, but we hadn't had any rain in months and the fire spread. Once it was put out, he and about half a dozen others needed places to stay. Some of the local hotel owners offered up free rooms, and Sam ended up here. But he wasn't comfortable taking one of the rooms without paying, so he did some work around the inn for your mom. He comes and goes from Fredericksburg, helping with various trail rides and taking different jobs throughout the region. They got to be close. I think Wanda looked on him like the son she never had."

That hurt enough to knock the breath out of Lorelei. Her mother had left her most valued possession to a man who was "like a son" instead of to the daughter she'd actually had?

Ava tilted her head sympathetically. "Oh, honey. Your mother loved you. She was so proud of you."

"Yeah. I hear that a lot," Lorelei said. What had Sam said when he'd found her sorting through her mother's pictures? That Wanda had looked for opportunities to brag about her?

"I think maybe she worried about Sam. I don't know the details of his childhood, but he doesn't seem to have anybody."

What about all those times after Lorelei's dad had died when *she* had felt alone? She dropped her head into her hands, the irony pounding at her temples.

"You have your life in Philadelphia, a job you love and I'm sure lots of friends there. And apparently a successful lawyer you're dating?"

"Rick," she said numbly. "Rick Caulden."

"What a shame your mother never got to meet him," Ava said.

Lorelei bit her lip, unable to imagine such an introduction—Rick, in his designer suit and Italian shoes, shaking hands with Wanda, in her tie-dyed tunics and lucky pig earrings. Would Rick have looked on the whimsical older woman with derision? Wanda would have clucked over his long hours and his devotion to the law practice. Lorelei could easily guess what her mother would have to say about his work schedule because Lorelei had heard similar lectures about her own life. *She didn't understand me.*

Which was mutual. Try as she might, Lorelei couldn't understand why her mother had changed her will.

"Are you going to be all right, dear?" Ava asked. "I could get you some coffee."

"No, thank you." Lorelei had put away so much coffee since her arrival that she probably had more caffeine than blood running through her veins. "I think I may go to my room for just a little while." That sounded so much like running away that she added, "To check my work email and voice mail. In case anyone needs me." But she was starting to worry…what if no one did?

Sam met his own reproachful gaze in the rectangular mirror above the old-fashioned dresser in his room. "Not your finest hour, Travis." Provoked or not, it was flat wrong to yell at a lady the day of her mother's funeral. His uncle, were he still alive, would have smacked him upside the head for that outburst in the library.

Although JD Travis had always been forthright about his contempt for his sister-in-law, telling Sam he was better off without a "gold digger who'd dump her own kid," even JD drew the line at being outright rude to a woman. On the few occasions when Rita Travis Hart had remembered she had a son, JD mostly limited his comments to grunts with "ma'am" tacked on the end. He certainly wouldn't have yelled at her, although Sam used to wish his uncle would.

Sam had been poleaxed by the unfairness of life— first losing his workaholic father to a heart attack, then being handed off to an uncle he barely knew so his grieving mother could "get herself together." Her recovery had included finding husband number two—a wealthy businessman from Dallas. Sam had been too afraid of alienating her further to lash out. But he'd dreamed of someone championing his cause and demanding to know how Rita could live with herself, cheerfully creating a second family as if her first one had never existed.

All of which was ancient history and didn't excuse his temper this afternoon.

Sam raised his gaze upward. "Sorry, Wanda." She would have been even less pleased over his behavior than JD. What had she imagined would happen when the news broke? Sam was equal parts touched and exasperated that she had chosen to leave him such a— *burden*—gift.

He went back to that moment when Robert Stork had made the announcement, the look of utter incredulity on Lorelei's face. Any sense of camaraderie they'd shared that morning had been annihilated in an instant. He experienced a twinge of loss almost like a paper cut, sharp and sudden. How much could it really matter if Lorelei Keller disliked him or believed he'd somehow maneuvered himself into her mother's will? He had no doubt Lorelei would be out of Texas as soon as humanly possible, back to her life up north and that Rick guy.

Good. Sam wouldn't be sorry to see her go. In the

meantime, however, he wouldn't let her rile him. He decided to go downstairs for a mug of coffee and one of Ava's apricot *kolaches*. If he was able to get a second with Lorelei when she wasn't surrounded by townspeople, he'd tell her he regretted his behavior.

Although some folks were beginning to leave, the crowd was still pretty thick. He nodded to a few people he knew on his way to the kitchen. Ava stood at the sink, drying dishes while Clare Theo washed.

He tapped Clare on the shoulder. "How about I relieve you for a spell, let you get off your feet, darlin'?"

The grey-haired woman smiled up at him. "I'd appreciate that, Sam." She handed him the platter she'd been holding. "I'll be back in a few minutes, okay?"

"Take your time."

Ava glared at him through her glasses. "Well, that was chivalrous."

As opposed to how he'd acted earlier, she meant. "After I'm done here," Sam said, "I thought maybe I'd look for Lorelei. You know where she is?"

"In her room. She mentioned checking in with her office."

On a Saturday? Under these circumstances?

The woman was unbelievable. Sam's father had literally worked himself to death, largely ignoring his family in pursuit of the almighty dollar, but even *he* looked like a slacker compared to Lorelei. Sam ground his teeth. Maybe now wasn't the best time to go looking for her after all. It would be difficult to apologize and actually sound sincere.

"You were pretty hard on her earlier," Ava said, in chiding counterpoint to his thoughts.

He'd thought so, too, but maybe they were both

wrong. Instead of regretting the times she'd told Wanda she was too busy with her job to visit, Lorelei had simply retreated to her room to work some more. He felt like shaking the woman.

But he hated for Ava to think badly of him. He ducked his head. "Forgive me?"

She pursed her lips in a stern expression, but, behind the spectacles, mischief danced in her eyes. "I can't stay mad at you. Even if I was angry, you've already received punishment enough for one day. After all, *you* are now the proud owner of that cat."

The day had been the longest of Lorelei's life, so why couldn't she sleep? Exhaustion seeped through her bones even as a contradictory restlessness left her tossing and turning. The bed was adequately comfortable, but rest eluded her. Maybe she needed some white noise. The quiet was tomblike after hours of chatter and sniffling and piano music and coffee percolating.

Or maybe she was restless knowing that Sam Travis, self-righteous usurper, was at the far end of the hall, probably sleeping like a baby. Despite their being the only two people under the roof, they'd successfully managed to avoid each other all evening. She hadn't seen him since his dramatic exit from the library. Considering the circumstances, she thought it was rich that *he* was in a snit.

Kicking off the covers, Lorelei gave up all pretense that she might fall asleep soon. *Forget this.* Instead, she decided it was time to try one of the many desserts in the kitchen. She could bring a piece of pie back to her room, maybe grab a book from the library while she was it. She'd already finished the only reading material she'd brought with her, a bound analysis on the mortality impact of medication interruption in post-disaster scenarios. Opening her door as quietly as possible, she crept out into the hall. The automatic nightlights Wanda had always kept plugged in for the guests illuminated the path to the stairs.

She almost missed a step when Oberon shot out of nowhere, zooming up the stairs in some inexplicable feline frenzy. Gripping the banister, Lorelei bit back a string of curse words—maybe her company should consider adding special life insurance policies for cat owners. Her heart was still racing when she reached the bottom of the staircase.

Seeing Sam Travis, shirtless in the arc of light that spilled from the open refrigerator, did nothing to slow her pulse.

What was he doing down here? The knee-jerk question was so dumb she didn't bother voicing it. Obviously he hadn't been able to sleep, either.

He must have heard her coming down the creaky staircase. Without looking back at her, he said, "I'm about to pour a glass of milk and cut into the German chocolate cake. You want a piece?"

Finding herself temporarily mute, she shook her head. At her silence, Sam turned around. Their eyes locked, and she was glad she stood in the shadows. Maybe he couldn't see the blush heating her cheeks. Although she'd been infuriated by the hateful way he'd spoken to her earlier, the anger didn't stop her instinctive female appreciation of his broad shoulders and bare chest. Knowing he'd defined those arms and abs working hard under the Texas sun somehow made them even more appealing than muscles honed through an expensive gym membership. It was a damn shame the man ever wore a shirt. Her gaze slid involuntarily down his body toward the denim waistband of his jeans.

The corner of his mouth kicked up. "You stare any harder, you're going to bore holes into me."

The warmth in her face ignited to full-on flames. She opened her mouth to snap that she hadn't been staring, but the lie stuck in her throat. Instead she advised, "Don't be conceited. Haven't you displayed enough character flaws for one day?"

His expression tightened. "Do you want any or not?"

Cake, she remembered. He'd offered her a slice of the German chocolate. "No, thank you. I'm not much for chocolate."

"One of those women who won't let herself enjoy desserts?" he inquired as he set the gallon of milk on the counter. He let the refrigerator door fall shut, taking most of the light with it. What remained came from a dim lamp above the stove.

"Not at all," she said as she came into the kitchen. "I just don't have a typical sweet tooth. I prefer desserts with extra bite to them. A really tart piece of lemon cake, or something spicy like—"

"Mrs. Hoffman's chili-powder dark chocolate brownies?" His tone was reverent. "Those kick ass."

She laughed. "Agreed." To the dismay of citizens and tourists alike, Bertha Hoffman held the exact recipe a closely guarded secret.

It was surreal to be standing in the dark discussing desserts with this man, when only hours earlier he'd been lambasting her in front of an audience for being a lousy daughter and taking ownership of the inn she'd assumed she would inherit. Would it be easier to talk about the situation now, rather than in a formal setting with an attorney present?

Sam picked up one of the many plastic food containers that lined the countertops and walked toward her in easy, long-legged strides. He moved with a rugged grace that was nearly mesmerizing. "Here." He stopped inches from her. "You might like these. Lemon curd cupcakes, made by one of the women who works at the visitors' center."

"Thanks." She gave him a tentative smile as she took the container, careful to keep her gaze raised and not ogle his body again. But looking him in the eye was, in some ways, worse. An uncomfortable awareness crackled between them.

He cleared his throat. "Lorelei... I'm sorry about earlier, with the attorney."

Her shoulders sagged as some of the tension she'd been carrying for the last few hours left her body. "Me, too. I know I wasn't very tactful. I was just so caught off guard. She was my *mother,* and she loved this inn." It had hurt far more than Lorelei ever could have predicted to learn that Wanda hadn't left something so important to her only blood relative. It had been like the death of an unvoiced dream, cementing that mother and daughter had never been close enough. And now they never could.

Sam reached out, cupping her cheek with a rough, warm palm. A shiver ran through her body, and he quickly dropped his hand to his side. "If it makes you feel better, I don't know what she was thinking." He turned back to the cake and milk he'd abandoned.

"You said your father died when you were young," Lorelei said softly. "Were you and your mother close?"

Maybe it was difficult for him to understand Lorelei's reluctance to visit Fredericksburg because he couldn't relate to how hard each visit had been. Every painfully awkward encounter had been another reminder that Wanda and Lorelei would never have the relationship that was supposed to come naturally to mothers and daughters. Worse, Wanda had never wanted to acknowledge the estrangement. Her cheerfully determined oblivion had only served to make Lorelei feel even *more* isolated.

Sam had tensed the second she asked her question, but he'd yet to answer it. Finally, he spared a glance over his shoulder. "No." He poured a glass of milk and cut a slice of cake without offering any further explanation.

Lorelei sighed inwardly. *The return of Monosyllable Man.* Oh, well. She wasn't sure she could have articulated her and Wanda's relationship, anyway. It was difficult to complain about a parent who had loved you and bragged about you without sounding crazy. Or, worse, whiny. She took a seat at the table and grabbed a napkin, prepared to indulge in a little cupcake therapy.

Directly opposite her, Sam scraped a chair back across the tile. But after a few bites, his fork clattered to the plate.

Lorelei looked up, surprised.

"My mother…" If his words were visible, they'd be the color of rusty water spurting from a faucet too long unused. "I was an only child. Considering the hours my father worked, I'm shocked they even managed to have me. But after he was gone, she sent me to stay with Uncle JD. Said it was just temporary." Sam looked away, but not before she glimpsed the bitterness etching its way into his expression.

"You were there longer than expected." It wasn't a question.

He stabbed at the cake. "'Til I left on the rodeo circuit at eighteen. Don't matter now, of course." His informal speech seemed like a forced attempt at casualness, and he continued without ever looking at her. "But when I was a kid, there would be these days when I was out in the field and I'd see the dust that meant someone was coming down the road and I—"

"You thought it was her," Lorelei added almost desperately. She felt compelled to rescue him from saying the words himself. She ached for the small boy whose hopes had been raised and dashed each time.

He scrubbed a hand over his face. "This sounds loco to admit, but whenever someone came down that dirt road and it *wasn't* her, I felt like they'd, I don't know, taken something from me. I hope that's not how you felt today, Lorelei. Like I took the inn from you?"

Like you took her *from me.* But it wasn't his fault that Lorelei and her mother had lost their chance to ever be close. A mass of conflicting emotions grew inside her like some malignant tumor.

"I don't even want the inn," Sam admitted with a short, self-deprecating laugh. "What the hell would *I* do with it? Wanda left a legacy of gracious hospitality. She put everyone at ease."

Lorelei's hands clenched in her lap. *Not everyone.*

He took a deep breath. "I can't give you your mother back. But if you want to step into her shoes, run the inn—"

"Run it? I'd be as inept as you!" When he quirked an eyebrow, she backpedaled. "I—I mean, I have a life in Philadelphia."

"Right. How silly of me to forget." He tipped his chair back on two legs, regarding her through narrowed eyes. "I'm sure your Rick is anxious for you to get back."

Rick didn't get *anxious* about anything but making partner. She waved a dismissive hand. They'd had a mutually beneficial and highly flexible arrangement, not an exclusive relationship. "More importantly, I have a career there. A job I worked hard to get and don't plan to give up so that I can come down here and fix tea and fold guest towels. No, we should sell the B and B. Split the profits," she offered, touched by the way he'd been about to turn over the whole kit and caboodle to her. He'd been important to her mother and, despite Lorelei's shock that afternoon, he deserved to share in the inheritance, too.

His chair hit the floor with a thud and he rose immediately. "Good night, Lorelei." There was no good reason, as far as she knew, for him to have snarled the words.

"Wait." She frowned. "I thought we were talking."

His words carried back to her, muffled. "And now we're not."

Frustrated, she strode after him. She could maybe excuse his storming out of the will reading—after all, he'd apologized for that behavior. But another rude exit in the middle of a conversation? This one actually ticked her off more because she'd thought for a few moments that they'd connected on some level.

"You're going to walk away again?" she demanded from behind him. "Is this a habit with you?"

Since she wasn't prepared for him to stop suddenly

in the hallway, she almost lost her balance trying to keep from plowing into him.

"Leaving seemed more polite than staying to speak my mind," he growled as he turned to face her. "You don't want to be in my company right now."

Aggravated past diplomacy, Lorelei rolled her eyes at his soft warning. "Oh, brother. Is that anything like 'you wouldn't like me when I'm angry'? You've already lashed out at me once today, and I survived. Go ahead, cowboy, tell me again what a lousy daughter I was. I'd love to have the stellar insight of someone who barely knows me and never had a single firsthand glance of what my relationship with Wanda was like. Let me have it," she challenged, poking her index finger right below his collarbone. "I can take anything you can dish out."

Chapter 6

She probably *could* handle anything, Sam reasoned. It was probably easy to keep your composure if you had ice water in your veins. He'd foolishly thought he was getting a look at a different Lorelei tonight, one who truly missed her mother and was capable of empathizing with people. She'd even somehow got him to open up about his own family history, which he never did.

So when she'd deftly turned the conversation to "profits" and shrugged off the possibility that there might be actual people in Philadelphia who meant more than her precious career... God. She seemed more like the biological child of *his* parents than a relative of Wanda Keller's.

"Well?" Lorelei taunted.

It seemed criminal that her expression could be so cold after he'd glimpsed a brief flare of unguarded heat earlier. Objectively, Lorelei was attractive—especially with her thick hair tumbling loose over her shoulders, her pink T-shirt and pajama shorts adding a rosy flush to a face scrubbed free of makeup. But the unmistakable desire he'd seen in her dark gaze had transformed her beyond a pretty woman to stunning, an enchantress from a man's dreams. He wanted to make her acknowledge what she'd felt, wanted to do *something* that thawed her the hell out.

Without consciously planning to, he backed her toward the wall. Her breathing grew hectic. Sam tried to ignore the rise and fall of her braless chest just inches from his body.

In contrast to her obvious physical awareness of him, her tone was deliberately bored. "I'm not impressed with the Neanderthal act." Her gaze dropped to his mouth, and Sam hardened.

"It's not an act," he said grimly. The thought of tossing her over his shoulder and dragging her back to his cave was far more appealing than it should have been. When had he leaned in so close to her?

He straightened. "I am going to bed. Alone."

She shoved at his shoulders with both hands. "I sure as hell wasn't volunteering to join you."

"I meant, don't follow me this time," he clarified. But he held her gaze, not stepping aside yet, as he waited for her to agree.

"We'll talk in the morning," she declared.

No, we won't. He turned toward the staircase. He'd already said more than intended to Lorelei Keller, and he didn't plan to make that mistake again.

He didn't bother telling her he'd been hired to help supervise a two-day trail ride out of Bandera. He was packed and planned to get an early start. Sam took the stairs two at a time, confident he'd be able to slip out tomorrow without encountering Lorelei. If he was uncharacteristically lucky, she might even be gone by the time he returned.

When Lorelei woke, sunlight was streaming between the curtain panels. She blinked, her mind groggy and her body tingling. Sudden embarrassment cut through her mental haze and she tried to stifle the memory of erotic dreams flavored with German chocolate kisses. She hurried out of bed, moving with impressive speed for someone with no coffee in her system, and headed for the shower, leaving the water colder than she normally would.

Forty minutes later, she was dressed, her damp hair neatly braided, and feeling in control again. She made her way to the kitchen, telling herself that if she should happen to run in to Sam Travis, he wouldn't make so much as a dent in her equilibrium.

Whether he was wearing a shirt or not. She even walked down the stairs with extra caution, lest Oberon decide it was time to race the Kitty 500 again.

But there seemed to be no sign of man or beast today.

She pulled out the coffee and a filter, then noticed a piece of scratch paper from the notepads Wanda placed in each guest room and by the kitchen phone. Sam's handwriting was an unselfconscious scrawl of black across the pale purple stationery.

L—

I'll be on the road for the next couple of days, so you'll have the place all to yourself until Tuesday night. If you head back to Philly before then, just

*lock up when you go. Wouldn't want anything to
happen to my inn.*
S.T.

She crumpled the paper in her hand. His inn? The
man was schizo. Last night, he'd seemed on the verge of
giving it to her. Then he'd done a complete about-face,
treating her to that obnoxious display of testosterone.
Her toes curled at the memory, and she gave herself an
impatient shake. She was not the type of woman to go
weak in the knees because some bare-chested cowboy
leaned over her, looking as if he were about to kiss her
senseless and carry her up the stairs.

No, that idea was not attractive at all.

"Rowrrr?" The meowed greeting, more inquisitive
than hostile, jolted her from her reverie.

"Morning, Obie." She glanced down. "Hope you
weren't looking for Travis. He's gone, and I for one
am thrilled. Turns out, he might actually be more of a
beast than you."

After an hour of the chuckwagon cook playing har-
monica to accompany a "cowboy balladeer," riders were
finally turning in for the night, disappearing into their
tents in groups of two or three. Armed with a padded
bedroll, Sam had opted to sleep outside, where he could
periodically check on the horses and the dying fire. It
was a beautiful clear night but cool enough that bugs
wouldn't be an issue. Away from big cities and towns,
the stars were magnificent in the inky sky—almost too
crowded for him to make out individual constellations.
Why spend the night beneath the colorless canvas of a
tent when he could savor this instead?

During Sam's early teens, he and his uncle had often camped in the open air. JD had died years ago while Sam had been working cattle on the other side of the state, but he could still hear the old man's voice in his head on nights like this.

"All you need is right here," his uncle had said. "Texas dirt beneath your feet, a sky full of stars overhead and the occasional Shiner beer—but not 'til you're older, boy. Don't know why my brother could never understand. Instead of appreciating the gifts he had in his life, he worked himself into the ground pursuing the almighty dollar. Your mama's no better, throwing herself at that country club king. But you won't make their mistakes, will you?"

"No, sir," Sam murmured nearly two decades later, his breath creating wispy puffs in the cooling air. The temperature had been dropping since the sun set, and he welcomed the crispness. It helped him think. Now that the riders were bunked down for the night and the peaceful rustling wind had replaced choruses of "Deep in the Heart of Texas" and "Home on the Range," he felt more clearheaded than he had since the morning he'd found Wanda. *I needed this.*

Maybe he'd simply been getting too stir-crazy in the B and B. That might explain his temporary insanity last night. He didn't know which was harder to believe— that he'd almost kissed Lorelei Keller, or that, unless his instincts were *completely* off, she would have let him. They had nothing in common.

Well, they'd both lost fathers at a young age and seemed to have complicated relationships with their mothers. But other than that…

Sam frowned into the blackness. For all that he'd resented his mother dumping him on JD, he had to admit that upbringing had probably saved him. What would he be like now if the Dallas country club king had raised him? Sam couldn't understand why Lorelei had habitually refused her mother's entreaties to come home, why she seemed so disdainful of her roots. Had she ever been lucky enough to see her birthplace the way he did? He folded his arms beneath his head, drinking in the raw beauty of the night.

The only things marring his peace were the unwanted thoughts of Lorelei, buzzing through his mind like mosquitoes. He'd seen real pain in her eyes when she talked about her parents and had glimpsed a wickedly tempting heat in her eyes last night. Was it too late for someone to save the number cruncher from up north? Despite how coldly efficient she could sometimes be, there was real emotion deep down.

Deep, deep down.

Not my problem. Sam put his hands behind his bed and looked up at the thousands of twinkling stars. He had a simple, uncomplicated life that provided everything he needed and it was a shame other people couldn't find fulfillment without their sixty-hour work weeks and cell phones and the ability to check email every ten minutes.

Still, as he drifted to sleep, his imagination provided tantalizing fantasies of what it would be like to show Lorelei the Texas he knew, to see the constant tension around her eyes relax and her mouth curve into a beckoning smile. A sight like that might actually rival the stars.

The storm that rolled in Monday afternoon was severe enough that Lorelei stopped packing boxes to assess the probability of a power outage. She rummaged through several kitchen cabinets and desk drawers in search of candles, matches and flashlights. Rain lashed the windows and the wind outside was howling more angrily than Oberon the summer he'd been sprayed by a skunk and Wanda had given him a bath. But the wind and rain were mere whispers compared to the house-rattling booms of thunder.

Shivering, Lorelei huddled deeper into her sweater. It was one of her rainy day favorites—forest-green ribbed chenille with a zipped-up neckline. She still felt chilled, though, either from the damp weather or the emotional havoc of digging through her mother's memories and trying to parcel them out to various acquaintances and charities. Maybe it was time she took a break from cataloguing and sorting Wanda's personal items and fixed herself a late lunch. It seemed like a good day for soup.

Armed with a flashlight, just in case, she made her way into the kitchen's walk-in pantry. Within minutes, she'd located pasta, broth and canned chicken. Onions hung in a mesh bag over the counter.

"As long as we've got all the basic seasonings and carrots in the fridge, we're in business," she muttered.

The last thing she expected to hear was an answering voice. "Hello?" A man, not Sam or the lawyer, called from the front of the house.

Lorelei was startled enough that she dropped a can on her foot. She sucked in a breath. "J-just a minute." Given the neatly typed sign posted in the front window about the inn not being open for business, she hadn't expected anyone to walk right in without knocking. *Should've locked the front door after walking down to the mailbox this morning.*

She set down her ingredients on the table and limped down the hallway to the entrance. Two men, both dripping water off their coats, stood at the welcome table. They were perusing not the official pamphlets on local attractions, but rather the spiral notebook in which Wanda had encouraged visitors to write about any "paranormal encounters" they'd experienced in the Hill Country.

"Ooh." The one with the receding hair line waved the little notebook in the air. "Read this part about the nearby Flagstone Guesthouse. It claims that doors open and close by themselves and that things turn on and off for no reason. Lights, faucets, television sets."

Lorelei cleared her throat, announcing her presence. "I'm sorry, but we're not renting out any rooms right now. Or arranging tours."

"Oh, we know." The other man, a shaggy, auburn-haired guy, beamed at her with baffling enthusiasm. "We're not here to check into a room, although that would be awesome. We stopped by because we heard someone *died.*"

"Right here in the hotel," his friend crowed happily.

Lorelei's stomach knotted. These two hadn't been drawn to the inn by stories of Wanda's legendary hospitality and the promise of hot coffee on a cold wet day. They were here because of morbid curiosity, because they were delighted at the idea that someone—*her mother!*—had died under this very roof.

"The woman you're referring to was Wanda Keller, my mom and the owner," she said stiffly. "Which is why—"

"Has she tried to contact you since she crossed over?" the redhead asked.

His friend groaned. "We've had this conversation, Dwayne. They haven't crossed if they're *still* here."

The bearded fellow, Dwayne, was too excited to debate the point. "Maybe Mrs. Keller could become famous in these parts for haunting the place, like Mrs. Mueller's ghost over at—"

"Show a little respect!" Lorelei snapped. She'd always hated conversations like this, but having to endure her mother's insistence that Lorelei's father wasn't truly gone hadn't been anywhere near as upsetting as these two idiots practically cackling with glee over Wanda's death. It had been less than a week since her death and they were reducing to her to some urban legend. *Where's Oberon when I need him to attack someone?*

The shorter man held up his hands, palms facing her, in a conciliatory gesture. "Your mother based this place on supernatural anecdotes and ghost stories, ma'am. She was interested in the same things we are. I don't think she'd mind our being here."

"I mind." Lorelei was starting to feel slightly crazed. She really should have taken a break to eat earlier. The few instances of spectacular temper in her past had frequently started with an empty stomach and low blood sugar.

"Uh…maybe we should go, Dwayne. We could always check out that Admiral Nimitz Museum over on Main. Some people say they've seen—"

"But we're here already," Dwayne whined. He shot Lorelei a rebuking look. "What could it possibly hurt just to let us look around while we wait out the storm? You don't even have to come with us. Have you experienced any cold spots? Unexplained electrical phenomenon? We just want to compile data on any possible paranormal—"

"Turn you two morons loose unsupervised? I don't think so," Lorelei said. "I want you out of here."

"Morons?" Dwayne gasped. "Now look here—"

"Ghosts don't exist! They're an invention of horror writers and superstitious people who don't know how to let go." *Or how to help their daughters let go.* Lorelei clenched her fists. "I suggest you stop obsessing over the afterlives of total strangers and *get a life* yourselves."

From behind her, a deep voice agreed, "You heard what the lady said. Don't let the door hit you on the way out."

"Sam!" Lorelei whirled around.

He was the last person she'd expected to see today—his note had said he wouldn't be back until Tuesday. His entrance through the back door must have been masked by the ongoing thunder. He looked so sane and solid, standing there in a black long-sleeve shirt and jeans, his customary hat tipped back just enough on his forehead for Dwayne and Dwayne's slightly less moronic friend to get the full impact of his glower.

Dwayne gulped. "When might be a better time to—"

Sam took half a step forward. "Goodbye, gentleman." Perfectly polite words, yet they were laced with enough menace to send the two unwelcome guests scrambling.

Once the men were gone, Lorelei turned back to her unexpected ally. "Thank you." She could have kicked them out herself—had been in the process of doing so—but Sam's presence had certainly expedited the process. What she appreciated the most wasn't even that the men were gone, it was the chance she'd been given to regain her emotions. For a second there, she'd wanted to yell and throw things and she wasn't even sure why. The two men had been a little insensitive, but the chasm between her and her mother had hardly been their fault.

He looked uncomfortable with her gratitude. "Don't mention it."

So what could she safely mention? They'd parted on rather tense terms. Was he disappointed that she was still here? Had he thought about their charged encounter in the hallway the other night? Lord knew she had.

Cheeks heating, she ducked her head. "Have you eaten? I'm about to make soup."

"Sounds good. See you after I change."

With his clothes being so dark, she hadn't immediately realized how wet they were. "Don't cowboys carry umbrellas in their trucks?" Back in Philadelphia, she kept two different size umbrellas in her car, as well as a first-aid kit, emergency cold weather supplies, a spare tire and jumper cables. She'd opted against a flare because of the potential fire hazards and dangerous gases.

He peered at her as if she were speaking a foreign language. "I've helped rescue cattle in flooding situations. I was pretty sure I could get from the truck to the inn without an umbrella."

"Right. Sorry. Carry on." Lorelei's face heated and she marveled at the fact that with one glance he'd made her feel as if perfectly sensible preparations were ridiculous. Or OCD. She couldn't relate to a man whose occupation—not that he seemed to have a steady, constant job—involved activities like riding in rodeos and rounding up cattle in storms. It seemed as if he deliberately sought out risk.

He disappeared up the stairs. Putting thoughts of Sam out of her mind, she studied the spiral notebook that had captivated the two men and sighed. *Speaking of people I can't relate to.* Was it possible Wanda had shared more in common with those men than with her own daughter? Wanda had always seemed more interested in fancy than reality—even though that reality included a scared little girl who needed her.

"What the hell?"

Wondering what had upset Sam, Lorelei hurried up the stairs. His door was ajar and she could see him—hatless, shirtless, but still wearing the damp jeans like a second skin—standing in the center of the room. "Everything okay?"

He shook his head and pointed, but she had to step farther inside to see what he was indicating.

She looked toward the bed. "Oh, dear." Her eyes widened, and she tried to suppress a laugh. "I guess Oberon wasn't too happy about you abandoning him." The cat had left several…mementos of his displeasure atop the quilted comforter.

"*He's* not happy?" Sam ground his teeth.

"Try to take it as a form of flattery," she suggested sweetly. "He must have really missed you while you were gone."

He picked up a white T-shirt from the back of a chair. She tried not to watch the ripple of muscles in his arms and back as he shrugged into it. "Do you think," he began, his words slightly muffled for a second, "that if we put demon cat in a box and left him on Ava's doorstep she's softhearted enough to keep him?"

"Ha! No way anyone's getting that cat into a box

without losing a limb." Not unless they laced his kibble with whiskey and waited for him to pass out.

"You might be surprised." Sam turned to face her, studying her for a moment with those hypnotic green eyes. His tone took on an uncharacteristic aw-shucks innocence she didn't buy for a second. "After all, I've had a lot of experience with livestock. Gentling the orneriest, feistiest creatures is pretty much my specialty."

While Sam cleaned his bed and carted linens to the laundry room, Lorelei returned to her soup preparations. She diced onions, carrots and celery. *Whack, whack, whack.* The thud of the knife against the cutting board was a bit harder than necessary but cathartic. *Arrogant cowboy.* Unless she was very much mistaken, he'd just lumped her in with his assessment of ornery livestock. *Whack.* If he made so much as one patronizing comment about breaking in fillies, she was going to—

"Smells good," he called as he walked into the kitchen.

She didn't bother answering as she scraped the vegetables into the pot of simmering broth, along with healthy doses of garlic and freshly ground black pepper.

"Impressive." Sam sounded surprised. "When you said soup, I assumed you were opening a can."

Because he didn't think she could cook? "It's only impressive when I have a whole chicken and make the stock myself." Although that took a lot longer, and she was hungry now. She cast a critical eye at the ingredients lined up on the counter. "That's not the pasta I would normally use, either."

He chuckled. "I grew up with a man who had exactly two specialties, only one of which was edible. I'm not picky."

With both of them in the kitchen, the rain outside didn't seem so dreary. It was almost…cozy. But that was an illusion, she reminded herself. After all, they'd been here before—and it hadn't ended well. In her career, she spent a lot of time looking at past trends and trying to minimize risk. She was smart enough to make that work for her in her personal life, too.

"I wasn't expecting you until tomorrow," she said. "Come back early to check on your inn?"

"I was helping with a trail ride. You may have noticed this isn't optimal riding weather." He leaned his elbows on the counter and watched her, his expression inscrutable. "Glad I got back when I did, though. You seemed upset."

"It wasn't a big deal. I shouldn't have let those two guys get to me." She spun away from Sam and his too-close scrutiny and began loading things into the dishwasher, her tone brisk. "That was…uncharacteristic. I normally have control of myself."

"And you think that's a good thing?" Sam asked softly. His tone wasn't argumentative, but it was difficult not to feel defensive.

"Of course I do. I built a career on analyzing facts, then making smart decisions. People need to do more of that and less uninformed reacting. Can you imagine how much better off we'd be if everyone stopped making emotional snap judgments?"

When he said nothing, she looked back at him and was surprised to see him shaking his head and grinning.

Why should she be stung that he didn't agree with her rational perspective? Growing up in this area, she'd always felt like the odd woman out. Sam was just continuing the tradition. "You find my outlook amusing?"

"No, ma'am. I wasn't laughing at you—just the irony. See, I made one of those snap decisions on the drive back. I'd been trying to decide how to tell you about it."

If he needed to tell her, then it obviously affected her. Despite the words she'd just spoken about not reacting until you had all the pertinent information, nervousness fluttered in stomach. "Wh-what kind of decision?"

"You don't like that your mama left me in the inn," he said. "And, truth is, I don't want it. I have other things in my life that are important to me, and I'm not looking for more. But it feels disrespectful to Wanda simply to hand the place over to you. She could have done that herself and chose not to for reasons of her own."

"Okay," she said slowly. She was following his logic so far; she just wasn't sure where he was leading. "So...?"

"Frederick-Fest kicks off this weekend. I know your mom really wanted you to be here for that."

Something painful twisted inside Lorelei. The last few conversations she'd had with her mother—the last conversations they would ever have—had been Wanda imploring her to come and Lorelei refusing. If Lorelei were the type to subscribe to mystical explanations, she might have questioned whether her mom had somehow had a premonition that this would be their last opportunity to share the town tradition.

"Here's what I propose," Sam began. "You stay for Frederick-Fest, run the booth your mother has already paid for and accompany me and a few tourists on the Haunted Trail Ride next Friday night. And when we get back, I'll sell you the B and B for a dollar."

"Plus there might be legal fees or closing costs for transfer of ownership," she said absently, still trying to wrap her mind around what he'd just offered. "I know the festival was a big deal to Mom, but she never mentioned any trail ride."

He quirked an eyebrow. "Afraid you can't rough it for a night, sleeping on the ground so far from civilization? Might do you some good."

"So this is what, simple pettiness on your part? A hoop I have to jump through before you'll let me have the inn?" *I can handle one lousy camping trip.*

"Is that really what you think? I was serious when I said it might be good for you. Being out there is…a balm to the soul." He said it challengingly, as if expecting her to mock his words. "More importantly, it's a 'haunted' ride—legends shared around the campfire, passing through areas where so-called ghosts roam. The kind of stuff your mother loved."

And I hate.

"Do this for her. You might even have fun."

"I don't understand you. Logically, it makes no sense for you to even give me the inn, much less care whether I stay for the week."

He regarded her solemnly. "Your mother cared."

Lorelei believed that if she met his bizarre conditions, he'd truly give her the place to sell. With the tourism in the area, she was confident she could find a buyer. Even she had to admit there were great attractions nearby. There were all kinds of activities and landmarks for nature enthusiasts; history buffs enjoyed the Pioneer Museum and National Museum on the Pacific War. The Fredericksburg Music Club and the Hill Country Film Festival added touches of culture. Then there was the boom in the regional food and wine industry. On highway 290 alone, leading into town, there were ten wineries, including Lorelei's favorite, Grape Creek. Plus, she'd heard that a major cooking competition was taking place in the area, drawing even more publicity.

Fredericksburg was a great destination. For people who didn't have her memories.

She cocked her head. "And are you planning to stay at the inn for the duration of the festival?"

"That's a problem?" The question seemed to catch him off guard. "We've been sleeping under the same roof so far."

Not for the past two nights. And that last night he'd spent at the inn, when she'd found him in the kitchen... She recalled the glint in his eye, the way he'd leaned toward her in the hall. Her breathing quickened, and she stirred the chicken in with the pasta and vegetables, keeping her gaze locked on the soup.

"No problem at all!" she chirped, mentally kicking herself for even posing the question. For the first time, she wondered about his usual sleeping arrangements. "Where do you stay when you're not here?"

"Variety of places. I have a trailer on some pasture land that's home base. For work in this area, staying with Wanda was always more convenient." He nodded toward the stove. "And the cooking here was always a hell of a lot better."

At that, Lorelei smiled. Her mother had been quite a cook. She'd always encouraged Lorelei to plan her own birthday menu, telling her no request was too extravagant. On Lorelei's eighth birthday, they'd had a four-course dinner of different kinds of German cookies, followed by a trip to one of the town's amazing chocolatiers. Looking back, Lorelei was stunned she hadn't ended up with a monster stomachache and a mouthful of cavities.

Reliving the memories made her feel strangely exposed, and she was glad when Sam stepped away from her.

He opened a drawer at the end of the counter and pulled out a deck of cards. "You play poker, by any chance? Blackjack? Figure we have a few minutes before the soup's ready."

She wrinkled her nose. "I don't gamble."

He smirked. "Thought as much."

So she was predictable? It was mildly annoying, but she was secure enough not to throw herself into a chair and say "deal me in," just to prove him wrong.

He sat at the table, long legs stretched in front of him, and started laying out the cards for solitaire.

Lorelei couldn't remember the last time she'd seen anyone play the game with actual cards. Usually, it was through a phone app or at the computer while waiting on hold to talk to someone. "You own a cell phone?" she heard herself ask.

"Sure." He flipped over a black ace. "Made a lot more sense for me than a landline. Why, you want the number?"

She shook her head. "I was just...wondering." *Idiot.* What had she thought, that just because Sam was good with horses and wore a cowboy hat he wouldn't know how to text? Fredericksburg might be a historic town, but Sam was not some pioneer frontiersman.

Frankly, she couldn't decide what he was.

He managed to do or say something that surprised her nearly every time they spoke and it irked her that she might be easy for him to peg while he remained a mystery. Her mind was naturally drawn to studying something—*or someone?*—until she fully understood it. Yet caution warned that prolonged observation of Sam Travis could lead to more complications than answers.

Chapter 7

Sam was too accustomed to waking before sunrise. Wednesday was a rare day off before he spent Thursday and Friday helping set up for the festival. Technically, he could have slept in—yet when his eyes opened at six-thirty in the morning, he knew he might as well start his day.

He could call Grace Torres after breakfast and let her know he had some time free. She'd asked him a couple of weeks ago about a few minor renovations she wanted to make to her family's restaurant, The Twisted Jalapeño. He liked Grace. The young woman didn't fuss and cluck over him like Ava and the other town matrons, nor did she size him up greedily like Barbara Biggins, as if she'd heard that "ride a cowboy" song one too many times. Grace was too preoccupied with her restaurant to have any romantic agendas, which made her easy to be around.

Interesting logic. Because, far as he could tell, Lorelei Keller was about the least romantic woman he'd ever met, but her company certainly wasn't "easy." Corporate priorities aside, she made him uncomfortable in ways he didn't entirely understand or care to examine.

He shook his head and swung his feet to the floor. Lorelei would be gone in less than two weeks. How she made him feel was irrelevant.

It wasn't yet seven when Sam left his room and headed for the kitchen to brew some coffee. But the minute he rounded the corner, the rich, heady scent greeted him and he realized Lorelei had beat him to it. She stood at the counter in a pair of skinny jeans and a cream-colored tank top. Her dark hair was wet, and Sam's body tightened at thought of her in the shower.

He cleared his throat. "You're up early."

She glanced over her shoulder. "Can't seem to shake the habit, even on days I'm not going into the office. But I actually have a reason this morning. Ava and I are going to caravan to San Antonio and drop off my rental car. Since I'll be staying longer than originally planned," she said pointedly. "I'll just have to bum rides off people for the duration of my stay."

"I can take you to and from the festival next week," he offered.

"Thanks." But from her dry tone, he guessed she was recalling that *he* was the reason she had to go to the festival.

"You've talked to your boss, right?" Did guilt motivate his question? Generally, Sam wasn't one for second-guessing himself, but he couldn't help wondering if his gentle blackmail had been such a good idea.

She nodded. "Yesterday. They approved the additional time and we agreed on some work I could do from here. I'll start compiling data for a trend study and— There you go again," she said, her tone laced with exasperation.

"What are you talking about?"

"Your intimidating scowl," she clarified, sounding not the least intimidated. "You do that when I talk about work. What do you have against actuaries?"

The corner of his mouth kicked up as he admitted, "Darlin', I'm not even sure what an actuary is." Although he'd overhead a joke in line at the bank once, that an actuary was an accountant, "but without the personality."

Instead of sharing that, Sam gestured toward the coffeemaker. "You know a watched pot never brews, right? How about I scramble us some eggs while we're waiting?" It seemed only fair. She'd made soup for him on Monday; then when he'd got in last night he'd found a note directing him to dinner leftovers that were easily microwaved. Turned out, Lorelei was a damned fair cook.

"I appreciate the offer," she said, "but I'll pass on the sit-down breakfast. Ava will be here soon and I still need to fix my hair and get dressed." She glanced down at her tank top, and Sam couldn't help following her gaze. Water droplets from her freshly washed hair had made the ivory material translucent in a few places, just enough to tantalize a man's imagination. "Finish getting dressed, I mean."

"Yeah." His voice sounded like a gravel road. *And I have no business going down that road.* "I'll, uh, pour you a cup to go as soon as its ready."

"Thanks. I should have been drying my hair instead

of standing here. Guess I was hoping I could breathe in caffeinated fumes to help get me going."

She brushed by him, smelling like an exotic flower blooming in the sun—her shampoo or some sort of body wash she'd slathered over her curves? With a hard swallow, Sam realized he no longer needed the coffee to get him going this morning.

Ava beamed at her from the driver's seat and Lorelei bit the inside of her cheek to keep from spouting statistics about how many wrecks resulted from people not keeping their eyes on the road. "I'm just so happy you're staying!"

"For the festival," Lorelei reiterated. *Keep your eyes on the road!* "Not permanently."

Ava pursed her lips. "We'll see. After all, you didn't think you were staying for the festival, either."

Lorelei sighed. "There's a big difference between taking a week off work and uprooting my life. I don't belong here, Ava."

At that, the woman jerked her entire head around to gape. "How can you say that?"

"Ava, would you like me to drive? After all, you made the trip clear to San'tone for me. Seems only fair for me to drive us back."

"Nonsense. My car can be a little quirky sometimes." She patted the dashboard affectionately. "No one understands her like I do. And stop trying to change the subject, missy. Why would you say you don't belong? This was home your entire life. People love your family in these parts."

They loved Mom. And I'm nothing like her. But Lorelei couldn't say that without crushing Ava, who was childless herself and probably did love Lorelei. The older woman just didn't seem to know she was in the minority.

Lorelei stared out the window, wondering what she would do differently if she had the chance. Come visit her mother, obviously. But that in and of itself wouldn't have been enough to change anything. *What should I have said to her?* Lorelei had tried as an adolescent to explain her feelings to her mother, who'd always offered a vacant smile and assured Lorelei that one day she'd understand.

"Ava, did you ever disagree with Mom?"

"What, you mean like fight with her?" Ava gave a startled frown. "Of course not. Your mother wasn't one for conflict. She was a gentle soul."

Lorelei sighed. *Gentle?* In this case, the apple had fallen so far from the tree, she'd landed in a neighboring orchard. Back in her teen years, she'd been fiercely competitive in her bid for valedictorian. And as recently as Monday, she'd wanted to throttle those two ghost-hunting strangers. Nor did "gentle" describe the way she'd argued with Sam the night before his trail ride. She caught her lower lip between her teeth. She'd been having less-than-gentle thoughts about Sam this morning, too. Not that they'd been arguing.

Maybe it was her morning-brain, often foggy before her first mug of the day, but had there been a moment when the tall cowboy had been undressing her with his eyes? Heat had spiraled through her, leaving her flushed and unsure how to react. One possibility? Pushing him up against the refrigerator and asking him to satisfy her curiosity about his kiss.

"You okay, hon?" Ava's maternal tone was like a well-timed bucket of cold water.

Lorelei couldn't believe she was allowing herself to fantasize about Sam *at all,* much less in Ava's presence. It was like making out in front of your parents.

"Missing your mother?" Ava asked.

The sympathetic question multiplied Lorelei's guilt exponentially. "I, ah, actually wasn't thinking about her just now."

"Oh?" The woman waited a beat. "Come on, tell Aunt Ava. You'll feel better."

"My mind drifted to Sam," Lorelei mumbled. "I barely know the guy but, for all intents and purposes, I'm living with him. The situation is…" Sexually frustrating? "Tense. Sometimes."

Ava cut her gaze toward the passenger seat. "You aren't still mad at him for inheriting the inn, are you? Now that he's giving it to you?"

"I wouldn't say mad, exactly."

"Is this why you asked if I ever fought with your mom? You think she left Sam the place because of some argument you and she had?"

"No, nothing like that."

What Ava said earlier about Wanda veering away from conflict had been entirely true. The closest mother and daughter had come to outright disagreements in over a decade was when Wanda had stubbornly decided that Lorelei needed to come home for this festival, which had been unlike her. And, after hearing Sam's abbreviated tale of his childhood—a veritable orphan with no mother and home to call his own—Lorelei could even understand why Wanda might feel moved to leave him the inn. Lorelei was still shocked that he'd told her about his upbringing, trusting her with something that had to sting even though he said it no longer mattered.

She had firsthand experience with how the past could wield power long after you'd moved on with your life.

"I need a drink," Lorelei blurted. She was half joking, rarely the type to indulge. Her favorite self-attributes were a calculator-like mind and control over unruly emotions and baser instincts. Alcohol tended to diminish those.

"Well, we are passing an entire string of vineyards," Ava said.

Oops. Lorelei didn't want "Aunt Ava" to think she'd turned into a lush since moving off to Philadelphia. "I was kidding."

"I wasn't."

"But don't you have sewing to do for the festival?" It had been Ava's idea to start their trip early, so she'd still have the afternoon to work.

"Festival doesn't start until Saturday." Ava lifted one shoulder in a shrug. "I'll get up a couple of hours early tomorrow. Or stay up an extra few tonight. Let's be impractical."

With effort, Lorelei managed not to shudder at the suggestion. Impractical was too close to careless, an invitation to risk.

"We can pull over, try out some local labels and toast your mother's memory," Ava coaxed. "Our version of an old-fashioned Irish wake."

"But you're driving."

"We'll wait until close to town and call Clinton to pick us up—you know there are at least four good places within spitting distance of the inn. What do you say, Lorelei? Your mother always worried you worked too hard and didn't do enough to enjoy yourself. When was the last time you let your hair down?"

Lorelei reflexively fingered her tight French braid. "I suppose a glass or two won't hurt."

Sam enjoyed physical labor. Normally, he could lose himself in the routine of whatever task he completed and wind up pleasantly exhausted from an honest day's work. But today's chores of painting, checking some wiring and changing lightbulbs in hard-to-reach fixtures and repairing rain gutters weren't demanding enough. While his body was busy at the Jalapeño, his mind wandered back to Lorelei. He kept remembering how alluring she'd looked fresh from the shower…although he might have added a few embellishments over the course of the day. He may have pictured even more water spots dotting her tank top before she'd covered it with a gauzy button-down blouse, may have imagined more heated interest in her dark eyes.

He was so focused on Lorelei that Grace had to say his name twice to get his attention, and he jerked himself out of his fantasies with a start—not a smart move for a guy on a ladder.

Grace smiled at him. "I really appreciate everything you've done, but we open for dinner in a couple of hours." During other times of the year, the restaurant was open for lunch as well, but since she was currently busy with the highly publicized cooking contest going on right now, she hadn't been opening until four each afternoon.

He should clean up his tools and get out of the way. "Be right down. This was the last bulb."

She glanced around her and gave a rueful shake of her head. "Considering some of the cracked booth seats and broken tiles that still need replacing, maybe

I shouldn't have added more light. Dim makes for better ambience."

He descended onto the floor next to her. "Grace, your enchiladas would be delicious even if guests had to sit in the dark on three-legged chairs." That was the truth, not empty flattery. But no matter how good a cook she was, he knew she was struggling to keep the place open.

He packed up all his stuff and set out a couple of Wet Paint signs, although he'd done the trim work when he first arrived so everything would be mostly dry before patrons began arriving.

"Thank you again," Grace said as she passed him an envelope of cash. He'd quoted the lowest possible price he thought her pride would accept. "I just wish I could afford bigger changes instead of small patch jobs."

"Hang in there," he advised. "Once you win that hotshot competition, you might be able to fix the place up more." He'd overheard enough other people talking about it to realize winning would be a big deal for Grace.

When Sam got back to the bed-and-breakfast, he wondered if Lorelei was inside. Now that her rental car had been returned, there was no way to tell. Not that it mattered. On the nights when she was locked away reading pages of facts and statistics or harassing coworkers by phone, he might as well be alone at the inn. Considering how preoccupied he'd been with her all day, maybe it was best if their paths didn't cross.

He unlocked the back door and stepped inside, resisting an insane urge to call out "Honey, I'm home."

The kitchen was empty, the house quiet.

Sam ignored a brief stab of disappointment and went down the hallway and stopped at the living room, surprised by the sight of two feet hanging over the arm of the couch. One sandal dangled precariously from the wearer's toes; its mate had already lost the battle with gravity.

"Lorelei?"

"Mmm?"

He walked around the piece of furniture and found not only his roommate reclined across the sofa, but also a purring Oberon curled up on her abdomen. Lorelei lazily scratched between the cat's ears. Sam was stunned by the cozy picture they made, but had to admit, if *he* were lying on top of her, he might consider purring, too. He blinked hard, as if he could unsee the mental image now stuck in his head.

She opened one eye, smiled up at Sam, then closed it again. Dark tendrils had slipped loose from her braid, framing her face softly. "Hey. You back from a hard day of riding the range?"

"Actually, I was working closer to oven ranges today. Appears that you two made friends while I was gone." Although Sam and Oberon were back on amicable terms after the cat's bedspread sabotage, Oberon continued to act as if he were doing Sam a huge favor whenever he allowed the human to pet him.

"Turns out, Obie's not so bad after all," Lorelei cooed. "You just have to know how to rub him."

"Uh-huh. So. You look…relaxed." He could have said comatose except for the rhythmic swinging of her foot and the dreamy half smile on her face. There was a day spa one block over; had she gone for a massage?

She arched her back in a full body stretch that made Sam's throat go dry and disturbed the cat, who hopped off the couch with a mew. Her transparent ivory blouse showed off her graceful arms and the swell of her chest beneath the thin tank top. Lorelei sat, frowning as she looked down. "Shoot, now I have cat hair on me." She set her hands just below the collar and ran them down over her body, and Sam forced himself to look away. He should mention that she needed brisker motions to brush off any fur—the slow slide of her fingers wasn't accomplishing anything. Or at least, not what she'd been trying to accomplish.

"Ava took me to a wine-tasting. Several tastings, actually." Lorelei rolled her neck, then leaned back against the couch's headrest. She frowned. "Think we missed lunch, though."

"Ava got you drunk?" he asked disbelievingly.

Lorelei's frown deepened, making her look more like herself and simultaneously making it easier for him to breathe. "Of course not! I do not get drunk. I just feel…" Her pinched expression faded into a slow grin. "Really loose."

Sam could hear his uncle's voice in his head. Before JD went out to dance halls or bars on the weekend, as he applied aftershave and tightened his belt, he'd always pronounced, "Thank the Lord for Lone Star Beer and loose women." It had been his version of "Thank God it's Friday."

"You do not wear expensive suits."

"What?" Sam mentally replayed the last few minutes of conversation, trying to make sure he hadn't tuned out while reminding himself that Lorelei was in no interpretation of the word a loose woman.

Lorelei jabbed a finger at him. "I know a lot of good-looking men who wear expensive suits."

"Like your boyfriend, Rick?" he asked sourly. If she

thought clothes made the man, her priorities were more whacked than he'd thought.

"Yes. No. Yes, Rick. No, he's not my boyfriend. But he does look very good in a suit."

"How nice for him," Sam snarled. "If you'll excuse me, I need to grab a shower, so—"

"Some of those businessmen?" She was still pointing her index finger for emphasis. "I think they need the suit to look that good. You don't."

Sam's jaw dropped at the unexpected compliment. He glanced down at the faded T-shirt he wore and the old jeans, now smattered with specks of paint. Then he looked back to her, hit full force by the avid admiration in her gaze. He wanted to express his own appreciation by leaning in to kiss her...except that her mouth was still curled in that crooked, non-Lorelei smile. She might not be flat-out inebriated, but she wasn't entirely herself right now, either. And he needed to get them away from this inn, with its many rooms and many, many beds.

"You know what?" He retreated slowly, as if she were a wild animal that might pounce the moment his back was turned. *I should be so lucky.* "I think you could use some food in your system. And as it happens, I know a great restaurant."

Chapter 8

After his shower, Sam changed into clothes not decorated with paint smears. When he went back downstairs, he found Lorelei in the kitchen gulping a glass of water.

He couldn't help grinning at her. "You need some aspirin to go with that?"

"No, I'm good." She scowled. "Not that I'm philosophically opposed to taking medicine when it would help me. I just don't happen to need any right now."

He raised an eyebrow at her emphatic tone and bizarre words but didn't pry. "Ever eaten at The Twisted Jalapeño?"

"Nope."

"It may have been called something else before, but I know it's been in the Torres family for years. You like Mexican?"

"Sounds fantastic. I probably should have eaten earlier today," she said sheepishly. "That's the last time I go wine-tasting on an empty stomach."

They walked out to his vehicle together, the gravel crunching under their feet. He opened the passenger door for her and she almost stumbled trying to step up into the truck.

"I'm guessing you're more used to luxury sedans." His words were involuntary and sounded too judgmental to be mistaken for lighthearted ribbing.

She glared over her shoulder. "I'll have you know that my little two-door is completely paid for and I intend to drive it until the wheels fall off."

As he walked around the truck to his own side, he chastised himself. While this might not technically be a date, she deserved some measure of charm—or, at least, not open hostility. He climbed into the truck and flipped the key in the ignition. A rock song blared out of the speakers, making both of them jump. He turned the volume knob as quickly as he could.

"Sorry about that." On the way home, he'd been trying to drown out his own thoughts. Plus, the radio had been playing a song he really liked.

Lorelei rubbed her ear. "Aren't you required by law to listen to country music in your truck?"

He laughed. "I'll make a deal with you. How about we leave our stereotypes here with Oberon and go to dinner—just you and me?"

"I'd like that, Sam. I think I'd like that a lot."

From the outside, The Twisted Jalapeño didn't look like much. There was a simple hand-painted sign, nothing that would light up at night and draw diners from the dark road, and the parking lot was scarred with potholes. Lorelei was undeterred, though. There was a small dive in Philadelphia, nestled among bigger buildings, where she could have happily eaten her own body weight in their cornflake-crusted macaroni and cheese.

Sam opened the door to the restaurant for her, and a hostess with black curly hair brightened at the sight of them. "Back so soon, señor Travis?"

"Working here all day made me crave the food. Rosie, this is Lorelei. Tonight's her first time at the Jalapeño."

"Nice to meet you," Rosie said with a welcoming smile. "If you'll follow me?" She led them to a mini-booth for two. "Your waitress will be out shortly, but I can go ahead and put in a drink order. We have an excellent beer list and daily margarita specials, including our signature chili lime 'rita."

"I'll stick with water and lemon," Lorelei said quickly. She had no intention of imbibing any more alcohol today. Her face warmed as she recalled telling Sam he didn't need a suit to look good. *Probably doesn't need* any *clothes to look good.* The heat blossoming in her cheeks flared even higher and she opened a menu, keeping her gaze lowered. Sam asked for a glass of iced tea and the hostess promised someone would be by momentarily with a basket of chips and the house salsa verde.

The food selections weren't limited to the tacos, nachos and fajitas Lorelei expected. Among the more commonplace favorites she could have found at a dozen other Tex-Mex places were dishes with an unexpected twist to them. Hence the restaurant name, she realized as she scanned the list of entrées. Pork with cucumberwasabi salsa, curried lamb burritos and spice encrusted chicken with Texas red grapefruits.

Lorelei's curiosity was piqued. "You like fusion food?"

"I have no idea what you just said," Sam said, still studying his menu. "But I like good food, and Grace's recipes are very good."

"She's the one in that contest Ava mentioned?" Lorelei was pretty sure the local chef entered was Grace something.

Sam nodded. "Her grandparents started this place, then her dad ran it for a while, but now it falls on Grace and her two brothers. I'm not sure either of them has been much help lately. One is getting divorced and the other is a police officer. He was injured on the job and is still recovering. In my opinion, this place should be packed every night. Grace has been busting her butt trying to reinvent it."

She couldn't help noticing that he sounded admiring of Grace's work ethic, instead of snarling the way he did whenever Lorelei's career was mentioned. "Well, if the food is as good as you say, I'll definitely be back a few times before I leave town."

A blonde waitress brought them their drinks and took their dinner order. Sam chose the fish tacos and Lorelei went with the chipotle-coffee buffalo steak fajitas.

"You hungry enough for an appetizer?" he asked her.

Lorelei nodded eagerly. All she'd eaten today was breakfast in her car, followed by a small selection of cheeses and some palate-cleansing crackers.

"We'll start with the pot of pork and peppers," he told the waitress.

She beamed at him. "Excellent choice! Personally, that's my favorite thing on the menu."

After the young woman had gone, he explained to Lorelei, "They slow-cook pork with jalapeños and serranos until it's practically mush. Uh, it tastes better than I'm making it sound."

Luckily, that turned out to be true. The spicy pork was incredibly tender and simply fell apart if she tried to stick a fork into it. Instead, she used her spoon to ladle some onto a warm flour tortilla, then nearly moaned at the taste. "Wow." She almost regretted that she had fajitas on the way. "I could happily eat a double order of this and call it a night."

Sam grinned. "I do like a woman with a healthy appetite."

As they ate, he pointed out some of the things he'd accomplished in the restaurant that day. Discussion naturally turned to her day and they chatted about the afternoon she'd spent with Ava.

"I always think about Ava being friends with Mom," Lorelei said, rolling up another tortilla. "I sometimes forget she and her husband knew my dad really well, too. It was nice to hear anecdotes about him when he was alive and still healthy. I don't know which is worse—losing someone suddenly or having plenty of time to fear the worst and dread it happening."

Of course, her parents had never wanted to talk to her about that possibility. They'd steadfastly insisted everything would be okay as they continued reading books on alternative treatments and miraculous cancer-fighting diets and consulting new age "healers" who were little better than charlatans in Lorelei's mind.

She glanced at Sam. "Did you have any warning that your dad was going to die?"

He gave a harsh chuckle. "My dad was an intimidating man who seemed larger than life, especially to a kid. Maybe he'd been warned by a cardiologist, told to watch his blood pressure or take a damn vacation for once, but none of that trickled down to me. Even if I'd known, I would have assumed he was mean enough to win a fight with the Reaper. He had a coronary at his office and was dead by the time the ambulance got him to the hospital."

"I'm sorry." And not just for Sam's boyhood loss, but for bringing up such a melancholy subject over great food. "I'm a lousy dinner conversationalist, huh? I guess listening to Ava talk about old times got my mind wandering down this path."

Sam seemed to understand her need to revisit the past. "Wanda told me your dad had cancer?"

"The diagnosis was grim from the beginning." They'd never admitted that to her face, but she'd strained to hear the whispers on the other side of closed doors. "My father refused the radiation and chemo, which he called poison. He'd read just enough 'spontaneous recovery' stories to believe something like that could happen to him. Mom kept chirping about the power of positive thinking, like all we had to do was *want* him to get better enough and he would. You've seen the Peanuts Halloween special where Linus waits in vain all night for the magical pumpkin to come, then vows to try harder the next year? I felt like that, like I just hadn't hoped sincerely enough. Dumb, isn't it?" Her mouth twisted in a bitter, self-deprecating smile, inviting him to laugh along at her childish folly.

But Sam's expression was somber. "Lorelei—"

"Here you go!" The waitress's voice seemed too loud and too perky. But the food she carried smelled wonderful, reigniting Lorelei's flagging appetite. After the woman had admonished them to be careful of the hot plates and gone on to her next table, Sam tried again to voice whatever he'd been about to say.

But Lorelei cut him off with an emphatic shake of her head. "You know what? This all looks fantastic, and I think we should dig in."

He watched her for a moment, and she thought he might speak his mind anyway. Lord knew he wasn't shy about doing so. But then he asked, "You want to try a bite of my tacos?"

"Yes. Thank you." Both entrées were delicious and she strove to enjoy them, putting aside her bleak reminiscing.

"So I've traveled all over the state," Sam began, "and know a lot about regional cuisine here in Texas. But I've never been up north. What's good in Philadelphia?"

She was grateful for the chance to talk about her adopted home, the place where she'd shucked her past and became the person she was meant to be. "I guess a cheese-steak sandwich is the most obvious. A lot of lifelong residents love turtle soup, but I haven't been able to acquire the taste." She told him about her favorite Stromboli vendor near her office and how much she loved holding a warm soft pretzel on a cold day. "And there are *many* cold days." The mornings when she had to shovel snow were the times she felt most nostalgic for Texas.

"They sell giant pretzels at the festival," he reminded her. "I'll have to get you one."

She flashed him a wry smile. "You're giving me the inn in exchange for staying. I don't need the added incentive of a pretzel."

"Y'all doing okay over here?" The bouncy waitress had returned. She refreshed their drinks, smiling extra brightly at Sam before departing again.

Lorelei laughed. "I think our server has the hots for you."

He blinked, looking startled by the observation. "What? Why would you say that?"

"For starters?" She dragged a napkin around her glass. "There's this puddle of water because she couldn't take her eyes off you long enough to pour." Lorelei watched him fidget in his chair. *Don't tell me the big, strong cowboy is embarrassed!* "Oh, come on, Travis. You can't be that oblivious. Women probably ogle you all the time. You're…"

He raised his head sharply. "Yes?"

She shrugged. "You know…*you*."

A slow, purely masculine grin lit his face, making his expression one of the sexiest she'd ever seen. "Uh-huh. Well, that certainly settled the matter."

She fought the urge to throw her soggy napkin at him. "Stop fishing for compliments. It's unbecoming."

"Not fishing," he protested. "I've already hit my quota of compliments for the day. What with your remark about how good I look even without a suit—"

She groaned. "It's not very gentlemanly to bring that up." Mellowed by the fading remains of her wine buzz, she had been far too open with her thoughts. If Sam hadn't left so soon to take a shower and change, would she have wound up confessing how often she'd thought about him kissing her? "I was hoping you'd forgotten."

"Forget an admission from you? You are many things, darlin', but forgettable is not one of them."

She was afraid to ask what the "many things" entailed. There was a good chance they wouldn't all be flattering. Conversely, anything too flattering could boost the simmering awareness between them. She was relieved they'd gone out for dinner tonight, somewhere safely public. The rest of her stay should be easier to manage with the festival to keep them busy.

"So, friendly waitresses aside, you have any ongoing romantic relationships?" Surely if there were someone serious in his life, he—or Ava—would have mentioned it by now. Lorelei certainly hadn't crossed paths with any women coming from the direction of Sam's bedroom.

"Not really. I travel a lot, keep an erratic schedule. I have lady friends in different towns who I'll maybe call for dinner if I'm coming through."

Dinner followed by breakfast? When he wanted to be, Sam was charming. It wouldn't be difficult for him to rack up a "lady friend" for every zip code he visited. Then again, he didn't really give off the vibe of a player. He was unabashedly plainspoken, not the type to string women along with slick phrases or insincere promises.

"I'm not looking for anything lasting right now." He made a face and added a muttered, "Although some women can't seem to get that through their heads."

He seemed too irritated for it to be a general comment. "You have a specific stalker?"

"As a matter of fact. But it seems impolite to tell you who." He affected a look of comical fear. "Besides, I'm pretty sure if we accidentally say her name three times, she materializes."

Lorelei laughed. "Well, we wouldn't want that."

"Sam!" A tiny, dark-haired bundle of energy in a bright red chef's jacket hurried to their table—obviously not an unwanted stalker, since he looked delighted to see her.

"Grace, dinner was wonderful, as usual. And you've made a new convert tonight." He swept a hand in Lorelei's direction. "Grace Torres, meet Lorelei Keller."

The chef's pretty features puckered in a frown. "Wanda Keller's daughter? I'm so very sorry for your loss. She was a lovely woman. She often visited my aunt in the nursing home and listened to her spin tales, like the time *Tía* Maria swears she encountered *La Llorona*."

At Lorelei's blank look, Sam explained, "The weeping woman, a figure in Hispanic folklore."

Grace nodded. "*Mi tía* looked forward to those afternoons. Your mother will be greatly missed. Dinner is on the house for you two!"

After what Sam had told her about the restaurant's struggles, Lorelei was touched by the offer but loath to accept. "Oh, let us pay! Please."

"Out of the question. Your money is no good here." Grace winked. "At least, not tonight. But you'll come again soon, yes?"

"Definitely," Lorelei agreed. "I was already planning to return while I'm in town."

"Will you be here long?"

"Only through the festival. But I may have to come back once or twice before the inn's final sale."

"You're not keeping it?" Grace asked, sounding surprised. "Taking over the family business?"

Lorelei recalled what Sam had said about this restaurant, how it had been passed down through three generations. "Mom didn't buy the inn until after I'd moved away for college. I don't really see it as the family business."

"Understandable," Grace said after a moment. "Well, good luck finding new owners. You two enjoy the rest of your meal."

At the back of her mind, Lorelei kept thinking about potential future owners. What kind of people might her mother want in charge of the inn—another empty-nester like Wanda herself, supernatural enthusiasts like the two who had barged in earlier this week? It wasn't until after they'd left the restaurant that Lorelei asked Sam, "When Mom left you the inn, do you think she really believed you'd keep it?"

Sam was quiet, and it was too dark in the cab of the truck to read his expression. "Hard to say what your mom thought. She…had her own way of viewing the world."

"That's the diplomatic way of putting it," Lorelei mumbled. Her peers in school had been less tactful about their opinions of her "kooky mom."

"I didn't mean it as an insult," Sam clarified. "My father and mother and stepfather all bought in to the same skewed keeping-up-with-the-Joneses values that thousands of other people share. I always liked that she was unique." A beat later, he added, "Of course, I didn't grow up with her."

It seemed like a big concession, his finally admitting that there might be more than just Wanda's side of the story, and the sympathetic note in his tone warmed her to the core. She stole a glance at his profile, thrown into relief by a streetlight, and repressed a sigh. In the week she'd known Sam, he'd demonstrated loyalty, humor and dependability—*and* he had the face of a rugged angel. Add in an ability to admit when he was wrong and it suddenly seemed a shame that he didn't want a girlfriend in his footloose life. Some woman might have been lucky to have him.

As they reached the back door of the inn, they simultaneously went to unlock it.

Lorelei drew up short to avoid a collision, and Sam stepped out of her way, moving to the side of the tiny concrete slab that didn't quite rate back-porch status. "You go ahead," he said. "It was just habit." In addition to each of their sets of keys, Ava had one, too.

She unlocked the door and preceded him into the kitchen, suddenly feeling awkward. If this had been a date, this would be the part of the evening where they kissed good-night. *Assuming we stopped with a kiss.*

Sam leaned against the counter, glancing at his watch. "It's still pretty early. Would I bother you if I watch television for a while?"

The individual rooms didn't have TVs, but there was a big screen in the living room. Lorelei knew her mother had often used the DVD player to do movie nights for the guests—not just films that suited the supernatural theme of the inn, but also holiday classics during appropriate seasons and romantic favorites when she had a houseful of couples.

"You're welcome to join me," he added belatedly. His tone seemed skeptical, though, as if he were trying to imagine what might appeal to both of them equally.

"You go ahead," she told him. "I plan to fire up my computer and work on the trend study." That was how she would have spent her afternoon if she hadn't come back lethargic from the wine. "'Night, Sam. Thanks for dinner."

Straightening suddenly, he stalled her with a hand on her arm. "Lorelei, wait."

His unexpected touch was warm through the insubstantial material of her blouse. Her mouth felt dry, and she licked her lips. "Yes?"

His hand slid off of her, and he shoved it through his tawny hair as he gathered his thoughts. "About your work." He flashed a teasing grin. "About my scowl?"

She grinned back at him, helpless not to in the face of those dimples. "What about it?"

"I said at the memorial service that most of my recollections of my father are hazy. But not all of them." He stopped, as if sharing this kind of thing didn't come naturally to him, then huffed out a breath. "You told me a bit about your dad over dinner. I should be able to return the favor. Especially since it indirectly affected you."

She raised her eyebrows, curious to hear what he had to say but sensing he might withdraw if she pushed.

"There's one very clear memory. I'd confronted him about breaking promises. He hadn't come to a baseball game, missed my hitting a home run or something. Seemed important at the time."

Looking at the powerful, broad-shouldered man in front of her, Lorelei couldn't quite picture him as a little boy. But even with the gruffness of his tone, she could hear an echo of that boy's crestfallen disappointment.

He shook his head. "I don't really remember the game. But I recall vividly the contempt on his face. He told me to man up, quit whining. Said I needed to understand his job was more important than a bunch of kids stumbling through nine innings and that when I got older, when I had a family to support, I'd be just like him."

"Clearly not father-of-the-year material," Lorelei

murmured. Was this one of the reasons Sam chose not to commit to a single steady job or work nine to five in an office somewhere, because he couldn't stomach the thought of fulfilling his father's prediction?

"In answer to your question this morning, I don't have anything against actuaries," Sam said ruefully. "Just a chip on my shoulder about people who seem married to their jobs. Which is no excuse for being a jackass to you."

It might not have been the most eloquent apology ever, but it had been incredibly personal. She didn't know how to respond. Part of her wanted to hug him, which startled her. Lorelei was so not a hugger. If she had been a gambling woman, she would have bet the farm Sam wasn't, either.

His lips quirked in a sardonic smile that never fully materialized. "Guess we both have some lingering anger toward our dads to work through."

She blinked, trying to make the transition from the unanticipated tenderness she'd been feeling to his bizarre assessment. She had memories of her father telling her long bedtime stories and tickling her until she shrieked—he'd been nothing like the cold businessman who made a child feel worthless. "I'm not angry with mine."

Rocking back on his heels, Sam shot her an incredulous look. "I was with you at dinner, remember? It's okay to be bitter about what happened."

"A good man got sick and died too young." She kept her voice level as she recounted the facts. It had been so long ago; bursting into tears now wouldn't change a damn thing. "I suppose I am bitter about the unfairness of the situation. But I'm not mad at *him*. My dad loved me."

"Just not enough to seek medical attention?" Sam asked softly.

Her entire body jerked. "How dare you? That's a horrible—"

"I'm not suggesting it's true," he said with exaggerated patience. "Just acknowledging how a daughter could feel that way."

Lorelei dug her fingernails into her palm. She'd agreed to stay for the festival—letting the world's least likely shrink psychoanalyze her in the meantime hadn't been part of the deal. Didn't he know she was having a difficult enough time with losing her mom this week? To drag up the past and relive losing her father on top of it...

She tried to numb the grief that threatened, her tone cool. "Even with treatment, there was no guarantee he would have made it. Second-guessing his decisions two decades after the fact would be completely irrational."

For some reason, her words seemed to rankle him. "I'm talking about emotions, not quantitative algebra."

"Like you know so much about quantitative algebra?" she snapped. What she really meant was, *Like you know so much about me?*

His body went still as his eyes narrowed. "Right. Because you're the Ivy League grad and I'm the dumb hick cowboy?"

"That's not—"

He took a step back, in the direction of the door behind him. "Changed my mind 'bout that TV. Think I'll shoot some pool in town. Don't wait up."

Lorelei gnashed her teeth as he disappeared into the

dark. The man might claim his specialty was taming ornery livestock, but as far as she could tell, his true expertise was in abrupt exits. She revised her earlier opinion about his dating life. Thank heavens he *wasn't* interested in a relationship. Any woman foolish enough to fall for Sam Travis would develop shin splints and bad knees from constantly having to run after him.

Since the two pool tables in the small bar were both in use and Sam had no interest in drinking, he ended up at the dartboard, playing Oh-One with a stranger who'd introduced himself as Ty. Sam wasn't sure whether Ty was a local, hired help for the festival or a tourist just passing through—the dark-haired man showed as little inclination toward small talk as Sam.

I've learned my lesson. Sam threw the first dart of his turn. He'd done too much yapping for the night already and planned to keep his trap shut going forward. Whatever uncharacteristic impulse had motivated him to share another piece of his past with Lorelei...well, that urge was long gone now. He was surprised he'd given in to it in the first place.

Wanda had always tried to coax him into "bonding" with other people. "Or at least smile more," she'd say. "If you're not careful, Sam, you're gonna scare away all my other guests."

Tonight was the second time he'd let himself get suckered into a false sense of connection with Lorelei, only to have his misreading of the situation turn around to bite him on the ass. He'd seen the pain in her face over dinner as she talked about her father's death, the guilt and hurt that she'd never been able to join in her parents' optimism. Even though he thought she'd been blessed to have Wanda as a mom, Sam did know what it was like to feel outside your own family. He'd always fallen a distant second in his parents' priorities. While Sam hadn't enjoyed talking about his father, he'd stammered through it. For a heartbeat of time, he'd felt he and Lorelei had found a patch of common ground.

Then the pity in her eyes—already galling—turned to annoyance and she haughtily informed him that *her father* had loved *her*. Then she'd become condescending and he'd had to leave before he lost his temper. It was ironic, really. He'd briefly dated a woman or two who'd tried their best to get him to open up, but he'd never been tempted to do so. Until Lorelei, who wasn't interested.

Won't happen again. Hell, he'd give in and date Barbara Biggins—a blue-eyed piranha in a miniskirt—before he made himself vulnerable to Lorelei again. He flung his third dart, and it went wide, bouncing off the rim of the board before falling to the ground. A growling noise sounded low in his throat, and Ty raised his eyebrows but said nothing as he walked to the throw line.

Several more rounds passed as each of them, lost in his own musings, whittled his score down to zero. Despite a few lucky throws along the way, Sam couldn't find the precision to hit the exact numbers needed. *Could be worse.* At least they weren't playing for money. He heard Lorelei's disapproving tone in his head as she'd informed him, "I don't gamble."

Of course she didn't. She also didn't relax, didn't visit her only family when she'd still had the chance, didn't let herself feel.

But even as he mentally listed those faults, he knew

they weren't true. Not entirely. If she were as cold as she sometimes appeared, she never would have gotten under his skin like this. It was those moments when the veneer cracked and he witnessed the emotion beneath...

"I'm gonna go out on a limb here." Ty broke the silence, his tone more resigned than curious. "Woman troubles?"

Sam dipped his head in a curt nod.

"Know the feeling." Ty tossed a dart and missed by a mile. "Good luck."

He didn't need luck. He needed Lorelei to sell the inn and go back where she belonged. But, somehow, looking forward to that didn't give him quite as much peace of mind as it should.

"Oh, Ava." Lorelei tossed the pamphlet she was supposed to be folding onto Ava's dining room table. Her creases were completely crooked, the tri-fold uneven. "I'm a bad person."

Coming into the room with a pitcher of lemonade, Ava paused in the doorway. "Is this about drinking wine in the middle of the day again? Because those tasting sizes are tiny. It's not like you had twelve actual glasses."

"I wasn't talking about wine." Lorelei would have laughed if she weren't plagued by the look she'd glimpsed in Sam's eyes last night.

After he'd first stomped out of the inn, it had been easy to hold on to her anger. But as she'd tried to settle into her work, she kept recalling that split second just before he'd announced he was going into town. When his green eyes had flashed with insecurity. *That I caused.* Until this trip, she'd firmly believed that the reason she didn't have a serious—and therefore time-consuming—romantic relationship was because she wasn't looking for one. Could it possibly be because she didn't deserve one?

Ava set the lemonade down next to the glasses she'd already placed on the side table. "So what heinous crime did you commit?"

Lorelei bit her lip. She knew Ava cared about Sam, even though she didn't know him as well as Wanda had, and Lorelei hated to admit that she'd insulted him. "Well, after you and Clinton dropped me off yest—"

The doorbell pealed, and Ava held up her finger. "Hold that thought, dear. Those must be the girls."

Lorelei heard female voices at the front door and greetings being exchanged. Then Ava returned with four other women. Ava's definition of *girls* applied to multiple generations. Gertrude Hirsch, Ava's mother-in-law, was in her mid-seventies. There were two middle-aged women, both of whom Lorelei recognized from the memorial service although she couldn't recall their names, followed by a round-faced redhead who probably still got carded when she bought a beer.

As soon as Ava had helped her mother-in-law into a chair, she pointed to the redhead. "Lorelei, you remember Tess Fitzpatrick? I believe the two of you were in the same graduating class."

Tess smiled brightly, her brown eyes warm. "Lorelei is the reason I passed geometry!"

"I was?" She was embarrassed not to remember, but then, Lorelei had spent most of her teen years preoccupied with getting away, counting down the days and weeks until college.

The redhead nodded. "Mrs. Sumner asked you to

tutor me when I was in jeopardy of failing. You were a hard taskmaster, but you certainly got me straightened out!"

At the behest of the math department, Lorelei had tutored multiple students during her four years in high school, and she suspected "hard taskmaster" was among the nicer things they'd said about her. She frowned inwardly, chiding herself for the knee-jerk negativity. Maybe there were others who, if not as instantly friendly as Tess, bore her no ill will. Not all of her former classmates had been as spiteful as Babs Biggins and her clique of friends, quick to label Lorelei a misfit math nerd and laugh about her zany mother.

"So should we work first and take a break for refreshments later," Ava asked, "or start with the snacks? I made a fresh batch of peach-pecan cornbread this morning."

The women were all here to help with various projects for the festival. Gertrude had originally founded a dance school in town called "The Hirsch Hoofers." It had undergone a name change and several shifts in management and Tess now worked there, teaching little girls tap and ballet. Ava and Tess had some last-minute sewing to do on costumes, as several of the classes would be performing this weekend.

"Lorelei came over with her brochures printed and needs some help folding them," Ava said. "She also needs some suggestions for decorating. No offense, dear, but you don't quite have your mother's imagination."

Lorelei couldn't help but chuckle at the colossal understatement. "Don't you think I should keep it low-key, though? After all, I'm not really trying to promote the inn. We're not even accepting reservations right now. I just want to do this as a goodbye to Mom." Maybe she'd first agreed to man the booth because it was an expedient way to get the inn, but attending the festival felt right. Even before Wanda had become a local business owner with her own booth, she'd always attended. Lorelei couldn't remember a year her mother wasn't there. *This'll be the first.*

Tears burned the back of her eyes as she pictured Wanda, her clothes smeared with powdered sugar from a warm funnel cake. Or Wanda cajoling her daughter to try on silly souvenir hats with her.

"Lorelei, dear?" Ava's voice was gentle. "Why don't you help me in the kitchen? Ladies, glasses are right there. Help yourselves to some lemonade."

"Thank you," Lorelei said once they were alone in the kitchen. She took a deep breath to regain her composure. "I appreciate the excuse to get away from an audience."

"Certainly." Ava reached up into a cabinet to pull out small dessert plates. She set them on the counter then stood there for a moment as if weighing her words. "But Lorelei? You know that no one in that room would think less of you for missing your mama or showing your emotions. Feelings aren't weaknesses."

"You sound like Sam." At Ava's questioning glance, Lorelei added, "He gave me similar advice last night." He may have been a bit more sarcastic about it once goaded, but the sentiment boiled down to the same thing.

"Then, he's a smart man."

Lorelei flinched, recalling his dead tone. *I'm the dumb hick cowboy.* That wasn't remotely how she saw him. She found him exasperating, even infuriating on occasion, but not unintelligent. If anything, he discomfited her sometimes because he seemed too perceptive.

Suddenly, she was eager to get through the festival preparations with the other women. As soon as they were finished, she had a cowboy to find.

Chapter 9

The wind whipped fiercely around Sam and the other workers dotting the Marktplatz, a landscaped public area that was home to the historic Vereins Kirche and considered by many to be the heart of town. Although there was already a permanent pavilion, along with many picnic tables, other tents and temporary stages needed to be erected. Tomorrow, sound systems would be wired and checked. The festival would host performances that ranged from dog-training demonstrations to four-year-old ballerinas to the live music of Praha Polka Party.

Sam was currently hammering in stakes along with Andy Schubert, one of the coaches at the middle school who'd come to help after classes were done for the day.

Andy eyed the sky, overcast with ominous clouds. Weathermen had been predicting another big storm. "Hope this holds off until we're finished up here."

"Holds off 'til tonight and blows over before this weekend," Sam added. He didn't think bad weather would kill attendance completely, but it could certainly make the festival muddier and less cheerful.

Andy grunted in agreement. "I'm guessing the Battlin' Billies Marching Band and everyone who's been building parade floats— Whoa. Who is she and why don't I know her?"

Sam wiped a hand on his jeans and looked up to follow Andy's gaze. *Lorelei?* He frowned, surprised to see her striding toward them across the lawn. Her long hair was loose today, swirling around her face and shoulders with each gust of wind. She had on a pale pink sundress with another one of those see-through blouses—this one the color of strawberries, with shiny collar and cuffs—buttoned over it. Her skirt kept flaring out around her calves and twisting between her legs. He found himself staring as if mesmerized by the motion. Or maybe just by her shapely legs.

Sam jerked his gaze away from her and back to Andy, who wasn't nearly as much fun to look at. "That's, ah, Lorelei. Keller. Wanda's daughter."

"Think she has any interest in being the future Mrs. Andy Schubert?"

"She's seeing a guy back in Philadelphia, where she lives." And if Lorelei had already explained that she and that attorney guy only dated casually…well, Andy didn't need to know all the nitty-gritty details of her life.

"Bummer," Andy said.

Sam stood. "I should go make sure everything's okay. Be right back." He walked off without waiting for an answer, wondering what was important enough for Lorelei to track him down. Had something happened at the inn?

She stopped, trying unsuccessfully to keep her hair from tangling about her face, and offered him a tremulous smile. "H-hi. I took you away from what you were working on."

"They won't fire me if I take a five-minute break. What's up?"

"I…" She broke their locked gazes, staring intently at the ground. "For the record, you made this look a lot easier last night."

He stiffened at the mention of the previous night, recalling his resolution at the bar to keep his distance from her. "Made what look easy?"

"Apologizing." She raised her eyes then, genuine regret clear in their coffee-rich depths. "Sam, I'm sorry about how I spoke to you. How I might have made you feel."

He was shocked by this overture but experience with Lorelei had taught him not to let his guard down. "Don't mention it. It's forgotten."

She reached out to clutch his arm, as if she was afraid he'd walk away from her. "Will you be done here soon? I'd like to buy you a drink. Or maybe something from one of the chocolatiers?" She swiped a thumb across her cheek. "I think that was a raindrop."

Had the rain begun already? All he felt was her grip on him. "You should get back to the inn, stay dry."

"Uh… I actually had a friend of Ava's drop me off on Main Street on the way to one of her errands. I was kind of hoping to get a ride back with you." She bit her lip. "No car, remember?"

He sighed, realizing he wasn't going to be able to

shake her loose. "Wait over under the pavilion. I should be finished up soon."

"Anything I can do to help?" she asked, her voice tentative and very un-Lorelei.

He wanted to squeeze his eyes shut and block out the earnestness in her gaze. Just as he'd acknowledged last night, it was these chinks in her normal armor that got to him. "Thanks, but Andy and I have it covered." If the skies truly opened up in the next few minutes and the scattered drops became a torrent, the flimsy material of Lorelei's blouse and thin cotton dress would be plastered to her body. "*Please* stay here."

She nodded. "Whatever you say, Sam."

He'd seen Lorelei coldly remote before and spitting mad, but like this—cheerfully accommodating and eager to please? This, he realized, was the woman at her most dangerous. *I am so screwed.*

At first, Lorelei had thought Sam would refuse her offer to buy him dinner or a drink. Yet once they were buckled into his truck, he'd relented. She breathed a little easier as he steered them toward a place where Sam said the barbecue was decent. Lorelei was an extremely independent person who was uncomfortable feeling beholden to other people—even sharing her workload with Celia had driven her a little nuts. After all Sam had done, from offering to give her the inn to his willingness to listen to her talk about her family, she desperately wanted to repay his kindness.

She hadn't meant to become bitchy and defensive last night when he'd brought up their fathers. His insight had simply thrown her. It sounded disloyal and illogical for a daughter to be mad at her father for contracting a disease he'd had no control over.

Somewhere between the Marktplatz and their destination south of town, the steady drizzle began pelting them with real force. Sam increased the speed of the windshield wipers twice before they pulled into a mostly empty parking lot. She guessed that the tables on the covered patio were a popular place to eat when the rain wasn't coming down in billowing sheets.

Sam's sudden laugh took her by surprise and she whipped her head around to find out what was funny. He gave her a sardonic smile. "I guess this evening would be the perfect time for one of those 'umbrella' devices I've heard tell of. Here." He leaned toward the steering wheel, shrugging out of his denim jacket. "It's not exactly waterproof, but it'll help."

She wanted to tell him that the gesture was sweet but unnecessary. Except that her words evaporated as she studied the muscles in his arms. It was ridiculous how good the man looked in a short-sleeved black T-shirt. The denim was still warm from his body, and when she shrugged into it, Sam's scent enveloped her. It was as though he'd let her borrow an embrace rather than just a coat.

He reached for his door handle and flashed her a rakish grin. "Ready to make a run for it?"

Laughing, they bolted through the rain. By the time they reached the entrance, Lorelei's hair clung to her face in wet ropes and she knew what little makeup she'd applied that morning was probably streaked unattractively across her face. But she couldn't bring herself to care. In fact, she felt breathlessly giddy in a way she hadn't since she was a young girl.

Inside, the country music twanging through the sound system competed with the rolling thunder and the rain splatting against the metal roof. This was a multipurpose place, serving as bar, restaurant and dance hall. There wasn't much of a crowd, but a few couples swayed on the red oak floor.

"You mind sitting at the bar?" Sam asked. "The food's good, but most of the tables are out on the patio."

"Bar works for me."

They found seats and consulted the menu, which was nothing like the complex offerings at Grace's restaurant. No, here the food choices were simple and limited: pork barbecue sandwich, pork barbecue ribs, coleslaw, baked beans, side salad and steak fries. Period.

Lorelei chuckled. "What, no dessert menu?"

Sam pointed toward the fully stocked bar opposite them. "I think they make some kind of chocolate martini thing on request. But you'd probably be more of a lemon drop girl. I know how you like a little tart with the sweet."

A ruddy-faced bartender with freckles peeking out around his dark red beard came over to them and greeted Sam by name. Then he took their orders of two sandwiches and a side of fries to split. By the time the food came out, people had started trickling into the bar.

Sam checked his watch. "Must be about time for happy hour."

Lorelei swiped one of the thick fries through ketchup and popped it into her mouth. She closed her eyes in bliss. "If I lived in Fredericksburg, I'd be here every night for the fries alone." When she opened her eyes again, she shook her head. "That settles it. I can't ever move back. Between Grace's restaurant and these fries and the chocolate shops on Main Street—"

"And the vendors at Oktoberfest and sausage from Dutchman's Market," Sam added.

"Exactly. I'd be the size of a house." She grabbed another fry. "But since I'm leaving soon, might as well enjoy it while I'm here!"

Sam leaned back on his bar stool, his expression pensive. "Do you ever think about coming back? Ever miss it?"

Lorelei paused, wanting to give him a real answer and not just a knee-jerk response. "I love Texas. In theory. But... I don't—I've never felt like I love who I am when I'm here." She glanced up from beneath her lashes to see if he was laughing at her inane answer.

But his gaze was contemplative, as if she'd said something worth considering instead of jumbled nonsense. "You love who you are in Philadelphia?"

People didn't openly mock her there and she wasn't reminded of the parents she'd lost every time she turned a corner, so that was a start. "I excelled in college in a way I didn't going to school here. I mean, I was always good at the academic part, but I didn't quite fit in." Especially after other students went out of their way to make sure of that. "At the university, I found other people like me, people who looked up to me. In Philadelphia, I feel like someone who's got her act together, someone who's respected and is going to move up at her company."

And here, she felt like a frustrated daughter trapped in a cycle with her mother constantly disappointing each other. Although, Lorelei supposed that cycle had ended now.

She pushed her plate away. "Ever since I got here, you and other people have been telling me how special Wanda was. I don't disagree," she added quickly. "She was completely her own person, comfortable in her skin in a way I envy. She was lively and free-spirited. But being so utterly different from her…"

"Did you worry you weren't special, too?" he teased lightly.

She graced him with a half smile, appreciating his attempt to keep her from getting too maudlin. "I tried to talk to her some about how I felt, how I didn't fit in at school, how much I missed Dad. But those conversations never made me feel any closer to her. Mom lived in her own happy bubble of denial. Like the way other kids treated me was irrelevant, like Dad wasn't really gone. He just 'existed on a different plane.' I stopped coming to her because she seemed so disappointed in my outlook, my inability to be like her. In Philadelphia, I can be Lorelei without feeling like I need to apologize for it every five minutes."

Winding down, she took a deep breath. "All right. This is twice we've gone out to dinner and twice I've unloaded on you. No more, I promise." But beneath the sheepishness, she felt a glimmer of satisfaction. She'd finally managed to discuss her family, a difficult topic for her, without getting short-tempered with Sam.

"I shouldn't have been so hard on you before for not visiting her," he said. "You have to understand, from my perspective… She missed you so much. I'm not saying that to make you feel guilty," he hastily assured her. "Just so you know, however different the two of you were, she loved you. And I can actually understand staying away. My mom lives in Dallas, and there's nothing stopping me from visiting her."

"When was the last time you saw her?"

"The twins' high school graduation. She got pregnant pretty quickly after her second marriage. It was one of the reasons she gave my uncle for not rushing right back to get me. First, it was they were newlyweds and needed time to make their union a strong foundation before adding me to the mix. Then it was that she was just so overwhelmed with having two babies at once and I was better off where I was than if I were uprooted again. My half sisters seem like nice enough girls, if too superficial, but when I'm at the house... Let's just say, I know what you mean about not fitting into your own family."

She reached out and squeezed his hand. "Thank you. It's nice to think someone kind of understands, even though I wish things had been different for you."

"I don't know. Our experiences shape us," he said philosophically. "I doubt I would have been happier growing up in the country club suburb than out on the ranch with JD. And if my past had been different, I'd be different, too. I might not be the delightful person you see before you now," he deadpanned.

She guffawed at that. "Yeah, delightful is totally the first adjective that springs to mind whenever I think of you."

He raised an eyebrow. "How—" He straightened abruptly, losing his smile.

"Sam? What is it, what's wrong?"

"Nothing, really." He stifled an aggrieved groan. "It's dumb. But you know how you were saying earlier you wanted to make up for last night? Save me from that woman, and we'll be even. More than even, I'll owe you!"

Lorelei laughed, remembering how uncomfortable he'd been at the Jalapeño when she'd speculated that the waitress had a crush on him. If Sam was going to swagger around town being a sexy six-feet-plus cowboy, he had to expect a little female interest. She swiveled her head to see who had him running scared. A woman with streaked blond hair and incredibly long legs was sauntering through the crowd, a predatory expression on her striking face.

A face Lorelei suddenly recognized. "*Babs?* Oh, hell no."

"I take it you've met my stalker?"

Chapter 10

Sam always dreaded being cornered by Barbara, partly because she was the adored younger cousin of a horse rancher who frequently gave Sam work. *And I'd miss working with those Thoroughbreds.* While Sam tried not to insult the woman outright, he brushed her off as firmly as courtesy allowed. Did she persist because she was that confident in her own charms, because she loved a challenge or because she was simply too spoiled to accept not getting something she thought she wanted?

Ironically, if Sam ever actually dated her, she'd probably dump him. Everything about the blonde screamed high-maintenance. Who spent hundreds of dollars on a pair of boots that would be ruined if you ever wore them into a barn?

Yet now, for the first time in memory, Sam felt something other than weary resignation when he spotted

Barbara prowling toward him. He was curious over the sudden bright spots of color in Lorelei's cheeks. She snapped her gaze back to him and pasted a wide, patently false smile on her face.

"Stick with me, cowboy," she muttered, barely moving her lips. "I've got this covered."

He grinned. *Things just got interesting.* Lorelei once again reached for his hand, the one she'd squeezed in empathy moments ago. This time she laced her fingers through his and dropped their hands atop the bar.

"There you are, Sammy!" Barbara's voice was habitually breathless. No doubt some men found it sexy, but it always left Sam biting back the advice that if she didn't wear such tight shirts, she could probably get more oxygen. It seemed at first as if she planned to ignore Lorelei's presence entirely, but then her blue eyes narrowed on their joined hands. Barbara's smile tightened. "Aren't you going to introduce me to your friend?"

"Why, Babs!" Lorelei's voice came out far more breathy than usual, and it was all Sam could do not to laugh at the subtle imitation. "I'm hurt you don't remember me. Lorelei Keller? We were in class together from practically kindergarten to graduation. Not that I'd expect you to remember me after so many years. High school was a lifetime ago, wasn't it?"

Barbara's nostrils flared slightly at the insinuation that they were no longer young women.

"I hear you're married now," Lorelei said brightly. "To Trace Collins, isn't it?"

"We're divorced, actually."

"After Trace, she married Vance Emmett," Sam inserted. "But they divorced, too."

"Oh." Lorelei's forehead crinkled in a sympathetic

frown. "But don't you worry, sugar. Pretty gal like you is sure to find your Mr. Right! I'd love to catch up more, but Sam was just about to take me out onto the dance floor." She winked and lowered her voice to a conspiratorial woman-to-woman pitch. "And when a guy like Sam wants to hold you…well, how could I pass up that?"

Lorelei slid off her stool, her hand still clasped with his, and led him onto the floor. He immediately tugged her into his arms, loving the excuse to bring her close. Keeping one hand at her shoulder, he slid his other hand down to her waist. It took real self-discipline not to let his touch drift farther, following the tantalizing flare of her hips.

As they shuffled into a basic two-step, Sam smiled down at her, his tone full of admiration. "You are a very bad person."

"You know, I was admitting that very thing to someone this afternoon." Her brown eyes gleamed, and no matter how obviously she tried, she couldn't stifle her grin.

Sam didn't think she'd ever looked sexier as she failed to quell her unrepentant mischievousness. "Thanks for your assistance. When I asked you to save me, I didn't realize you'd throw yourself into the task with so much gusto."

There were a lot more dancers circling the wood floor than there had been when Sam and Lorelei had first arrived this evening. As they took a turn, he had to pull her tighter against him. Her chest brushed his, and he momentarily lost his rhythm in the soft press of her body. Their legs tangled, her skirt swishing against his jeans. Logically, he knew he couldn't feel it through the denim, but his skin prickled as if she'd stroked his flesh with the silky material.

"I was happy to help," Lorelei said. "Probably too happy. I didn't realize I was such a petty vindictive person. It's a little depressing, really."

"From what I know of you—and of Barbara—I'm sure she had that coming."

"Back in the day, she had a lot of not very nice things to say about me. And said equally unkind things about Wanda," she added darkly.

Well, that cinched it—Barbara's chances of winning Sam over were officially lower than the odds of a man who'd never purchased a ticket hitting the Lotto Texas jackpot. Wanda had been a nurturing soul who'd always managed to find good in people. What possible reason could someone have for running her down?

He didn't want to glance toward the bar to see if they had an audience. He'd much rather look into Lorelei's eyes. "She still there?"

Lorelei bobbed her head in the affirmative. "Glaring daggers into me over the top of her martini glass. Maybe she's changed over the years, but the Babs I remember doesn't give up easily."

"Are you saying we should try harder to dissuade her?" He steered Lorelei toward the edge of the floor, out of the path of other dancers.

"Whatever you need," Lorelei said blithely. "I'm just here to play decoy. And, apparently, act out juvenile vengeance."

He stopped moving, steadying her when she almost stumbled. She glanced up reflexively, her brows drawing together in question. He slid the hand on her shoulder behind her neck, through the rumpled waves of her hair, and leaned down. He could actually see her pulse stutter in the hollow of her throat, hear her breathing change.

She made no move to discourage him or duck away, though. Far from it—the barely banked wickedness in her eyes blazed back to life, but there was no accompanying humor this time. Only heat.

Oh, God. Sam's about to kiss me. Shock and desire bloomed within Lorelei. And then, just like that, he *was* kissing her. Without any fumbling hesitation, his mouth had covered hers. Lorelei froze temporarily, surprised this was actually happening. It was entirely unlike her.

Was it?

She'd imagined this plenty, and now she had the opportunity to experience it firsthand. He teased his tongue over her lower lip. The sensation that quivered through her jolted her from her trance. She parted her lips, and he took the movement for the invitation it was. As their kiss deepened, Lorelei started to feel light-headed, flushed with warmth and a greedy craving for more. Sam's mouth put to shame all the wines she'd tried yesterday, intoxicating in a completely different way.

A sharp moan escaped her and she dimly registered that his palm was cupping the back of her head as if he was trying to press her closer. Which was funny, really, because she'd already voluntarily moved as close as two fully dressed people could physically be. That thought led to imagining them *not* fully dressed and sheer need stabbed through her.

Without relaxing his hold on her, Sam tilted his head back, resting his forehead on hers as they caught their breath. Lorelei was practically panting. She should probably feel embarrassed about that—they'd been making out like hormone-crazed teenagers in front of an audience! But right now the rising lust far outweighed any mortification.

Sam eyed her with a combination of awe and wariness, as if she were some dangerous temptress. "You may be bad, but you are one hell of a good kisser."

Back at you, cowboy. Her mind seemed to be in working order, but her body was still too dazed for her to form words. They just stared at each other. Lorelei didn't know how long they would have remained there, motionless, if a sudden burst of thunder hadn't made her jump. She'd completely forgotten about the storm. Which wasn't surprising, since she'd also forgotten about the roomful of people, including Barbara.

Lorelei heard herself giggle, a very unsophisticated sound.

"Please tell me you're not laughing at the way I kiss," Sam said. "The male ego is very fragile."

She rolled her eyes. "Yeah, I noticed how shy and uncertain you were. You expect me to believe women haven't already told you that you kiss like a pagan god?"

"Ah." The word was a rumble of satisfaction. "My ego thanks you. So what's funny?"

"I just don't think that when Barbara made her beeline across the bar toward you that *this* was the end result she imagined."

Sam brushed his knuckles over her cheek. "It's not exactly what I imagined, either."

Meaning that their kiss was better than what he'd envisioned, or that he never would have thought anything like this could happen between them?

"We should get off the floor," Sam said. "We're a traffic hazard."

She followed him through the crowd and back to the bar. When she attempted to settle their tab, he objected. The bartender laughingly sided with Sam. "I realize, ma'am, that in this day and age, women should be able to pay, but we're just not that enlightened here."

Maybe some feminist part of her should be annoyed, but how irritated could she be with a man who'd just kissed her senseless *and* wanted to buy her dinner? They made it to the exit without running into Barbara again, which suited Lorelei just fine. Though she'd taken an unexpectedly naughty joy in tweaking the woman earlier, right now she didn't want to be reminded that Babs had been the impetus for that soul-shaking kiss. Besides, Lorelei's brain was currently liquefied. If she got into a verbal sparring match with her former nemesis, she'd be at a loss for a single timely comeback. *High school all over again.*

Sam held open the door for her and she saw that the storm had grown worse while they'd been inside. Small hailstones littered the front walkway. The parking lot was one big mudslide.

"We could stay here," Sam mused, "but we're under tornado watches later tonight and I'd just as soon get on the road before anyone with a few beers under their belt heads home."

"I'm game." The inn was only ten minutes away under normal conditions.

"Hang on tight," was all the warning Sam gave before swooping her up into his arms. Hurrying, he carried her through the rain toward the pickup truck.

Though Lorelei tried to maintain some discipline

about diet and exercise, at five-eight she was never going to be a delicate armful. It was impossible not to be impressed with the way he cradled her. But he had to set her down to unlock the door. Holding her against the side of the truck, he let her slide down against his body. Her body tingled at the contrast between cold rain sluicing over them and the heat of him surrounding her. If they hadn't been standing in a public parking lot and lightning weren't flashing all around, she'd be tempted to brace herself against the truck and wrap her legs around his waist.

"There you go." He popped open the door. "You okay?" he asked when she didn't immediately jump in the dry shelter of the cab.

She swallowed. "Dandy." Except that she was losing her mind.

What was she doing, fantasizing about jumping a man she'd known for a week outside a bar? That scenario offered health risks, emotional risks *and* legal risks. While she wasn't one hundred percent up to date on Texas public indecency laws, she was pretty sure sex while standing in a parking lot was against code. Still, the picture of what making love to Sam might be like flashed through her mind again, and she shivered.

"You chilled?" Sam asked solicitously. "I've got the heater on, but it'll take a minute to be effective."

"Actually, I'm not as cold as you'd expect."

He half turned to her as though about to respond, but then simply shook his head and focused on peering through the windshield. There was some debris on the roads, mostly in the form of small tree branches. The silence that fell between them felt natural at first, more an attempt to concentrate on careful driving than awkwardness over his kissing her. Yet, the longer they were in the car and the more time Lorelei had to dwell on her ardent response, the more difficult it became not to say anything.

A few minutes ago, she'd been thinking about how good it would feel to have Sam inside her. And here they were on their way to a hotel where they'd be alone together all night. Did he think that when they reached the inn, they might continue where they'd left off? Mild panic fluttered in her chest. *Definitely panic.* Not *excitement, you hussy.*

She waited until he'd safely crossed a path of road covered in standing water before she broached the subject. "What I said earlier, about you kissing like a god? I meant it. That was—" Hotter than a Lone Star Fourth of July "—nice. And you know I was happy to help out with your stalker."

"But it was an isolated incident," Sam recited as if he were a student spouting memorized facts. "You're not the type of woman to be ruled by your passions, making impulsive mistakes that you'll regret when you're in a more rational mood."

"Uh, yeah." Pretty much in a nutshell. Lorelei didn't know whether to be impressed that he understood her so well or vaguely insulted. The way he described her, she sounded dull and inflexible.

"Agreed. One-time deal."

Well, that was easy. She blinked. "So you weren't planning to try and kiss me later?" At all?

He kept his eyes on the partially flooded road, but his mouth curved into a devilish grin. "Disappointed, darlin'?"

"Wh— No. I'm relieved we worked through it logically. Thank you for being so considerate of my point of view." She slumped down in her seat, proud that she and Sam, despite their brief history of hostile miscommunications, had reached such a sensible accord. Yep, she was pleased. And not at all despondent at the thought of his mouth never again taking hers.

By the time Sam pulled his truck behind the inn, the lightning had died down. But an eerie wind howled over them. Lorelei knew that tomorrow morning, the small buds that had started to blossom on flowering trees would be floating in mud puddles like soggy confetti. She just hoped the destruction would be limited to flora and fauna, not people's roofs and fences.

She and Sam filed into the kitchen and she paused at the door to the laundry room, shrugging out of the borrowed denim jacket. "I'll wash and dry this and have it back to you by tomorrow." For now, she planned to wash and dry herself. "I think I'm gonna sink into a hot bath for a little while." All of the guest rooms contained private bathrooms with shower stalls, two of which were specially equipped for handicapped visitors, but the only tub in the place was in the master suite that had been her mother's. Right now, the huge square tub sounded like heaven.

Sam nodded. "See you in the morning. And Lorelei? Thank you."

For tracking him down this afternoon to apologize? For running interference with Babs? For telling him he kissed like a god? Lorelei thought it best not to ask, since she was striving to forget just how addictive his kisses were.

She went to her room and grabbed her most comfortable nightgown, a pale yellow dress that fell to midthigh from wide shirred straps. It was her favorite because of the ultrasoft fabric, but when she'd packed it, she hadn't known she'd be sharing the inn with someone else. The sweetheart neckline and high hem were a bit more revealing than she was comfortable with Sam seeing, so she also pulled the guest robe out of the closet. She'd just finished tossing a couple of toiletry items into a duffel bag when her cell phone jangled.

"Hello?" Holding the phone between her ear and shoulder, she gathered up her stuff and padded barefoot into the hall.

"It's Ava, dear. Please tell me you're in safe for the night and not out in this humdinger of a storm?"

Lorelei smiled into the receiver, touched by the woman's maternal concern. "Yeah, Sam and I are both—"

"And what is all this I hear about the two of you making out on the dance floor?"

The abrupt interrogation surprised Lorelei so much she nearly tripped over her own feet. "Uh…" *Word travels fast.*

She hurried down the stairs, hoping she was out of earshot of his room. It would be humiliating to get caught discussing him on the phone like some teenager dishing to a girlfriend. "He said Barbara Biggins has been stalking him, and he's had a tough time convincing her he's not interested. It was an act for her benefit." And also the most stirring kiss Lorelei had experienced in her adult life, but that wasn't relevant.

"Just an act?" There was a flat note in Ava's tone. Skepticism or disappointment?

Lorelei pushed open the door to her mother's room— she couldn't think of the suite as anything else, even after days of packing away Wanda's belongings. "He's an attractive man and a good kisser, I grant you. But it's not as if we have much in common. Including the states we live in, remember?"

"All right. Just checking. I didn't want to step on your toes when I introduce him to my niece this weekend."

Lorelei blinked. "Your niece?"

"Emily. She's a paralegal who lives in San Marcos." The city Ava mentioned was right here in the Hill Country, famed for its river and springs. "She's coming to town for the festival. Emily broke up with her fiancé last year. I didn't want to push her while she was recovering but I think she's lonely. And she's such a nice girl! You know, your mother and I always used to say Sam needed a good woman in his life."

Lorelei felt a wholly irrational twinge. Wanda had wanted to set him up with someone but had never once mentioned him to her single daughter? Of course, logically the idea of Lorelei and Sam together wouldn't have made a lick of sense, but normally that wouldn't have stopped Wanda.

In the bathroom, she found a jar of lavender-scented foaming bath salts that claimed on the label to "soothe away stress." Lorelei dumped a ton of it into the running water.

"Hello? Lorelei?"

"I'm here."

"Oh. Thought maybe the call had dropped for a second there."

She sat on the edge of the tub, sticking out her hand to check the temperature. "Ava, does Sam know you plan to shove an available woman into his path? Because he was just saying the other night that he doesn't want a relationship."

Undeterred, Ava made a dismissive *pfffft* noise. "Honey, every man says that until he meets the woman who changes his mind. He can't discount Emily if he's never even met her."

Lorelei frowned, trying to follow that reasoning.

"I am more than capable of handling Sam," Ava continued confidently. "I just wanted to make sure *you* were okay with it."

"Sure. Of course. Why wouldn't I be? Hope it all works out for those crazy kids. Look, Ava, I appreciate you checking on me, but I was just getting ready to sink into a bubble bath, so…"

"Talk to you tomorrow, then."

Lorelei set the phone on the linen shelf and undressed, wondering absently who'd tattled to Ava about the kiss. After being gone from town so long, Lorelei couldn't imagine anyone here caring what *she* did. No, she suspected Sam was the primary person of interest in any gossip that got passed along. Just because Barbara was his most aggressive admirer didn't mean dozens of other aspiring women weren't also keeping tabs on him. *Brace yourself, ladies.* They were about to have another rival for Sam's affections in kind-hearted but lonely Emily.

She clipped her hair up into a haphazard knot. Tendrils of steam beckoned from the bubble-filled tub and Lorelei sank into the water with a contented sigh. Her body had been thrumming with electric tension ever since Sam put his arms around her on the dance floor. Now, her muscles finally started to loosen. She closed her eyes, only to have them pop open again when she heard a sound at the door.

"Hello?" She cocked her head and realized that the

noise was scratching. A paw batted from beneath the door, insistently demanding entrance. Lorelei recalled her mom saying that when she brushed her teeth in the mornings and evenings, Oberon liked to follow her into the bathroom and sit on the vanity, mewing conversationally as if he were telling her about his plans or recapping his day.

Should've closed the outer door. Though she'd locked the bathroom door, she'd been preoccupied by her conversation with Ava and hadn't closed the door between the bedroom and the rest of the house.

"Sorry, Obie," she muttered. "I bathe alone."

The scratching became more frantic, and she flicked a handful of water at floor level, hoping that if his paw got wet, he'd retreat. Instead, as if she'd declared war, he retaliated with a shrill battle cry that made the hairs on the back of her neck rise. Lorelei found herself wondering if Lonely Emily might like a cat for company.

"Go away," she insisted.

She wanted to believe she could simply ignore him, but Oberon did not accept defeat. Any minute now, he'd launch into a peace-shattering caterwaul. Not willing to cede her serenity to a freaking feline, she stood. She grabbed her towel off the brass hook and wrapped it around her. She planned to boot his fuzzy butt from the room and shut the master suite door. Let him yowl out in the hallway—she'd turn on some music before resuming her bath.

When she opened the bathroom door, Oberon took off like a shot. But she didn't doubt he'd try to return. Time to shut the door and flip on the radio. Lorelei had only taken two more steps toward the door when the entire inn was plunged into blackness. There was also a jolting silence as appliances and ceiling fans stopped functioning. She stood still, waiting for her eyes to adjust before she tried to find a candle or matches. Blundering around in the darkness could lead to her stubbing a toe on a piece of furniture or tripping over the cat.

But before she'd had a chance to reorient herself, a beam of light flashed down the hall and Sam rounded the corner, stopping short at the sight of her in a towel. She blinked against the brightness.

His voice was hoarse. "Power..." He coughed into his fist, tried again. "The power went out."

"I noticed." She shifted her weight, careful not to drop the towel, hyperaware of the suds dripping along her collarbone and the fact that her topknot was flopping limply to the side of her head.

Sam took a step closer, flipping the flashlight away so it wasn't shining directly at her. "Here. You might need this."

"Thanks." Tightening her grip on the towel with one hand, she reached out the other one, grateful but perplexed. "How'd you get here so fast with a light?" It was as if he'd just been hanging out in the hallway, waiting for them to lose electricity.

"I was on the way already and grabbed the emergency flashlight out of the outlet where it was charging. I thought I heard you shriek. I was afraid you might have hurt yourself or seen a critter." He gestured to the towel she wore. "I would've knocked before I came in."

The image that sprang to Lorelei's mind was in direct contrast to his words. She could too easily picture herself reclining in the bubbly water when suddenly the door opened...

She swallowed. "You came to save me from a potential critter? I live alone in Philly," she reminded him, unused to anyone riding to her rescue. "I've had to deal with critters on my own."

"Yeah." His lips twitched. "But everything's bigger in Texas."

Unbidden, her gaze slid down his body. When she caught herself, she yanked her eyes back up, hoping it was too dark for him to have noticed. But he was staring so intently she doubted she could hide anything from him. He reached out a hand as if in slow motion and brushed away a line of frothy soap that had been winding toward the towel and the crevice between her breasts. Lorelei's breath caught. Why hadn't she tried harder to talk Ava out of any misbegotten matchmaking attempts? *Maybe I should warn him. As his friend.*

But she couldn't quite dredge up the nerve to discuss Sam's love life while she stood there wearing no clothes. "That noise you heard wasn't me. Oberon was throwing a tantrum because he was locked out. He wanted to keep me company while I was in the tub."

Sam smirked. "Then he—"

Click, whir. Light poured through the room. Lorelei gasped, her towel slipping a couple of centimeters before she caught the top of it. Sam's expression was so deliciously predatory that she was torn between fleeing and letting the towel hit the hardwood.

Backing away, she stammered, "I—I should finish rinsing off now."

He nodded. "Maybe I'll go take a shower, too." As he turned the corner, she heard him mumble, "A very cold one."

Chapter 11

The kickoff day for the festival, Saturday, also happened to be St. Patrick's Day. Irish or not, luck was definitely with the town. The day dawned clear and bright, all of the week's previous storms having rolled through. The sky was a brilliant blue and although the early morning hours were cool enough to warrant a sweater, temperatures were forecast to reach the high seventies by noon. After spending much of Friday indoors with bankers and real estate agents, Lorelei looked forward to being outside today.

Tess Fitzpatrick, who had generously come over last night to help fill giveaway bags with calming incense and potpourri, promised to stop by the booth during downtimes when she wasn't organizing pint-size dancers for their next show. From her spot on the spacious public lawn, Lorelei watched dancers from the high school stretch and a group of musicians set up their instruments and sheet music. Lorelei was situated between a trio of women selling handmade jewelry and a middle-aged couple who were unpacking boxes of jars. Closer inspection revealed the jars were full of marinade, including one made with red wine from a local vineyard and another that was intriguingly labeled "madman moonshine marinade."

Lorelei knew her version of the Haunted Hill Country booth wasn't quite what her mother would have done, yet she felt Wanda would approve. To honor her mother's lifelong faith in pig figures as lucky talismans, Ava and Lorelei had found a novelty tablecloth—probably meant for BBQ events—that was covered in smiling pigs. Lorelei had also put together a scrapbook celebrating the inn and surrounded it with pamphlets on some of the area's other B and Bs, spotlighting those her mom had liked the best. And Lorelei had printed and folded the brochures saved on her mom's PC that offered advice on dealing with Hill Country spirits.

Included were a reminder never to slam doors (lest you injure a ghost crossing the threshold and antagonize it into haunting you); the reassurance that most ghosts are benign but should you run across one you'd like to shake, try imitating a rooster's crow (the specter may fade away if it believes dawn is breaking); and the advice to turn your pockets inside out whenever passing a graveyard (to keep the spirits from sneaking into your pockets and hitching a ride).

At festivals past, Wanda had playfully attempted "readings," either through cards or tea leaves. Lorelei refused to go that far to entertain booth visitors, but she had purchased a large bag of fortune cookies at a party supply store in a neighboring county. She'd filled a green plastic bowl with the cookies and set it among the goodie bags.

She'd just finished reassuring a little girl in a flashing shamrock necklace that the cookies were free when she looked up and saw a familiar bearded face. Dwayne, the would-be ghost hunter, angled two fingers at her in wry salute. Today, sitting out in the cheery sunshine at a display table that reminded her how enthusiastic Wanda had been about the supernatural, Lorelei wished she'd handled Dwayne and his friend with more benevolence.

"Hi," she called.

His auburn brows rose but after a moment, he ambled toward her. "Hello. Mind if I take one of these pamphlets?" He gestured to her stack of Hill Country spirits brochures.

"Please do." She handed him two, including one for his friend. "I don't want to have to take all these back with me at the end of the day. Is your buddy here, too?" she asked, scanning the crowd.

"Jerry." Dwayne nodded. "He's over by the water wheel, interviewing a man who's lived here all his life. Man claims that his twin brother died in 2002 but always visits on their birthday."

Lorelei thought she kept her expression neutral, but Dwayne cocked his head, studying her as if he'd seen a flash of something.

"You really hate this paranormal stuff, huh?"

She leaned back in her folding chair. "*Hate* is a strong word."

"But accurate?" he persisted.

"My mom was really into it. I guess I just…"

He held up his hands. "Say no more. Both of my

parents are into surgery. Performing it, not getting it done. They wanted me to go to medical school. Not my thing, though."

She tried to picture him in a white coat and consulting a patient file but failed spectacularly. "Well, even though ghosts aren't my thing—largely because I think it's all bunk—I didn't mean to go ballistic on you guys the other day."

He grinned at her. "Right before we left, you *did* look like you were going to shoot lasers out of your eyes. Kinda terrifying. It was our bad, though. I was all hyped up on energy drinks and should have been more compassionate. Forgive me?"

"If you'll forgive my wigging out."

"Done." He winked. "Besides, me and Jerry like scary entities."

That made her chuckle and she was still smiling when Sam approached her table. His green button-down shirt made his eyes sparkle like emeralds beneath the brim of his cowboy hat.

"You look like you're enjoying yourself," he said. "Didn't I just see that guy we ran off from the inn the other day?"

"Dwayne. He stopped by to grab some pamphlets and tell me I was scary."

"He's got that right," Sam drawled.

"Hey!" She reached out to swat him on the arm, and he grabbed her hand.

"You're supposed to be wearing green today," he said, his voice stern with mock-reprimand.

She tried not to be distracted by his continuing to hold her hand. "This is green." *Ish.* She'd paired a lace-trimmed sweater with a short black skirt.

"No, it's one of those weird not-quite-blue colors only women know the names of. Turquoise or something."

Teal. When she'd packed a suitcase for Texas, she'd been in shock over her mother's death. The last thing she'd considered was the upcoming St. Patrick's Day and whether she'd be in town that long.

"Tradition says you could get pinched," he continued.

She arched an eyebrow. "Try it and die, cowboy."

His only response was a wolfish smile.

She snatched her hand back. "Aren't you supposed to be busy roping dogies?" As in, *get along little?* He was working over at the fairgrounds today, participating in interactive demonstrations of roping and saddling.

"Headed that way now," he said. "Just thought I'd say hi first." He turned to blend into the crowd but only got a few vendors away before he stopped, exchanged greetings with an elderly woman and leaned down to pick up something off the table. Then he pivoted and retraced his steps to Lorelei.

He crooked his finger at her with a grin. "C'mere." He leaned across the table, and she met him halfway. He dropped two strands of bright green shamrock-bead necklaces over her head, letting his hands slide down over her. His breath was warm against her ear as he murmured, "There. Now you're safe."

Interesting word choice. Lorelei had always associated "safe" with security and seat belts and comfy socks—not a spike of adrenaline at the feeling of a man's touch and the giddy uncertainty of whether he might kiss her again.

As he walked away, she tried not to appear overtly

fascinated with his jeans. But her admiration was echoed in a hearty sigh behind her.

"*Mmm,* that man. You are a lucky lady," Tess said.

Lorelei turned to smile at the redhead. "Hey, Tess."

The woman shrugged a large macramé purse off her shoulder and set it under the table. She was wearing a white tennis skirt with a dark green polo and had accessorized the outfit with green polka-dotted suspenders and lime-colored canvas shoes. She looked like the peppy head cheerleader for Leprechaun U.

"Very cute," Lorelei said.

"Thanks. I had considered just wearing a green leotard and tights under a sandwich board that said, 'Kiss Me, I'm Irish,' but thought that might be a touch desperate." She plopped into the other folding chair. "If I weren't so eternally grateful to you for helping me understand geometry proofs, I might have to hate you. I've been depressingly single for the past six months and, in a single week back, you snagged the interest of Sam Travis." She grabbed one of the B-and-B brochures off the table and fanned herself dramatically.

Lorelei looked away, nibbling on her bottom lip. It was one thing to act as Sam's human shield where Barbara was concerned, but Lorelei was usually honest to a fault. Painfully blunt, she'd been called. Letting Tess, who'd been so genuinely kind to her, believe something untrue discomfited her.

"There's not anything between me and Sam, not really. It's just a matter of close quarters while we're both staying at the inn."

"Y'all may not be picking out china patterns, but he was interested enough to kiss you in front of everyone over at the Star the other night. That's further than most women around here have gotten with him." Tess's brown eyes twinkled. "And trust me, plenty have tried."

Lorelei laughed. "That I can believe. So he really hasn't dated much?"

"A woman here or there about a year ago, but nothing that ever lasted past a few dates, far as I know. Since he doesn't live here full-time, I can't say he doesn't have a steady girl *somewhere,* but if that were the case, he would have said so. He's turned Barbara Biggins away more than once. Hell, if I were him, I might have lied about having a girlfriend in parts unknown just to throw Barbara off the scent."

Lorelei sat forward, elbows on her knees, and lowered her voice to a confidential whisper. "That's why he kissed me—to con Barbara into thinking we were together."

"Really? Outstanding." Tess rubbed her hands together. "Wish I could have seen her face. She was the quintessential mean girl back in school and has not improved with age. Still, I'm kind of bummed about you and Sam. Rather, the fact that there is no you and Sam."

"Bummed? Two minutes ago you were acting jealous and implied my being with him was reason enough to hate me."

"True. But the two of you would make a very cute couple."

"We'd make a very *temporary* couple," Lorelei corrected. "As you said, Sam doesn't make his home here. Neither do I. He's a good-looking guy—"

"And a good kisser?" Tess prompted. "Tell me he's as good as he seems like he'd be."

Better. "People don't have relationships based on that." Not successful ones, anyway.

"Maybe not relationships. But people have had flings based on less," Tess said matter-of-factly.

Lorelei choked back a laugh. "I'm not the flinging type."

No, she was apparently the solitary type. This friendly bantering with Tess heightened her awareness of how few people she'd spoken to from Philadelphia in the past few days. The office receptionist had emailed condolences, on behalf of the entire staff, and Lorelei had talked to Celia a number of times—until the woman had started dodging Lorelei's micromanaging phone calls.

She'd been here over a week. Weren't there people who were worried about her, people she should be missing more? Lorelei sometimes went jogging with one of her neighbors, and the woman had texted her that morning to say she'd just achieved her personal best for a 5K. When they did their cool-down laps, they had no trouble making small talk, but it wasn't as if Lorelei had thought of calling the woman when she was upset over picking up Wanda's ashes. Rick left a voice mail that he'd been given tickets to a sold-out show and to let him know ASAP whether she'd be home by the date of the performance—otherwise, he'd find someone else to take.

The closest thing she had to a romantic relationship boiled down to first right of refusal of theater tickets? She couldn't work up any rancor over it, though. It wasn't as if she'd been pining for Rick. With an inward sigh, she realized that when she got back to Philly, she should break the habit of doing things with him. Their convenient friendship was never going to develop into anything deeper. What if their constant partnering at events prevented them from meeting potential lovers?

Before now, Lorelei hadn't been seeking more intimacy in her life. Yet a burgeoning sense of longing was beginning to take shape. As devoted as she was to her job, work wasn't everything. It might be nice to have a man in her life who listened to her talk about her day, who made her laugh, who had broad shoulders she could lean on, were she ever so inclined. *A man whose kisses make me dizzy.*

She was grateful for the distraction when several tourists came by the table, expressing their regret that they'd never been able to stay at the B and B, which they thought had a "cool theme." They asked her about some of the superstitions in the pamphlet and Tess joined in with some of the folklore tidbits she'd heard growing up. The women from the jewelry table came over to snag a couple of the miniature bags of potpourri, followed by a man who introduced himself as an official photographer for the event and asked Lorelei to smile for the camera. As Tess excused herself to organize a line of preschool-age tap dancers, a proprietor from one of the inns across town came over to say how glad she was Lorelei had decided to include the Haunted Hill Country booth one last time.

"It's like Wanda is here with us, saying goodbye," the woman said affectionately.

Lorelei had spent what felt like a solid two hours talking to people. It wasn't until she hit a lull and had a moment to herself that the surrounding scents really penetrated her conscious mind. Lunchtime was approaching, and the food vendors were doing a brisk business. She breathed in the buttery ears of corn, the smoky fragrance of giant roasted turkey legs, the nearly eye-watering sharpness of hot peppers and the nutty malt aroma of beer being poured into souvenir steins. Her stomach gurgled.

That's it. The booth is officially closed for lunch. She made sure the stacks of paper were weighted down with some of Wanda's topaz crystals and small chakra stones and left the fortune cookies and incense out where people could help themselves. Then she hoisted her purse and texted Tess to see if the woman wanted to meet up in one of the food pavilions.

Now that she'd realized how hungry she was, Lorelei didn't know where to start. Booths stretched across the entire length of Main Street. She grinned, suddenly very grateful that the festival spanned a week. As much as she looked forward to tomorrow's chili cook-off, for now, she decided she was in the mood for German cuisine. After piling a plate with brats, potato salad and dilled cucumbers, she got a message from Tess saying We have a table, saved you a seat.

Sure enough, as soon as Lorelei entered the designated pavilion, she saw Ava standing and waving. Also present were Ava's husband, Clinton, a young woman with hair so pale it was almost white, Tess, Sam and another man in a cowboy hat. Once she was closer, she took in details of the other man's outfit, from the feathers in the band of his hat to the longhorn skull pattern on his colorful shirt to his bolo tie and a gold belt buckle that probably weighed more than Oberon. *He shouldn't sit next to Sam,* she thought almost pityingly. The man looked like some demented cliché of a "Texas cowboy" while Sam was emphatically, quietly, the real thing.

Sam stood and pulled out the chair between him and Tess.

"Thank you." It occurred to Lorelei that she was

going to get spoiled here and would need to remember how to open her own doors and scoot back her own chairs when she left.

"Lorelei, this is my niece, Emily Hirsch," Ava said, introducing a pretty woman with a too-solemn expression. Her stick-straight platinum hair was held off her face by a wide red band, and her high cheekbones were better defined than words in a dictionary.

"Nice to meet you," Lorelei said, her imagination preoccupied with the idea of this woman and Sam. Did Emily seem perhaps a bit too frail and ethereal for him, a man who worked with his hands and tromped through mud and rain with no umbrella?

"We've been meaning to come by your booth all morning," Ava said apologetically. "We just haven't made it that far yet."

"Aunt Ava must know everyone in town," Emily said, sounding awed. "She can't go three feet without someone stopping us to hug her or ask her opinion on something."

"If you two get a chance, stop by after lunch," Lorelei invited them. "You can tell me any ghost anecdotes you know. I'm tired of repeating the same three over and over."

Ava shook her head. "Have you asked Sam for help? He's the tour guide for the 'haunted' trail ride, for pete's sake. You should see him spellbind the tourists with stories."

Lorelei shot him a sidelong glance. When he was in one of his reticent moods, it was impossible to picture him as an engaging storyteller. But this morning, when he'd teased her about wearing the wrong color, his face had been so expressive, a pure joy to watch. And when he'd brought her that flashlight during the inn's power outage, his voice had been husky enough to make her shiver. There would be worse ways to spend an evening than sidled up to a campfire listening to that voice.

Ava had turned to Sam, her cheerful tone bordering on manic energy. "Emily here is a storyteller, too! She volunteers twice a month at a library, working with kids. I just know you'll make a great mother someday," Ava told her niece warmly.

Lorelei almost winced at the uncomfortable expression on Emily's face. The paralegal was squirming in her chair, obviously wishing her aunt would stop her matchmaking attempts—or at least be more subtle about them. For his part, Sam had hunkered down over his plate, attacking his food with a single-minded ruthlessness, as if eating would give him a socially acceptable excuse for ignoring conversation altogether.

In an attempt to dispel the awkwardness, Lorelei interrupted Ava's rhapsodies by turning to the man with the belt buckle. "I'm sorry, but I don't think we've met."

"Dickie Gebhart at your service, ma'am. I manage one of the clothing stores here in town."

"One of the Western wear emporiums?" she asked.

His smile flashed white beneath his dark mustache. "What gave it away?"

"Speaking of clothes—" Ava turned to her niece "—you have to go shopping with me while you're in town. Emily has such an eye for color and detail. Why, when Clinton and I decided a couple of years ago to redecorate, Emily practically designed the new living room for us. Didn't she, Clinton?"

"Uh-huh." Clinton dutifully nodded his gray head without ever looking up from his spaetzle.

Lorelei resisted the urge to smack her forehead with her palm. Ava was a very dear woman—looking back, Lorelei wasn't sure how she would have survived this week without her—but as a Cupid, she lacked finesse. After Tess gave an humorous recap of one of the morning's dances, Ava launched into a memory of one of Emily's recitals, her proud tone suggesting that Emily could have been a prima ballerina if she hadn't chosen to be a paralegal instead. Ava didn't seem to notice that her niece was looking at her as if she were off her meds.

"Aunt Ava, I only took dance for six months. Because Mom made me. I was *horrible* at it, hated every minute. Two left feet," the woman confided across the table to Tess.

This news inordinately cheered Lorelei. Sam was an excellent dancer. It seemed that Ava might be grasping at straws in thinking Emily and Sam were compatible.

While they were clearing the table at the end of the meal, Sam remarked on Lorelei's mood. "What's got you so happy?" he asked as they carried their trays to a nearby trash bin. "You're whistling."

"Was I? Guess I've just had a lot of fun today." That was true. She'd enjoyed it more than she could have predicted. Even Ava being a little bit kooky had a certain rightness to it, reminding Lorelei of her eccentric mother. "I miss Mom."

Sam stared at her, uncomprehending. "Okay. See, that sounds like a sad statement. Missing her put you in a good mood?"

"No. I just… I feel close to her here. I'm really grateful you convinced me to do this."

"Grateful enough to help me fake my own death and

get into some kind of witness protection program? Ava has lost her ever lovin' mind."

Lorelei smothered a laugh. "Don't worry. I'll protect you from the oh-so-scary retired lady and her pretty niece."

Instead of acting offended by her mild ridicule, Sam surprised her by dropping a kiss on top of her head. "Thanks, darlin'. I knew I could count on you."

After accepting a ride from Tess, Lorelei arrived at the inn shortly after sundown. Oberon met her at the door with his best woe-is-the-neglected-cat impression. She'd sorted through the mail and was filling a glass of ice water when Sam came through the back door.

He hefted a brown paper sack. "I hit a few stalls on the way to my truck—figured both of us would be too tired to cook tonight."

Lorelei groaned. "No more food. Ever." But a moment later, she heard herself ask, "Just out of curiosity, though, what did you bring?"

Laughing, he carried his bounty over to the table and began pulling out various cartons. Lorelei took a seat to better inspect the offerings, but she doubted she could eat anytime soon. This afternoon, Ava had worked a couple of hours at Wanda's table so that Emily could "hang around someone her own age," leaving Lorelei and the quiet blonde free to sample lots of festival snacks. After a few stymied attempts at conversation that went nowhere, they seemed to have reached a mutual unspoken agreement that as long as they were eating, they weren't required to speak.

Lorelei grinned at a sudden memory, thinking there was one person out there tonight who should feel even more stuffed than she was. "I kept spotting this same family throughout the day," she told Sam. "They had the cutest little boy, probably around three years or four years old, and you wouldn't believe this kid's appetite! I swear every time I saw him, he was devouring something almost as big as he was—an entire sausage on a stick, a ginormous ice cream cone. Tess and I passed them on our way out. The kid had a pear in one hand and a bag of gourmet nuts in the other. God help those parents and their grocery bill when he hits his teen years!"

Rampant appetite and ice cream smears around his mouth aside, he really had been an adorable little boy. Lorelei didn't normally think of herself as a "kid person," but she'd found herself smiling at quite a few in the crowd.

"I might want to have a baby," she said, testing out how the words sounded and felt—more an exploratory statement than a declaration.

Sam shot back in his seat so hard the chair skidded on the tile. "Uh…"

She rolled her eyes. He acted as if she'd just suggested getting pregnant tonight. "Get a grip. That wasn't my bizarre attempt at a come on. I was just realizing for the first time I might actually want kids someday in the far flung future. Unclench." Did he have any idea how panicked his expression was?

"Right. I knew that. Congratulations. In advance," he said weakly.

"You know, up until now, I've thought it was kind of funny how you avoid women and, by extension, commitment, but this is starting to seem a little pathological. Does the thought of having a family really rattle you that much?"

Instead of shrugging off her question with a macho denial that he could be scared, he shrugged. "There was a small barn at the edge of property where JD and I worked, more like a shed, really, and we cornered the occasional copperhead inside. Whenever I had to go in there for some reason, I'd get this nauseous kind of dread. I got nothing against the institution of marriage in the abstract but pondering myself with an actual wife and kids? Well. I have a venom extractor in the first-aid kit in the truck, should I ever need it, but family's a permanent condition."

She crossed her arms over her chest. "I don't buy it, the whole desperado loner vibe. You had a soft spot for Mom and you were annoyed I didn't visit her more. You do have a sense of family obligation."

"Wanda was a good woman, good to me, and I liked her. But I saw how much she missed you, how wounded she was that you weren't closer. And now that I've gotten to know you better, I see that you've got wounds of your own. Family does that. Why create more obligation for yourself and the potential for hurting one another?"

"I know your parents disappointed you," she said, softening her tone when she imagined the one-two punch of losing a father only to be abandoned by his mom. "But you got along with your uncle, right?"

"Sure. JD did his best by me. He's dead now." Sam said it simply, without a trace of self-pity, but his point was made. JD was just one more loss he'd suffered. The actuary in her completely identified with Sam's position; deeper entanglements equaled more risk. Wasn't she a believer in safeguarding oneself however possible?

Lorelei felt guilty for even pursuing the argument. What business was it of hers if Sam preferred to stay a bachelor? Yet once again, she thought of that laughing, pink-cheeked preschooler she'd seen today who'd looked so much like his own adoring father. It took shockingly little imagination for her to imagine an equally cute boy riding *Sam's* tall shoulders, mischievous eyes shining the way Sam's had this morning when he'd razzed her about not wearing the right shade of green.

She shook herself out of her reverie. Maybe this was just her heretofore unknown biological clock buzzing at her—next time she'd smack the snooze button and ignore the damn thing. "So I'm out of fortune cookies," she said, clumsily changing the subject. "I was surprised by how many people asked me about fortune-telling or reading their auras or whatever. One woman came by the table to specifically invite me to her house for a Ouija board attempt at getting in touch with Mom. I'm going to have to come up with something for tomorrow."

"What, you mean like taking a crystal ball to the booth with you?" he asked, an unmaterialized grin flirting around the corners of his mouth.

"I was thinking more along the lines of printing out tomorrow's horoscopes and reading the pertinent signs to anyone interested."

"Guess that's technically more interactive than the fortune cookies," he said dubiously. "But it lacks showmanship."

"Sorry. We weren't all born with your inherent skill for hamming it up in front of crowds, Mr. In-The-Center-Ring." Despite her teasing tone, she'd been impressed when she and Emily had caught one of Sam's lasso demonstrations this afternoon.

His talent and focus were…sexy, she admitted to herself. He'd shown intense concentration on what he was doing but at the same time a total awareness of the crowd, playing to them with his smiles and his tricks. After that display and Ava's earlier remarks about him telling stories around a campfire, Lorelei was starting to look forward to their trail ride. She and Sam spent so much time alone together, it was a revelation of sorts to watch him relate to an audience. Then again, was it really a surprise that Monosyllable Man could charm folks when he wanted? After all, it wasn't the general population that spooked him, it was one-on-one connections.

"I could give you tips," he offered in a lazy drawl.

"Thanks, but no matter how good you are, I don't think you can teach me roping by tomorrow."

"Not what I had in mind. You should try your *hand* at palm reading." He emphasized his pun by waggling his fingers at her.

"Ugh," she complained. "That was beneath you."

"You didn't like the joke?"

"It's only a 'joke' if it's funny, Travis."

In response, she got the full-on grin this time instead of just the hint of one. Her toes curled inside her black ankle boots.

"For palm reading," he told her, "you don't need any of the props. Wanda had fun with her mystical cards and stuff, but you'd just be uncomfortable."

"I'll be uncomfortable anyway," she groused. "I am not holding hands with strangers all day and pretending to see the future in the wrinkles of their skin."

"It's not that bad." He held out his hand. "Here."

"You want me to pretend to read your palm?"

"Other way around. I was going to demonstrate."

She extended her arm, feeling dumb but playing along. The sights and sounds of the festival had invigorated her; the idea of retreating alone to her room wasn't nearly as enticing as sharing this lighthearted moment with Sam.

He traced light circles over her wrist with his thumb, and pleasure rippled through her. *What is wrong with you?* Hands were not erogenous zones. Or maybe they were—it had been so long since she'd had sex, she probably wouldn't remember. Then he smoothed his thumb over her palm, peering at her with mock intensity. A lock of hair fell across his face, making him boyishly enticing. For a second, she could forget that he was a jaded man who seemed to think poisonous snake bites were preferable to letting someone get close to him.

His touch feather-light, he followed a line on her palm. Her eyes closed involuntarily.

"This is your wealth line," he told her quietly.

She played along. "And do you see lots of money in my future?"

"Is money the kind of wealth that's important to you? I see you rich in other areas—rich in intelligence, the respect of your peers, the affection of your friends. And the total devotion of your husband."

Her eyes popped open. "There's a husband?"

"Definitely. Your wealth line intersects with your love line. You'll meet him soon after your return to Philadelphia. At a coffee shop. He'll bump into you and spill hot espresso down your skirt—"

"Be still my beating heart," she said drily.

"—and you, of course, will rip his head off for not watching where he was going. Luckily, he has a thing for passionate brunettes and he buys you dinner to make up for his clumsiness. A great new Italian place, where he tells you that he works for the IRS, which intimidates most women but not you. You're married within a year and have three brown-eyed children who are all able to ace the math portion of the SAT by the time they're twelve."

She drew her hand back. "Very informative. Thank you." Aside from the three kids—she was just starting to adjust to the idea of one or two—the fantasy would have sounded pretty good a week ago.

She found herself unenthusiastic about the Italian restaurant. Because she was so full, or because she suddenly had a newfound appreciation for hole-in-the-wall Mexican fusion restaurants? And the IRS agent didn't sound as appealing as he once would have, either. In fact, Sam's entire silly prediction left her feeling a bit depressed.

Or maybe that was just the hormonal letdown after being inexplicably aroused while he was touching her hands.

"Now you have to do me." He flopped his hand down on the table. "What do you see?"

A man who had a lot to offer but who wasn't going to let himself believe that.

She slid her fingers around his and stared down, then rubbed her temple with her free hand as if she were receiving a psychic message. "Oh! Well…this is a surprise. To the shock of pretty much everyone, Barbara Biggins wears you down. You fall madly in love and have eight children. You meant to stop with five, but then came the triplets," she said sweetly.

He snatched his hand away, recoiling in horror.

"Throw some salt over your shoulder or something, woman!"

"I didn't want it to sound too on-the-nose," she said, defending herself. "I thought I'd go for the unexpected."

"Sheesh." His green eyes were reproving. "If you don't want to marry the IRS guy, just say no when he proposes. Don't shoot the messenger."

She gave a hollow laugh as she stood. "You are a nut. And I...think I'm going to turn in early. Good night, Sam."

"Sweet dreams," he called after her.

His words bothered her because, with her skin still tingling from his simple caresses, she feared her dreams would be very enjoyable, indeed. And Lorelei eschewed dreams in favor of reality. She always felt better after taking stock of the situation and assessing the bare facts.

So, reality check. You will be gone within a week and even if you were staying, Sam wouldn't want you.

Oh, yeah. Now she felt *much* better.

Although Frederick-Fest ran all week—and tourists kept coming each day—the hours for general booths weren't as long once the weekend was over. And after all, it wasn't as if Lorelei was trying to drum up business for the inn. So by midweek, she'd pretty much packed up shop and was using her time to either make plans with her newly hired real estate agent or enjoy the festival.

On Wednesday, there was a public cooking demonstration featuring the four finalists in the televised chef competition. Lorelei spent a few minutes beforehand chatting with Grace Torres, but could tell the chef was frazzled by the pressures of trying to win this contest.

As Lorelei watched from the crowd of onlookers, someone lightly grasped her elbow.

"Got a minute?" Ava whispered.

Not wanting to distract the chefs, Lorelei ambled off to the side, motioning for Ava to follow.

"What can I do for you?" Lorelei asked.

The older woman fiddled with her glasses, looking sheepish. "It's not for me, it's for Em."

Lorelei heaved a sigh at the mention of Ava's niece. "Oh, honestly. You're not still trying—"

"No! Definitely not. Sam's been avoiding me for days, and Emily gave me quite an earful Sunday night. I suppose I shouldn't have meddled. It was a long shot that they'd take to each other. It's just difficult, to love someone and see them squander their potential for happiness. It's like, ever since she ended things with that pig of an ex-fiancé, she's afraid to even try."

Despite herself, Lorelei sympathized. She recalled the look on Sam's face when he'd maintained he was better off alone. Didn't he have any idea how happy he could make the right woman—how happy said woman might make *him?*

"It's okay, Ava. I understand why you were behaving like a lunatic."

Grinning, the woman thumped Lorelei on the shoulder. "Smart aleck."

"So if you're not trying to foist Emily on Sam and vice versa, what is it that you need?"

"Today's her last day of vacation. She's going back to San Marcos after lunch tomorrow. And I'm not sure she's had a very good time, which is partly my fault. I thought maybe people closer to her age could take her out, show her some of the nightlife."

Recalling the blonde's expression when she mentioned her two left feet, Lorelei decided dancing was out of the question.

"Did you already have plans tonight?" Ava asked. "I know you and Sam have been getting ready for that camping trip." She'd agreed to come by and take care of the cat for the two days they'd be gone.

"I'm free tonight. But are you sure Emily will want to do something with me?" Lorelei didn't want to mention how awkward the girl had been while they toured the festival Saturday and again during the chili tastings on Sunday. But surely Ava must know how painfully shy her niece was? Frankly, Lorelei was a bit surprised Emily had managed to get engaged to someone in the first place.

"If you extend the invitation, I think she'll accept." Ava's cheeks reddened. "I don't want her to feel like I put you up to this."

"Got it."

In the past two weeks, Ava had been there for Lorelei in countless little ways, and Lorelei was actually glad to have an opportunity to return the kindness. It occurred to her that, assuming all went smoothly with the sale of the inn, Lorelei might not see her mother's friend after this week. Oh, they'd exchange Christmas cards and maybe the occasional email. But Lorelei's entire goal had been to put her past in Fredericksburg *behind* her. She had no plans to visit. And as far as she knew, Ava hadn't set foot in Philadelphia a single time since the fall Lorelei had gone away to college.

A knot of emotion rose in Lorelei's throat. Acting on impulse, she threw her arms around Ava and hugged her tight.

"Uh… Lorelei?" A second passed, then Ava returned the hug, patting her lightly on the back.

"I'll miss you when I leave," Lorelei mumbled. "I hope Emily visits you a lot. Someone needs to check on you and keep you out of trouble."

Ava laughed. "That might be a bigger job than one person can handle, dear."

Releasing her hold on the other woman, Lorelei promised, "I'll come up with something for tonight and give Emily a call." Ava had passed along her niece's cell phone number a couple of days ago.

Lorelei decided that Tess would be a valuable resource to consult. After all, Tess knew a lot more about the local "nightlife" than Lorelei did. Hopefully the cheerful redhead could come with them. There wasn't a single intimidating thing about Tess; maybe she could help coax Emily from her paralyzing shyness.

Today, Tess was working in a face-painting booth where children could have their face whimsically decorated for free. "We can't charge them, or we'd end up having to refund everyone," Tess had joked last night. "Every animal I draw somehow ends up with a grotesquely long neck. Even my ladybugs look like giraffes! And don't even ask me what my attempt at the state of Texas resembled."

As Lorelei stood behind a group of children and watched her friend apply a misshapen pink blob on a little girl's cheek, she had to concede Tess's point. It was a good thing the woman made her career in the performing arts, because she seemed to have no aptitude whatsoever in the field of visual arts. Still, Lorelei wanted to be encouraging.

The pig-tailed girl admired herself in a hand mirror, then slid off her stool to rejoin her waiting parents. None of the other kids rushed to vacate the empty seat.

Lorelei stepped forward, telling Tess in a stage whisper, "I particularly liked the glittery sparkles you added to her...unicorn?"

"Close. Butterfly."

Huh. "Maybe you ought to stick to simple shapes like smiley faces and the Lone Star flag," Lorelei suggested.

A woman who was cleaning off brushes and small sponges at the other end of the long table said, "Whoever you are, tell me you came to help!"

"Not exactly." Lorelei doubted she'd be much better at this than her friend. "I actually just wanted to talk to Tess for a minute, but I can wait if you guys are too busy."

The woman sighed. "Take her. Petey Kendall is next and I can tell you from experience he's gonna want a T-Rex."

A boy standing nearby tried unsuccessfully to blow a bubble with his purple gum. "A T-Rex for the right cheek and a stegosaurus on the left!" His Witte Museum T-shirt also featured dinosaurs.

Tess tossed her arms up in defeat. "We're officially outside my skill set, so—"

"*What* skill set?" the other woman demanded.

"—I think it's time for my break. Wanna get some food?"

Lorelei laughed. "All we've done for days on end is get food!"

"That's not true." Tess sniffed. "At the vintner lecture on Monday, I also got libations."

The two of them took a lazy stroll around the playground, smiling at children's antics as they passed.

"So what did you need to talk about?" Tess asked. "And please let it be that you came to ask for my expertise in the art of seduction."

Lorelei snorted. "You consider yourself an expert?"

"Not the point. Do you realize you're leaving after this weekend and that you've yet to make a move on Sam?"

"That's because I have no intentions of making a move."

"But your chances of a mind-blowing vacation fling are dwindling! Staying under the same roof as that man is utterly wasted on you." Tess expelled a breath, looking peeved. Well, as peeved as anyone with freckles and a perpetual smile could. "I don't get it, Lor. I've seen the two of you together and deny it all you want, y'all have the hots for each other."

"I don't deny there's an attraction." Although she wondered if it had faded on Sam's part. Whenever their paths had crossed during the past forty-eight hours, he'd seemed prickly, strangely aloof after their former bantering. "But this is not what I wanted to discuss with you. Are you free tonight?"

Tess brightened. "I don't suppose you're asking because you want to set *me* up with Sam?"

"No." Lorelei took care to enunciate the word as forcefully as possible.

"Well, then yes. I'm very disappointed, but I'm also free."

Chapter 12

As soon as Sam helped the little girl atop the saddled pony, she began whooping and swinging her cowgirl hat in the air. "Yahoo! Giddyap, pony."

Most of the parents he'd seen today would start snapping pictures now, taking advantage of the pony's steady plodding gait to get some great "action" shots. But the mother and father of the towheaded child who'd introduced herself as Molly were too fixated on each other. The woman was standing with her hands on her hips, talking in a low, clipped voice. Sam couldn't make out any of her words, but the tone was unmistakable. Her husband was equally angry; he kept interrupting, gesturing wildly as he spoke. Damn shame, considering the beautiful day, the jovial surroundings and the fact that their adorable daughter was enjoying a ride on one of the sweetest-natured ponies Sam had ever known.

Yet even in the midst of a sunny Texas afternoon filled with the promise of spring, these two radiated stress and hostility. Practically anything could have set them off. Perhaps the man objected to how much money was being spent on food and festival tchotchkes or maybe the woman was concerned about how much beer he'd imbibed and wanted him to cut back on his refills. Or either one of them could be miffed that his or her spouse had spoken to flirtatiously to someone in the crowd.

A billion things that could go wrong, in Sam's opinion. And sometimes it was no discernible thing at all. When he'd asked Grace Torres one day how she was holding up, mostly just intending to ask after the restaurant business, she'd taken the opportunity to vent her frustration over her brother's separation from his wife.

"I just don't understand!" Grace had railed. "They love each other so much. Whatever else happened should be secondary to that, right?"

Lots of things in life "should" be, but weren't.

He conjured a smile for the little girl. "Sorry, darlin', your time's up." He helped her slide her feet from the stirrups and walked her back to her bickering parents. The mother took the girl's hand and stalked off, followed closely by the father, whose volume was increasing with each passing word.

"Cute kid. I especially liked her hot pink cowgirl boots," Lorelei observed from his left. "Wonder if they make those in my size."

Sam gave her a weary smile of greeting over his shoulder. "Hey."

"Wow." She took a step closer, squinting up at him. "That bad, huh?"

He shrugged. "Long day. I enjoy the festival, but I'm ready for it to end after about day three. I'm getting restless."

"Ready to leave town?" she asked.

Ready to do just about anything that didn't involve going "home" to her each night. It seemed as if she'd infested every corner of the inn in countless maddening ways. Her scent lingered in rooms long after she'd passed through, teasing him. The sight of a rosy lipstick ring on a tumbler in the sink had made him think about her mouth—more specifically, about kissing her. Even Oberon, the tiny traitor, had abandoned sleeping at the foot of Sam's bed in favor of curling up with Lorelei. *Cat's no fool.*

"What do you want, Lorelei?"

She scowled. "Have I done something to upset you?"

"I'm not upset, just busy."

She turned her head to the left, then to the right in exaggerated slow motion. "You mean because of this huge line of children waiting for a ride?"

"Things will pick up again after the lunch hour's over," he said defensively.

"Tess suggested I find you. We're going out tonight—me, her and Emily Hirsch."

"Are you kidding me? How did Ava recruit you to this groundless cause?" He hadn't been too surprised when Ava had gone out of her way to introduce him to her niece. At least once every three or four months, either Wanda had suggested the name of some nice girl he should take out, or she'd put one of her friends up to the task. But he'd thought that Lorelei had understood his position, that he emphatically was not looking for any serious romantic entanglements. Timid Emily was far too sweet a kid for him to lead on when he had less than zero interest in her.

"Take a breath," Lorelei ordered. "You looked like you were about to reach for your six-shooter and riddle me with bullets. Ava's already apologized for throwing her niece at you. Trust me, Em's not interested. Tess and I just wanted to do something nice by taking her out on her last night in town. And Tess suggested you come along."

"Why?" he asked suspiciously, still apprehensive about a feminine plot.

Lorelei rolled her eyes. "Must be because we wanted the privilege of your gallant and delightful company."

He grated out a laugh. "I did warn you it had been a long day and that I'm cranky."

She regarded him for a long moment, her lips twitching. "You never said anything about cranky."

"It was implied."

"Look, you've been working long hours at the festival and talking to lots of tourists all day. That can be draining."

She was right. Even though he mostly enjoyed interacting with the people who came to the festival, the smiling alone made his face hurt by the end of the day, to say nothing of the small talk. How in the hell did politicians do it?

"You could probably use some fun tonight," she continued. "Unwind, recharge your batteries. And Tess and Ava both live in the opposite direction of the bar than the inn. If I can ride back with *you* instead of asking Tess or Emily…"

"Which bar did you guys pick?" If she thought she

could talk him into line-dancing, she didn't know him at all.

She rattled off the name of one of the local places with no dance floor. "Thought we'd keep it low-key. Tess says tonight is trivia night. We can play on teams."

He wasn't sure that he wanted to go, but at least he'd be away from the inn and the dozen distractions that were Lorelei. If they were out in public, he had a better chance of keeping his hands off of her. *Maybe.* "And you're sure I won't be intruding on girls' night?"

"We'd like it if you joined us." She bit her lip, looking vulnerable, and he regretted how surly he'd been. "*I'd* like it."

He nodded sharply. "Just tell me what time to be ready."

Sam hadn't said much on the ride from the B and B to the tavern. Lorelei wondered if she'd done the right thing, letting Tess talk her into bringing Sam.

"You swear this has nothing to do with your thinking I should make a move on Sam?" Lorelei had asked one last time before she'd tracked him down at the festival.

"I swear," Tess had vowed. "If I had any ulterior motives, it would be about *me* getting a love life. Guys are more likely to approach us if we have a man around." Her theory had been "too intimidating if it's all chicks. But mostly, I just think it would be fun if Sam joins us."

Stealing a glance at his profile in the cab of the truck, Lorelei thought "fun" might be too high an expectation. She was disconcerted by his mood. For a few days, he'd been so playful that she'd almost forgotten his taciturn side, but it had returned with a vengeance. *Pity.* With her leaving soon, this wasn't how she wanted to remember him. But it was probably for the best that she saw him with no illusions.

By the time they got to the bar, Emily and Tess had already been seated at a U-shaped booth. The four of them ordered sodas and an assortment of appetizers for the table to share. A man with a microphone introduced himself as Andy Schubert and explained that in a few minutes, they would get started with T.E.X.A.S. trivia. All questions fell into the categories of Today (pop culture and modern life), Entertainment, "X-tra" Credit (really tough questions to help separate the average from the champions), Ancient/Not-So-Ancient History and Sports. Waitresses were circulating with pencils and slips of paper for answers.

"So you guys put together your teams," Andy announced, "and get ready to battle for our great prizes, generously donated by local sponsors."

After the man was finished recognizing the sponsors, Sam unfolded his long legs and he rose from the booth. "I'll let you ladies decide on the team name. I'm going to say hi to Andy."

Tess plunked a tortilla chip into the spicy, black-bean-based "cowboy caviar." "I don't care what we call ourselves as long as we win," she said merrily. "The gift certificates are all for places in town and since I'm the only one who truly lives here, I figure I get to keep them."

Lorelei laughed. "So basically, we're just your minions, here to—"

"Lorelei Keller?" A dark-haired man in slacks and a white button-down shirt stopped next to them, smiling down at her with warm familiarity. And he was smiling down from quite a height. The tall stranger had at least a few extra inches on Sam.

I should know who he is, shouldn't I? Drat. She quickly skimmed through her memory bank. Honestly, you'd think someone around six-five would stand out.

Across the table, Tess saved her. "Brody! I don't think I've seen you since high school."

Right. The name clicked into place. Brody Jenkins.

"It has been a while," Brody agreed. "I'm with an engineering firm in Austin now, but I came to town for the festival. I just completed a hellacious project at work and thought I needed a few days off, so I came to stay with my parents."

"Good to see you," Tess said. "This is our friend Emily, from San Marcos, and of course you remember Lorelei."

His hazel eyes returned to Lorelei's face. "How could I forget? You're the one who got away."

That announcement startled her. "I am?"

He grinned. "I meant to ask you out all through high school, but I was busy with basketball. And possibly a little daunted," he admitted. "You were one of the only students who could beat my scores on math exams."

She smiled but was distracted from answering by Sam's scowl. He'd returned to the table and stood impatiently behind Brody.

"Oh, sorry, man." Brody followed her gaze and stepped aside. "Am I in the way?"

"This is Sam Travis." Lorelei made the introductions as Sam reclaimed his seat next to her. "Sam, Brody Jenkins. He went to school with Tess and me."

Tess turned her head, looking around the room. "Are you here with someone, Brody?"

He shrugged. "I met a buddy for a beer, but he just left. Newly married, didn't want to be out late. They're still in that honeymoon phase." His gaze flickered from Sam back to Lorelei, specifically to her left hand. "Are you two…?"

"Ha! Not at all," Lorelei said.

She knew from the way Sam stiffened next to her and Tess's quizzical look that her denial had been a bit too resounding. But really, the idea of Sam Travis doing something as crazy as getting engaged or, heaven forbid, getting married? *It is to laugh.*

"You should join us," Tess invited. She beamed. "Yet another person who doesn't live here who can slave for me. My diabolical plan is to surround myself with people who can answer the questions, then selfishly reap the rewards. You're smart, right? Went to UT on scholarship?"

"Basketball scholarship," he clarified. "But I held my own on the dean's list."

"Awesome, you're hired. Scooch over," Tess instructed Emily. The quiet blonde slid farther toward the middle, leaving room for Brody on the end, directly across from Lorelei.

Tess turned to Emily with a suddenly stern look. "Wait, I didn't check your credentials. You're smart enough to win me prizes, right?"

"Salutatorian in high school. But it was a graduating class of like fifty," the woman added with a modest grin. "So I'm not sure that counts."

"Good enough for my purposes," Tess declared. "I think our team name should be Empress and the Minions. Hey, it's better than Three Chicks and Two Dudes."

"Only marginally," Lorelei said.

Andy tapped on his microphone and announced they were getting started, lobbing out an "easy" question to get the crowd warmed up. It was about an award-winning actor and Emily announced in an excited whisper, "I know this one!" before Andy had even finished reading from his card. A few minutes later, Lorelei found herself thinking that they should have taken Emily out for trivia days ago. Knowing half the answers was obviously good for her confidence, and it allowed her to interact with others without struggling for appropriate personal conversation.

Emily's increasingly bright smile was a nice counterpoint to the dark thundercloud over Sam's head. *Inviting him was a mistake.* He'd barely said two sentences since he'd come back to the table and found Brody chatting with Lorelei. And Sam remained stonily silent through most of the questions. Because he didn't know the answers or because he didn't want to be here?

When Andy announced that one of the extra credit questions, worth two points, was a math problem, half the people in the bar groaned.

Brody, however, rubbed his hands in glee, grinning across the table at Lorelei. "We got this one, Ivy League."

At the end of the first round, answer sheets had to be turned in at the bar so standings could be calculated. And, the owners hoped, so that people had a good window of opportunity to spend more money on drinks and food.

Sam grabbed the piece of paper Tess had been using to record answers. "I'll take it up there. Might as well contribute something, right?"

Lorelei's heart squeezed. She couldn't help watching his progress to the bar, her attention only half on Brody as he talked to her.

"So how often do you get down here?" he asked. They'd established earlier that she'd remained in Pennsylvania after college.

"Almost never," she said absently. "But I've really been enjoying this trip." She caught herself and shook her head at the bizarre statement. "Well, not the part where I had to say goodbye to my mom! But..."

"We knew what you meant," Tess assured her. "And you know Wanda would have wanted you to enjoy your visit. She loved the festival."

Lorelei nodded. "If you guys will excuse me? I think I'm gonna run to the ladies' room before we start the next round." She swept up her purse but instead of heading for the restrooms in the far corner, she detoured through the center of the room, pulled toward Sam as if by a giant, unseen magnet.

He doesn't need a magnet to draw women to him. Not when he has those eyes.

He'd already turned back toward the table and they almost collided. "Sorry, didn't realize you were behind me," he said.

"I wanted to talk to you. Away from the others. You're not having any fun, are you?"

"Is that your polite way of saying I'm raining on everyone else's parade?" He shoved a hand through his hair. "I shouldn't have come. If I cut out early, do you think..." He glared in the direction of their table. "I'll bet Jenkins would be happy to give you a ride."

Beneath his brusque demeanor, some emotion had glimmered in Sam's expression. *Jealousy?* Lorelei was dimly ashamed of how happy that possibility made her. She couldn't help herself, though. The idea that Sam might want her felt really, really good.

Because I want him.

No matter what she'd told Tess or what logical reminders she gave herself, her unwise attraction to Sam had only grown this week, not diminished. And the idea of him leaving her here tonight, when they had so little time left together anyway…

She put a hand on his arm. "Actually, I think calling it a night might be a good idea. This place is a little too crowded for me." She cast a glance back at their table, where Tess and Emily were both giggling at something Brody had said.

Sam's expression was pained. "You don't have to humor me. You should stay with them, enjoy yourself."

"But…" She stopped and took a steadying breath. *Just do it.*

What did she have to lose? She and Sam were going to part ways soon so even if she abjectly humiliated herself in the next sixty seconds, it's not as though it would have any bearing on the rest of her life. Except, of course, for the deep and painful emotional scars, she thought wryly. The words she wanted to say were risky—even knowing he had some physical attraction to her, she couldn't know whether he'd reject her.

He'd stilled, his body thrumming with a new tension she could practically *hear,* like the electricity currents running through power lines. He studied her with those green eyes that seemed to see more of her than anyone else had before. "But what, Lorelei?"

"I don't want to stay and 'enjoy myself.' I'd rather go back to the inn. And enjoy you." The daring announcement might have been more effective if it hadn't been delivered in a whisper.

Then again, maybe not. Judging from the way Sam sucked in his breath, her words had definitely had an effect.

"Lorelei." Her name came out as a groan. And it had never sounded sexier. "You don't belong with me. You deserve someone like him." Sam jerked his chin in Brody's general direction but never took his eyes off of her.

Warmth unfurled inside her. That was his argument? Not a reminder that he wasn't looking for any romantic complications in his life, just "you deserve..." Didn't every woman deserve, at least once in her life, to be with a man who made her body tingle and her pulse race? A man who could make her forget how to breathe with his incomparable kisses?

Emboldened, she took a step closer. "I know you don't want a girlfriend. But do you want me? I'll be gone soon, but for now... Let's look at it as my being on vacation. Would a vacation fling really be so bad, something for us both to remember fondly after the inn is sold and we've both moved on from here?" He would come back, she was sure, but he'd made it clear that he wouldn't put down roots.

His dazed eyes were locked on her mouth and he was breathing more heavily. But he was obviously conflicted. "You just lost a parent. That's enough to leave anyone emotionally vulnerable. I won't take advantage of you," he said raggedly.

She grabbed hold of his black T-shirt, the cotton soft in her hands. "This isn't about my being needy or being afraid to be alone, I swear. I can't stop thinking about what it would be like. I've been—"

The rest of her words were lost in his kiss. His mouth crushed hers, the intensity of his embrace proving that she hadn't been the only one thinking about them together. Her fingers tightened on his shirt, and she arched into him, kissing him back for all she was worth.

"You have *got* to be kidding me!" Barbara Biggins made a derisive, unladylike harrumphing noise. "Will you two just get a freaking room already?"

Sam met Lorelei's gaze, his words for her ears only. "Sounds like a good idea to me."

As Lorelei fiddled with the truck's radio dial, Sam made a concerted effort not to floor the accelerator. A speeding ticket would delay their getting back to the inn. And his getting Lorelei into bed.

His heart thumped in an irregular pattern as he tried to process what awaited him. For the past three days, it seemed as if he'd been fantasizing about her constantly. It was difficult to believe those fantasies were finally going to come true.

She wants me? Didn't she know she could do better than a cowboy with calloused hands and a couple of semesters of community college? With women like Barbara, he could understand the pursuit. It wasn't about him as an individual, it was about the hunt. He'd garnered a reputation for being aloof; breaking through that would mean a woman had *won.* Even though he'd continue freely roaming the streets instead of having his head mounted on a wall, he'd still be little more than a trophy.

But Lorelei hadn't been pursuing him. She'd spent her first few days in town snapping at him. And if she'd wanted to seduce him, she wouldn't have passed up a golden opportunity like the other night. When he'd turned the corner and found her dripping wet, with only a piece of terry cloth keeping her naked body from his sight... Sam's fingers tightened on the steering wheel and he shifted uncomfortably, his jeans no longer the relaxed fit they'd been an hour ago.

Say something. Making conversation might help distract him long enough to get blood to his brain. And talking to her seemed like the gentlemanly thing to do. It would be creepy to drive in silence for ten minutes, then pounce on her the minute they set foot in the B and B.

"So, uh..." He cleared his throat. "They were pretty understanding about our bailing on the team."

They must have witnessed his and Lorelei's kiss from the horseshoe-shaped booth. Emily had been gaping at them and Tess had been grinning from ear to ear. Sam had studiously avoided glancing toward Jenkins; he'd worried he wouldn't be able to keep the smugness out of his expression and Lorelei was more than some conquest to gloat over.

"Understanding?" Lorelei echoed. "Tess chased us away so fast you'd think she owed us money."

True. The redhead had no semblance of a poker face. For a moment, he'd actually thought she was going to admonish them to have fun but not to forget to use condoms. He frowned. It had been a while—did he *have* condoms? *Nightstand.* Thank goodness.

In his peripheral vision, he noticed how lights from outside glinted off the jet buttons on her dress. The casual outfit—which stopped a couple of inches above her knees, hardly revealing—had been driving him nuts all night. In a bar of women wearing tight jeans and a few low-cut tops, he'd been obsessed with a flowing black dress with loose, elbow-length sleeves. Probably because it buttoned from just below the vee neckline straight down to the hem. He hadn't been able to look at her once without thinking about *un*buttoning. A few quick movements of nimble fingers, and she'd be—

Lorelei leaned forward again and resumed messing with the radio stations.

"Can't find any songs you like?" he asked.

"Nervous energy," she confessed. "Guess I'm just looking for something to keep my hands occupied."

He had several suggestions. None of which were appropriate while he was operating a motor vehicle. By "nervous," he hoped she didn't mean she regretted her impulsive words at the bar. How did he let her know he understood if she changed her mind without making it sound as if he didn't want her? Because he couldn't recall wanting a woman this badly before.

Moments later, they drove behind the inn. Sam squeezed the steering wheel. "You're still good with this? I mean, if you were just caught up in the moment earlier…"

She gave him a dumbfounded look. "Caught up in the moment? Sam, when I propositioned you, we were in the middle of a trivia game and you were stomping around like a grouchy bear. With that backdrop, you're worried I was so overcome with lust that I talked myself into something I'll regret?"

"When you put it like that…" He unfastened his seat belt and reached for her, pulling her closer on the bench seat. She seemed startled but came into his arms.

"You know, there are some comfy beds inside," she teased, even as she tilted her face up for a kiss.

He was stalling out here because it was too tempting to rush her into one of those beds. Sam had been around enough of the local vintners to hear lots of commentary on properly tasting wine. Talk of "bouquets" and "citrus tones" and "complexity" had always sounded a little pretentious to him. But after tonight, he might have a better appreciation for a slow, measured sensory approach because he truly wanted to savor Lorelei. He wanted to breathe her in and let her taste linger on his tongue. He wanted to close his eyes and lose himself in her.

Threading his fingers through her hair, he kissed her thoroughly, deeply, but he didn't hurry, letting the need build for both of them. She began wriggling in an unsuccessful attempt to get closer and making *mmm* sounds that were somewhere between a whimper and sigh. The only flaw in Sam's plan to kiss her out in the truck and stoke the desire between them? In order to get inside, they would have to *stop*. He couldn't bring himself to, not yet.

He did move away from her mouth, though, sketching quick light kisses along her jaw before moving to the soft skin of her neck. When he nipped slightly just below her ear, she rewarded him with a low moan that had him as hard as a rock. He rubbed a thumb over her collarbone, then traced a deliberate line down into her cleavage before cupping a breast through the satiny fabric of her dress. She arched against his palm and Sam fumbled behind him for the door handle. As they slid out of the truck, he realized his truck windows were fogged up, as if they'd been a couple of high school kids parking. Not that Lorelei would ever have gone out with him when they were teenagers—they would have had nothing in common, and he suspected she'd been too busy trying to get into the right college.

Well, we're adults now. And tonight she was his.

Holding her tucked in the crook of his arm, as if he couldn't bear any distance between them, he steered them toward the door. They were already kissing again by the time the cat met them in the kitchen, meowing at them like some incensed chaperone, as if to say, *And just what do* you think you two are doing?

"My room?" Sam asked.

"Fine with me," she murmured, her eyes glazed with need.

At the top of the stairs, he scooped her up. Her arm went around his neck and she nuzzled his chest.

"Don't distract me or you might get dropped," he warned. Did she have any idea how good she felt against him?

He kicked the door shut behind them and righted her at the foot of the bed. He bent his head to kiss her but missed. She'd already dropped into a sitting position on the edge of the mattress. Looking up at him through her lashes, she reached for the top button of her dress. His mouth went dry.

"I like that dress," he said. "Do you know it has exactly nine buttons? I counted."

Her lips curved in a slow grin. "So that's why I felt your eyes on me tonight, purely numerical interest?" She slid the first button free, then the second. By the time she reached the third, he realized it was a good thing *she* was unfastening them. His hands felt shaky.

Luckily, his own shirt was simple to remove. He whipped it over his head, then reached for her, raising her to her feet with only half of the buttons undone. He tucked his fingers inside the gaping panels of fabric and shoved lightly. The material whispered down her body and pooled at her feet. She stood before him in sandals and a matching set of a black bra and panties. The lingerie was simple, but curves like hers didn't need any extra embellishment to be mind-numbingly erotic.

"Lorelei." It felt like a prayer on his lips. He reached for her, kissing her hungrily. His hands were just as greedy, wanting to touch every inch of her warm skin. He skimmed over her back, down the graceful length of her spine to cup her butt, holding her closer as he rocked his hips into hers.

She raked her fingernails across his chest, then toward the denim waistband of his jeans. His entire body tensed in anticipation. Finally, she brushed over his erection and Sam hissed a breath through grated teeth.

"Gotta get out of these jeans," he said.

Instead of helping him, she kicked off her shoes and reclined across the bed, watching avidly. Seeing how clearly she desired him was nearly as powerful a turn-on as her touch had been.

Stripped down to a pair of boxer briefs, he joined her on the bed. He drank in the sight of her then surprised them both by almost laughing.

She propped herself up on an elbow. "What's funny?"

"You remember that day you went to the wine tastings? I came back and you were lying across the couch?" Her relaxed body had seemed so pliant and welcoming, her smile when she'd seen him so unrestrained. "At the time, I wondered what could possibly be sexier. But this is way better."

She ducked her gaze for a moment, incongruently

shy after she'd shucked her clothes. "I'd been thinking of you all that afternoon. I could blame the wine, but…"

"You remind me of wine." He gently pushed her onto her back.

She narrowed her eyes. "Say 'full-bodied' and die."

He ignored the crazy talk—her body was perfect—and kissed her neck. "You smell good," he murmured against her skin. Like honeysuckle, only naughtier. "I detect floral notes," he deadpanned.

She chuckled but the amusement in her eyes dissolved into heat when he reached for the front clasp of her bra. He ran his thumb over the swell of her breast. "Pale, perfect color." In ever narrowing circles, he swept his finger around her puckered nipple, listening to her breathing grow more frantic. He leaned over her breast, not touching but close enough that she could feel his breath. "And these remind me of berries. Exotic and—" he scraped his tongue over her "—delicious."

She writhed and Sam drew her into his mouth, lost. He'd wanted to woo her, but he had no words left now, only a need to touch her, to be inside her. By the time he eventually sheathed himself in a condom and thrust into the slickness of her, the only word he knew was her name.

Lorelei woke up slowly as if she didn't want to leave a particularly pleasant dream. She was exhausted and could tell even before she opened her eyes that it was still dark. Moonlight peeked through the blinds on the window, falling across Sam's face. He looked utterly at peace and she grinned, glad to have done her part in relaxing him.

When she tried to slide out from under his arm he

made a small noise of protest and snuggled her closer into his bare chest. If she weren't so thirsty, she probably could have happily stayed there for hours—days—on end. Come to think of it, though, she was hungry, too. Neither of them had eaten much at the bar and they'd left early. She should treat herself to something down in the kitchen—heaven knew they'd worked off some calories. They'd made love twice before falling asleep.

He'd surprised her in bed. Monosyllable Man could be poetic when he was duly inspired. Also, for a man who seemed so intent on keeping control of his life—by keeping others at a distance—he'd had no trouble at all ceding control to her when they'd had sex. The second time, she'd wanted to set the pace. She'd explored his taut body before straddling him and guiding him into her.

She bit her lip at the memory, thinking that if she didn't hurry up and get out of this bed, she might not make it down to the kitchen for something to eat after all. Stepping over their discarded clothes, she headed into the bathroom and grabbed the robe off the brass hook. When she came back into the bedroom, Sam was gone.

Like minds? She wondered. He had to have worked up an appetite, too.

Downstairs, she found him pulling containers out of the refrigerator. She stopped in the doorway to admire the view of his ass in the form-fitting gray boxer briefs. Maybe food could wait after all.

His body stilled suddenly; she must have made a noise to give herself away. As he slowly turned toward her, he drawled, "You keep starin', you're gonna bore holes in me."

She laughed. "We've been here before, haven't we?" It seemed like a long time ago, that night she'd come down here for a midnight snack and had ended up arguing with Sam about who should have the inn. Then, she couldn't have imagined wanting to stay in town a day longer than absolutely necessary. And now? She would be sorry to leave.

It wasn't just the green-eyed cowboy and great sex she'd miss—although, right now, those topped the list. She was also enjoying the people and the food and the pace. Though she'd always claimed to love her job, she hadn't realized how much it could drain her—the long hours, the stressing over whether a project was absolutely perfect, whether it would be enough to help her move ahead.

That's it, she decided in a flash of insight. As far back as she could remember, her life had been about moving. Moving past her dad's death, moving out of Texas to go to school, moving to the top of her classes in college, moving ahead at work…

When was the last time she'd simply stood still and enjoyed where she was? Savored the moment?

"Lorelei?" He'd set the food on the counter and was studying her with naked curiosity. "You still with me?"

"I'm here." *Here and now. And happy.* But two in the morning didn't seem like the time to share the revelation she'd just had. Besides, they'd been having a spectacular night. If she told him that suddenly she wasn't so eager to return to life in Philly, he might worry that she'd recanted her "fling" philosophy and was looking for something more permanent. "I was just thinking about that night we ran into each other in the kitchen and you offered me cake."

He came toward her, his expression wicked in the shadows. "That reminds me. There was something I wanted to do that night." He kept walking and didn't stop when he reached her, instead backing her into the wall without actually touching her.

Lorelei licked her lips, her heart thudding faster. "Yeah? What's that?"

In answer, he reached for both her hands, raising them over her head and holding them against the wall. When he kissed her, her body went so liquid she wouldn't have been able to stand without his support.

Food would *definitely* have to wait.

Chapter 13

Lorelei was glad this trail ride was only a two-day event. She hadn't brought many pairs of jeans with her. Sam had grunted his approval when he saw her bag that she knew how to "pack light." Truthfully, it wasn't as though she'd had that many options.

He was outside putting their stuff in the bed of the truck and she was taking the quiet moment alone to re-group. When they came back, this would all be over. Sam had other jobs lined up, other places to be, and the real estate company would begin showing the inn to po-tential buyers. Even though Lorelei would be back here after the campout, this felt like goodbye.

She looked around the sun-filled kitchen, memories swirling together. While she and her mother might have had their differences, Wanda had loved her and had tried to make her trips home fun-filled. She remembered three Christmases ago, when her mother had finally coerced her into sharing some spiked eggnog, and they'd attempted to build a gingerbread house together. They'd giggled at the "structurally unsound" results while licking frosting off their fingers.

"No way would any company ever allow home-owners insurance on this wreck," Lorelei had said on a laugh.

More recently, Lorelei had joked with Ava and Tess in this same kitchen. And, night before last, made love with Sam. Heat blazed into her cheeks as she recalled the intensity with which he'd taken her against the wall. Even if she hadn't wanted to run this place, and certainly couldn't envision herself organizing ghost tours year-round, she felt a fondness toward the inn she'd never experienced before.

"You were right, Mom," she whispered. "I'm glad I came for the festival." Lorelei almost laughed when she heard the soft tinkling of the dragonfly chimes, even though she knew it was simply the breeze through the window, not a reply from the Great Beyond.

Wait. Didn't Ava have those chimes now? She whipped her head around to glare at the empty hook over the kitchen sink.

"Knock knock?" The back door swung open and Ava stepped inside. "I just came to tell you guys to have a nice trip and promise that I'll actually interact with Oberon. Even if I have to wear gloves and football pads to protect myself."

Lorelei laughed. "Believe it or not, he seems like he's mellowed. Sam and I both pet him on a near daily basis and still have ten fingers each." Of course, the cat had been furious when they'd locked him out of Sam's room again last night. She frowned suddenly, making a mental note to close her and Sam's bedroom doors before they left. Just in case Obie objected to being left behind.

"I also wanted to stop by before you left to make sure you were feeling okay. Emily mentioned that you and Sam left rather abruptly the other night?" Ava raised her glance to the ceiling, not meeting Lorelei's eyes. "And no one's seen either of you since."

Though it was obvious by Ava's forced nonchalance that she'd already deduced what happened, Lorelei couldn't bring herself to acknowledge it. "What do you mean no one's seen us?" She did her best to sound mystified. "We've been around. Just, um, a little busy getting ready for the trail ride."

"Uh-huh."

Lorelei was utterly grateful when Sam came inside, putting a damper on Ava's questions.

"All ready?" Sam asked. Lorelei nodded and they both said goodbye to Ava.

They were several miles down the road before she realized she'd forgotten to close the bedroom doors. Oh, well. If the cat was moved to show his displeasure over their being gone, it wasn't as if there weren't targets all through the inn.

"Hey, Sam? I've been thinking about Oberon. What are we going to do with him? Mom mentioned that the inn is his home, but neither of us are staying. And I don't think Ava's bonded with him quite like we have."

"So what do you suggest, some kind of split custody arrangement? You take him year-round and he can stay with me for the summer and Christmas break?"

"Ha-ha. I was being serious."

He hesitated. "You know I'm not very stationary. I

have my trailer, but he's used to a lot more room. Plus, there are coyotes nearby and if he were ever to get out... I, uh, I've gotten kind of used to the little bugger. I didn't mean to, but it'll be tough to see him go." Braking at a red light, Sam turned to capture her gaze with his. "Probably best for me not to hold on, though."

The backs of her eyes burned. So did her throat, making it difficult to speak. Then the light turned green, Sam looked away and the moment passed.

A few minutes later, when the silence felt oppressive, she said, "I guess I'll take him, then." It came out sounding resentful, which she didn't mean. She'd grown accustomed to having the cat around, too. Seeing his fuzzy face when she came through the door after a long day would make her feel a lot less lonely back in Philadelphia.

"You sure you don't mind?" Sam asked. "I recall your saying something once about not being cut out to own pets."

"Yeah." She stared out the window. "But I've... changed since I got here." *In more ways than you want to know about.*

Owning a cat was the least of her worries.

Sam's eyebrows were raised as he took in Lorelei's fretful expression. Keeping his voice low enough that none of the tourists or ranch hands in the long barn overheard, he whispered, "You told me you liked horses, that you've been riding before."

"I have. Maybe it's been even longer than I realized, but... I'm good with the horses."

He leaned in close enough that he could smell her shampoo beneath the sweet, earthy scent of hay. "Then what's the problem? You looked upset."

She sighed. "I was just analyzing all the things that could go wrong on a trail ride like this! Bad habit, I know. But do you have any idea the kind of *liability*—"

He laughed then, barely resisting the urge kiss her. So she was worried not as an equestrienne, but as an actuary? "Everyone's signed their waivers, darlin'. And we'll be careful, I promise."

On the hour long drive to the ranch, she'd explained to him in detail what she did for a living. *Still don't get it.* But he understood the gist, which was good enough. Especially since she was leaving in the next couple of days. It wasn't as if there were going to be a pop quiz.

Now, if he had to pass a test on the exact shade of Lorelei's eyes or the gamut of sounds she made as she approached an orgasm, he knew he could ace it.

He gave himself a mental shake. A distracted trail boss was no way to prevent those accidents she feared.

The ranch and horses were owned by a family who'd hired Sam for a variety of odd jobs in the past. The family's patriarch was approaching seventy now and no longer did the overnight trips. His son headed them up frequently but a couple of years ago, when his wife had been going through a difficult pregnancy, he'd entrusted a group to Sam. Since then, Sam did several a year so that the man wouldn't have to be away from his spouse and two young children so often.

"I know it's just for the night, but you'll understand when you have kids of your own. At this age, it's too easy to miss a first smile, first word, first step."

All milestones Sam had no intention of ever experiencing, but he hadn't wanted to sound like a child-hating cynic. The truth was, he was fond of kids. In the generic sense. Some of the trail rides he worked were specifically geared toward young riders—just not this one, with its spooky stories this evening and bat expedition. This ride was only for eighteen and up, but he couldn't help grinning inwardly at how panicked Lorelei would be if children, with all the potential mishaps they could cause, were added to the mix.

Kids were fun. As long as he didn't have to parent them. He wasn't sure any of the male role models in his life had been helpful. There was his biological father who'd worked himself into an early grave; Lorelei's father had also died young, but at least he hadn't ignored his only child her entire life. And his stepfather was a shallow, superficial man who cared more about appearances than family bonds. Even JD was a questionable influence. The womanizing bachelor had only had relationships that lasted from Friday night until Monday morning.

If Sam had seen more evidence of how to make a relationship work, how to balance the responsibility of providing with the joys of being together, would he be less wary of relationships now? Would he be able to let himself fall in love?

His gaze skittered back to Lorelei and he rubbed his chest. Something that felt like heartburn hampered his breathing for a second, but then he walked away from her, telling himself he had a job to do. The eleven tourists gathered needed to get acquainted with their mounts. Standing here and playing what-if wasn't going to accomplish anything.

By four o'clock that afternoon, Lorelei was really having to bite her tongue to keep from whining, "Are we there yet?"

No one else was complaining. Then again, she was probably the only person who'd spent the thirty-six hours prior to climbing into the saddle having energetic sex. There had been a brief period this afternoon when she'd been only pleasantly sore. The rolling gait of the horse beneath her had simply made her aware of the places she still tingled from Sam's touch.

But now there was no "pleasantly" about it. *Ow, dammit.* All she wanted was to throw herself from the mare's back, catch a cab—which seemed unlikely out here in the middle of nowhere—and get back to the inn, where she could soak in the tub with some mineral salts for her sore muscles. She didn't even care if Oberon came into the bathroom to keep her company. Hell, he could swim around in the tub as long as he left her alone to whimper in peace.

When Sam announced that they'd reached the spot where they'd be making camp for the evening, she could have kissed him. Except, probably not, because that proved to lead to other things and her body ached far too much to even contemplate that.

People began dismounting. The chuckwagon cook and the rider Sam was training to be an eventual trail boss himself were helping to secure the horses.

Sam came over to assist Lorelei. As much as she'd been looking forward to getting down off her horse, she found that she had to do so very gingerly.

"You okay?" To his credit, Sam tried to sound and look concerned. But other emotions were seeping into his expression—knowing amusement and sizzling desire, as he obviously recalled how she'd come to be sore in the first place and how much he'd like to do that again.

"Not gonna happen," she growled.

"I don't know what you're talking about," he said innocently. Then he gave her an evil grin. "'Course, if what you meant was that I have to keep my hands to myself, it's only fair to let you know that I have some really great cream to rub on sore muscles. And I had planned to offer to massage it in personally."

"You're supposed to be solicitous of the riders under your care, not looking for ways to get them out of their jeans," she scolded. "Are all trail bosses this one-track-minded?"

"When they have a woman who looks like you to share their tent? Absolutely."

Despite pretending to be appalled by his ulterior motives, she had to admit his desire wasn't one-sided. Seeing Sam out here, clearly in his element, was incredibly sexy. All through the day, he'd shared historical anecdotes, such as the Texas "camel experiment" in the mid-1800s and the Mason County Hoodoo War. If their trivia game the other night had included any questions about Texas government, the Civil War, Native American tribes from this region, livestock or weather phenomena, Sam would have cleaned house. He had an easy confidence in the saddle and seemed to truly love the land he was showing them.

And Ava had been right. He was definitely a natural-born storyteller. He'd led them through a narrow pass earlier that day and told them in quiet, somber tones that had somehow carried down the line of riders that the area was reputed to be haunted by a brokenhearted woman who'd been betrayed by her family.

"She fell in love with a Chanas brave and planned to sneak away from her family in the night to join his nomadic tribe. But her brother caught her and her father, in a rage, shoved her from that peak, declaring that he'd rather see his daughter dead than turn her back on who she was. It's said that when her father realized what he'd done, he shot himself and that both her uneasy spirit and his remain here, never able to find peace with each other. Their ongoing anger is the explanation for many strange happenings."

With Sam as their leader, Lorelei didn't think twice about what kind of bugs might be buzzing about their tents tonight or the seasonal allergies that sometimes plagued her when the weather turned warm. He was mesmerizing.

The group was instructed to set up tents while it was still plenty bright outside. Then they were going to take two hiking excursions while the camp cook fixed dinner—the first to a nearby natural cavern, the second to see a bat colony.

"It's still a bit early in the year, but they do start returning to the area in March," Sam told them. "So cross your fingers."

He took time assisting everyone, checking the horses' shoes with a middle-aged man who was a Houston stockbroker in his real life "but always wanted to be a cowboy." Then he helped a woman taking this family trip with her two college-age daughters pitch their tent. A man and wife in their early sixties were obviously veteran campers; the couple didn't need technical support so much as they needed a good-natured referee for their squabbling. Otherwise, they'd never finish setting up before dark. Finally, Sam came over to inspect the job Lorelei was doing.

"Tent looks good, Ms. Keller. Nice job," he praised.

"Which is important. Because it would be *such* a shame if this collapsed in the middle of the night and you had to bunk with someone else." The look he gave her tent left her half alarmed that he planned to sabotage the stakes as soon as her back was turned.

"A male someone," he added. "You know, to protect you from beasties. Wolves, javelinas. The occasional *El Chupacabra.*"

"Bunk with a man? What kind of example would that set for those college girls?" she chided lightly. How far into the night would it be before she caved to the temptation of snuggling into Sam's sleeping bag with him?

"Right, because being college girls, they've probably never heard about sex," he scoffed.

"Well, they didn't hear about it from *me.*"

He laughed. "Such a virtuous and pure-hearted woman. Must be why I love you."

Lorelei was highly intelligent; she knew he was kidding and meant nothing by the words, knew it straight to her core. Yet she couldn't prevent the way she trembled inside at the declaration. *Why I love you...*

Worse than her involuntary emotional response, he *saw* her react, if only for a millisecond. Sam's playful mien froze in place like a mask, a caricature of itself.

Oh, please don't. She braced herself for his stilted apology, his polite explanation that he'd only been kidding. That would be too humiliating to endure—not only a rejection, but also his thinking she was so unreasonably deluded she might actually be seeking more from him. If nothing else, she hoped he respected her intellect more than that. She was smart enough to embrace the truth: it would be a monumental mistake to fall for Sam Travis.

That just hadn't stopped her from doing it.

* * *

Once again, Lorelei was the outsider. And that camp-fire revelation stung so badly that she realized she was no longer accustomed to this feeling, could no longer shrug it off. Sometime during her stay in Fredericksburg, she'd started to feel as if she belonged.

Wish I were back in town now.

Around her, the tourists fell into two groups. Those who lounged in that particular boneless lassitude stemming from any active day in the open air, and those who were literally on the edge of their seats—in this case, portable foam mats—tense with expectation as Sam wove another tale. His narratives tonight had begun with a mix of supernatural ghost stories alongside explanations of natural marvels, including a mass of granite that had once terrified superstitious settlers because of the noises it made when the granite contracted in the cool night air and the blue sparks it could generate. As the sun had dipped lower on the horizon and stars began to twinkle overhead, he also pointed out some constellations and threw in some Greek myths for his captive audience.

Lorelei, however, was neither relaxed nor able to lose herself in Sam's baritone. She was seething.

Ever since that awkward moment this afternoon, Sam had been growing more aloof with her. When they'd hiked to a cave after camp was set up, she'd stopped at one point to take in the breathtaking view and Sam had come after her to make sure she wasn't injured or too tired to keep going. She'd reflexively reached for his hand as she told him how beautiful it was here, and he'd stiffened.

"We're holding up the group. We should move on,"

he'd chastised her mildly. Though his tone hadn't been harsh, it had been far from tender.

He'd been subtly pushing her away for hours now. Apparently, his slip of the tongue had been enough of a reminder for him that this—that *she*—wasn't what he wanted in the long run. Did he think it was kinder this way, to withdraw so that she got angry or that her ego was stung enough she no longer wanted to be with him? Maybe he thought it saved them from a messy goodbye, but all it was doing so far was ticking her off. They were both adults and they'd had an agreement going into this weekend. She would have honored his feelings; there was no need to act like a boyfriend who'd lost interest and was trying to give her the brush-off.

"...but of course, the Germans have lots of legends, too," he was saying. She realized she'd tuned out some Hispanic folklore he'd shared. He had now moved on to other cultures with major influence in the region. "Including a seafaring legend that shares its name with one of our campers." He met her eyes then, raising his cup of water in wry salute.

"There's an 'echoing rock' on the Rhine River called the Lorelei that has been the site of many boating accidents. Skeptics say the murmuring 'voice' associated with the rock comes from a nearby waterfall, while others believe stories of an otherworldly female with a beautiful voice. A siren or mermaid who lures sailors in, bewitching them until they knowingly steer right into their own ruin."

As if a woman by dint of being confident enough to call out to a man and let him know he was wanted was a nefarious enchantress, a threat? *Screw this.* Though Sam's voice was smooth, his expression bland, she heard his words as an indictment. She hadn't been plotting his seduction, hoping to snare him. Frankly, she didn't think *he* was the one who'd been hurt by their short-lived affair. Because you had to let yourself care to be hurt.

Lorelei loudly faked a yawn. "Fascinating stuff. But I'm afraid I'm beat." She stood, trying to look relaxed instead of stalking to her tent. "'Night, everyone."

As soon as she was zipped in for the night, she'd check to see if she had enough bars out here to text Tess and beg her for a ride. If her friend couldn't come pick her up from the ranch tomorrow, Lorelei would devise a Plan B. Because no way in hell was she riding with Sam Travis, spinner of tall tales and emotional coward.

Chapter 14

It was time to go home, back to her real life. Lorelei stood in the driveway of the Haunted Hill Country Bed-and-Breakfast with Ava, who would be driving her to the airport, and Tess, who had come to say goodbye.

Lorelei hugged the redhead whose friendship she'd come to value, especially when Tess had shown up at the dude ranch three days ago with a steely glare for Sam and a box of tissues in the car for Lorelei.

After the two women had left, Tess had asked quietly, "You want to talk about it?" At Lorelei's emphatic head shake, Tess had sighed. "For what it's worth, I'm sorry I encouraged you to make a move."

I'm not. Which was the problem in a nutshell. She didn't regret what had happened with Sam. In fact, she craved more. Whereas he was backpedaling so fast that he could have biked the annual Hill Country 600 in reverse.

Tess had promised to stay in touch and maybe even

visit Lorelei—and Oberon—in Philadelphia. The cat was not happy about his current location in the carrier.

"Thank you for everything, Tess. I owe you."

"Are you kidding? After you spent all yesterday afternoon working on my taxes? I should name my firstborn after you!"

Ugh. So that a jaded man could one day accuse said firstborn of luring men to their dooms? "Let's just call it a draw."

Ava shuffled her feet. "Guess we should be going, huh?" But she didn't move toward her car. Instead, she remained in place, clutching her keys and scanning the street every few seconds.

He's not coming, Ava. Sam had already said goodbye, more or less. When she'd told him after the trail ride that she was going back to town with Tess, he'd nodded. "Probably a good idea," he'd said with no inflection whatsoever in his voice. The only time she'd seen him since was at the lawyer's office when paperwork for the inn had been handled. Afterward, he'd nodded to her and told her to take "real good care" of herself and the cat. And the jerk had actually sounded more choked up about the cat.

The B and B was officially hers now. And she was giving it away. She cast one last glance at the building, trying not to feel guilty. As if she were abandoning the place.

"Come on," she told Ava. "I'm ready." Which wasn't true, but it sounded better than *let's get the hell out of Dodge before I fall apart.*

As she climbed into the car, she felt an unexpected spark of kinship with her mother. Lorelei had been frustrated by her mom's seeming inability to move on after her husband's death, but Wanda had shared years of marriage and a child with the man she loved. All Lorelei had spent with Sam was a couple of weeks, some unexpectedly heartfelt confidences and the best sex of her life. Yet it felt as if she were leaving her heart in Texas. Would *she* be able to move on?

If Lorelei heard "good to have you back" from one more person, she was going to scream. She knew her coworkers at the insurance company meant well, but all they'd been doing for the past week was reminding her that it *didn't* feel good to be back.

She was trying to have a good attitude. It just wasn't working out very well. On her first day in, she'd dropped by Celia's office with a cookie basket to thank her for all the extra work she'd done in Lorelei's absence. She'd had half-formed plans of inviting the woman to have dinner sometime.

But she'd never issued the invitation because Celia had acted really weird, skittish even, glancing from Lorelei to the door as if considering making a run for it. Then she'd refused the cookies.

"If I ate stuff like that, I wouldn't be a size four." That had been the only time during the strange encounter her gaze settled on Lorelei, as if noting that Lorelei was categorically not a four.

Big deal, she'd found herself thinking. *My body looks great.* She knew this because Sam had told her, in various ways, about a hundred times in a forty-eight-hour window. She'd almost smiled at the memory until she realized that she wasn't supposed to be thinking about Sam Travis, much less grinning over him like a schoolgirl with a crush.

Lorelei had hoped that throwing herself into her job would distract her, but she wasn't getting her usual satisfaction out of it. As she looked at trends and calculated the odds of disaster, she felt annoyed. Was it healthy to spend so much time expecting the worst? Sure, being prepared was smart, but why were people always bracing themselves for bad things? If there were a thirty percent chance of something horrible happening, didn't that leave a seventy percent chance that it wouldn't? *Maybe we should play those odds for a change.*

She was sitting at her desk reevaluating her career on Thursday evening when her phone buzzed and Rick told her he was in the lobby.

"Can I come up?" he'd asked. "I haven't seen you since your trip." The only contact they'd had at all was when he'd emailed to tell her that those event tickets had fallen through, so never mind.

"Sure." She couldn't say she'd missed him, but he'd certainly never done anything to warrant her being bitchy. They could be friends.

Moments later, he strolled into her office, every bit as debonair as she remembered. Not a hair out of place, not a smudge of lint on his expensive suit. *Boring.*

"Lorelei." His voice was grave. "How *are* you? Holding up okay?"

If he'd been that worried, he could have called her.

"I'm fine." It wasn't strictly true, but it was a concise answer.

"Good. Look, Lorelei, my reasons for being here are twofold. First, I wanted to check on your well-being, of course."

Mental eye roll. "Of course."

"But I also felt I should discuss our relationship with

you. You know we've always been free to see other people?"

"Mmm." She made a vague sound of agreement, trying not to remember just how much she'd seen of another man.

Rick linked his fingers behind his back, pacing in front of her as if her desk were the jury box. "I don't want this to be awkward for you, Lorelei. It certainly wasn't planned—"

"Rick." Her lips twitched and she wasn't sure if she was feeling more amusement or impatience. *Cut to the chase already.* "Are you trying to tell me you've found someone?" *Because, no offense, but she's welcome to you.*

He nodded, looking pained for a second. "And she works here. You know my gym is just around the corner? It turns out she goes there, too. Celia Warren?"

Is that why Celia had acted so squirrelly? Maybe the woman had felt guilty, stepping into Lorelei's shoes at work and then going out with a man Lorelei sometimes dated. *Good grief. She's Lorelei 2.0.*

"I think that's terrific news," Lorelei said sincerely. "You and Celia have a lot in common. Enjoy each other! Now, if you'll excuse me, I was about to head home and feed my cat."

Rick's forehead crinkled into perplexed lines. "You're not a cat person."

"That's okay, he's probably not technically a cat. More demon spawn than feline," she said with a fond smile. She should go home and see what Oberon had destroyed today. Yesterday, he'd knocked a glass award off the bookshelf. The day before, he'd shredded a roll of toilet paper into confetti. Prior to that, he'd hacked up a fur ball in her bathroom but hadn't actually mangled anything. Oberon liked to mix it up, keep things fresh.

When she'd squirted him with a water gun last night for clawing at the curtains, she'd threatened, "Watch it, or I'll mail you to Sam. And I might not poke holes in the box lid." A laughable threat on many levels. And Sam the nomad probably didn't even have a mailing address.

As she crossed the parking garage to her car, she wondered if Sam missed her at all. *Probably misses the cat.* And why not? Sometimes people who had trouble relating to others did better with animals. Look at how good he was with horses!

A horse wasn't likely to abandon you for a better barn or dump you on an estranged relative and never come back.

Lorelei told herself that thoughts like these were a dead end. It didn't matter if part of her sympathized with *why* Sam felt safer without any attachments. He, by his own choice, was no longer part of her life. But just as her car sat stuck in traffic, her mind seemed stuck on him. Everyone he'd cared about, including Wanda, had either died or left him. *Like me and the cat.* Assuming that he'd cared about her.

But she knew he did, whether he'd admitted it or not. He'd been candid with her about his past and about his fears. That couldn't have been easy for a man who had trouble trusting others. And he'd liked her enough to let his guard down at times, laughing with her and making her laugh. She still believed that Sam had a lot to offer a woman.

Unfortunately, he didn't see it that way. *Maybe because no one's ever tried to show him.* Lorelei bit her lip. Had she given up too easily? Where was the determination that had gotten her into a highly selective college and earned her ACAS?

Oberon met her at the door when she got home. He flopped on his back and yowled pitifully. She looked around but her preliminary search didn't find any new destruction. He followed her from room to room, meowing and sounding unhappy.

She scooped him into her arms and petted him. After a moment of token resistance, he stopped squirming and let himself enjoy it. Although he wouldn't give her the satisfaction of hearing it, she felt certain he was purring on the inside.

But as soon as she set him down so that she could look through the day's mail, he began complaining again. Lorelei shook her head. "You don't like it much here, do you? Want to know a secret? I'm not sure I do, either." Philadelphia had served a purpose in her life, had been a refuge, her method of running away.

How could she stay mad at Sam for fleeing emotional complications when she'd done the same thing for so long?

"Maybe," she told the cat, "it's time we call our real-estate agent."

"Hey, Travis!"

Sam turned on his bar stool to acknowledge a man he knew from his rodeo days, Bryan Wilton.

"Caught you in the shootout today," Bryan said as he took the seat next to Sam.

Sam was currently in Burnet, Texas, for their April festival. As part of the entertainment, tourists were treated to an old-fashioned bank robbery where the sheriff and his deputy chased thieves on horseback and justice prevailed in the end. Sam had first been offered the part of deputy, but these days he felt more like a bad guy, so he'd gone with that.

"Knew you were good with horses," Bryan said. "But I didn't know you could act."

"Oh, I'm quite the actor," Sam said, wondering if only he heard the self-loathing in his voice.

Those last couple of days Lorelei had been in Texas, he'd acted like he didn't give a damn. He figured that was better than a messy goodbye where he admitted he didn't want her to go. Part of him had wanted to hold on to her, but he knew that wouldn't last. Either she would have resented how little he had to offer and eventually dumped him or he would have bolted, his natural aversion to committing himself to one person or place too ingrained to overcome.

"So what are you up to these days?" Sam asked as the other man signaled the bartender. "Still on the rodeo circuit?"

Bryan shook his head. "No, I'm managing a tack shop now. I needed something more stable before I could convince my girl to marry me."

Sam almost spluttered beer. "You're married?"

"Engaged." Bryan beamed. "And couldn't be happier. I know, I know, I said it would never happen, but I just hadn't met the right woman yet. You'll see! One day you'll meet someone and it will change you."

He already had. And it had definitely changed him. Oh, in most ways, he was still the restless loner he'd always been. But now he was painfully aware of what he was missing.

Working trail rides after the festival shootout was a difficult transition. Sam found that blasting at people—

with fake guns, of course—suited his current mood more than being patient with tourists who had signed themselves up for three hours on horseback even though they seemed to have no knowledge whatsoever of riding. *Gonna have to take it really slow today.* Thank God this was just an afternoon jaunt and not one of the overnight trips.

A stable hand named Dave was helping check riders in and compiling all the signed forms. Two other stable hands were introducing guests to their mounts. Sam had been checking on the horses and equipment to make sure everything was in working order. Against his will, he remembered that ride with Lorelei when she'd asked with wide eyes if he had any idea of everything that could go wrong.

For a woman who'd been so preoccupied with accidental injury, how had she not understood the hazards just her smile posed? Sam had been falling for her before they ever left the B and B, but once he'd seen her astride a horse, out in the sunshine, grinning at him, he—

"Yo, Travis!" Dave snapped his fingers. "Did you hear me?"

"Sure," Sam lied.

Dave leaned against a stall door, smirking.

"But, uh, just in case I misheard, maybe you should say it again."

"I just checked in a woman for the ride who asked to speak with you personally. She's at the front of the barn. Guess she has some questions about the trail."

Sam sighed, telling himself that even if the questions turned out to be an affront to common sense, he'd answer them patiently. He couldn't take his black mood out on every random stranger.

But as he blinked against the sunlight that backlit her, he realized this was not a stranger. His chest constricted painfully. "What are you doing here?" In his mind, he was screaming the question. Thankfully it came out as a whisper others wouldn't overhear.

Lorelei fisted her hands on her denim-clad hips, raising her chin in challenge. "I think you meant to say, 'Hi, Ms. Keller, nice to see you again.'"

Nice? That was the most asinine description he'd ever heard. It was incredible to see her again, to look into those dark eyes that had haunted his dreams—and, let's face it, most of his waking moments. But having her this close to him also hurt like breaking a rib or getting kicked in the gut, knocking the breath out of him as pain radiated through his body.

"I've signed up for today's ride," she informed him, as if this were an everyday event.

"You should be in Philadelphia."

"That would make my commute a little difficult. Hard to run my bed-and-breakfast from there."

"You took over the B and B?"

She couldn't do that to him! While Fredericksburg may not be his permanent home, he spent time there regularly. Now just driving past the town would be a torment.

Lorelei continued as if blithely unaware that he was in hell. "I'm not using my mom's theme, of course. I'll have to come up with something new. Between that and opening my own bookkeeping service, I should stay pretty busy."

"Sounds like," he managed to spit out. "I wish you all the best with everything."

Her eyes narrowed, sparks of anger beginning to

show through her composure. "Oh, no. I've already heard that brush-off, the one where you tell me to take care and have a nice life. If you want to be rid of me this time, you'll have to come up with something more original. Otherwise..."

Otherwise?

How could one word sound so ominous yet conversely make his heart kick into an excited rhythm? Some foreign emotion welled within him, and Sam ruthlessly tamped it down. "I'm not sure what you mean."

"Then I'll spell it out for you. I am fighting for us. Because *you*," she said, jabbing him in the chest with her finger, "are too much of a... How would you cowboys put it? A lily-livered coward. If you won't put it on the line for us, then I will."

He wasn't angered by her old-fashioned insult, but the truth in her sentiment infuriated him. Dammit, he *knew* he was scared, had warned her of that. Eventually, his negative feelings would sabotage their relationship, assuming something else hadn't first. People broke up with each other every day for a million different reasons, and a lot of those people were better adjusted than he was.

But instead of voicing any of that, he said as calmly as possible, "There is no 'us,' Lorelei."

"Well, there's gonna be," she declared. "Because we love each other. Not being together is just plain stupid."

That strange emotion surged again, like a river flooding its banks, and he identified the feeling this time. *Hope.* Hope he hadn't asked for and didn't want. "What is with you stubborn Fredericksburg females?" he growled. "First Barbara stalking me, now you?"

Her cheeks flushed, but she didn't rise to the taunt.

She merely shook her head. "I'm not like Barbara. I'm being like my mom, all those times she called me last month and the month before that. I'm being persistent when it comes to someone I love."

He flinched at her use of the word. She truly loved him?

"I wish I'd given in to Mom," she said softly, "that I'd visited her more, tried harder while I still had the chance. You're going to wish that, too, Sam. If you let me leave here today, you'll regret it."

"So what's the alternative?" he asked her hoarsely. "The way I see it, no matter what happens, there will be regrets." He'd rather get them over with now than in a year, a decade. "You're the one who told me people should make more decisions with their heads, not with their hearts. That they should calculate the risks and protect themselves accordingly. You can't guarantee a happily ever after."

She ducked her gaze and he thought he might have won the argument by using her own reasoning. But when she looked up, he could see there was still plenty of fight left in her expression. He had an out-of-body moment where he almost wanted to grin because he felt proud of her.

"There is one guarantee," she protested. "You've heard the line about death and taxes? Nobody lives forever, Sam, and you and I both know life can be short. We've lost people close to us. Is this what they would have wanted for you? You're the most extroverted hermit I know. Even in a crowd of tourists, you're alone. If your life came to an end tomorrow, would you be satisfied with the way you spent it?"

No. God, no. He wanted to spend about a million

more hours in her arms. He didn't need an impressive corporate career or social prestige or fancy belongings. He was beginning to think he needed Lorelei, though.

She reached up to caress the side of his face, her touch like a brand. "I won't stalk you, Sam. But if you decide love is worth the risk, you know where to find me." She gave him one last long look before walking out of the barn.

"Dude." At the sound of Dave's incredulous voice, Sam turned and realized that at some point during the conversation, they'd garnered an audience. "You're not just gonna let her go?"

Was he? Lorelei had told him repeatedly that she didn't believe in fairy tales. Neither did he. But he knew lots of cowboy legends, and very few of them ended happily.

Then have the courage to write your own damn story, Travis.

A wide-eyed middle-aged woman standing next to Dave made shooing motions with her hands. "Go after her, son. Before she gets away!"

That spurred him into motion as no other words could have. Ever since the last time Lorelei had walked away, he'd felt like a husk of a man, going through the motions of his life with no real purpose or enjoyment. Could he endure that again?

He raced into the sunshine, quickly catching her. "Lorelei, wait!" He spun her around, hating himself for the tears that sparkled on her lashes. "Oh, hell, don't cry. I'm not worth it, darlin'."

She smacked him on the arm. "Yeah, you *are*. That's kind of the point."

"I love you." He blurted it fast before he could lose his nerve.

Her jaw dropped but she quickly regrouped, affecting a smug expression even though tears rolled down her face. "I told you so!"

His eyes felt suspiciously damp, too, and he pulled her against his chest so that she didn't see. "Know-it-all Ivy League pain-in-the-ass," he said affectionately. He smoothed his hand over her hair. "But I do love you."

She tilted her head back. "Love you, too."

Giving in to the emotions swamping him, Sam framed her face and captured her mouth with his. Applause and hoots of approval sounded behind them. Lorelei grinned against his lips but didn't move away. Their deep, thorough kiss felt like an unspoken vow. A promise of new beginnings and happy endings and, most important, being there for each other to weather everything in between.

* * * * *

New York Times bestselling author **Virna DePaul** was an English major in college and, despite a passion for Shakespeare, Broadway musicals and romance novels, somehow ended up with a law degree. For ten years, she was a criminal prosecutor for the state of California. Now she's thrilled to be writing stories about complex individuals (fully human or not) who are willing to overcome incredible odds for love. She can be found on Twitter, @virnadepaul, or at virnadepaul.com.

Books by Virna DePaul

Harlequin Romantic Suspense

Dangerous to Her

It Started That Night
Deadly Charade
Texas Stakeout

Harlequin HQN

Shades of Desire
Shades of Temptation
Shades of Passion

Visit the Author Profile page at Harlequin.com for more titles.

TEXAS STAKEOUT

VIRNA DePAUL

For James. I miss you!

Chapter 1

U.S. Marshal Dylan Rooney was on a stakeout. Only in the hill country of Texas a stakeout didn't mean sitting in an unmarked sedan, drinking coffee and eating donuts. Nope. A Texas stakeout meant sitting on the back of a horse. And Dylan, who was a mediocre rider at best, had drawn the short straw in more ways than one. As a marshal, it wasn't uncommon for him to work away from his home base in California. It was, however, uncommon for him to be this bored. And this sore.

He much preferred traveling by plane, train or automobile—the faster and sleeker the mode of transportation, the better—than relying on a four-legged best from hell.

While two other marshals from Dylan's five-member team, and several other marshals from various states, scoured the country for Jackson Kincaid, a prisoner who'd recently escaped transport in California, Dylan was on his third day in Nowhere, Texas, binoculars trained on the ranch owned by Jackson Kincaid's sister, Rachel. Besides the sheer boredom of it all, it wouldn't have been a bad assignment, but he hadn't counted on his damn horse having anxiety issues. Ginger, the horse he'd rented from an adjacent farm, wouldn't stop dancing in the red Texas dirt, kicking up a cloud of dust in Dylan's face.

It would be the height of stupidity for Kincaid to run here, especially given that it was where he was first taken into custody, but it still had to be covered. Dylan and his team would do whatever it took to apprehend Kincaid, even if it meant endless hours of watching Kincaid's ten-year-old nephew popping soda cans off fence posts with a BB gun.

The kid wasn't a half-bad shot, Dylan thought just as his mother came into view. Dylan sat up higher on the horse and pressed the binoculars tighter to his face, watching as she made the long hike up the western fence line and across the field to where her kid stood, BB gun at his side. Just as it had when he'd first seen her picture—hell, every time he'd caught a glimpse of her in the past few days—Dylan's pulse accelerated. Rachel Kincaid was nothing like the sophisticated women Dylan normally dated, but she was hands-down gorgeous. Willowy and tall, she had a dark Texas tan and dark eyes that clashed with the vibrant near white of her blond hair. She worked hard—too hard—and there was no doubt she loved her son, Peter, to distraction.

Too bad she had lousy taste in men, her brother and deceased husband included. Her husband's alcohol problem and subsequent drunk driving accident had left Rachel a widow.

And her brother?

He'd taken everything his sister had sacrificed for him and flushed it down the toilet the minute he'd agreed to transport drugs across state lines.

Now Rachel was basically running the ranch by herself. She had some help, but not much.

Earlier, the woman had been conferring with her only ranch hand—records listed him as Josiah Pemberly, age sixty-three—down at the natural spring. Though Dylan hadn't been able to hear their conversation, it had appeared pleasant, with both parties smiling a lot. Now that Rachel had reached her son, the conversation going on between them seemed far from pleasant. As Rachel spoke, the child stood motionless, his back to her. Frowning, Rachel lifted a hand as if to reach out to the boy, then stopped. Shaking her head, she wheeled around and strode quickly back to the ranch house, her entire posture stiff with frustration.

The woman was sexy as hell, Dylan thought, but it was obvious she had no control over her kid. And she'd obviously lost control of her brother, whom she'd essentially raised, a long time ago. Dylan just hoped her kid didn't end up taking the same path in life that his uncle had.

Dylan dropped the binoculars so they hung on their leather strap around his neck. Day three in the stakeout for Jackson Kincaid, and all Dylan had seen at the Kincaid ranch was one gorgeous yet overworked woman, her sullen brat, one elderly ranch hand and a bunch of weird-looking llamas. At least, he figured they were llamas. Texas was getting too froufrou. Whatever had happened to sheep and cattle ranching?

The next fifteen minutes passed in a drone of boredom. The ranch hand kept mending the fence. The kid continued popping soda cans off fence posts. Dylan gulped down water until the wind picked up, snapping more dust into his eyes and sending a tumbleweed straight at his horse.

"Whoa," he murmured, tightening his grip on the reins with one hand and wrapping his other hand in Ginger's mane. The mare shied, as expected, but Dylan managed to hang on and focused on maintaining his seat and keeping his feet in the stirrups. He fought for control, working to recall the instructions his camp counselor had taught him the year the state had sent him to summer camp in the boonies.

"Keep your seat. Don't yank on the reins. Dig your heels down."

And then he heard a shriek wend its way upward from the valley below.

The kid? The mother? Dylan wrapped the reins around his fist to control the horse and brought the binoculars back to his eyes. The kid had dropped his BB gun and was running toward the house. Dylan panned the lenses over to the house but didn't see the porch door swing open. In the few days that he'd been spying on the Kincaid Ranch, Rachel had always come running whenever the kid wanted her. Now? Nothing. Had something happened to her?

"Mom!"

The single word caught on the edge of the wind and whipped up the ridge to Dylan. Desperation filled the boy's single word.

Dylan loosened his grip on the reins and squeezed with his knees, yelling, "Yiya!"

Ginger responded by leaping forward. Immediately she settled into a gallop and headed down the ridge to the valley. The ranch house was only about a quarter mile away as the crow flies, but the trail down the ridge zigzagged like a pinball machine. Still, even with all the switchbacks, he'd probably be able to reach the kid in time to help.

Assuming he didn't get thrown and break his neck first, of course.

Rachel Kincaid let her long hair drip water down her back. The cold shower had felt good and had taken the biting edge off her nerves. With their higher elevation, the Texas heat usually stayed away from the ranch, but not this summer. This summer the heat got to her. Or maybe it was that Peter kept getting to her.

God, she loved her son, but he'd never been an easy kid. Often affectionate and sweet and funny but also hyperactive. Defiant. Impulsive.

Six months ago he'd been diagnosed with attention-deficit hyperactivity disorder. At the time, she'd been relieved to have an explanation for his moodiness that didn't come with being labeled a failure of a parent. But she'd also been overwhelmed and uncertain of her ability to do right by her son. After doing tons of re-search on the subject, she'd reluctantly agreed to get him on medicine, something that had seemed to help right away. Putting Peter on a schedule that still provided him lots of downtime had helped even more. By the time the school year had ended, he'd been doing so much bet-ter and their relationship had become downright rosy.

Now, however, the prolonged time they'd been spending together over summer vacation was beginning to take its toll. So was the fact that Peter missed his uncle Jax; even if he didn't know the real reason Jax had left last year, he was confused by Jax's failure to visit or call. Peter missed him, and he was bored with just her and Josiah for company. And Rachel? She missed her brother, too. Missed him terribly. She was also tired from working the ranch. From working Jax's appeal. From her frequent battles with Peter. It made her feel guilty, but she wanted summer to be over. Wanted the heat gone. Wanted Peter back in school where he could sass his teachers for part of the day instead of her.

She stepped into a worn but clean pair of Levi's jeans and pulled a tank over her still-dripping hair, knowing it wasn't fair to compare Peter to what her brother, Jax, had been like at ten but doing it, anyway. Jax had been…easy. Then again, Jax hadn't had ADHD. And, when Jax had just turned ten, their parents were still alive and she was in her first year in college; she probably wouldn't have noticed if Jax had given her parents attitude, anyway. Afterward, with their parents gone before he turned eleven, Jax had been so grief-stricken it had taken months before he'd smiled again, let alone thrown attitude.

Peter, on the other hand, had been offering up enough sass to fill a silo. The way he'd turned his back on her earlier when she asked him to stop shooting the pellet gun and fill up the alpacas' water trough had just about driven her out of her skin. She'd had to walk away before she lost it and started yelling at him.

She grabbed her boots but stopped when she heard something.

Peter calling her. The tenor of his high-pitched voice came through the open bedroom window, urgent and scared.

Her heart leaped into her throat. Her baby needed her.

She didn't bother with the boots, and instead rushed down the stairs and burst out onto the porch, looking for her son.

There, racing from the western fence line where she'd left him only fifteen minutes ago, came Peter. And coming toward him from the opposite direction, in a cloud of red dust, rode a stranger on a galloping chestnut quarter horse.

"Peter!" she screamed, and ran to him. She stumbled as the rocks on the drive bit into her feet but kept on going.

"Mom, you've gotta help!" Peter cried out when she reached him. He wrapped his arms around her and sobbed into her shoulder.

Heart pounding, Rachel held her son tight and faced the rider who brought his horse to an ungainly stop next to them. He seemed about her age, or maybe just a few years older—maybe early thirties. Wide shoulders, legs long against the barrel of the horse. Blue jeans, a plaid snap-front long-sleeved shirt rolled to the elbows and his Stetson said *cowboy,* yet his unscuffed boots and the clean felt of his hat screamed of falsehood.

Wait. She knew his horse: Ginger. A horse from her neighbor Aaron Jacobson's herd. The same neighbor harassing her about the fence line. Hell. Today of all days she didn't need to deal with a stupid land dispute. And she didn't need some city slicker to give her a hard time about the spring.

"I don't know who you are or why Aaron sent you to hassle my kid," she snapped out at the stranger, "but I swear to God, if you don't get off my property, I'll call the sheriff on you. You and Aaron leave my kid alone," she nearly growled, holding a sobbing Peter even tighter. "Whatever issues that man has with the property line can be handled in court—not by intimidating a child."

The man slid off Ginger in an awkward motion and stepped forward, palms held upward in a universal gesture of peace. He came closer and she stood shaking, watching his every step, until he stopped a few feet in front of her. His deep blue eyes were steady and without malice. Didn't matter. He was tall—at least six foot two—and he towered over her and Peter; his wide shoulders and military posture screamed *intimidation.*

But she was a mother. She wouldn't let him intimidate her. Not when her kid was crying against her shoulder.

"My name's Dylan, ma'am," the man said. "Dylan Rooney. And I'm not here about your neighbor. I was riding the ridge, uh, bird-watching, and I saw the kid playing with his BB gun. Next thing I knew I heard him screaming and running to the house. I figured something had happened and came down the hill to help. Kid—" he directed his statement to Peter, who'd raised his tear-streaked face away from her shoulder "—are you hurt?"

Peter pulled away from Rachel and swiped futilely at the tears that kept streaming down his face. "No, it's not me. It's…it's…" Anguish froze his expression, his mouth gaping and open, shutting off whatever he'd been about to say.

Rachel reached for him, but Peter took another step

away from her. The distance, a mere two inches, ripped yet another hole in Rachel's heart. He'd needed her—and then he hadn't. She couldn't help thinking of all the family she'd lost—her parents and even her brother in a way. She swallowed the lump of emotional pain down and said, "I heard you ask for my help, Peter. What's wrong?"

The man—Dylan—came forward and placed a solid hand on Peter's shoulder. Somehow the masculine grip held Peter together in a way Rachel's soft hold hadn't, because Peter took a shaky breath and the tears stopped flowing.

"It's Josiah…"

Josiah. Her ranch hand. And friend. A sensation like a cold hand slid up her back. Twenty minutes ago she'd checked in on him as he repaired the fence on the property line she shared with Aaron Jacobson. Had Aaron gone too far this time? Was Aaron causing Josiah trouble?

Her neighbor had been a real pain in the neck ever since he discovered a natural spring right on her side of the fence line a couple of years ago. He'd been digging around the courthouse records, trying to prove the spring was actually on his own land. She'd been too preoccupied with running the ranch, keeping Peter in line and working on the appeal process for her brother to deal with Aaron's constant haranguing, but she'd finally referred him to Julia Rickel, her friend and lawyer, who'd threatened lawsuits and police action and whatnot if Aaron didn't back off. Aaron had made it clear he hadn't liked what he considered to be Julia's threats.

She opened her mouth to speak, but the stranger beat her to the question she was about to ask.

"Kid," Dylan said, "what happened? Where's Josiah?"

Peter hitched a breath and pointed back to the fence line. "He's over there. B-b-but it's too late. We're too late."

The cold hand on Rachel's back now gripped her throat. *No.*

"Too late for what, Peter?" she whispered.

"Too late to help. Josiah's dead."

Chapter 2

Rachel's face had turned so white that Dylan expected her to faint at any moment. He reached out a hand, offering to steady her, but she waved him away. Of course she did. He was a stranger. She had no reason to trust him.

He turned to Peter, whose expression was still alight with panic. Had Jackson Kincaid snuck on the property without Dylan noticing? Seemed unlikely, but…

He followed the kid's pointing finger with his line of sight.

The boy's voice shook as he said, "Way up the fence line, next to the spring."

"Did you see anyone up there with him?" Dylan asked.

The boy shook his head.

"Are you certain he's…dead?" Rachel's voice came out on a whisper of a breath.

Peter swallowed and nodded, his eyes filling back up

with tears. "He has a big hole in his head and there's a lot of blood and his eyes are open and not moving and he doesn't have a pulse," he said breathlessly. "I checked. Then I ran to get you."

Oh, hell. This wasn't some kid making a desperate bid for attention. This was real. "You and the kid get into the house and lock yourselves in," he ordered even as he mentally cursed. As if that would do a lot of good if Jackson Kincaid was on the ranch. He was her brother, for God's sake. It wasn't as if she'd view him as a threat to her or her son. And truth be told, Dylan had no reason to think Jackson would hurt them. Still, the man had proven himself to be violent and if he'd killed Josiah...

Rachel started, staring at him with wide brown eyes, pupils dilating. "What— Why?"

"Just to be safe. Call 911. Use the landline. Tell them to get an ambulance here immediately."

Rachel looked from Dylan to her son, then raised her chin. "Peter, do as he says. Lock all the doors and wait for the ambulance, okay? I'm going to check on Josiah."

"I can do that—" Dylan began, but Peter was already running into the house.

"Not without me," she said. She watched the house until Peter had slammed the door behind him, then strode toward Ginger. She put a bare foot into the stirrup and easily swung herself up onto Dylan's horse, then kicked her feet out of the stirrups. "You coming?" she asked. "Because I'm not leaving you here alone with my kid."

Dylan struggled with indecision. He wanted to insist he check on the ranch hand by himself, but this was her private property and what reason could he possibly

give for thinking there might be something or someone dangerous out there? Not the truth, certainly. Not
yet. Not when the most likely explanation was that her
ranch hand had had some kind of accident.

When Rachel raised her eyebrows impatiently and
leaned forward, he slid his booted foot in the stirrup and
pulled himself up behind her. Ginger danced for a few
seconds, then settled as he used his knees to nudge her
forward. He wrapped an arm around Rachel's waist and
pulled her in tight to his chest. She was stiff but didn't
resist. The quarter horse, her hooves steady despite the
added weight, settled into an easy lope.

"So, are you a friend of Aaron's?" Rachel asked over
her shoulder. "Did he send you out to spy on us? Did
he tell you about the crazy widow and her bratty kid?"
Bitterness edged her words, which came out jumpy and
breathless as Ginger continued to cover the uneven ter-
rain.

Not exactly, Dylan thought. The Department of Cor-
rections had told him about her brother and his brazen
escape, and research had informed his team about Rachel, the sister whom Jackson Kincaid thought of as his
mother, and Rachel's son. Of course, Dylan didn't tell
Rachel that. Lying to her wasn't his first choice, but he
also didn't want her clamming up and getting irrational
when there was a potential crisis to deal with.

"He just loaned me a horse. We're not friends. Does
Josiah have a history of any sort of heart condition?
Stroke?"

"No health issues. He's older, but healthy. He's repaired the fence line time after time. I don't know what
could have harmed him."

Dylan immediately thought of her brother again.

"Maybe your son is wrong about him being dead." In his arms her body loosened fractionally, and she twisted her torso to face forward again. Whether she completely believed him or not didn't matter—she trusted him enough to help her ranch hand.

"I'm not holding out hope. Peter's been raised on a ranch. We raise alpacas for wool, so we don't do a lot of butchering, but he's seen dead animals. He knows what lifeless eyes look like."

So did Dylan. Personally and professionally.

Professionally? The duty of a marshal was to bring in fugitives whether they claimed to be innocent or not. It wasn't his job to investigate their crimes, nor to believe them or not believe them—that was for the cops, the courts and the jury system to decide. Fugitives didn't see it that way. They wanted their freedom. Sometimes they fought to keep it

Sometimes they died.

Personally...

He fought to erase the dead eyes staring dully at him in his mind's eye, but he couldn't.

Dead eyes all looked the same: unblinking and missing life's sheen. But the first set of dead eyes he'd ever seen—his mother's—haunted him every day of his life, reminding him of what could happen to a person who refused to accept the bad in others before it was too late.

"So your son's name is Peter. And you are?"

"Rachel. We're almost there," she said. "Down the gulley to the right. Then the spring's a few hundred yards south."

He knew how to get to the spring already but kept silent, and instead neck-reined Ginger in the direction Rachel had given. The horse headed downhill and Rachel leaned back to compensate for her weight on the horse's shoulders. Her still-wet hair brushed his face and he breathed in the scent. Soft and floral, with a hint of freshness. Ginger stumbled and Dylan tightened his grip on Rachel, appreciating the soft weight of her breasts on his forearm. *Get a grip,* he mentally chided himself. Yeah, Rachel was one hot woman, but she was also the sister of the fugitive he was hunting, and they were on the way to find out if her ranch hand still lived. Appreciating her sweet smell or the luscious weight of her breasts was the last thing he should be doing.

He reminded himself it had been three long months since he'd bedded a woman. Before that, he'd been in a long-term relationship with Ashley, a deputy D.A. back in San Francisco. They'd dated for several years and she'd been pressuring him for more. She'd wanted to move in together. Wanted to move toward marriage. He hadn't been able to commit. He'd cared about her. Appreciated her in bed and out. But he'd known she wasn't the one, just as the handful of women he'd dated before her hadn't been the one. The ones he'd dated after her?

They'd been beautiful. Smart. Urban chic. But they'd bored him. Body, mind and soul. It had been far easier to immerse himself in work. Now there was Rachel Kincaid. Stimulating him in so many different ways and distracting him from his duty. It not only surprised him. It was beginning to piss him off.

Dylan grabbed his binoculars and scanned the surrounding area. It looked clear, but he was still conscious of the presence of his firearm inside his boot. Knew it would take mere seconds to draw his weapon if he needed it.

"There!" Rachel exclaimed, pointing to a spot of

blue, deep down among the green rushes that surrounded a bubbling spring. She grabbed the reins herself and pulled Ginger to a halt.

Dylan swung himself off the horse, then helped Rachel to her feet. She stumbled and he caught her—their faces inches from each other. Her eyebrows swung together in a V before she pulled away.

"Josiah?" she called out, pushing through the rushes, gray mud sucking at her bare feet.

She came to a halt next to the bright spot of blue they'd seen, and Dylan came up behind her. When she sank to her knees in front of the crumpled figure, Dylan knew Peter had been right.

The man was dead.

On her knees, Rachel swallowed against the heave in her stomach. Josiah lay at an odd angle, a few yards from where the spring water bubbled to the surface. Coagulated blood stained his face, no doubt from the severe wound on the side of his forehead. Next to his head, a large jagged rock protruded from the ground. He must have slipped. Hit his head.

She hated that Peter had seen Josiah's open eyes, so devoid of life. Was that what Jax saw when the school bus had dropped him off and he'd come home to find their parents, dead from carbon monoxide poisoning? She reached a hand out to close his eyes but was stopped by a firm grip on her elbow.

"Don't touch him," Dylan growled.

For a second, the timbre of his voice and the weight of his touch made fear shoot through her. This was a stranger, a stranger who'd appeared as suddenly as Josiah had been hurt. Killed. Dylan Rooney claimed he'd been riding after Peter because he'd only wanted to help, but what if that wasn't the case?

But just as panic and fear started to choke off her breath, she reminded herself that he'd told both her and Peter to stay at the house to call 911. Someone bent on trouble would hardly want more witnesses to deal with, and he would most likely have tried to separate them.

After taking a deep breath, she slowly pulled her arm away from his grip. "I only want to close his eyes. Give him some dignity," she argued.

"We can't disturb the scene any more than we already have. This man is dead. We need to back up and wait for the authorities."

Dylan's words buzzed inside her head. Two phrases hung in the air, as if a spotlight was on them. *Disturb the scene. Wait for the authorities.* Then she remembered the way he'd initially ordered her and Peter to go inside the house and lock the doors after them. As if he'd wanted to make sure whatever had hurt Josiah couldn't hurt them.

Aaron had been beastly over the past month, demanding rights to the water he'd found on her land. Even before that, he'd always been a bit of a jerk, which was why she'd initially wondered if Aaron had been causing Josiah trouble.

But she hadn't been thinking murder. Now, based on the position of Josiah's body next to the rock, the most logical assumption would be Josiah had fallen and hit his head.

Clearly this man suspected foul play.

Why?

Dylan held out a hand and after a slight hesitation,

she took it. He tugged her upward and she came to standing, facing him.

"Why can't I touch him?" she asked hoarsely. "What do you mean, 'disturb the scene'?"

"I'm sorry. I didn't mean to frighten you," he soothed. "It looks like he fell, but it's always possible something else happened to him."

"Like what?"

His fingers tightened around hers right before he ran his hands up and down her arms in a comforting motion. Her first instinct was to push him away and tell him she needed answers, not sympathy. But that would be a lie.

She suddenly felt on the verge of collapse. Wanted nothing more than to rest her cheek against his chest and beg him to hold her. Comfort her.

He sighed and lifted one hand to run his knuckles against her cheek. "There are always those who want to hurt others, Rachel. There's always a possibility that there's danger where we think we're the safest. But I'm here. And I'll help you. You just need to let me."

Chapter 3

"I don't understand," Rachel said even as she pulled away from him. Fear had made her large eyes grow rounder, and Dylan barely suppressed a curse. Scaring her was the last thing he wanted, but he couldn't dismiss the possibility that her brother had killed this man. For all he knew, Kincaid was still on the property somewhere, a threat to them all.

And yet for all Rachel knew, Dylan was the threat. He needed to extinguish the fear in Rachel's eyes. Sometimes only the truth could do that.

"I told you my name is Dylan Rooney, ma'am. What I didn't tell you is I'm a U.S. Marshal and I'm here on important business."

Rachel backed farther away from him, her bare feet sinking even deeper in the mud that his boots protected him from. She winced, and once again he held out a hand to provide stability. This time she ignored it, staring at him warily.

"Business that has something to do with what's happened to Josiah?"

"Could be. I'm not certain."

"But you think he's been murdered."

"That remains to be seen," Dylan said. She shifted, then winced again, reminding Dylan she'd run out of the house barefoot. She had to be in pain. "Here, let's get you back up on the horse while we wait for help. No sense in you continuing to beat up your feet if you don't have to."

He moved toward her, but she held out her hand. "Stop. You think I'm going to just take your word you're a cop? That you have any legitimate business being here?"

"I can show you my credentials. Will that help?"

She frowned, then nodded. Slowly, he reached into his back pocket for his wallet. He held it out and she took it. As soon as she flipped it open, she saw his badge and official ID. Her shoulders seemed to relax somewhat and she held the wallet back out to him. When he'd pocketed it, she turned and started walking toward Ginger, limping the whole time.

He placed a hand on her shoulder. "Let me help you, ma'am. Please."

She looked up at him, silent and looking a little lost, obviously numb from the shock of finding her ranch hand dead. She didn't protest when he scooped her up in his arms and walked her the few yards back to Ginger, who was calmly grazing on green grass. Tall as Rachel was, she didn't weigh much, but she did remain stiff in his arms while he raised her up onto Ginger's back. Apparently dead bodies had no spook value the way tumbleweeds, bees and the occasional butterfly did, because the horse stood still.

When he settled Rachel onto Ginger's back, she slumped in the saddle, as if all the strength had seeped out of her bones. "You were spying on us. Josiah? Or me?" she asked, her voice hollow, as if she'd forced the words out using what little energy she had left.

That was an answer he didn't want to give just yet. Not until after Josiah was dealt with and he knew he'd have some uninterrupted alone time to explain everything to Rachel.

The sounds of sirens in the distance gave him an out. "Will Peter be able to lead the EMTs here?" he asked.

Rachel nodded, then sat up straight, agitation showing in her blanched face. "But I don't want him to see—"

"I won't let him near the spring. I'll make sure he stays back, okay?"

A faint smile of gratitude curved the corners of her lips upward. Dylan realized that was the first time he'd seen even the hint of a smile on the woman's face.

Rachel Kincaid was beautiful, but when she smiled it made him long for the rest of the world to disappear so he could spend hours simply staring at her.

"Thanks for that," she murmured. "He's just a kid. Seeing death at a young age can be so harmful. So destructive."

Yeah, he knew.

In less than a minute, they heard the voices of the EMTs and he left Rachel to clamber up the gulley, intent on holding Peter back from going to his mom. From seeing Josiah's body again.

But Peter wasn't with the EMTs, who said they'd instructed the kid to go back to the house after he'd brought them close enough so they could find their own way to the spring. Silently, Dylan cursed. Now that he'd confirmed Josiah was dead, he was regretting letting the boy go off on his own. He wanted him near. To ensure his safety, yes, but also to settle Rachel's worry about him.

Dylan showed the EMTs his badge. They confirmed Josiah Pemberly was deceased and made the appropriate calls to the police. Within a few minutes, a deputy from the sheriff's department showed up. Dylan and the other man, whom Dylan had met days earlier, exchanged tense looks.

Deputy Mark Todd was one of the three sheriff's deputies Dylan and his team had contacted when they first arrived in town. He knew who Dylan was and why he was here. Thank God he also knew better than to say anything in front of Rachel.

By the time a half hour had crept up and passed them, the deputy had agreed to make sure the body made its way to the medical examiner. He'd also agreed to call in another deputy so they could do a thorough search of the property together.

Dylan walked Ginger back to the house, an emotionally drained Rachel still perched on her back. He'd get her into the shower, bandage up her feet if need be and check in on the kid. Then he planned to see if Rachel had any whiskey in the house, pour her two fingers and tell her why he was in Texas, scoping out her house with high-powered binoculars on the back of a borrowed horse.

The odd thing was, part of him didn't want to tell her.

Instead, he wanted her to smile again. And he wanted to do whatever it took to keep that smile going, not extinguish it.

Rachel wasn't sure what to make of Dylan Rooney. Correction: U.S. Marshal Dylan Rooney. By the way the sheriff's deputies had deferred to his authority, he appeared to be law enforcement, just as his credentials indicated, but was there truly any reason for him to think Josiah's death had been the result of foul play? Some reason to think that she needed his help?

Maybe he was simply being paranoid because of the work he did. At least that was what she told herself as the marshal led Ginger, with Rachel in the saddle, back to the ranch. When they got there, he gently lifted her off the horse and put her on the front porch, then told her he'd take off Ginger's tack and set the mare up in one of the empty corrals.

Rachel immediately went in search of her son. She found Peter sitting on the floor in a corner of his room, his arms wrapped around his knees. "I was right. He's dead, isn't he?"

"Oh, baby," she whispered, knowing there was no easy way to break the news. Peter had loved Josiah. She fell to her knees beside her son and reached out to place a hand on his shoulder. "I'm sorry, Peter, but yes, Josiah's dead."

"I knew it," he choked out. Shooting to his feet, he pushed her arm aside and bolted away.

"Peter," she called, jumping to her feet to follow him. But her feet hurt and she was blinded by tears and her son was so much faster than she was. By the time she reached the top of the stairs, he'd barreled down them and had slammed out the back door. She had covered her eyes with one hand, choking back sobs, when the front door opened and Dylan Rooney stuck his head in.

"You want me to bring him back?"

She shook her head. Peter often hid out in the huge cottonwood by the creek—he'd always liked to process difficulties alone, and she'd always respected his needs even before she came to understand that because of his ADHD, giving him extra space was important. Now, however, she wanted him by her side. Safe. She'd shower, get some clothes and shoes on, deal with Dylan, then find Peter and keep him with her so they could grieve Josiah's passing together. "He'll be fine," she said. "I—I just need to clean up and then we can talk. You can wait in the living room."

Before he could reply, she headed into the master bedroom and quickly shut the door behind her. Then she rushed to the bathroom and shut that door behind her, as well. Only then did she lean back against the door and allow herself to break down, trying her best to stifle the sounds of her sorrow. She cried for Josiah, taken too soon. For Peter, who'd seen the stare of death. And she cried for her parents and for Jax. Jax, too, had seen empty, lifeless eyes when he returned home from school and found their parents. She hadn't been able to protect him from that pain any more than she'd been able to protect her son.

Some mother she was turning out to be.

For the second time in as many hours, she stepped inside the shower and let the cool water wash her clean. Her feet were a mess, cut by the sharp stones she'd run across on her way to comfort her crying son, then sliced again by the knife-sharp reeds at the spring. Jackson

Pollock-ish designs were painted in gray clay from her feet to her calves.

Numbly, Rachel stared at the water sluicing down the drain and, even though part of her hated herself for it, her thoughts drifted to the practicalities of Josiah's death. After her husband Phillip's death so long ago, the only way she'd been able to afford a ranch hand was that Josiah had been happy to do extra chores for a place to sleep and three meals a day. He'd been with her for years, and was the only alpaca shearer her flock tolerated. Between her and Josiah, they'd been able to shear the entire flock in a couple of days. With spring upon them and shearing season right around the corner, she'd have to find some way to come up with the money to hire a professional outfit.

Money she didn't know where she'd find. Money had always been scarce; Phillip's parents were still alive, adored Peter and would help if they could, but they barely got by on a minimal fixed income as it was. Rachel had used what little money she'd had in her bank account for Jax's appeal. Her friend Julia had insisted on taking on Jax's second appeal pro bono, but even with Julia offering her services for free, money was tight. And Josiah had no one in his life besides her and Peter—she'd need to pay for a funeral. It was the least she could do to pay homage to a man who'd been a loyal employee for years. A man who'd tried to steer her son right when Peter acted out. A man who hadn't deserved to die.

A man who, according to a U.S. marshal, could have been murdered.

Broken and choked sobs wrenched their way out from her body, the harsh sounds clashing with the soft raindrop lullaby of the shower spray. Her legs turned to jelly and she dropped to the tiled floor of the shower with a crash.

Strength seemed to have left her, so she sat, knees tucked in tight under her chin and arms wrapped around her shins, and sobbed. She closed her eyes, only to see Josiah's vacant stare as he lay in the green reeds, his blue-checkered shirt covered in wet mud. "No, no, no," she choked out, repeating the word until it became a mantra. Something that took her away from this place. Something that let her drift away from conscious thought, into the ether of nothingness where she could feel no stress, no pain. No fear.

"Rachel."

Dimly, through the fog of pain and anguish, she became aware of someone calling her name.

"Rachel."

There it was again. Her name. Spoken in a soft, male voice. A voice full of compassion and sorrow. A voice close by.

She forced her eyes open to see the shadow of a tall form standing outside the steamed-up glass shower walls.

U.S. Marshal Dylan Rooney. In her private bathroom. Invading her space. How dare the man? "Get out," she managed to say. Instinctively, she cringed, then realized she was curled into herself, all the important stuff covered up, even if he could see anything more than her shadow through the foggy glass.

"I heard a thump and you crying out. Are you all right?"

"My son just saw his first dead body, and you told me my ranch hand and friend has possibly been murdered. No, I'm not okay."

Silence followed her statement. Finally Dylan spoke again. "I meant, are you okay physically? I want to make sure you didn't hurt yourself."

"I'm fine," she sniffed.

"Yeah, right, and I'm Santa Claus," he muttered. A deep exhale of breath followed his words, and then he said, "I guess you sound okay. When you're done crying—I mean, when you're done taking a shower—I'll be in your kitchen. We need to talk," he said, his voice grim. "You need to know why I'm here. And why I think Josiah may have been murdered."

With dread, Rachel listened as he walked out of the bathroom.

Her mother had always told her to be careful what she wished for. Learning the truth about why U.S. Marshal Dylan Rooney was here was what she'd wanted.

But now she wasn't so sure. Now she'd give almost anything to believe he really had been birdwatching…and she desperately wished he'd turn around and leave—not just her house, but her ranch— just as abruptly as he'd appeared.

Chapter 4

Rachel stared at the man who'd claimed to want to help her only to then deliver the killing blow that might finally defeat her. "No," she said. "I don't believe you. Jax would never have escaped prison."

Rachel's heartbeat thudded so heavily her chest ached. She glared at Dylan, who sat across her kitchen table, flicking a thumbnail against the rough-hewn wood. Her father had made the table when she and Jax were young. Jax had insisted on using the hand planer and ended up slicing off the tip of his finger, right on the spot Dylan was toying with.

Innocent, sweet Jax, who'd followed their father around as though their dad was his own personal hero. Rachel knew that sweet boy was still inside her brother even though he'd refused to show him in the past year. Even though he'd confessed to police that he'd knowingly transported drugs across state lines, a crime that had landed him a prison sentence.

According to police, Jax had been contacted by someone who'd heard he was looking to make a quick buck. All Jax had to do was drive a package from Texas to east L.A., give the package to the man at the drop site, receive a package in return and drive back to Texas. All for two thousand bucks and the cost of gas. He'd been told the package contained vital documents needed for signatures to sell some high-level computer tech company to a big conglomeration. But he'd known better than that. He'd known the package contained drugs.

When he'd arrived at the drop site, men with guns came storming into the warehouse. Jax had managed to escape and had hopped a freighter back to Texas.

Rachel hadn't known any of this was happening. Jax had told her he was going out of town to look for work. She'd been so proud of him she'd been willing to let him go off for a few days, even though the ranch desperately needed his help.

Then DEA agents and the local sheriff, Howard Ryan, had arrived at the ranch a few days after Jax had taken off, scaring the hell out of her and Peter with their guns and yelling and stomping about. The sheriff had found Jax near the barn and handed him off to the DEA. With her crying and begging them for information, the agents had handcuffed her brother and hauled him away, leaving her with unanswered questions. Jax had refused to look at her. He'd refused to say one word to her. After he'd confessed, he'd refused to say another word to the police.

The last time she'd seen her brother was the day of his sentencing, before they took him away. The two times she'd tried to visit him in prison, he refused to see her.

She didn't know why—whether he was ashamed of what had happened to him or whether he blamed her for his troubles. One thing was for sure in her mind—Jax's confession had to have been coerced.

No matter how bad things looked, she had faith in her brother. He was a good man. And he had to know Rachel was doing everything in her power to get him out of prison—legally. He'd never put everything she'd done for him on the line by escaping his prison sentence.

Numbly, she stared at the bottle of whiskey and two tumblers Dylan had placed on the table. He'd obviously thought she'd need something to soften the news he was about to give her. The mistaken news, she told herself again. He was wrong about Jax. He had to be.

"There must have been a mix-up in the head count or something," she insisted. "The wrong name answered during roll call. Jax didn't run off."

"Rachel," Dylan said, setting an elbow on the table and leaning closer to her. "Your brother's a fugitive. Has been for a few days now even though we've managed to keep his name out of the press. The U.S. marshals—including my team back in California—got the notification he was being transported from High Desert State Prison to San Quentin for overcrowding when he escaped custody. I'm the one who ended up stuck out here on top of Ginger with binoculars glued to my face and no bathroom for miles, on the off chance Jackson turned up."

"And what were you planning on doing if he did?" she asked, anger revving her words to a fast tempo.

"The same thing I'm still planning to do. Watch and

wait until capturing him doesn't present a danger to you or your son, then nab him and bring him back into custody."

"What do you mean wait until capturing him doesn't present a danger to me or Peter? Were you planning to come in with guns blazin'? Have the big shoot-out at the O.K. Corral on my property?"

Instead of answering, Dylan stared at her, holding her gaze with his. She'd noticed before how startlingly blue his eyes were, but the expression he held now, one mixed with pity, compassion and a hint of fury, made the blue seem all that brighter. He shifted, and his plaid snap-front strained against the breadth of his shoulders. Under different circumstances, she'd label him a hunk. If she'd met him at the grocery store or the post office, she'd probably check for a wedding ring. And if she was being completely honest, she'd admit she'd already done the labeling and checking several times.

She mentally chided herself when her gaze once again dipped to his left hand. His ringless left hand. Damn it! This was not some friendly guy seated next to her at a Back to School Night. This man was the enemy.

She pushed her glass forward and waited as Dylan unstoppered the alcohol and poured her a drink, then used a finger to push it back across the wooden table to her. Despite wanting to down the entire glass in one gulp, she forced herself to sip elegantly, letting the firewater drift down the back of her throat, wishing she could be sharing the drink with Josiah. Tears filled her eyes and she tipped her head upward. She cried easily, always had, but she didn't want He-Man to see her tears. Not after he'd watched her sob, naked, on the floor of her shower. Granted, the glass of the shower surround had been so fogged Dylan hadn't actually seen her naked. But still…

Dylan cleared his throat. "I don't understand why you think it's so unbelievable your brother would run from the law. He's a convict."

"A convict who was falsely accused. A convict whose case is under appeal. A convict who will win that appeal and be fully acquitted."

Dylan shook his head slowly, his gaze piercing hers. "You can't possibly be that naive, Rachel."

"And you can't possibly claim to know me. Just because you did the whole gallant-knight thing today, riding in on a charger, coming to the rescue, doesn't make you the good guy. It doesn't make you right."

The corner of his mouth tipped upward in a crooked smile. "So I was a gallant knight, then?"

Funny how that curl relieved some of the tension of the day. The man probably made women melt and teenage girls swoon. But Rachel was far from a teenager, and she wasn't in a melting or swooning mood. She wasn't sure if she wanted to rip Dylan's head off for being against her brother or spend the night crying into her pillow over Josiah's death.

She let out a deep sigh, allowing the alcohol to blur her emotions, smooth the jagged edges. But then a thought suddenly occurred to her, and the jagged emotions were back with a vengeance.

"Josiah," she breathed. "You implied he might have been murdered. You can't possibly think…"

But he did. She could see it in his eyes.

"Josiah fell," she said baldly.

"Maybe," Dylan said. "Maybe not."

She stood abruptly. "I think you've said all you

needed to say. My brother's escaped, and he might be on his way here. The U.S. marshals have my place staked out. Now I need to find my son and go about our evening chores. Tomorrow's a big day—I have a funeral to start planning, and I need to figure out how to hire a ranch hand I can't afford. So I think it's time I thank you for your help with our crisis today." She gestured to the front door.

The man remained seated.

"Seriously, did you not get what I said? I'd like you to leave now."

He nodded. "I heard you. And yes, I understood the subtext without the need for added direction. But I'm not leaving. Not until you understand what kind of threat your brother truly represents. Not until you understand that you and your son may be in mortal danger from Jackson Kincaid."

Dylan figured no one wanted to hear someone they loved could hurt them, but he'd seen too many instances of domestic violence not to know that sometimes the ones you loved the deepest were the ones who could cause the most harm. He also figured Rachel Kincaid had heard and experienced all she should have to in one day. Unfortunately he couldn't give her the reprieve he wanted to.

He had a duty to the citizens of the United States to keep them safe.

Justice. Integrity. Service.

The motto of the U.S. marshals wasn't simply words on letterhead. Those words meant something to him. If he did his job, fugitives were brought to justice. He did his job with integrity, respecting the rights of all concerned, be it family, victim or the fugitive himself. And he did it all for personal satisfaction, yes, but mostly to be of service—to his country and to its inhabitants.

Right now being of service meant convincing Rachel Kincaid her brother could harm her.

He wished he didn't have to. The woman had gotten under his skin in just a few hours. If he were a lesser man, he'd say his connection to her was simply physical. The woman was a looker, no doubt. And although those glass walls in her shower had been steamed up pretty well, he'd seen the swell of her breasts, the roundness of her naked hip, when he went to check on her.

But he knew there was more to his feelings for Rachel than physical attraction. He admired her. She certainly put up with a lot from her son. Before that... According to the files he'd read, she'd taken over running the ranch when her parents died, and had raised her younger brother, Jackson. He'd been ten and she'd just turned eighteen. She'd quit college and moved back to the ranch. Six months later she'd married a local boy— Phillip Wright—who'd killed himself a few years later in a drunk driving incident, leaving Rachel a widow with a three-year-old son to raise even as her teenage brother got himself into more and more trouble. She'd been struggling to do the right thing for all of them ever since.

"I know you raised him, Rachel. That you were little more than a child yourself when your parents died. You had your hands full with him, didn't you?" he asked.

She shot him a hard look. "Jax was like any other teenager. He got screwed by life and screwed things up in response."

"Detention throughout high school. He didn't even

graduate—had to take his GED. Then two DUIs and a few minor drug busts followed. All that I could see blaming on losing his parents so young. Typical messed-up kid stuff."

"So?" Rachel snapped at him.

He paused before going on. "Then a B-and-E that he got a light sentence on because he was a juvie. Then another B-and-E. Again, maybe you could blame the loss of your parents on him acting out. Being stupid. But then there was the bust for possession of marijuana for sale. His first potential felony. He got off on that one on a technicality. Still sounding like a screwed-up kid to you?"

Rachel sagged back down in her chair and let her hands fall into her lap. She stared at the floor. He followed her gaze to the cracked checkerboard floor tile that had her transfixed. At least she was listening. Not running. Not fighting.

He sucked in a deep breath. Time to wake up Rachel Kincaid. "But what convinces me he isn't some stupid screwed-up kid anymore was the drug deal gone south. Your brother took a job delivering heroin to a drug dealer in Los Angeles. When the DEA showed up to raid the place— Well, you know what happened." He let his words hang in the air.

"Jax never had a chance to fix the tile," Rachel said, dully, still staring at the floor. "That week Peter had the flu. We needed money desperately—I couldn't even afford to take Peter to the doctor. I was exhausted, trying to tend to Peter and the livestock. Jax was trying to help. He was making me a sandwich when he dropped the mayo jar and shattered that tile there." She nodded to the broken tile. "Three days later he was arrested.

Poor Jax. He hadn't even turned twenty before he was taken from me and now he's barely twenty-one. He's spent the past year in prison. He's been without his friends. His family…"

"Rachel," he said softly, "Jax isn't a victim. He admitted he knew what he was doing. He confessed. His first appeal was rejected for that very reason."

She raised her gaze to meet his, her eyes nearly as dull as Josiah's earlier in the day. "He was harassed into giving that confession. Scared."

They stared at each other until Dylan sighed. The day had settled into evening. His teammate Eric Haynes had the night shift and would probably already be in position to spy on the ranch. No sense in staying any later. He didn't want to ride Ginger back to Aaron's ranch in the dark.

Besides, if Rachel was naive enough to believe her brother wasn't the drug-dealing scumbag he knew the kid to be, he knew nothing he could say right now would change her mind. Hell, his own mother had been handed irrefutable proof that his brother was bad to the core, time and time again, and she'd never accepted it, even up to the day she died.

"I can see you've got your mind made up about Jax. But sooner or later, Rachel, you're going to have to face the truth." Dylan stood and headed toward the door.

"Where are you going?" she asked, her voice catching in her throat.

Hand on the door handle, he stopped. "The Sleep-E-Z Motorcoach Lodge."

"So the U.S. Marshals will be leaving me alone now?"

"Nope. The sheriff's deputies swept your property— it's clear. They're gone, but my teammate Eric is already in place. He'll keep watch until I show back up in the morning."

"Jax is a good kid," she stated. "He's innocent. And if he did escape, and I'm not saying he did, he must have had a good reason, if only that he was scared."

At that, he turned and caught her gaze with his. "A good reason? He—" He bit off his words. He was pretty certain that Rachel would collapse under the weight of any more bad news. He'd be back to tell her the rest of the story. Until then, maybe some rest would enable her to see reason come morning. So Dylan contented himself with saying, "Good night, Ms. Kincaid." He stepped outside into the humid Texas evening air, frustration crawling around inside his skin. As he slammed the door behind him, he heard a crash and the breaking of glass.

Then he heard her crying.

Again.

He stood there a long time before he found the will to walk away.

Chapter 5

After Dylan Rooney left, Rachel threw herself a very brief pity party and then went looking for her son. Just in case he'd snuck back inside without her knowing it, she combed the inside of the house first. When that proved fruitless, she headed outside and to his favorite tree. Down at the creek, even with dusk not yet set and cool light still diffusing the air, Rachel could tell the cottonwood's branches hung empty. No Peter.

She called Peter's name, but only the trickle of the creek and the rise and swell of the cricket and frog chorus rose around her. A nearby bullfrog stopped its low bellow, but no boy's voice responded. She doubted Peter was in the barn—the grass hay gave him allergies— but she'd try there.

She'd crumbled when she saw Josiah's dead body.

Peter had to be freaking out. He liked to be alone when he got upset, but still, this was going on too long.

Fifteen minutes later, with all the light from the fading dusk gone, she headed back to the house. Peter hadn't been in the barn, either. Nor in the toolshed, or in the woodshed or in any of the corrals.

Upstairs, she paused in front of his closed bedroom door. She'd deliberately left it open before she headed outside to look for him. Relief swamped through her even as she braced herself and knocked on the door. "Peter?" No answer. She knocked again. "Peter, honey, I know you're upset, but we need to talk. Peter?" When there was still no answer, she opened the door.

She let out a cry of dismay upon seeing it was still empty. Immediately she saw the piece of paper propped on Peter's pillow. There, in Peter's dismal scrawl, was a note addressed to her.

Mom. I wasn't paying attention to where I was shooting the BB gun. I think I killed Josiah. I don't deserve to live here and decided to be a railroad bum. I have a hat and extra socks and I took five dollars from the cookie jar. I'll pay you back some day. Your son, Peter Kincaid.

An empty ache filled her heart as she realized what Peter must have felt, thinking he'd shot Josiah. She'd seen the wound on Josiah's head. No BB could have done that kind of damage. It had never dawned on her that Peter could have assumed he'd killed a man.

"Oh, God, Peter," she murmured, staring at the note she now held in her hand. She'd thought she was doing the right thing by leaving her son alone to work through his pain, when she really should have been seeking him out, making sure he was okay. Instead, she'd spent time wallowing in her own grief and arguing with a U.S. Marshal over her brother.

What kind of mother was she?

And where the hell was the rulebook on how to be a parent? Why didn't kids come with a user's guide?

Within minutes she called the sheriff's department and reported Peter missing. The call didn't go well. Sheriff Ryan expressed frustration over how many times Peter had run off in the past few years and how many times he'd been caught trespassing. Disturbed by the edge of warning in the lawman's voice, Rachel listened with growing trepidation and worry for her son, then called her best friend, Julia. Her brother—and now maybe even her son—needed a lawyer.

Rachel needed more than that.

She needed a friend. A break. A hint of hope that her life was finally going to take an upward swing.

But given everything that had happened today, given everything that U.S. Marshal Dylan Rooney had told her, she couldn't imagine her life going anywhere but completely downhill.

Hours later, morning brought bright Texas sunlight streaming through Rachel's kitchen window, but there was still no sign of Peter. She'd searched the surrounding area of the ranch until it got dark, and then she'd paced and worried and paced some more, praying for her son to come home. He'd run off before, but never for this long. The sheriff had called just over an hour ago, indicating his men had searched her property and the adjacent land—no signs of Peter.

Peter knew how to take care of himself, but Rachel's

mom Spidey senses had the creepy crawlies making their way up her spine. Even if Josiah hadn't been murdered, Texas hosted a number of bad things that went bump in the night. Rattlesnakes, cougars, scorpions and brown recluse spiders. And the occasional bad guy. Scary stuff she didn't want to think about. Not with her son out there, alone and thinking he'd killed a man.

Rachel busied herself making two foaming lattes. One for her, and one for Julia. Thank God for Julia, who'd shown up fifteen minutes after Rachel called her, then taken over with lawyerly efficiency, querying Rachel about U.S. Marshal Dylan Rooney's presence and why Peter had run off. Then she'd shoved Rachel in the direction of her bedroom and promised to bed the alpacas down. Of course, Rachel hadn't slept a wink, but she didn't tell Julia that.

"Thanks again for spending the night," Rachel said, handing over Julia's latte. There wasn't anything she could do to find Peter, and until she heard otherwise, she had to assume he was okay. She needed, however, to distract her mind from her worry, and working on Jax's case would help. "Did you find anything out?" She nodded to the open laptop on the kitchen table.

"Some," her friend said, blowing on the foam of her drink. "According to the internet, this guy Dylan Rooney is who he says he is. U.S. Marshal. Part of a special ops team."

"What makes him so special?" Rachel asked. Besides his wide shoulders, long legs and tendency to rescue kids and widows in need. She gave herself a mental smack. This marshal might be sexy as sin, but he was still after her brother. That meant he might have rescued them, but not because he'd wanted to keep them safe. He'd done it because he wanted something else. He wanted her brother, and she and Peter were just means to an end.

"His team usually goes after the really bad guys. International drug cartel kind of people. I'm surprised they're interested in Jax. Yeah, the bust was big and two people were injured, but it's not like Jax held the smoking gun or anything."

"Have you found out anything about an escape?"

Julia grimaced. "I'm sorry, Rachel. I wish I had different news. But according to prison officials, Jax managed to escape during transport and the only reason they told me that is that I'm on record as his lawyer. He really got himself into a world of trouble with this escapade. Legally, he's screwed himself, big-time."

Rachel groaned and slumped against the refrigerator, letting the metal cool her skin. How was it she'd failed her brother so badly after their parents died? "How bad is it for his appeal that Jax took off?"

"Bad. Completely, totally, I-really–hope-there's-been-some-kind–of-mistake bad."

"There's no mistake," a male voice boomed out. "Jackson Kincaid is bad news. And if you want to keep yourselves and Peter safe, you need to accept that right now."

Dylan knew he shouldn't be staring, but wow—Rachel Kincaid had excellent legs. Dressed in purple cotton sleep shorts and a white ribbed tank, barefoot yet again, and even with her hair in a wild and disheveled ponytail, she looked delicious. His gaze traveled up her legs to meet hers.

She looked delicious and pissed.

And she wasn't moving from where she leaned against her refrigerator, giving him the glare of death. Only her body had tensed, tightened. As if she were expecting a fight.

"Planning on letting me in, or doesn't Southern hospitality extend this far west?" he asked, grabbing the handle of the latched screen door and giving it a rattle.

"Southern hospitality is reserved for gentlemen. And since you're staring like a largemouth bass at a lady in her pj's, you're obviously no gentleman," Rachel snapped out.

She'd shown some backbone yesterday, too, although the ordeal with the dead ranch hand had about done her in. Tough exterior, soft heart, he thought, remembering how devastated she'd been, crying for her friend in the shower. And how heart-wrenching her sobs had sounded as he'd stood outside her door, wanting nothing more than to stride back inside, gather her in his arms, and comfort her.

"Seriously, though, we need to talk about your brother. I'm happy to wait outside while you dress." *There. Gentlemanly behavior, right?*

Ignoring him, Rachel headed up the stairs. The woman Dylan hadn't been able to see popped around the corner and unlatched the screen door and held it open.

"I'm Julia Rickel," she said. "I know why you're here. I'm Rachel and Jax's attorney. And Rachel's best friend."

"U.S. Marshal Dylan Rooney. Rachel's...well..." Rachel's what? Yesterday, she'd sarcastically referred to his knight-in–shining-armor routine. And that was before he'd told her that her brother was out to get her. Before she'd flipped on him and thrown a bottle of booze at what most likely was his head. "Rachel's nemesis."

Julia flashed him a quick grin, then stuck her hand out. He shook it, noting the lawyer's strong grip. She looked to be about ten years older than Rachel. Nice looking, with short brown hair and a trim figure, and with very much a lawyer-type attitude, he realized as she checked him out just as thoroughly.

"Mind if I grill you while you wait for Rachel?" she asked, pulling her hand away and then motioning for him to sit at the rough-hewn kitchen table.

No polite chitchat for this woman. But if she was truly Jackson's lawyer, he probably couldn't say much in front of her. "Grill away," he said, anyway.

"What on God's green earth made you stake out the Kincaid place on horseback? And on Ginger, of all horses?" she asked.

He shrugged. "We didn't want to call attention to ourselves. Aaron Jacobson had a notice in the paper that he rented out horses, so the team's operations officer rented one for me, saying I was a bird-watcher."

"Lame," Julia said, then focused her attention on her laptop.

"Completely lame," Rachel agreed, walking back into the room, this time wearing shorts that covered just an inch or two more than the other ones had, and a bra under her tank.

"Agreed," he said, bringing his gaze from her rounded breasts up to her face. "I would have gone for a hiker so I could have stayed on foot. But at least Ginger got me down the ridge and to your place when Peter started hollering. My partner, Eric, told me some sheriff's deputies came back to search for Peter. They told him he has a habit of running off. He's not back yet?"

Rachel's eyes welled up with tears and her muscles seemed to lose their strength, contradicting her earlier rigidity. "No."

She turned and crossed the kitchen, then opened the refrigerator door, as if looking for ingredients. But he could see her swipe at her eyes. Once again, the woman was crying.

"Look, if he runs off a lot, then—"

"He doesn't run off 'a lot,'" she snapped out, slamming the refrigerator door shut and glaring at him, but tears still glistened in her eyes. "But in addition to being a kid and needing some space sometimes, he's got ADHD. We've been working on different coping skills and it helps being able to run. To move. He knows this land. He always finds his way back safely, but..."

"But he's grieving," he said quietly.

"More than that. He came back when I didn't know it, but only to grab some things and write me a note. He thinks he killed Josiah with his BB gun."

Holy hell. Dylan shifted on the bench seat. The kid thought he'd killed someone with a BB gun? Those things could maybe take out an eye, but not a human. "The M.E. called late last night. Cause of death was a cerebral hemorrhage. Although we don't yet know if he fell or was hit in the head, I can assure you, your kid and his BB gun had nothing to do with Josiah's death."

"I never thought Peter shot Josiah," she snapped out. "He fell. He hit his head. End of story."

"It's just the beginning actually. He could have been murdered. The coroner's running more tests. If Jackson is here, there should be—"

"Jax," Rachel ground out, her face going red. "His name is Jax. No one calls him Jackson. And you're not going to find any evidence that he's here or that he killed Josiah. How many times do I need to tell you he's innocent?" Her words revved up, adrenaline ramping up the speed. "Get it through your thick head—even if my brother escaped, he did it because he was scared. Jax is not a killer."

He waited, allowing her time to calm down, to get her emotions back in check. Quickly, he shot a glance at Julia. Jackson—Jax's—lawyer. Like him, she sat on the bench seat, only she'd pulled her knees up to her chin. Her fingers had stopped their dancing across the keyboard and instead she stared at the screen as though riveted. Interesting. Had the lawyer found out the real reason Dylan was there? Did she now know what he knew?

What Rachel obviously didn't know?

If she did, that meant the information had finally leaked to the press.

"I raised him," Rachel said, breaking the silence, pulling his attention back to her. "Whatever decisions Jax made, I led him there. I know he's not perfect. But if he's made mistakes, it's partially my fault."

Dylan snorted. Barely stopped himself from cursing and snapping at her. She was acting just like his mother. Making excuses for someone else's bad behavior. Blaming herself. "Listen to me—"

On the other side of the table from him, Julia snapped her laptop shut and rose to her feet. "Rachel," she said, sliding the laptop under her arm and coming around to face her friend. "How long will you keep taking the blame for what Jax did? And are you really going to take the blame for what he's done now?"

"So he ran away from jail. I know that's bad, but it's not like he's killed anyone."

"You have to tell her," Julia said.

Dylan caught the woman's full-on glare. Worry and not a small amount of anger shone in her eyes.

Justice. Integrity. Service. Those words meant something to him.

Neither Rachel nor Julia could see that. Rachel was worried about her son and brother. Julia was worried about her friend—with good reason. He wasn't here to hold the hand of a widow who refused to accept her brother was dangerous.

Even so, what he had to say was going to devastate Rachel. He had to tell her, if only to get her to take this situation seriously. To take him seriously.

He had no other choice.

Chapter 6

"Tell me." The deepness of Rachel's own tone sent a vibrato through her throat. What did the marshal know that he hadn't told her? What was her best friend keeping from her?

In front of her, Julia shifted from foot to foot, her laptop slung under one arm, the other arm crossed in front of her chest. As if she was on guard. From Rachel? Or from what they were about to tell her?

Dylan had risen to his feet, as well. Unlike with Julia, his arms were wide—hands fisted and placed on his hips. With his feet apart, he reminded her of some top-notch official in the military. Or a bully.

Neither spoke.

Rachel fought back a swearword. "I said tell me. Tell me what's happened to Jax."

Julia took a tentative step forward. "You know what?

Maybe I was wrong. You're dealing with too much, Rachel. Maybe you should focus on Peter right now. Let your concerns about Jax go for a bit. You've had a shock, with Josiah passing away and Peter running off. I'll handle Jax's situation."

Rachel turned on her. "I handle Jax. Me. You're his lawyer, not his mom."

"And you're not his mom, either," Julia pointed out. She'd used a soft tone, but the words pinpricked Rachel's heart. "Your son needs you. Be there for Peter. Let me and the marshal handle Jax."

Rachel fought for control. "How did you get my best friend to suddenly be on Team U.S. Marshals?" she snapped out at Dylan. "I know my son needs me. And I know my brother needs me. He's alone out there, scared."

"Who are you talking about, Rachel?" Dylan asked, his voice low. "Peter or Jax?"

She slumped. Both, she thought. How was she supposed to be a mother to two boys who needed her—one who was her biological son and still a kid, and the other whom she'd parented for the past eleven years and who could barely be considered an adult?

Tightening her spine, she stood straight, then stalked out of the kitchen and onto the wooden porch, letting the screen door slam behind her. The wind, light and gentle but stronger than a breeze, ruffled the tops of the grass in front of her. Peter needed to run the mower over the lawn. The alpacas needed feeding, the babies needed worming, the chickens and pheasants needed to be fed and watered and to have their cages cleaned. The horses needed to be turned out into the pasture. And it was just her. No ranch hand. No son. No brother.

Tears pricked her eyes. She ached to hold her son in her arms. To rock him and tell him Josiah's death was not his fault. But the days when she could rock her son were long over. He'd be home soon. He always came home—either willingly or yanked by the ear by one of the deputies. But he wouldn't want a hug. Would deny comfort, both for himself and for her.

And what of her brother? How could Rachel fix things for him this time?

The squeak of the screen door and the heavy thud of boots on the porch let her know Dylan had joined her. She remained standing, staring into the distance at the faraway creek, at the brush that rose on either side, and at Peter's favorite cottonwood.

"Julia's headed back to her office. She said she has some paperwork to file on your brother's behalf." Dylan stepped closer, his heat emanating off his chest and meeting her back. It made her feel as if a warm blanket of comfort and care had been placed on her.

Although he didn't touch her, her hair was up in a high ponytail and the hairs on her neck quivered. She shivered involuntarily as she imagined him touching her—massaging the back of her neck with his strong fingers, his warm palm pressed against her skin.

And her body responded.

Aching in long-forgotten places that emphasized how different they were. How strong and masculine he was. How perfect he was made to press against and inside her softer more feminine parts.

God, how she wanted to lean back and rest her weight on this man. The man who'd come riding to her son's rescue. The man who'd stood by her when she dealt with the death of her ranch hand and friend. The man who smelled of mint and melon.

The man who thought her brother was a scumbag drug dealer who'd kill an old man and endanger his family.

His very presence was a threat to her and those she loved.

She turned and shifted away from him, making him frown. The rough wood of the porch railing dug into her back. "Tell me," she said quietly. "Please."

His jaw clenched before he abruptly nodded. "I'm sorry, Rachel, but there's not much a lawyer can do for Jax now. I'm afraid it's bad. Jax didn't just run off, though believe me, that would be no small matter to deal with. During the escape, two U.S. marshals who'd been transferring him to another prison were shot."

"Oh, God…are they…" She couldn't bear to say the word.

"One's dead. The other's been in a coma and is in critical care."

She dropped her gaze to the faded wooden planks of the porch floor. The bones in her legs threatened to break into a thousand pieces and the shaking started. Surely he wasn't telling her that Jax—

He slid a finger under her chin and tipped her head up.

"Rachel, I need you to look at me. I need you to understand."

Unwilling, she met his deep, dark gaze.

Dylan continued, saying, "The reason we have such an intense operation targeting your brother is that he's dangerous. He's a killer. And we need your help to trap him."

* * *

Rachel jerked her head away from Dylan's touch and barreled into the kitchen, the loud crack of the screen door swinging shut behind her sounding like thunder. Dylan's entry through the door was notable but much softer.

"Rachel—"

She shook her head as she paced alongside the kitchen table, the floor cold against her bare feet. The sensation was in complete opposition to the heat running through her veins: the heat of anger, of fear and of…denial?

She'd raised Jax since he was ten. Held him in her arms when he'd woken up with nightmares about their parents' dead and empty eyes. Admonished him and yet felt a sense of pride when he stayed up all night with his favorite alpaca when she was about to give birth. Got annoyed with him over the countless frogs and baby birds he brought into the house to rescue.

And she'd been there when the troubles in school had started. Then the troubles with the law. It hadn't mattered.

Jax saved baby jackrabbits from coyotes. He didn't kill people. No way would she ever believe otherwise.

And no way in hell would she help the U.S. Marshals trap her brother.

A whinny came from the barn—a subtle reminder it was well past time to feed the livestock yet one strong enough to act as a lifeline. She grabbed on to it for all she was worth.

Trying to convince Dylan of her brother's innocence was a waste of time. She knew her brother; he didn't.

She turned, strode outside once more, then headed down the patio steps and toward the barn.

Once again, she heard Dylan following her. Heard him say, "Damn it, Rachel, stop."

When she didn't obey him, he gently took hold of her arm, halting her progress and turning her toward him.

With a vicious tug, she ripped her arm away. "Don't touch me," she shrilled.

He immediately put his hands up in a placating gesture. "Rachel, you have to listen to me—"

"No! I don't. Because you refuse to listen to me. No way is Jax a killer. And no way will I help you trap him. Please leave. I have animals to feed. After that, if he hasn't come back on his own already, I'll go looking for Peter."

He put his hands on his hips, his expression radiating impatience. "Have you considered that maybe if you help me, I can help you?"

"I don't want your help!"

"You sure about that? Because the U.S. Marshals have resources, Rachel. One call and I can get a chopper in the sky, looking for your son."

An incredulous bitter laugh tore out of her. "You're telling me you have the resources to find a kid, lost and alone somewhere out in the wilderness of Texas, and you're refusing to put those resources to use unless I help trap my brother? Isn't that called blackmail?" When the man refused to answer, she showed him her back and continued marching down the trail to the barn, aware of Dylan on her tail.

"That's not what I meant. Look—I was going to get the chopper in the sky whether you agreed to help us trap your brother or not. I'd already asked my team administrator to look into it before I got here, just in case Peter hadn't returned. She's likely got a pilot at the ready."

"Ready to move if I do what you want," she said with a sneer.

"No," he snapped. "I won't put your kid's life in jeopardy by playing games. I'm just pointing out that our relationship doesn't have to be contentious. You don't have to fight me because you think I want to hurt your brother. I don't. I just want him safely returned to custody."

She stopped and whirled, facing him with arms crossed over her chest. "So you…what? Think we can be friends and do each other some favors? You'll help me find Peter and you expect me to believe you won't expect something in return? Something like me handing over my brother?"

He stood only a few feet in front of her so that she could almost feel the fire burning in his eyes. She forced herself not to retreat.

"I know you'll never hand over your brother," he said. "All I want is your cooperation, Rachel. No, strike that. That's all I can ask for. Because anything else I want from you has nothing to do with your brother."

She sucked in a breath. Looked away. Refused to acknowledge the heat in his eyes that seemed to flare a thousand times brighter as he'd finished speaking. He wasn't admitting he was attracted to her. And even if he was, so what? Sexual attraction meant nothing; family did. "How, exactly, do you want me to cooperate?"

"Don't treat me like the enemy. Don't do anything to warn Jax away. Let me help. Him and you."

"By putting him back in prison for a crime he didn't commit!"

"He's going back to prison," he said quietly. "He was convicted for transporting drugs. The evidence suggests he shot those marshals, but he hasn't been convicted of those crimes yet. He still has a chance to tell his side of things. You want to help him? Do it the way you have been doing. By working inside the law. Anything else is going to end badly and you know it."

She did know it. Jax would never be safe, not labeled an escaped convict.

"You think he murdered Josiah."

"I can't ignore that as a possibility, but it's a slim one in my mind. And I do give great weight to the phrase 'innocent until proven guilty.'"

She stared at Dylan. Took several deep breaths. Took a couple of steps back to put some distance between them physically even if she couldn't run and hide from what he was saying.

"So don't warn him away. That's all you want from me?"

"Not quite. Let me stay here, on the ranch. Pretending to be a ranch hand. That way if Jackson—Jax—shows up, he won't be suspicious. He'll think I'm hired help. We can take him in easily—no ugliness."

A ranch hand. Dylan was proposing to pretend to be her ranch hand. Right. As if a city slicker like him—a man who didn't even know how to ride Western, for God's sake, could be an actual ranch hand. She snorted.

She didn't need his help. Peter was fine. He'd be home soon and then she'd lock them both inside the house. Away from this man and his ugly accusations. First, however, she needed to get her chores done.

"My answer is no."

Using all her strength, she strode to the barn and raised the iron bar that held the doors open. When sunlight streamed into the darkened barn, the livestock grew agitated. Usually Josiah had fed, watered and turned them out by now.

"Hungry babies," she murmured, then grabbed a pitchfork. First went oat hay to the quarter horses, Anchor and Row. Next she distributed pellets down the alpacas' trough, taking time to ruffle soft necks or murmur to the babies—the crias. All the while she was aware of Dylan following her.

"How much longer will you be?" he finally asked.

She refused to turn around. "I work until sundown. And now that I'm missing two helpers, I'll be working even longer."

Behind her, she heard rummaging and the clanging of metal against metal. She craned her neck to look around a stack of hay bales to see Dylan, feed bucket in each hand.

"Tell me what to do."

"I told you. I'm not betraying my brother by letting you stay here."

"I heard you. I want to help, anyway, okay?"

She stared at him suspiciously. "Sure you do. Do you think Jax is hiding underneath some hay?"

"I think you need to get that I'm just doing my job, Rachel. If you don't willingly allow me to stay here, I'll go right back to sitting on the ridge on Ginger, binoculars trained on every move you make, my teammates at the ready to take your brother down by force if he shows up. Before I do that, why not let me help?"

Help. Hanging around ready to nab Jax wasn't exactly what she'd consider help. But if she didn't agree, Dylan and his team would still spy on her. How much of her privacy could she afford to give up? She'd need to call Julia—find out what her legal rights were. Julia's specialty was appellate law, but she'd probably be able to advise Rachel on the legalities of the U.S. Marshals spying on her property. On her every move. Every move her son made.

Peter.

"Weren't you going to call a chopper?" she asked. "I mean, I know Peter's fine. But the sooner he's back, the better I'll feel."

Dylan set the buckets down, then reached into his back pocket and pulled out a phone. Swiftly, he arranged for a chopper to sweep the immediate area around Rachel's ranch.

When he disconnected the call, he stood silent. Waiting.

Rachel cleared her throat. Forced out, "Thank you. I appreciate you doing that."

"I want your son found, too, Rachel. I'm not here to harm either of you. I wish you'd believe me."

But he is here to harm me. How could he think otherwise given what he was accusing Jax of? Her head suddenly started pounding and all she wanted in the world was to lie down, cover her head with something until the world dimmed to nothing and sleep.

That, of course, wouldn't accomplish anything. Not for Peter. Not for Jax.

And not for her.

She could deny and hide all she wanted.

Dylan Rooney wasn't going away any time soon.

She swallowed, then said, "I do believe you. It

doesn't change much between us, but I do believe you want to keep Peter and me safe."

"And your brother, too. I want to bring him into custody but I want to do it in a way that's best for everyone. Him included, Rachel. Like I said, the best chance I have of doing that is if he thinks I'm on the ranch helping you out."

"God, you don't give up."

"No, ma'am."

Rachel studied him. "He hasn't been here and he's not going to come here. He didn't kill Josiah."

"I hope that's the case. I really do. Even if it is, you can still use my help. Free of charge. What do you say?"

Rachel hesitated. Struggled with the knowledge that if she didn't give in to Dylan's request, he'd still keep an eye out for Jax. Maybe the best thing she could do was keep Dylan close and do her best to convince him of Jax's innocence.

"Fine," she said. "The alpacas get a full bucket of pellets, sprinkled all the way down the feed trough. There's a hose on the other side of the barn, outside. Empty the water bucket, scrub it out and fill it with fresh water. Then join me back in the house. I'll…I'll think about letting you stay on the ranch and give you my answer then."

"Yes, ma'am." For a brief second, she thought she saw a smile quirk his mouth sideways.

What stunned her most was how, despite everything, she felt that smile in her bones. It made her want to smile back. And worst of all, it made her want to feel the press of his lips against hers.

Chapter 7

Rachel left Dylan to feed the remaining livestock and headed back to the house. She was supposed to be inside, at her computer, paying bills and tallying receipts for the alpaca wool she'd sold over the internet, but instead she responded to the hard tug in her gut and brought her laptop out to the porch, where she settled onto the porch swing.

There, she could see the driveway, the creek and the ridgeline. Keep her eye out for her son. And her brother.

But out in the fresh air, surrounded by the hum of bees and the bubbling rush of the creek, warm sunlight slanting through the chinks in the porch roof, made focusing on bookkeeping near impossible.

Not that she'd have been able to concentrate even if she were inside. Despite truly believing that Peter was fine, she needed her son. Needed to see him, to feel him, to smell the top of his head the way she used to when he was little. Once Peter was back, she'd be able to focus on helping Jax. And how she was going to deal with the U.S. Marshal currently working in her barn.

Briefly, she closed her eyes. Dylan said he'd intended to call a chopper to find Peter whether Rachel helped him catch her brother or not. As much as she wanted to believe he was a heartless monster bent on destroying her life on a whim, she knew that wasn't true. He was here to do a job. He worked hard to protect the public from criminals. He wanted to keep her and Peter safe.

Her instincts told her he was a good man.

He was just mistaken about Jax.

Once again, she told herself that letting him act as her ranch hand would mean she could keep her eye on him and have more time to convince him of Jax's innocence.

Unfortunately she'd also have more time to feel the tingles he inspired whenever he was around. Even as mad as she'd been, when he gripped her arm to stop her from walking away from him, she'd felt his touch in places that hadn't been touched since her husband had died. And even now she could remember the lure of his smile. She could envision them kissing.

Touching.

Caressing.

Exploring and tasting and surrendering to a passion that had nothing to do with anything or anyone but the two of them, naked and hungry.

Those blasted tingles shot through her. Her breath caught in her throat. *It's been too long,* her body cried. *I want him.*

Rachel's eyes jerked open and she let out a cry of

dismay. *Stop!* she told herself. *That will never happen. Never. Never ever.*

She was whispering those two words when she heard the rotor of a helicopter whistling its way up and down the valley and across the ridge.

"You said he's found his way home before."

She jumped at Dylan's voice. He must have snuck up on her while she was daydreaming about them. Although he had no way of knowing her private thoughts, she blushed, anyway, something he apparently noticed given the way his eyes narrowed on her face. What had he said? Oh, right. Peter. "He's been taking off ever since he could walk. At first he'd be gone for about ten, fifteen minutes. Then he started staying away hours. There's not a lot I can do to keep him here. And trust me, I've tried. When he was really little, I built that corral over there—" she pointed at the corral almost abutting the house "—just so he could play without me tethering him to my own body."

Dylan gave the corral a curious look. "And that lasted how long—until he learned how to climb?"

A burst of laughter escaped her. She clapped a hand over her mouth, aghast.

"Don't feel bad for experiencing human emotions, Rachel. You're in grief over your friend, in turmoil over your brother and now you're worried about Peter. You've got a lot to stress you out. But find release where you can."

"Easy for you to say," she responded.

He shrugged. "Maybe. But your brother has a lawyer, which is good, and my team takes pride in bringing fugitives back alive. He's not in any danger from us. And as far as your son goes, if he's run off as often as you say, you're right—he's probably doing fine."

She knew Dylan was right. Peter knew the dangers of the Texas wilderness better than any kid around. Precisely because he'd gone on so many of his walkabouts when he was little, she'd seen to it he knew how to take care of himself in the great outdoors. But she still worried. And hated that she couldn't control Peter's every move.

"When I first got the diagnosis that Peter was ADHD, I was scared. But mostly I was relieved. The more research I did, the more I realized I could help Peter. Be more understanding. In many ways we've gotten closer. But being here on the ranch with me all summer…he's pulling away again. Testing me. I think it's because he misses Jax."

"Does he know—"

Rachel shook her head. "I told him Jax got offered a job too good to pass up. A job doing something he's always loved." Rachel smiled slightly. "Writing songs for an up-and-coming country star who's planning his debut. Until then, he's keeping his identity a secret. The country star, I mean."

Dylan's eyebrows shot up. "Your brother writes songs?"

Rachel nodded. "Jax plays the guitar. Loves it. Loves composing."

"Is he good?"

She shrugged. "I think so. But then I'm biased, right? Unable to be impartial."

At her slightly bitter tone, Dylan sighed. Shifted. "No one's ever slipped up and said anything to Peter about the real reason Jax is gone? No one from school?"

"Not that I know of. Peter's never said anything to me about it, anyway."

"Right. So when he comes back and finds me here..."

She closed her eyes for a moment, then did what her instincts were telling her to do. "I'll let you stay on as a ranch hand. But I'm only doing it so I can keep an eye on you."

"I understand."

"I'll tell Peter I needed help. You offered it. I don't want him knowing why you're really here or you can leave right now." Her chin tilted up defiantly. "You're not going to use my son to—"

"It's okay, Rachel. I agree with you. We won't say anything to Peter. Not unless there's a reason to. And if that turns out to be the case, I'll talk to you first. I promise. Okay?"

She hesitated. Nodded. "Okay."

"Did Josiah have a trailer somewhere?"

"He has...had...a room in the house. The ranch doesn't have separate quarters for employees." She frowned as she realized for the first time that if she agreed to let him act as her ranch hand, it would only make sense for him to take Josiah's old room. That was a little too close for her. Josiah had practically been family. This man was...not.

"I won't be trouble, Rachel," he said. "I'll give you your privacy. But..."

"What?"

"Will Peter wonder if there's another reason I'm staying?"

"What do you mean?"

"Will he wonder if we're dating? Lovers?"

Her mouth went dry and she jerkily shook her head. "No. He won't wonder."

"Why's that?"

"Because he knows I'm not interested in dating. Jax and Peter and this ranch are my life and Peter knows it. Now I really need to get back to what I was working on."

"No problem," Dylan said. "I'll be as quiet and unassuming as a mouse."

She snorted.

He smiled slightly, then settled his large frame into an Adirondack chair next to the swing. After a few minutes of silence, she relaxed and pretended to work on her laptop.

They sat that way for twenty minutes before a billow of dust down the drive caught her attention. She stood, shading her eyes against the late morning sun. A sheriff's car. Good news, or bad?

The car came to a stop in the drive and she recognized the grizzled head and lanky frame that emerged from the vehicle. It was Sheriff Ryan, hat in hand. He slammed the driver's door behind him and walked toward the house. Alone.

Disappointment weighed heavily on her chest. So he hadn't found Peter.

At the edge of the porch, the sheriff paused, and looked at her then. Gray wrinkles stood out against his tan skin. He caught her gaze, then shook his head.

"Oh, God, no," she uttered, even as her knees buckled.

Two strong arms caught her around her waist.

Knights in shining armor didn't usually get an elbow to their solar plexus. Dylan let go of Rachel, who had used a backward jab to let him know she didn't need his help.

But she was wrong. He could help.

He would help.

He just didn't know how. Not yet.

Before them, the sheriff waved his hat at Rachel.

"Peter's fine. I'm sorry if my expression said otherwise. I'm just unhappy these little escapades of Peter's are costing the taxpayers money."

Dylan cursed softly. He knew what Rachel had thought when she'd seen the sheriff's doom-and-gloom expression. Hell, Dylan had thought the same thing. The sheriff should know better and as he assessed the man, Dylan began to understand that he did. He'd wanted to scare Rachel.

Instinctively, he stepped to her side and put his arm around her shoulders. The sheriff's eyes widened slightly, but as Dylan stared back at him, he knew the other man had caught his silent message. Do not mess with this woman or you will be sorry.

Next to him, Rachel glanced at him in confusion before pulling away. "You found him, though? He's coming home?"

Another shimmer of light moved toward the ranch along the road, dust forming billows behind. The sheriff waved his hat in the direction. "Deputy Loren is bringing him home right now. That chopper you got up in the air—" he nodded at Dylan "—scoped him out down on the tracks, about seven miles away. We got him, but that damn whirlybird probably spooked all the livestock in a ten-mile radius."

And if Jax had made it from Los Angeles to Texas, and was hanging out in the nearby woods, waiting for his chance to come onto the property undetected, he could have been spooked, too, and Dylan and his team might have lost a chance to pin him down. Dylan could only hope that wasn't the case. But at least the kid was safe.

A sheriff's patrol car came to a halt in front of them. Within moments, Deputy Hank Loren let Peter out of the backseat, then handed the kid a backpack and gave him a pat on the back, pushing him toward his mom.

Sullen, the kid walked up the steps of the porch, gaze glued to the ground, averted from his mother, then brushed past Dylan.

No way, no how was this kid getting off that easy. Not after Dylan had called in a chopper to rescue his ass. Not after the kid's mother had spent the past eighteen hours worried sick. Dylan reached out, gently took hold of Peter's skinny arm and turned him around.

"Listen, kid," he said, tightening his grip when the kid made to pull away. "I think you owe me and the sheriff's department a thank-you, and you definitely owe your mom an apology. She's been worried sick." He flashed a glance at Rachel, who stood stiff, arms curled in around her chest. Not as if she was frightened—as if she was protecting her heart.

"I didn't ask anyone to find me," Peter snapped at him. "I was fine. Caught myself a trout for dinner and ate berries for breakfast. Used iodine in the water to purify it. And I was about to hop a freight train to someplace west."

Kids Peter's age thought they were invincible, but of course, Dylan knew better. He also knew how they could blame themselves for things that weren't their fault. Emotional pain radiated through him before he found control and shoved it back. "In case anyone hasn't told you yet, you didn't kill Josiah. He died from a head wound, not from being shot by a BB gun. His blood isn't on your hands."

The kid's shoulders dropped and his eyes went from bright and snapping to round and glistening. Dylan's heart expanded. The kid had really thought he'd killed a man. Poor thing. That wasn't a weight Dylan would wish on anyone's shoulders.

"But you still owe your mother an apology, and apparently there are a ton of chores to do."

"Sorry, Sheriff. Sorry, Mom." Peter made to move off, but Dylan squeezed his arm tighter.

"Not good enough. A man looks someone in the eye when he apologizes. A man doesn't use a snotty tone. A man accepts his responsibly and carries the burden of blame on his own shoulders."

"I'm ten," the kid threw out. He didn't look at his mother or the sheriff, but at least stared Dylan square in the eye.

"The way I look at it," Dylan said quietly, "you're either young enough for a spanking or old enough to accept responsibility on your own. Which is it to be?" Personally, Dylan didn't believe in spanking, but he wouldn't tell that to the kid.

Rachel cleared her throat and Dylan flashed a glance at her. She stared at him, mouth firm, eyes narrowed. She was obviously pissed at him for interfering with her son, but that was too bad. As he'd thought earlier, he was going to help her whether she liked it or not. He looked back at the kid, who held his gaze for a moment, fight building in his eyes, reminding Dylan of his mother.

Then something changed in his expression. Resignation setting in? Or acceptance? Dylan couldn't tell.

The kid squared his shoulders and faced the others. "I'm sorry I ran off. I'm sorry I made everyone worry. I'm to blame for making you all scared."

Good enough for Dylan. He dropped the kid's arm and turned to Rachel.

"I'm going back to the motel," he said softly, silently communicating that he was doing so to pack up his stuff and move into the house.

Rachel's house.

Where she lived with her son. Peter might not assume she and Dylan were sharing a bed, but an outsider, someone like the sheriff, might.

"Thank you for your help," she said quietly.

He nodded and left Rachel to deal with her kid.

He found himself not wanting to leave her at all, which confused him.

He admired Rachel. He wanted her. He couldn't have her.

The most he could have was her help tracking down her brother.

He knew it.

What he didn't know was why the hell it pissed him off so damn much.

An hour later, Dylan was packed up and had reported in to his team.

"The fugitive's nephew could be a problem," Marco Hernandez said. "He doesn't know you're a U.S. Marshal, right?"

"Nope. As far as the kid knows, I'm a stranger who raced a horse down from the hill to help when he started screaming. He has no clue I'm with law enforcement," Dylan said.

"I'd like to keep it that way," Marco said. "Could be if he gets wind you're out to capture his uncle, he might warn his uncle off."

Could be, Dylan mentally agreed. Could also be that if Jackson was as dangerous as he appeared, he could use the kid as a human shield. "I'm making progress, but I don't want to push things too far too fast. I'll talk to Jackson's sister. Tell her to send her son to stay with a relative for a while. At least until Jackson is brought in." It made sense. The fact that it would result in him and Rachel being the only two people in her house together was beside the point. He was attracted to her, but it wasn't as if he could do anything about it, even if she wanted him to. Which she didn't.

"Do that. And good job getting the woman to agree to let you work the ranch. Sitting around on a horse pretending to be a bird-watcher has got to be the most idiotic stakeout I've ever heard." With that, the team leader dropped off Skype, leaving Dylan still online with two members of his team.

"But I thought bird-watching sounded plausible," Stacy, the team administrator, said. "People do it all the time where I'm from."

Dylan snorted. Stacy Johnson was from Napa, only an hour out from where Dylan grew up in San Francisco. "Texas is not California, and I'm finding that out the hard way. I'll keep in touch, Stacy."

"Take care, Dylan," she said before she terminated their connection.

"So you'll be staying at the gorgeous widow's place round-the-clock." This came from Dylan's partner,

Eric, who was holed up in a hotel a few miles from Dylan's—something they'd arranged to avoid attention from small-town busybodies. Even with Dylan staying with Rachel, Eric would remain in town as backup and would continue to scope the ranch from afar. Right now, however, Eric wasn't thinking about the job. Even on the small screen of Dylan's iPad, Eric's smirk showed up bright and clear. "Sleeping under her roof. You always were a glutton for punishment, Rooney. And the luckiest son of a bitch I know."

"Bust my chops another time. The list of chores she has for me is a mile high. And a hell of a lot of those chores have to do with manure."

"Fair trade as far as I'm concerned," Eric said before signing off.

Definitely a fair trade, Dylan thought as he double-checked the room to make sure he hadn't forgotten anything. Having to do some heavy lifting on a ranch was child's play in terms of what he was willing to do to get the drop on Jackson Kincaid.

Of course, he knew that wasn't the kind of trade-off Eric had been talking about. He'd been referring to the fact that Dylan would get to spend more time with Rachel. A smart, beautiful woman who worked too hard and didn't get enough respect from her son or brother. A woman who, regardless of the fact that she'd agreed to let Dylan work her ranch, viewed him as the enemy. She'd been up-front about the real reason she'd agreed to let him help her—to keep an eye on him. Dylan was betting she'd also use their time together to try to convince him of her brother's innocence. Hell, maybe she thought she could work out some kind of deal. Get him to go easy on her brother.

He wondered how far she'd be willing to go. If she'd be sweeter. Friendlier.

If she'd offer him her body.

But as soon as the thought crossed his mind, he dismissed it.

Rachel would never use her body to manipulate him or any man, even if it was to help her brother. He didn't know why he was so sure; he just did.

And while he knew he wasn't the type of man who'd ever go easy on a fugitive even if Rachel did offer him her sleek, tan body to do so, he knew turning her down would be one of the hardest things he'd ever have to do.

Chapter 8

After Peter returned home, Rachel ordered her son into the shower and spoke with a local minister on the phone about Josiah's funeral. She spent the next few hours with Peter, then mentally preparing herself for Dylan's return. By early afternoon, when he returned carrying a single duffel bag, she felt composed. That composure fled when he found her in the kitchen preparing dinner, leaned against the counter and asked if she had relatives Peter could stay with.

He wanted her to send Peter away? She'd just gotten him back.

"The fact is, Rachel," Dylan said, "there is a chance Peter is in danger. There is a chance you're in danger, too, although I doubt I could say anything to make you leave this ranch."

Plus, she thought, he needed her on the ranch to increase the chances Jax would show up. The same wasn't true for Peter.

"My son is not in danger from my brother."

"He's believed to have shot two U.S. Marshals in cold blood."

"You said you believed in being innocent until proven guilty."

"I do. But I also believe in working with the information we have, and right now the only information we have is your brother escaped. During that escape, two men were shot. The only natural conclusion is that your brother shot them."

"With what?"

"Excuse me?"

"What did he shoot them with? Were the marshals shot with their own weapons?"

"No."

"So where'd he get the gun to shoot them? He was a prisoner, for God's sake. He didn't have a weapon."

He folded his arms across his chest. "Prisoners sneak in contraband all the time, Rachel. Guns and drugs."

She frowned, knowing the point he was making by mentioning drugs. "Yes, my brother had started experimenting with drugs before he was arrested. Yes, he even confessed to transporting them. But he was deathly afraid of guns. He probably wouldn't know how to shoot one."

Dylan shook his head in mock amazement. "You just won't give up thinking your brother is innocent. He's the only one who escaped that day, Rachel. Who else do you think shot those marshals?"

"I don't know. But I know in my gut it wasn't Jax," she said quietly, just as she'd promised herself she would the next time she said it. Keep calm. Keep emotion out of it. The less hysterical she acted, the greater likelihood he might actually begin to listen to what she had to say.

"What's that?" Dylan put a strong hand on her arm and looked up the valley, his head cocked to the side. "Do you hear that?"

She listened but heard nothing.

Then she did. Under her feet, felt vibrations. It sounded like a...

Peter stuck his head inside the kitchen doorway. "Stampede!"

"Cattle?" Dylan asked.

Rachel nodded. "Peter," she said. "Stay in your room, okay?"

"But, Mom—"

"Do as I say, young man. Now," she snapped. "Or I promise I'm giving every single one of your video games to charity. I did it before. Do you really want me to do it again?"

With a glower, Peter obeyed her, running up the stairs and slamming his bedroom door shut. Praying he stayed inside the house, she ran outside and Dylan followed.

There had been a couple of times in the past few years when Aaron's herd escaped their pasture and headed to the streambed. From there, they'd take off down the natural pathway, which led through her property. After the last stampede, she had made sure the fence line had been thoroughly reinforced, which should have kept the cattle out even if they escaped from Aaron's property.

Now, however, the vibrations were heavy under her

feet and she could already hear the lowing and bellow-ing of cattle in distress.

Had something startled Aaron's cattle into a wild enough stampede that they'd taken down two solid fences? Were her alpacas in danger of being trampled?

She couldn't take the risk.

Breaking from Dylan's grip, she raced toward the grazing herd of alpacas, which stood between the barn and the creek bed. If the cattle hadn't been turned by the fence line, they would come straight through this area—and the alpacas wouldn't have a chance. Behind her, she could hear Dylan's heavy breathing. Although she ran at full speed, he passed her within seconds.

As he ran, he called out over his shoulder, "Go back! Keep yourself safe! I'll herd them into the corral, get them out of danger."

"You can't do it alone. You're faster than I am—you go around the far side and start herding them out toward me, and I'll cut them off and get them into the corral."

"Damn you, woman, do you have to control every-thing?" But Dylan didn't stop and kept running full out, waving his arms and yelling at the alpaca herd. One by one, they stopped their grazing to look at him, then communicated together with flashing ears.

"Run, babies," she whispered. They needed to move—now. Dylan put his fingers in his mouth and let out a piercing whistle. At that, the herd shifted, turned and as one, started to run toward the corral she'd once built for her son to play in. From behind, she could hear the herd of cattle growing closer, at a full run, but she refused to move, and instead stood locked in place, her arms out wide, creating a barrier the alpacas would un-derstand.

Smart creatures. She had to bank on their intelligence. They grew closer, still not turning to the corral, but she held firm. Then the herd shifted and streamed into the small fenced-in area, Dylan right behind them. He slammed the gate shut and barred it in place and then turned to look at her. His eyes went wide.

"Rachel, move!" he shouted.

Oh, God. The cattle.

She ran, but could she outrun the thundering herd? Almost at the corral, the swirl of dust from heavy hooves choked her.

"Here, grab my hand!" Dylan reached out and grabbed her, then in one swoop, hauled her up onto the top board of the corral right before fifty head of Texas longhorns crashed through her property.

The two minutes it took for the cattle to pass by seemed like two hours. She sat with Dylan on the wooden fence, waiting for the danger to pass. When the cattle trotted out of sight, Dylan swung himself down. He reached his hands up, an offer of help. A gesture of peace.

Still shaking, she let him help her down, his hands holding her rib cage firmly. But once her feet touched ground, she found she still needed his grip. Her bones seemed to have lost density.

"Rachel," Dylan murmured.

Their faces were so close she could see the small scar at the corner of his mouth. Could see how his nose angled a little to the right, as if he'd broken it more than once. Could feel his heartbeat thudding against her chest. His scent swept up around her, replacing the stench of cattle with the smell she'd come to recognize as being uniquely Dylan.

Again, he said her name. Soft. Quiet. And she didn't back off. Didn't move away. She moved closer instead, hungry for the sensation of a strong man against her. Needy for a man's touch.

His mouth crashed down on hers—his lips firm and warm and velvety. His tongue silken. His breath and her breath combined to make magic. She slid her hands up his back, grasping at his shoulders and pulling him in closer, starving for his touch. For his mouth. For his heat and strength.

And feeling desolate when he pulled away and stepped back, leaving her standing alone, shaking with the release of adrenaline, the rush of desire and the intensity of sexual arousal.

He pushed back a strand of her hair as he gazed into her eyes. "Rachel. Peter...Jax..."

His words instantly snapped her out of her desire-induced malaise. She took several shaky steps back. "Oh, God. I'm sorry. I can't believe..." She stared at the ground, tears of frustration welling in her eyes. "What you must think of me. The sex-starved widow. Ready to take on any man, including the one who thinks her brother is a murderer. You must be laughing yourself sick inside." She blinked furiously. Swiped at her eyes.

"Rachel, look at me."

She ignored him.

He stepped closer until she had no choice but to look up.

"I'm not laughing myself sick. Even if I wanted to laugh, I'd be too blown away by that kiss to do it. We have chemistry. That's been obvious from the start. The stampede got our adrenaline going, that's all. We'll forget that ever happened. Agreed?"

As easy as that? she thought. Maybe for him. For her, who hadn't wanted to kiss a man in seven years? She doubted she'd forget the feel of his lips and body against hers any time soon. But all she said was, "Agreed."

"Right. So…how'd those cattle get here?" he asked, his voice rough. He stared at a spot over her head.

"I don't know. The fence line is reinforced. At least, it was. They had to have broken through it." Which meant she had to repair the line. And she didn't have the money to do it. She'd have to keep her alpacas in the lower field until she could find another solution.

"Let's saddle up the horses. It's time we go for a ride."

"Where?" she asked numbly.

"Where those cattle came out. I want to look for a break in the fence line."

But she didn't. She didn't want to spend any more time with him. She wanted to hide under her covers in the dark. She wanted to figure out what the heck had just happened between her and U.S. Marshall Dylan Rooney. "Can't it wait until tomorrow?"

"No."

"Why not?"

Dylan's mouth set in a grim line. "I don't think it's a coincidence those cattle ran through your property. I think this was deliberate."

Chapter 9

What on God's green earth had possessed him to kiss Rachel Kincaid? Dylan adjusted his seat on the back of Anchor, one of Rachel's quarter horses, as they rode to the fence line to see how the cattle had broken through.

He knew the rules inside and out about fraternizing with fugitives. You did not make out with fugitives. And you did not make out with the sister of a fugitive. Yet fifteen minutes ago, Dylan had practically thrown her up against a corral and had his way with her mouth. He'd wanted to have his way with far more of her. Had almost given in to temptation.

But then he'd remembered her son was in the house. And the reason why Dylan was even on their ranch to begin with.

One of his fellow marshals was dead because of Rachel's brother and another was barely clinging to life.

He had to keep his mind focused on his mission. Bring in Jackson Kincaid, no matter what. Yeah, Rachel Kincaid's body, mind and heart triggered him in all the right ways, but now was not the time to indulge.

Ahead of him, Rachel had come to a stop and dismounted. He nudged Anchor up to her horse, the one she called Row, and did the same. Then he checked out the fencing.

Was his suspicion correct? Had the stampede been deliberate?

Clean, sharp nips ran down a straight line on two sections of her heavy-duty barbed wire fence. Wire sat rolled up, off to the side.

Deliberate, then.

No way could anyone think the stampede had been an accident.

He flashed a glance at Rachel. The wind picked up, whipping a strand of her white-blond hair into her eyes. She used the excuse of brushing her hair away as a way of wiping away the tears he saw glistening in her eyes.

She had a soft heart. She cried easily. When she was sad. Angry. Frustrated.

She was so tough, but also vulnerable.

Someone had tried to cause her harm. That same someone had probably killed Josiah. He wanted to beat the bastard to a pulp.

"Let's go check out Aaron's line," Rachel said. "After the last property line dispute, we both agreed to put an acre's length of land between our fence lines. His is due west." At his nod, she mounted Row, then squeezed him into a trot. Dylan followed on Anchor, and in a minute, they were an acre west, at Aaron Jacobson's fence line.

Again, the fencing had been deliberately cut. Both

Dylan and Rachel dismounted, and Dylan came close to examine the cuts. Aaron's fence line had been older than Rachel's—rusted—but still strong. Dylan ran his finger across a clean slice. Wire cutters. Someone had set up the stampede.

Could that person have been Rachel's brother? After all, causing a stampede was nothing when compared to breaking out of prison and gunning down two marshals to do it. But why would he do it?

Did he know Dylan was on the ranch? Had he guessed he was law enforcement and wanted to warn him off? Warn Rachel off? But if he knew Dylan was a cop, he'd know a stampede wouldn't run him off. And why would he want to get his sister off the property?

No, it didn't make sense.

Chances were the stampede was unrelated to the hunt for Jackson Kincaid. That didn't mean it didn't need to be investigated.

"You said you're in a property line dispute with your neighbor." Dylan bent down and pulled on a section of wiring, taking care not to cut his finger on the rusted barbed wire.

She nodded. "Aaron Jacobson. The guy who rented you Ginger. This is his fence line. His property. But if you're thinking he'd let his cattle stampede all over my property to get me back over wanting the spring, you're wrong."

"How so?"

"He loves his longhorns. Besides, half are pregnant. Running like that, all panicked, could compromise the pregnancies."

"Okay, how about anyone else that might want to

cause problems for you? Because if there's no other suspect…"

"No. I know what you're going to say. But this isn't Jax. It's not. He'd never…" Rachel slumped, as if suddenly exhausted—probably too much stress and not enough sleep. She found an old stump and sat, picking at the grass below.

The woman needed a break. He wanted to help—to make everything okay for her. What was it about her that triggered his inner knight in shining armor, just as she'd snidely accused earlier? Dylan came to sit next to her on the stump, then made a zigzag pattern on the ground by flattening new grass with his boot.

Her horses were trained to remain in the same place when their reins were dropped, and now stood nose to tail, swishing flies from each other's faces. Spring in Texas brought beautiful things: bluebonnets, songbirds, green grass…and bugs.

A ladybug landed on Rachel's bare shoulder. Dylan gently lifted it, then held it out on his index finger in front of her face.

"Make a wish and blow it away," he said.

She smiled weakly. "I thought you were supposed to tell it to go back home. Something about its house being on fire and its children alone."

"Seems harsh. I like asking it for a wish instead," Dylan said.

Rachel held the silence for a moment, then took a deep breath and blew the ladybug off his finger.

"What did you wish for?" he asked.

Her face grew clouded. "For this to all be over."

That was what he wanted, too. But probably for much different reasons than the ones Rachel had. He said,

"I don't have all the pieces of the puzzle yet, Rachel. But something's going on here." He gestured to the cut fence. "Until I can figure out what, you have to admit getting Peter someplace off the ranch, just like I suggested earlier, makes sense."

Rachel blew out a long, measured breath. Dylan waited.

"I can't," she finally said. "Peter is all I have. I can't be away from him. The safest place he can be is with me."

She was wrong. But she was also right. Without more evidence that Josiah's death, the stampede and her brother's escape were linked, he didn't know what he could say to make Rachel change her mind. "All right," Dylan said.

He stood.

"That's it?" Rachel asked. "You're not going to fight me about Peter?"

"He's your son. You know what's best for him and I can't force you to send him away. You agreed to let me stay with you and that's enough for now. But get used to the fact that I'm going to be staying very, very close to you and Peter, Rachel."

"In case Jax comes by? Because you want to catch him?"

"That's one reason."

"What's the other?"

"You said Peter is safest with you? Well, right now the safest place for you and Peter is with me. And I'm going to make sure no harm comes to you, whether the threat is from your brother or someone else."

Chapter 10

Later that day, Rachel leaned back in the leather seat that faced Julia's desk and drew in a deep breath through her nose. At the edge of town, tucked in between a bakery and coffee shop, the lawyer's office smelled heavenly. Although at early afternoon the bakery had already finished its day's worth of baking, the scent of yeast and sugar snuck between the walls, reminding Rachel how little she'd eaten. She'd shown Dylan to Josiah's old room, given him a list of chores, driven Peter to a friend's house to play, then come to town to confer with Julia.

And to get away.

"You willingly agreed to let a U.S. Marshal who has every intention of capturing your brother live on your property?" Julia asked incredulously.

"If Dylan stays on the property, I'll know where he

is at all times. I hate that the marshals are watching the house. I'd rather watch them watch me."

"And?" Julia prompted, as if waiting for more explanation.

"And...with Josiah gone, I desperately need help on the ranch."

"And?"

Irritation set Rachel's spine a little tighter. "And what?"

"Your decision doesn't have anything to do with the fact that the man is drop-dead gorgeous?"

"Get serious, J," Rachel snapped out, irritated. "He wants me to send Peter away until Jax is caught."

"It's not a bad idea."

"What?"

"Let's just talk possibilities. If you decided that was what was best for Peter, where would he go?"

Rachel wrapped her arms around her middle, guarding against a hollow ache forming in her stomach. "If I decided that was best for him, I could send him to his father's parents."

"Then do it. I think Dylan is right. Peter could be at risk, especially with a bunch of U.S. Marshals trampling all over your property, the valley and the ridge. And if the marshals are gunning for your brother, you don't want your son in the line of fire."

Again, Rachel's first instinct was denial. But because it was Julia making the suggestion, she forced herself to reconsider. She had to think of what was best for Peter. She hated losing the little bit of control she still had over her son, but his safety came first. And despite what she'd told Dylan earlier, if someone had intentionally caused the stampede, Peter wasn't safe on the ranch no matter how close she stayed to him.

"I'll drive him down tonight," she said. "Tomorrow I'll call the school and let them know where he'll be. I don't want the sheriff's office after me for truancy." She made a face. She'd just about had it with law enforcement.

"And what about you? I don't want you in the line of fire, either. Haven't you considered that you might not be safe? Maybe you should take a few days off— go away for a while."

"I can't. The ranch is the only future I can give Peter. I can't abandon it." Although she had taken online courses and had earned her B.A. in agricultural sciences from a reputable university, she was trained in nothing other than ranching.

She refused to surrender control of her own ranch.

Plus—and she knew this was what was really keeping her from leaving the ranch—Dylan seemed convinced Jax was coming to her. If he was, she needed to be there for him.

Although the drive to Peter's grandparents' house took three hours, Dylan insisted on coming along, which had surprised her.

"Aren't you afraid Jax might show up while I'm gone?" she asked before they left.

"My partner can cover the ranch while we're gone. Like I told you before, I think that stampede was intentional. I'm not willing to risk your safety."

Her heart warmed at his words, but she reminded herself that while he'd admitted he was attracted to her and had enjoyed their kiss, he was probably more concerned with keeping her alive because she was his best bet to getting Jax. Still, he insisted on driving, for which Rachel was eternally grateful.

Twenty minutes into the drive, Dylan surprised Rachel once again, this time by making an obvious effort to engage Peter, who sat between them in the cab of her old Ford pickup. He asked questions about various things, including skipping stones and climbing trees and school-age bullies, which reminded her he'd also been a ten-year-old boy once. That had her imagining what he'd looked like and what kind of mischief he'd gotten into at that age. Those thoughts then led to her wondering what his life had been like since. What kinds of girls (then women) he'd dated. Whether he had family. Where he lived when he wasn't chasing down fleeing prisoners in Texas. More than once she had to quash the urge to join the conversation and ask. She already felt too drawn to Dylan as it was—the more she focused on Dylan as an officer of the law and less as a man with human experiences and connections, the better off she and Jax would be.

At first, Peter mumbled and barely kept up his end of the conversation.

Then Dylan nodded at the BB gun Peter had clutched in his hands.

"Cool Red Ryder. Had one just like it when I was your age. Your mom teach you to shoot?"

Peter actually smiled. "Nah. Josiah did."

Dylan smiled back. "Didn't want you to get one? Afraid you'd shoot your eye out?"

Peter looked at Rachel, and Rachel winked at him. Then he turned back to Dylan. "Your mom worry about that, too?"

"I think it's part of some secret moms' club ritual to

worry about that. But just like Ralphie Parker's mom, and my mom, looks like your mom finally came around. She trusts you to have fun, be safe and be responsible. That tells me a lot about you. Good things."

Peter didn't respond directly, but he did say, "We always watch *A Christmas Story* on Christmas Eve. Me, mom and Uncle Jax. But Uncle Jax missed it last year. He's away."

It was the first time Peter had directly mentioned Jax in front of Dylan, and as soon as he did Rachel stiffened. Her tension increased as Peter commenced to tell Dylan more and more about his uncle.

"Uncle Jax taught me how to ride."

"Uncle Jax is great at tracking jackrabbits."

"I want to learn how to play the guitar like my uncle Jax."

Eventually Peter seemed to run out of breath and accolades.

"You know," Dylan said, "your uncle Jax…"

Rachel stiffened and Dylan's gaze caught hers.

"…sounds like a really fun guy," he finished.

"You'd like him," Peter said. "And…" Peter bit his lip and hesitated before saying, "I think he'd like you."

Rachel's eyes widened. In Peter's world, that was a huge compliment.

Dylan seemed to get it. "Thanks, kid. But why do you say that?"

"Because you helped me. You tried to help Josiah. And you're helping my mom."

Again, Dylan looked at her. There was a message there. One she didn't miss. *Your son gets it,* it said. *Why can't you?*

Because you're not trying to help Jax, she thought.

And if Peter knew that, you wouldn't be winning him over right now. Not ever.

Of course, Peter also wasn't old enough to truly understand the mistakes Jax had made, her rational side told her. Or how Dylan was just doing his job. Heck, even she had trouble with those concepts.

But Rachel didn't want to deal with logic and reason right now. Not when she was having to send her son away. Not when she didn't know if and when she'd ever see her brother again.

Eventually they arrived at their destination. It didn't take long to drop Peter off. Her former mother-in-law came out front to greet them, but though she gave Rachel a hug, she didn't invite her or Dylan into the modest ranch house. Told that there were warm cookies waiting for him inside, Peter gave Rachel a kiss and ran to the front door, where his grandfather waited. There, he turned back and waved. Then he yelled, "Bye, Mom. Bye, Dylan."

"Love you," Rachel shouted back as Peter disappeared from view. She turned to Maureen and almost winced at the lack of spark in her eyes. Before Phillip's death, this woman had practically glowed with vitality. But after…she looked as if she'd aged two decades instead of seven years.

They spent about ten minutes going over Peter's routine. Although Rachel had told Maureen about Peter's ADHD, he'd never spent more than a few hours with his grandparents since, and even then Rachel had been present.

"Don't worry," Maureen said. "We'll keep a close eye on him."

Rachel nodded. "Thank you for keeping him."

"It's our pleasure, Rachel," Maureen said. She smiled wanly, then followed Peter inside. Her husband, Tom, stood at the front door. He stared at Dylan a long time, his gaze curious. And sad. Then he nodded at Rachel before walking into the house and shutting the door.

Rachel and Dylan drove away. With every mile they traveled, she felt anxiety building inside her as if she were a balloon. She squeezed her hands together tightly, wanting nothing more than to command Dylan to turn around so she could retrieve her son. She reminded herself that she'd sent him away to keep him safe, but now she didn't have her brother or her son.

She was completely alone in the world.

Either Dylan sensed Rachel's need for silence or he was working something around in his own head, because they talked very little on the ride back. When they were about five miles out from the ranch, however, Dylan cleared his throat.

"Rachel, I know we discussed that kiss and agreed to forget about it, but…if you're uncomfortable with me staying in Josiah's old quarters," Dylan said, "I can always borrow a sleeping bag and stay out on the front porch. Your call."

She kept her eyes closed, considering her options.

Keep your friends close and your enemies closer. Wasn't that it?

Years of being a mother had taught her to sleep lightly—she would know if he got up in the middle of the night. Plus, if Jax was to sneak in at night, he would sneak in through the French doors in the master bedroom—where he'd always snuck out of the house as a kid. And where she was now sleeping. She would be able to get to Jax before Dylan could.

Besides, she wasn't afraid Dylan would try to sneak into her bed. Truth be told, she was more afraid she'd try to sneak into his. "I don't mind," she said. "Like you said, that kiss was just the result of adrenaline. I know I'm just a job to you. And you...well, you're nothing to me." She said it despite how harsh the words sounded. She said it to try to convince him but also herself.

She cracked her lids opened and peered at Dylan between her eyelashes. He shifted his seat, and his grip tightened on the steering wheel. Had she insulted him? Or was he taking her words as a challenge and thinking of proving her wrong? Was he thinking of their shared kiss? She hadn't been able to get it out of her mind. In Julia's office, when Julia was interrogating her over her intentions for letting Dylan act as her ranch hand and stay on the property, she had hoped her cheeks had not betrayed her desire by turning bright pink.

"Are you sure?" Dylan asked, his voice sounding tighter than before.

Not at all. But she also knew how alone she felt right now. At least if he was in the house with her, she could pretend there was someone who cared. Someone who'd listen to her if she needed to talk, even if she had no plans of doing so. "Absolutely."

Headlights from a car behind them grew closer, illuminating the cab of the truck. With the added light, she could see the lines framing Dylan's mouth grow deeper.

The headlights grew even brighter, and Dylan growled under his breath, then flipped the rearview mirror down to dull the glare. "Assholes," he swore.

Odd. Rachel had not heard him swear before, except when he was speaking of her brother. Did the man hate all rule breakers?

A bump from behind jolted them forward. Rachel's seat belt caught her up short, the sudden jerk forcing air out of her lungs.

"Damn it! Rachel, here—" Dylan reached in his leather jacket pocket, pulled out a cell phone and tossed it to her.

"Do you want me to call 911?" she asked.

"No. Just put it on speakerphone and hold down the number one button for a moment." With that, he leaned down, reached into his boot and pulled out a handgun. Steering with one elbow, he released the safety.

Eyes glued to his gun, Rachel held down the number one on his phone. A woman who identified herself as Stacy answered.

"I'm driving Rachel's truck and we're getting rammed." He proceeded to give her their location and instructed her to get them backup.

"Got it," Stacy said quickly. "We'll have help there as soon as we can."

"Right," Dylan said, and Rachel disconnected the call.

Twice more they were rammed. Dylan fought to keep the truck on the road. Rachel fought to breathe.

"Rachel, lean in front of me and take the wheel," Dylan ordered.

She didn't stop to ask why. To question. To snivel or whine or cry. Instead, she leaned in close to his body and grabbed the steering wheel as he twisted, keeping his foot on the gas, and leaned his upper body out the driver's-side window, gun pointed straight back.

"When you have a straightaway, steer a bit toward the left. That'll give me a clear shot."

Copper filled her mouth. Blood. She'd bitten through her lip. "Straightaway coming up. Two seconds."

Dylan floored it, and there they were, in the straightaway. She steered slightly left, heard popping sounds, then a squeal of rubber on pavement. Dylan eased his frame back into his seat and took over the steering wheel from her. She sagged back into her seat as he continued to drive.

"Got both front tires. They won't be going anywhere for a while." He used her cell to call Stacy and confirm the location of the car and the fact deputies would be on the look-out for the men who'd rammed them. After disconnecting the call, he shot her a glance. "You did good, lady. Are you all right?"

Was she all right? She fought back a gag response. Her world had been turned upside down. She'd never be all right again. "Who was that? Why were they ramming us?"

"I don't know."

A thought occurred to her and she grabbed his shirt in a panic. "Were they following us? Did they follow us when we dropped off Peter? Maybe we should head back—"

"They weren't following us, Rachel."

"But how do you know?"

"I'd know if someone had been following us. I'm trained to pick up on those kinds of things. I promise, we weren't followed. That car only came on us once we got off the main highway."

"So were they drunk? Dumb kids playing chicken?"

"I don't know," he said again.

"Great. You don't know. At least you don't think it was my brother," she snapped out bitterly.

"There were two men in the front seat of that car. Both their silhouettes were all wrong. Neither was your brother."

She sat in silence for a while. Ramming a moving vehicle at seventy miles an hour wasn't a prank. Something serious was going on. But what?

"At least they weren't shooting," she said, trying to lighten the mood.

Dylan didn't laugh.

She looked at him and saw his lips pressed in a grim line. Those lines on the side of his face were deep, and his eyes narrowed. "What is it?" she asked, hesitantly.

"That's why I told you to get in front of me," he said.

"I don't understand…."

"They hadn't started shooting yet. But if I hadn't gotten to them first, that would have been the next thing coming at us. I couldn't see much, but I could see both men held guns."

Dylan had barely parked the car before Rachel was out of it and heading into the house. With a quiet curse, he called Stacy, who told him law enforcement had found the car with its tires shot out, but no sign of the two men who'd been driving it. "Keep me posted," he said before disconnecting.

Slowly he followed Rachel through the front door. He expected to see her climbing the stairs to her bedroom. Instead, she stood inside the foyer, frozen, staring at the kitchen doorway in front of her, her arms straight by her sides. Dylan stepped next to her so he could see her profile. He winced at the blank, almost robotic look on her face.

"Rachel," he whispered. Unable to help himself, he

lifted his hand and caressed her cheek with his knuckles. Her skin was soft but cold, as if despair was freezing her from the inside out. "Baby," he said.

The endearment seemed to jolt her out of her paralysis. With a frown, she turned and looked at him. Confusion flashed across her face, as if for a moment she didn't even know who he was. Where she was.

"I'm alone," she said, her voice thin and reedy.

"No," he began, but her bitter laughter interrupted him.

"Yes. I'm alone. No parents. No husband. No Josiah. No Jax. No Peter. Right now I'm alone and weird things are happening, things that scare me, but no one can help me."

He took her by the arms and gave her a small shake. "I'm here to help you, Rachel. I won't let anything happen to you."

She tried to jerk away from him, but he wouldn't let her. "You can't help me," she cried. "Not when you believe what you do about Jax. Not when you want to take him away from me forever, which is what will happen if he's blamed for shooting those marshals."

"I have a job to do, Rachel, but that's not going to stop me from helping you. From keeping you safe."

She placed her palms on his chest as if she wanted to push him away but couldn't bear to do so. She shook her head. "You can't keep me safe. You can't. You can't. You can't."

She kept repeating the words and something snapped inside him. He couldn't take it anymore. Couldn't take the grief and desolation he saw in her eyes. He needed to erase it. Needed to make her forget her troubles and how unsafe she felt. "I will keep you safe, Rachel," he said fiercely. "I know you don't believe me, but I will."

"You c—"

Before she could once more deny what he'd said, he covered her mouth with his.

For a split second, she stiffened.

But only for a second.

Almost immediately she softened in surrender, her body melting into his and her mouth opening to the strong thrust of his tongue. Even so, Dylan wrapped one hand around her neck and one arm around her back, ensuring that she couldn't pull away as he explored her sweet taste. He wanted to fill her up with his strength and shoot his essence inside her again and again until she couldn't help agreeing that she was his. That she wasn't alone. That she'd never be alone as long as he had a single breath left in his body.

His body hardened more and more the longer they kissed. He couldn't remember ever wanting a woman as much as he wanted her. Couldn't remember feeling as if he'd die if he didn't bury himself inside her. His hands went in search of her curves—first, her full, rounded breasts. Then the dip of her tiny waist and the flare of her womanly hips. Finally he palmed her rear, pushing her closer even as he bent his knees slightly so he could rub his erection against the vulnerable juncture of her thighs.

He was lost in the feel and taste of her, so much so that it took a while to register the sound of his own ragged breaths and the sweet erotic cries of pleasure she was making. He wanted to ratchet those cries into screams as he brought her to orgasm. Automatically, his fingers moved to unsnap the button of her jeans. He growled in frustration when her hand covered his and she broke their kiss.

"Dylan. We can't. I want to, but we can't."

Their gazes met, her brown eyes fiery with desire but also clouded with regret. His hand trembled beneath hers. He wanted to argue with her. Opened his mouth to do so. But the words wouldn't come. She was right.

They couldn't give in to their desire. If they did, he knew Rachel would regret it. And the last thing he wanted to do was cause her more pain.

Even though it nearly killed him, he nodded. "You're right. We can't. But I can hold you. Just hold you for a minute more. Can I do that?"

Her eyes filled with moisture before she buried her face in the crook of his neck. Wrapping his arms around her, Dylan did as he'd promised.

He held her. He also stroked her hair. Told her things were going to be okay. That she was going to be okay. And he prayed that he was telling her the truth.

He had no idea how much time had passed before she pushed away from him.

Briefly, he tightened his arms around her, not wanting to let her go. But letting her go was something he was going to have to get used to. This beautiful courageous woman wasn't his.

He let her go.

"You okay?"

"Yes." She cleared her throat. "Are you?"

No, he thought. *This woman is killing me. And all I want is more of her.* "Yes," he said. "But I've got to check in with my team. Find out what they've learned, if anything, about the men who tried to run us off the road."

She nodded. "Do you want to use my office?"

"Thanks, but I noticed I get the best remote internet connection out in the barn. In the tack room. I'll head out there and give you some privacy so you can get to bed."

She stared at him for a moment, probably thinking that he wanted to talk to his team where she wouldn't overhear him, and she was partially right. But he really did want to give her some privacy, as well.

"I'm tired," she said suddenly.

"You're tired," he agreed. "You need to rest. Go to sleep and things will look better in the morning."

She smirked and cocked an eyebrow. "You really believe that?"

Once again, he brushed his knuckles against her cheek. "I hope so."

With a sigh, she nodded and turned away. He watched as she climbed up the stairs, looking as if she were carrying the weight of the world on her shoulders. At the top, she paused and looked over her shoulder at him. "We keep complicating things," she said.

"Yep," he agreed.

"I know in the morning I'll regret it, but right now I don't. Because for a moment, I didn't feel alone, Dylan."

He wanted to say he didn't regret kissing her, either, but he couldn't. Complications, he reminded himself. Instead, he said, "I'm glad, Rachel. Now go to bed."

Her smile indicated she understood what he *wasn't* saying.

She lifted her chin and said, "Good night, Dylan. I'll see you in the morning."

"Good night, Rachel."

He watched as she walked into her room and softly closed the door.

He waited almost twenty minutes before checking in on her. He knocked softly on her door. When she didn't answer, he peeked inside. He didn't enter her room, but from the doorway he could see she was asleep. In slumber, her face wore an expression of serenity, as if all the worries of the past two days had been erased. Rachel in sleep was as beautiful as Rachel awake. He fought the urge to climb into the bed beside her and simply hold her again.

With a sigh, he closed the door and headed out to the barn. Even though he knew Eric had eyes on the ranch, Dylan still made sure he had a clear view of the house, however, so he could see anyone coming or going.

Five minutes later, Dylan was talking to Stacy over Skype.

"Wish I could tell you more," she said, "but all we know so far is the SUV was stolen in Hartford, about forty miles away."

Dylan swore. "So no way to tell if they're related in any way to the Jackson Kincaid case?"

"I can't find the link—but that doesn't mean there isn't one. I have local law enforcement on the lookout for two Caucasian males, about six foot two, and weighing around two hundred pounds. Bodybuilder types, is that right?"

"We were driving at least seventy and it was night, so I couldn't make a positive ID, but they had the dome light on in their SUV, so I'm confident of the description I've given you."

"So neither man was Jackson Kincaid?"

He shook his head. He wanted to capture Jax, sure,

but he also didn't want Rachel to get hurt, either physically or emotionally. She seemed unable to believe her brother capable of any wrongdoing. Although the facts suggested otherwise, he harbored a small hope in his heart that somehow Rachel was right—at least, right in the fact that her brother would not hurt her.

"Dylan?"

He brought his attention back to the screen. "Kincaid doesn't have gang tats on his neck. Those guys did." He blew out a breath. "There have been two threats against Rachel Kincaid and a suspicious death on her property, all within forty-eight hours, and I don't like it. I'd like to get her out of here. Force her to leave."

Stacy tilted her head. "No can do. Boss man wants her on the property and there's really no reason to think the incidents are related. Not yet. The death of her ranch hand has not proven to be a murder. She admitted to having a feud with her neighbor over the property line, so that cattle stampede you told me about could have been prompted by that feud. And as far as the SUV ramming you goes?" She shrugged. "I'll admit, that looks hinky, but since neither man in the SUV was Jackson Kincaid, we cannot link the incident to him."

He knew she was right. Without more, there was no reason to move Rachel off the ranch. Especially when it was still possible Jackson Kincaid might be heading to Texas to get to his sister. "Got it. No convincing Rachel to leave her property." He didn't like it, but between him and Eric, Rachel would be safe. He'd make sure of it.

"It's 'Rachel' now, is it?" Stacy gave him a leering wink. "I think someone's got a crush on the widow Kincaid."

More like a hard-on, he thought, then forced himself to be honest. He was insanely attracted to Rachel, yes, but there was more than that when it came to his feelings for her. Despite the fact that she was just like his mother—always blaming herself for the mistakes her family made—she was also stronger in many ways. And it hadn't escaped him that when she ordered Peter into his room to keep him safe from the stampede, she'd shown a maternal background inconsistent with the excuses she constantly made for her brother. He liked her. Hell, he more than liked her. By the way he'd stared at her while she was sleeping, he knew he *was* crushing on her.

"Any sign of Kincaid from the others?" he asked.

"Trying to change the subject?"

Trying to get Rachel out of his mind and focus on the job. He did not need the distraction. "Just answer the question."

"No sign of Kincaid."

"Right." He sighed. "Thanks. I'll check in tomorrow."

"Sounds good," Stacy said. "Now go play cowboy. Gotta say, I'd love to see you in spurs and a whip."

He managed to smile but just barely. Dylan was a city boy, born and raised in San Francisco. No matter. A whip and spurs weren't what it would take to bring down Jax Kincaid. If Kincaid showed up, however, his ass would belong to Dylan. He just had to keep Rachel safe in the meantime.

Chapter 11

Good God, Dylan thought the next morning. How tight could a pair of shorts get on a woman? In the barn-yard in front of him, Rachel chopped wood—the round moons of her butt peeking out at him from under the frayed denim of her shorts every time she finished a stroke of the ax.

Last night, he'd dreamed of her. At first, the dreams had been dark. Her in danger. Him trying to protect her. Her refusing to believe she was in danger and running to her brother instead. Eventually the dreams changed because *he* changed. He no longer asked to help her; he simply refused to leave her side. That meant they fought. But it also meant sex. The Rachel in his dreams loved to give over control to him, but she loved taking it, too. There wasn't a position she shied away from, but her favorite was when he powered into her from behind, fisting her hair with one hand while the other played between her legs. Her second favorite was riding him, teasing him with tender shallow thrusts followed by fast deep ones that had him shouting her name.

By the time he woke, he felt her in every pore of his body. He swore he could smell her. Taste her on his tongue. In the shower, he'd tamed his erection, dressed and gulped down the coffee Rachel had prepared. When she'd come in from outside and she'd seen him, his hunger must have been reflected in his eyes, because she blushed. For a second, her eyes ate him up and he could plainly see reciprocal desire reflected in their depths. She stood there, cheeks flushed, mouth parted slightly, breath exhaling on quick puffs. Then her expression went blank. She told him she'd talked to Peter, who was doing fine with his grandparents, and then she told him to meet her in the barn.

Where she handed him an ax.

And handed him humiliation on a plate.

He'd admitted to never having chopped wood before. Now she was giving him a demonstration. One he liked very, very much. Those cheeks triggered his fantasies from the night before. Fantasies involving him on his knees behind a naked Rachel and—

"Are you paying attention?"

Rachel's voice brought him out of his reverie. So much for fantasizing over the widow Kincaid. There was wood to chop. And his manliness to reclaim. "Yeah. I got it. Left hand holds close to the bottom of the ax handle. Right hand holds the top. Sling the ax back, then over your shoulder and start sliding your hands together at the apex. Then—smack."

She handed him the ax.

He grabbed the wooden handle and imagined giving it a sudden tug, pulling her off balance. And against him.

Heat rushed to his crotch. Another hard-on formed.

Damn, but he wanted to kiss her again. Wanted to drop the frigging ax and take her in his arms. Unbutton her shirt and unhook her bra and let his hands wander over her breasts.

Instead, he did none of those things. He simply stepped forward to the chopping block and placed a quarter round on top, then backed up, visually measuring the distance. He lifted the ax, sensing the weight and heft of the wood and iron, balanced between his widespread hands. Then, following Rachel's directions, he slung the ax back, high and down, in one swoop.

He hit the log dead center, and two pieces shot off the chopping block. He let a grin slide to the surface, and turned and faced her. Inane pride filled his chest. "I did it!"

She smiled, wide and full, and Dylan thought it again—Rachel smiling full-out was a thing of pure beauty.

"If you were eight years old," she said, "I'd tell you how proud I am and pat you on the back. I took Jax out for ice cream the first time he chopped wood, and bought Peter a video game for his first. Instead, I'll just ask. Think you can chop all those quarter rounds there?" She pointed to the side of the barn, where a good fifty quarter rounds sat piled high.

"Yeah, I can do it. No choice, since it has to be done. There's so much to do around here. I can hardly believe you've been getting by, even with Peter and Josiah's help."

Rachel sighed. "None of this is easy. Jax used to help until he started getting into too much trouble. Peter helps—has done so since he was a little one. Josiah—" her voice caught "—Josiah put in a good forty hours a week on the ranch work. Now it's just me."

So she was back to that again. He wondered if she said it to remind him to keep his distance. To remind herself. "I'm here now," Dylan said knowing that wasn't enough for her. Wishing he could give her more. But he couldn't. She was cooperating with him, but in her heart, Rachel still believed Jax was innocent. She refused to accept his true nature, just as his mother had refused to accept his brother's. And for that reason, she wasn't what Dylan needed, no matter that she was what he wanted. Even putting all that aside, he had no doubt that once her brother was back in prison, whether Dylan was the one who actually brought him back there or not, she'd be done with him.

The knowledge made him want to take the ax to the waiting quarter rounds and keep going. And how crazy was that? He'd known Rachel a couple of days, but the way his body reacted to her, it was as if they'd not only kissed but spent weeks exploring each other's bodies and trading intimate secrets.

"Well, when you're gone, I'll have to figure out how to either manage this place on my own or pay for a ranch hand. Heck, maybe this time instead of an elderly man like Josiah, I'll look for some young handsome thing to muck out my stalls." She said it with a twist of her mouth, probably meaning it to be a self-deprecating comment rather than the challenge his body heard.

Ignoring the spark of jealousy that immediately ignited at her words, Dylan said, "Whoever you get, I'm glad you'll have help. That you won't be counting on your brother to come home anytime soon."

She folded her arms over her chest and set her jaw. "He'll be back soon enough. Julia will prove he's not a murderer. And as for the fact that he ran? Maybe he had a good reason."

Same old song and dance, he told himself, but then something Rachel had said drifted into his head—that her brother didn't like guns. That he composed music. Did that really sound like someone who'd be able to get the drop on not only one but two U.S. Marshals to engineer his own escape? So far there'd been no evidence that anyone else had been involved in the prison escape, but it wasn't as if the marshals had a lot of witnesses to interview. Their only one was still in a coma fighting for his life. If he woke, what would he tell them? That Jackson Kincaid had indeed had a good reason to run? Or that Rachel didn't know her brother as well as she thought?

And why was he even considering the possibility that Rachel was right about her brother's reasons for running? She couldn't even accept that he'd been involved in the drug deal to which he'd confessed. She was beautiful, but she preferred to walk around blind to the flaws of those she loved.

He just hoped that tendency didn't end up killing her the way it had killed his mother.

Rachel left Dylan outside, chopping wood, and headed indoors to her office to pay bills. As she did, Dylan's handsome visage haunted her. In his soft and faded jeans and a plaid button-down rolled up to his arms, she didn't know what she enjoyed feasting her eyes on the most: Dylan's tight butt or his wide shoulders.

Both.

She entered her office, sat down at her ancient roll-top desk and turned on the computer.

And then promptly turned around to stare out the window at a wood-chopping Dylan.

She wanted him. Well, at least her body wanted Dylan's body. Her mind argued firmly against the idea.

Run, her mind told her. *Take him,* her body screamed.

She listened to her mind and turned away from the window to once again focus on her computer screen. Enough of dreaming about a man she could never have. Would never have.

A few clicks and hits of the return button later, and her emails popped up. Bill. Bill. Another bill. A reminder from her veterinarian's office that it was time to order vaccines for her alpaca herd. And an email without a subject in the subject line. Spam, most likely. She hit Delete, then froze. There was something familiar about the return address.

Hurriedly, she opened her Trash folder. There, at the top of the dumped emails, sat the one she'd just deleted.

An email from her brother.

Tears filled Rachel's eyes and pain radiated outward from her chest. She hunched forward, almost cradling the computer monitor, and read the email from Jax.

Sis. By now you probably know about the jailbreak during transport. How I ran. I swear I didn't shoot those men. As long as you and Peter are safe on the ranch, I'm coming. We can work out a deal. I'm coming home, but promise on the memory of Mom and Dad you won't tell anyone. Love, Jax.

Fear, relief and confusion slammed into her all at once. Dylan was right. Jax was headed home to her. But Dylan was also wrong. Jax hadn't shot those U.S. marshals. Yet she knew how much detail he took in composing his music, and the odd wording of his email suggested they'd been deliberately chosen, as well. That he was sending her a message. But what? That she and Peter would be in danger if they left the ranch? Or that they'd be in danger if they stayed on the ranch? Did he know the marshals were here?

Rachel closed the email and filed it in a folder labeled Taxes.

Her first instinct was to call Julia, but Jax had begged her to promise on the memory of their parents not to tell anyone. What was Jax involved in? Why, after all this time, had he finally decided to contact her again, as if the past year of silence and rejection hadn't happened?

She propped her elbows on the scarred desk and sank her head into her hands, suddenly weary. The desk wobbled, the loose leg in the back one of the many items in need of repair. But she didn't have the money.

That was what had landed Jax in this mess in the first place. If he really had transported that package knowing it contained drugs, he'd done it because he'd been trying to make money to help her out.

Maybe history would repeat itself and Jax really would come to the ranch, just as he'd said in his email. If that happened, she knew which trail he'd use to come up to the house. Which door he'd use to sneak in. What time he'd try to sneak in.

She hadn't been his mother for ten years for nothing. She knew most of his secrets, even if she didn't know them all.

The question was who'd be here when Jax arrived. Just her? Or her and U.S. Marshal Dylan Rooney.

"Rachel, are you okay?"

At the sound of Dylan's voice, Rachel jerked in her chair and raised her head. She blinked, noting the light sheen of sweat that covered him, making him look even more sexy than normal if that was possible. A man like that who could work so hard outside bed? He'd only have that much more stamina in bed.

And what a silly thought for her to have when she knew her brother was on his way and might be walking directly into Dylan's waiting hands if Rachel allowed that to happen.

That might be the best thing for everyone. Dylan had said he wanted to take her brother into custody without anyone being harmed. It was always better to face problems head-on, within the confines of the law, than to make matters worse. "Dylan—"

"I've finished the wood and was about to move on to my next chore, but I wanted to check in on you first. Make sure you're okay."

"You mean because of Josiah and the stampede and someone trying to run us off the road. Those were just weird coincidences," she said.

"That's what you've decided to tell yourself?"

"Unless you can prove they're connected somehow. Can you?"

"You know I can't. Not yet. But I don't like the sight of you sitting in here, head in your hands, radiating weariness and vulnerability, either."

She raised her chin. "We all need to take a break sometime. I'm fine. And I can handle myself. I've done it long before you were around, and I'll continue to do it when you're gone." When his mouth tightened, she sighed. "I'm not trying to be difficult, honest. But, Dylan, I just showed you how to wield an ax, remember? I'm not exactly a fragile flower."

"No, but you remind me of a wildflower. Delicate. Beautiful. But strong enough to withstand the elements, too."

Her mouth parted at his unexpected compliment. A flare of something in his eyes made her want to stand and go to him, as if she were a moth and he a flame. Instead, she looked away and gripped the edge of her desk tightly, praying for the willpower to withstand temptation.

"You taught me how to wield an ax. How about I teach you something now?"

Her gaze met his once more. "What's that?"

"You said your brother doesn't know how to shoot a gun. Do you?"

"I can shoot a rifle. On an isolated ranch, it's important to be able to protect my family and livestock."

"Right. But can you shoot a handgun?"

"You mean, like the kind of gun you carry around in your boot? No."

"Want me to teach you?"

"Because you think I might have to shoot my brother to protect myself?"

"Because you've never shot a gun before, it could be fun and maybe, just maybe, it might come in handy someday."

"You're serious?"

"It's better than sitting in here feeling sorry for yourself, right?"

She narrowed her eyes. "Now you're just trying to make me mad."

He grinned. "Is it working?"

In the field acres from Rachel's house, Dylan put a soda can on a wooden fence post, then moved six feet down and placed another can on the next post. Headed in the opposite direction, Rachel did the same.

"How many cans are we putting up?" he called out.

"As many as you want to shoot." She finished placing her last can on a post and returned to Dylan.

The sun caught the light in her hair. Running his fingers through it suddenly seemed so appealing, but that wasn't why they were here. He was here to teach Rachel how to shoot a gun. Because whether she wanted to accept it or not, weird things were happening around the ranch and he liked the idea of her being able to protect herself if need be. Not that he was going to hand her a loaded weapon to carry around after one shooting lesson, but it would be a start. He could teach her a little every day, and when he left, she could continue with the shooting lessons.

He frowned at the idea of leaving the ranch. Her. He knew it was coming. That he couldn't stay here indefinitely on the chance that her brother showed up. But one thing was for sure, he wasn't leaving until he knew she and her son would be safe. And hopefully by that time she'd be on her way to feeling better so that he wouldn't walk in on her and find her looking beaten and defeated the way he did when he'd walked into her office earlier.

On her way back to him, Rachel stumbled but quickly

corrected herself, her hips swaying as she regained her balance. Her incredibly sexy hips, with her firm, tight butt held by the soft, well-worn denim. When she reached him and turned to face their targets, he came up behind Rachel. "Ready?" At her nod, he placed the handgun in her hands. He'd already gone over the basics of the gun's mechanisms with her. "Feel the weight?"

"Yes."

"Good. Now here. Take the safety off."

"Am I standing correctly?"

Shooting a gun wasn't like playing golf. A marshal never knew what position he or she would be in when having to discharge a weapon. Assuming a perfect position wasn't necessary. But Rachel didn't know that. He stepped right behind her and slid his arms around hers, covering her hands with his. Her backside fit perfectly against his front—molded to him. He breathed in her scent, that breathtaking mixture of rose and cinnamon and nutmeg.

"Are you planning on smelling my hair all day, or will you teach me to shoot?"

He chuckled. Spunk. With her world falling apart at every corner, Rachel still had spunk. He dropped his hands but stayed behind her, their bodies maintaining a subtle connection. "Okay, then. Sight down the barrel. See the target?"

"Shiny red, dead ahead."

"Squeeze."

A shot sounded and the can popped off the fence line. The energy dispelled from the weapon sent Rachel back somewhat, against his chest, and he held firm. Chemistry radiated outward, almost visible. He ran his hands across her shoulders. "Sore?"

"Somewhat."

"Want to try again?" he asked.

"Absolutely!"

Even though he'd wanted to give her a distraction from her pain, the flippancy of her tone gave him pause. He gripped her shoulders tight. "Rachel, you were raised on a ranch. You know guns aren't a game. Just like how you treat the rifle and shotgun with respect, you need to treat a handgun the same way. It's not a toy."

She pulled away from him. "I know that. I'm not an idiot."

"I didn't say you were."

At that, she turned to face him. "No, you were just playing the big, bad law enforcement dude. I don't need a lecture."

"What's with the 'big, bad law enforcement' part of that statement? Do you have issues with authority?"

"Both my brother and my son seem to keep getting in trouble with the law. So yeah, I guess I do have an issue with authority."

"Christ, Rachel, I'm here to do a job. Your brother's the one who escaped. My job is to be here when he shows up. I haven't given you any reason to mistrust me, have I?"

She tilted her head down, studied the thin shoots of new green grass at their feet. "You're right," she murmured.

He resisted the smile that seemed to want to tip the corners of his mouth up. "What was that?" he asked, knowing full well he was goading her.

Rather than growing irked, Rachel instead looked back up at him and flashed a grin. "You're right. *R-I-*

G-H-T," she said, spelling out the word. "I can't fault you for how you're handling your end of things."

He reached out and gripped the handle of the handgun, twisting it to point back at the target. "Another?"

A quick nod, and then Rachel was lining up another shot. That one went wide, as did the next, but over the course of twenty minutes, Rachel ended up hitting a good 90 percent of all shots she took. The ones that didn't hit the soda cans weren't all that far off. Dylan found her accuracy a relief.

"That's it," he said after she emptied the last chamber. "I'm out of practice ammo."

Rachel gave a tight nod, then handed him the empty handgun and looked around, as if she'd suddenly recalled where they were. "We've still got a lot of chores to do. But thank you. This was fun."

When she turned away, he grabbed her elbow, unable to help himself. He didn't want their time together to end just yet. "Was it just firing the gun that was fun?"

"What else is there?" she asked.

As he stared at her, her gaze dropped once again to the ground…only to rise a second later to rest on his—

Oh, yeah. The widow Kincaid was checking out his crotch.

Heat flooded him, and he fought back the desire to grab her and cover her mouth with his. Palm her breasts. Slide his knee between her legs and press against her mound. Nope, wasn't gonna happen. Not again.

"I'll go get the horses," he said tightly, not allowing himself to say more. After all, what could he say? That her mouth tasted like heaven? That the way she softly exhaled while squeezing the trigger was enough to make a lesser man come? That he'd woken up with an erection because he'd been dreaming of her naked body? He stomped over to Anchor and Row, who refused to so much as look up at him as he gathered the reins. Each horse kept its muzzle buried in the soft new grass, munching away.

Five hard tugs on the reins later, coupled with a few curse words on his end and a soft giggle that came from Rachel, Anchor and Row both lifted their heads and reluctantly stepped in line behind him.

"I'll give you a lift up," he said when he finally came to a stop in front of Rachel.

She reached out, slid the reins over Anchor's neck, then grabbed the saddle horn. "Thanks," she said softly, placing a hand on his shoulder as he bent before her.

Anchor shifted, and Rachel stumbled against him. He grabbed hold tight, holding her steady, his head now pressed tight against her belly. An audible gasp slipped out from between her lips. Under her thin button-down shirt, he could hear her heartbeat. One-two. One-two. One-two. The pace rapidly increasing.

"Dylan," she whispered.

And suddenly his shirt was being bunched up in her fist, and he was rising to his feet, and Rachel was bending underneath him like a strong sapling in the wind, and then his lips were on her neck. For a moment, the earth faded away into a shimmery gray, the crickets' hum evaporated and all he could hear was Rachel's heartbeat. All he could feel were Rachel's fists against his shoulders and her hips pressed hard against his. All he could see was Rachel's hair, her ear, the line of her jaw, the lush red of her lips.

He kissed her then. Hard. Wrapped one arm around her lower back to wedge her tight against his hips and the other arm around her neck to hold her head in place as he teased her lips, asking without words for her to open to him. His own heartbeat matched the rhythm of hers and suddenly they were one—tongues sliding, lips touching, teeth nipping.

The kiss seemed endless. As did the others that followed, each kiss a universe of its own. Again and again. And again.

Hiding his erection became a thing of the past. Instead, he ground it against her and felt a rush of desire tugging deep within him as she met his movement with a heady groan. He drew his hand from behind her head and palmed her breast, her heat soaking through the thin layer of cotton. With dexterous fingers, he unbuttoned her blouse, tugging it free from where she'd tucked it into her jeans, then slid his fingers under the wispy lace of her bra. Her groan turned into quick pants as he rolled her nipple between his thumb and finger. Hungrily, he bent down and sucked the tightened bud into his mouth, nearly coming undone when she ground her crotch against his knee, which he'd shoved between her legs.

Just the way he'd fantasized.

He slid his hand lower to cup her butt and pull her hips in tighter. She mewled and torqued, twisting as if to climb up his body and settle her crotch on his erection. He met motion with motion, bending at the knees to dig the head of his erection against the apex of her thighs, seeking to connect their heat. He sucked, hard, drawing her breast deep into his mouth. Her body, wrapped in his arms, shook, the vibrations growing stronger with each pant emanating from her lips, until finally she shuddered and cried out his name.

Damn. She'd just come. From nothing more than the pressure of his mouth on her breast and the press of his body against hers. He pulled his head up but kept his arms wrapped tightly around her. She kept her face, which was flushed a blazing pink, averted.

"Are you okay?" he murmured, stroking her hair.

She closed her eyes, but nodded just before straightening. He remained close, his hips nudging hers to provide support, sliding his hands up to her shoulders to keep her steady.

"God, I'm sorry. We keep… I keep…" Her voice quavered with tears. "I don't know why…"

"I know why. Because we're attracted to each other. And you're a beautiful, passionate woman. A woman I want desperately. Don't feel embarrassed because of the pleasure I gave you, Rachel. I don't. And I know you don't believe me right now, but everything is going to be okay. You're going to be okay."

Her eyes flicked open and she stared at his chest. "Nothing will ever be okay again," she said in a small, tight voice, "but I appreciate your concern. Really, I do." She released the fabric of his shirt that she still held in her fists and slid her hands down until they rested on his belt, slung low around his hips.

"Rachel?"

Her chin rose, and slowly, so did her gaze, until she made visual contact. She cleared her throat, the sound delicate yet deliberate, then spoke. "Like you said, we're attracted to each other. I thought my reaction to you was a fluke. But this…"

"But this was real," he finished for her. "No aberration. No fluke." He knew not to press her, but rather to let her draw out her own conclusions.

She shook her head, sending her hair flowing in the gentle evening breeze. "I want you and you want me."

He wove his fingers under her hair and stroked the soft skin covering the back of her neck with the pads of his thumb. "That's a truth I would never deny. But my job. Your brother. Our feelings complicate things, Rachel."

"I know." She took a step back, breaking their contact, and blew out a sharp breath. "So, while this was fun…" She waved her hands in the air, as if gesturing to their momentary lapse of judgment.

"So, while this was fun, it's over now," he said firmly.

"Exactly."

Yeah, they could both wish that were the case. But he knew in his bones it simply wasn't true. This wasn't over between him and Rachel, but it had to be.

He couldn't be like Rachel, hiding his head in the sand from the realities of life. Some people were bad and deserved to be punished for their bad deeds. That was the case for her brother, just as it had been for his. She wanted to make excuses. He couldn't.

He knew what kind of tragedy came with continually making excuses for another. So no excuses about what he and Rachel had done. He'd take full responsibility.

But he'd also have to make sure he had the strength to keep it from happening again.

No matter how damn bad he wanted it to happen again.

And over and over and over again.

Chapter 12

Two hours after Dylan's impromptu gun lesson, Rachel sat in Julia's office, staring at her friend. After their wild make-out session, both Dylan and Rachel had gotten back to working on the ranch when Rachel's cell buzzed. Her friend's voice mail on her cell phone had sounded urgent, so she'd dropped paying the bills and headed out without telling Dylan where she was going. She did, however, leave him a note so he wouldn't worry.

He had a list of chores as long as her arm—he'd stay busy. Wasn't as though she needed to give him her itinerary, anyway. As he'd reminded her, anything between them personally was impossible. So then, he was just a guest on her property. She owed him nothing.

"So I got some new information today," Julia said. "That's why I called you in."

"And?" Rachel prompted, fingering the brass studs on Julia's leather office chair.

"I'm sure I've never mentioned this before, but I have a friend…my college roommate…her father was a bigwig with the U.S. Marshals in Colorado. Retired now, but I gave my friend a call and asked if her father could put an ear to the ground about Jax's escape."

Rachel leaned forward. "And?"

"And he couldn't find out anything more than we already knew. At first. But he kept digging. And it turns out he has a friend who's a bigwig with the DEA. He asked questions about Jax and the drug raid last year and discovered something that's been kept under wraps this whole time. About the man who Jax delivered those drugs to in L.A."

"Lou Parker?" Like Julia, Rachel had gone over Jax's trial transcripts hundreds of times during the appeal process, so she knew the major players that had been identified during the DEA's raid. "He was arrested on a bunch of outstanding warrants. He was sent to prison before Jax was."

"Right. Only he never gave up information about who he was working for. If he was working for anyone. What we never knew was the DEA believes he was working for the leader of an American drug cartel. A man named George Evans. Big into cocaine, Ecstasy and heroin. High-end stuff. The kind of stuff celebrities get caught smoking or snorting."

"I'm not seeing how this is related to Jax."

"The DEA believes Evans was at the raid but escaped before he could be apprehended. Just like Jax. The big question is which one of them left with the money."

"Money? What money?"

"The million dollars Lou Parker was supposed to pay Jax in exchange for the drugs he delivered. The drugs that Evans never got. But the DEA thinks Jax took his money, anyway."

Rachel lifted her hand to her temple. She felt disoriented. As if the world was spinning around her. "Jax never said anything about any money. And they arrested him at the ranch. He didn't have any money on him."

Julia just looked at her until Rachel understood what she was silently communicating.

"You think he hid this money on the ranch before he was arrested? That *that's* the reason he's heading home?" Not for family. Not to make sure that she and Peter were okay. But for drug money? "And this is what Dylan thinks?"

Julia shook her head. "According to my friend, the DEA hasn't shared the information about the missing money with anyone, including the marshals."

"Maybe that's because they know Jax didn't take it," Rachel said. "There were all kinds of criminals arrested that night. And you said yourself George Evans got away. He probably took the money with him."

"That's a possibility," Julia conceded. "But it's not the only possibility, Rachel."

Rachel's mouth tightened. "You're Jax's attorney. You're supposed to be focusing on the possibilities that can help him, not hurt him." *You're not supposed to be focusing on the possibilities that will hurt* me. Why was Julia doing this? She had to know how much it would hurt Rachel to think that Jax would come to her only because of money. It was on the tip of her tongue to tell her about Jax's email—that he only wanted to make sure that she and Peter were safe—but she held back. She felt she couldn't trust anyone anymore—even Julia.

"Rachel," Julia said, her tone soft, "I know you love your brother as both a sibling and a parent. And I know that love can go deep. But consider the facts. Jax has just escaped federal custody, and during the escape, two U.S. Marshals were killed. Whatever happens, you need to protect yourself. If Jax comes home, turn him over. Do *not* harbor a fugitive. Do you understand? Because if you do, and you're caught, you could get a prison sentence yourself. And who would raise your son then?"

Dylan stood, one hand on the pitchfork and the other on his hip, watching as Rachel drove up to the ranch, twin clouds of red dust following her beat-up pickup truck like two Tasmanian devils racing after her back tires. She hadn't told him she was leaving, and when he first realized she was gone, he'd been pissed. Beyond pissed. But only because he'd been worried. Someone had tried to drive them off the road last night and she was off on her own doing God knew what. But then he'd found her note just before he got a call from Eric that he'd seen her leave the ranch and had followed her into town. She'd indeed stopped to see Julia, and her drive into town had been uneventful. Eric had promised to follow her until she got back home safely.

Knowing Rachel was safe, Dylan had worked most of his anger off doing the chores she'd asked him to do. The entire time, he told himself Rachel wasn't his and he had no right to expect her to check in and out with him.

At least Rachel had a friend during all this. He couldn't imagine her not having someone to talk to, to confide in. Had to be so lonely for her, out here on the ranch, miles from town, with only her son and her ranch hand to share her day with.

He grimaced, thinking of the ranch hand, and wiped a hand over his brow, swiping off the rivulet of sweat that had started to pour. Fifteen minutes earlier, Stacy had called with the coroner's preliminary findings of Josiah's death. He had to speak with Rachel, although this was yet another conversation he didn't want to have.

He resumed shoving the pitchfork into the pile of discarded hay the alpacas had left behind after their morning feeding. Rachel had told him to pitch the remnants into a wheelbarrow and dump the load off at a compost pile covered by a tarp at the edge of the barn. He hadn't realized how many wheelbarrow loads were involved. Apparently Josiah only cleaned up the remnants once a week, and this was his fifth and final wheelbarrow load. How on earth Rachel would keep the ranch running after he returned to California, he didn't know.

And if it involved the young stud she'd talked about earlier, he didn't *want* to know.

Rachel drove up parallel to him and slowed the truck, putting it into idle. She rolled the hand-cranked window down and stuck her head out the window, gazing at the area he'd already cleaned up. She smiled tightly. He knew immediately she was upset but trying to hide it. "Wow," she said, her voice dripping with false cheer. "Can't believe how tidy you've made the corral. Josiah does—*did*—a good job, but he always left quite a bit behind. It's almost as if you've taken a broom to the place. Were you in the military once?"

"Nope. This is just what you get when you put law enforcement on the job. We're pretty damn thorough."

As soon as he said the words, he regretted them. Her attempts to look cheerful gave way to a pinched expression that made her look as if she'd just licked a lemon.

He'd take it. At least it was honest. Real. He didn't want her hiding her troubles from him. And by the same token, he couldn't hide what he knew from her either.

"Rachel..." He stopped speaking. What could he say? That he was sorry he was out to get her brother? He'd be lying if he voiced the words. Jackson Kincaid was a fugitive who'd confessed to his crimes. He deserved to be behind bars, not gallivanting about the countryside, worrying his sister and costing the taxpayers loads of money trying to get his sorry ass back in prison. But he was sorry her brother, and by necessity his job, was causing her pain.

"I have things to do," she said quickly, taking her gaze away from his, staring straight ahead through her dust and bug-spattered windshield, and grinding the gears as she put the truck into first. Suddenly she frowned, then turned her attention back to him.

The intensity in her eyes caught him off guard, and his heart skipped a beat. How beautiful she was. God, he needed to keep his damn focus—this was not a pickup in some bar. This was a woman whose brother had done a very bad thing, and he had a job to do.

And part of his job was to inform her about what had happened to her ranch hand.

"I know you need to get back to work," he said, as a way of apology. He was about to continue, but she cut him off with a wave of her hand.

"I just realized...did you do the list of chores in order, the way I asked?" she said.

He nodded, unsure where the conversation was headed.

"Wow. That means you've already stacked a cord of wood, repaired the broken board on the side of the barn, dug the ditch for the new watering system *and* mucked out the chicken coop, right?"

This time instead of nodding, he grimaced. That chicken coop had been no pretty picnic, that was for sure. He wasn't sure he'd ever forget that particular stench. "Yes to all the above," he said, swinging the pitchfork onto the now-full wheelbarrow. He picked up the wheelbarrow handles, ready to resume his trek to the compost pile. A pile he was becoming far too intimate with, in his mind. "This is the last of it. What else do you want me to do today?"

For a moment, Rachel simply stared at him in silence, her brow furrowed, her eyes narrowed, as if taking in the very measure of him. Finally she spoke, saying, "Color me impressed." She blew out a quick breath. "It would have taken me a week to get all those chores done. I owe you."

"You don't, though. I'm just doing my job."

"Right. I remember. But you could have dinked around, pretending to do your job. But you didn't. You actually did the work. I'm…I'm grateful."

He knew by the way her throat bobbed up and down that the word *grateful* had been a difficult one for her to squeeze out. He appreciated it. She didn't have to like him, and certainly didn't have to be nice to him, but here she was, telling him she was grateful. There was more to Rachel Kincaid than met the eye, and her complexity intrigued him. Probably more than it should.

Too bad she couldn't have instilled more values in her criminal brother.

The air shifted, bringing with it the pungent odor of the compost pile he'd left uncovered. Damn. He needed to hurry up and get the tarp back on it before the entire ranch was drowned in the nasty scent. "I need to talk to you."

She looked wary, then resolved. "I'll go park the truck and can meet you on the back porch with lemonade. Just give me about ten minutes, okay?"

He tipped his head in agreement, and watched as Rachel gave the truck gas and eased past him, the open window letting the breeze toy with her near-white hair.

Fifteen minutes later, the compost pile thoroughly covered by the tarp, and his hands washed in the outside faucet, Dylan strode onto the back porch. Rachel was already seated, a magazine illustrating heavy equipment open on her lap, a pitcher of lemonade, a bucket of ice and two glasses on the small table by her side. For a moment, he simply enjoyed the picture she made and imagined he was coming home to her. That she was his. That there was nothing between them but desire and affection.

His core stirred, and he allowed himself the indulgence of picturing her naked in his mind's eye. Of covering her with his own naked form. Penetrating her. Stroking her with his shaft and his hands and his tongue…

She glanced up at him and he clenched his fists even as he drove his lustful thoughts from his mind. Every time he saw her, it was the same thing. He wanted her. And not just her body. Her company.

She was a good woman. She stimulated his mind

and his body. She wasn't like the sophisticated city women he normally dated, and to him that was nothing but good. She was real. Fresh. Sensual in a Mother Earth kind of way that made him want to take her on the ground, surrounded by trees and wildflowers that couldn't begin to compare to her beauty.

He could easily see himself falling in love with her. In fact, sometimes it felt as though he was already halfway there....

No, he mentally growled. *Do not go there.* So she was good. Sexy. So damn beautiful. He couldn't love her. He wouldn't. First, he didn't believe true love could form in such a short amount of time. Second, how could he love someone he didn't totally respect? He respected a lot about Rachel, but her inability to see the truth of her brother's flaws? Her willingness to bury her head in the sand so that she was endangering not only her life, but her son's?

No.

How many times did he need to remind himself that he couldn't have her before it stuck?

He lowered himself down onto the empty Adirondack chair next to hers, then filled both glasses with ice and poured what appeared to be fresh-squeezed lemonade until the ice bobbed to the surface. Handing one to Rachel, he gave her a soft smile. At least he tried to. But given his recent thoughts, combined with the type of news he was about to deliver, he was betting his smile was strained.

Damn, but he hated having to tell her about Josiah. So he'd wait. For a few minutes, anyway. No need for him to hurt her right off the bat, not when she'd gone to the lengths to squeeze lemons for fresh lemonade.

"You and your brother have the same last name. But you were married," he commented. "You kept your maiden name, then?"

Rachel sipped from the glass in her hand and made a sour face. "I should have put more simple syrup in. The lemons are extra tart this year." She twirled a lock of her long, straight hair with her fingers, the sliver of sunlight that hit the back porch causing shimmers to glint off the highlights. "When I got married, it wasn't really out of love, but more to provide Jax a good home. I'd known my husband for years—we'd gone to school together." She gave a light laugh. "He was the kid who pulled my pigtails, you know?"

"Cute."

"Clichéd," she said. "But still, he was sweet. And when my folks died and I needed help with Jax, he stepped up to the plate. Offered to marry me and help out on the ranch. Only problem was, he was still a kid himself. When he discovered I was pregnant, he freaked out and started partying with his friends. Wouldn't come home all night sometimes. Ended up driving drunk and killing himself by the time Peter was three."

Some of the story he'd known by researching Jackson Kincaid and his sister. But the sorrow in Rachel's eyes spoke of something research could never tell him. She hadn't loved her husband—not the passionate, "in love" kind of love you would expect from a marriage—but she'd cared for him. That was clear.

"And your name?" he prodded. He didn't know why the fact that she used her maiden name intrigued him, but it did.

"Peter has his father's last name, but I felt like I'd

never really been married, so taking his name would have felt like a lie."

Interesting. She'd exchanged vows with a man, had signed a contract before God and the law, had made a child with the man, but never considered herself married. Warmth suffused his chest, then spread down to his belly, where it transformed into a tingle.

Despite his best intentions, she was worming her way inside him again. Making him want her. Making him think he could love her....

Once again, he pushed those feelings away.

It was time he shared the information he'd been holding on to. Information he knew for certain Rachel wouldn't want to hear.

After a few more minutes of idle chitchat about the weather—unseasonably hot and oppressive—the alpacas—sweetly humming in the distance—and the tractor Rachel wanted to buy—expensive—she finally gave him a flat glance and let out a deep sigh. "You haven't said what you wanted to tell me yet. Is it bad?" she asked.

"Bad enough."

"Is it about Jax?"

"It's about Josiah." He waited, watching her expression go from guarded and worried to sad and concerned. She toyed with her drink, pushing one ice cube around in circles with the tip of her finger, staring at the lemonade as if it held the secrets of the universe.

"He was murdered," Rachel said, not asking a question, but rather making a statement.

"Yes," he said, in confirmation. No sense skirting about the issue. Not when Rachel already knew the answer.

"Oh, God," she said quietly, almost to herself, and stared off into the distance, not meeting his gaze. She set her glass of lemonade down on the table and folded her hands in her lap, staring down at her entwined fingers. He didn't press forward, but instead gave her space to process the news.

A loud snort caught his attention, and he turned to gaze at a few of the alpacas Rachel had put in the corral by the barn. These five were expecting any day now, she'd explained, and she wanted them nearby, not out in one of the bigger pastures, in case they went into labor. They'd seemed agitated, being cut from the rest of the herd, and he'd suggested they could maybe be let out on the far pasture with the remaining herd, let nature take its course. Rachel had responded almost angrily, insisting that they needed to be close, where she could control the situation in case something went wrong. He'd backed off but still felt a pang of empathy for the penned-in fuzz balls.

It wasn't lost on him that she had a thing for control. Of course she did. She'd had to take control of her brother after her parents died. Had to take sole control of this ranch and her son. Taking control was her way of making sure everyone stayed safe.

But she couldn't control everything.

"How?"

Her single word startled him. No wailing, no moaning, no gnashing of teeth. No hysteria. Just the quiet, factual question. If it hadn't been for her glistening eyes, or the way she clenched her arms tightly around her chest, he would have thought she didn't care. But that pulse at the base of her delicate throat said otherwise. Rachel was grieving. In pain. But keeping it to herself. He had to admire her resolve.

"He died from a cerebral hemorrhage, as we already knew, but what we didn't know was that it was brought about by a heavy, sharp object hitting the top of his head."

"The top of his head," she repeated dully.

Damn. She was beautiful, compassionate, loyal to a fault and shrewd. She'd caught the clue he'd unwittingly handed her. "Yeah. There was no way he could have fallen and hit himself on the top of the head that hard. He'd have to have fallen from a height and landed on a rock straight on top of his head."

"But why would someone kill Josiah? The man was a simple ranch hand. Everyone around town knew him. Loved him." She turned suddenly in her seat and speared him with a sharp look. "And don't go saying my brother killed him because Josiah somehow stumbled across Jax. First, Jax would never, ever kill anyone. And second, Josiah would have helped Jax hide from the law—from you, if he'd known about you—and Jax knows that. Josiah was like family to us, Jax included."

He held up a hand. The woman was a force to be reckoned with. He eased forward, the deck chair squeaking under his shifting weight, and said, "I won't tell you I think your brother killed Josiah. I can say, though, that I've seen family members kill one another over the most trivial of things—I once had to track a woman who'd run off while out on bail who was accused of killing her husband because he didn't put away their kid's LEGOs the night before."

Rachel winced involuntarily. "Ouch. Stepping on a LEGO in the dark—I've been there. If you don't have kids, you don't realize how murderously painful that can be."

Her words suggested she was trying to lighten the mood, but her expression was tense and unsmiling.

"I don't have any evidence as to who killed your friend, Rachel. And I'll give your brother the benefit of the doubt. My job here is to bring him back to face justice, not to try him for a theoretical crime."

"I know that. I like that you're at least willing to give him the benefit of the doubt. Some people aren't. Hell, even Julia—"

She stopped speaking abruptly.

"Even Julia what?" he asked.

"I don't believe it," she said. "And I don't want you to, either."

Whatever it was Julia had told her was eating at her. Would she trust him enough to tell him? Was it possible she was beginning to see him as more than the enemy?

Dylan reached out and took her hand. "Do you remember what I said about keeping you safe, Rachel?"

She bit her lip and nodded.

"I meant it. I can't tell you what's going to happen to your brother, but you can trust that I want to help."

"I don't know why, but I can't deny it. I do trust you."

"Then tell me what Julia said."

Chapter 13

An hour later, in the tack room in the barn, Rachel sat on a Western saddle, supported by a saddle tree, using it as a seat. After she told Dylan about George Evans's missing money and the DEA's ludicrous theory that Jax had taken it, Dylan had looked ready to explode. Instead, he'd stood, thanked her for confiding in him, then told her he needed to get in touch with his team.

Twenty minutes later, he'd come back to the house and asked her to join him in his makeshift office. She'd obeyed, but only after taking her time to slide her arms into the sleeves of a chambray shirt and button it up. A breeze had picked up, and even in the barn a chill prickled goose bumps along her arms. She shivered, but whether from the sudden cold or from the way Dylan gave her a sidelong glance, his eyes smoldering with what she'd swear was possessiveness, she wasn't sure.

But then he turned his attention back to his tablet, and she continued to stare at him, and any cold she was feeling disappeared under a spreading heat.

It had felt good, confiding in him about what Julia had told her. The fact that he clearly hadn't known about the DEA's theory and was angry about being kept out of the loop had made her relieved he hadn't been keeping a secret from her and had made her feel that they were finally on the same side for a change. Maybe that was why she couldn't seem to take her eyes off him. His strong jaw. His blue eyes framed by such thick lashes. The soft dark hair she wanted to run her hands through. The ears she wanted to lick and nibble…

She sucked in a breath. *Focus,* she told herself. Stop gaping at the lawman as if he were an ice-cream cone on a hot summer day. Shifting in her seat, she brought her focus back to the situation. She'd told him about the DEA's theory. Maybe she should tell him about Jax's email. Let him know that Jax was coming so they could talk about the best way to help her brother. Only she was too used to protecting her brother to make that leap. Not yet.

Dylan's tablet buzzed, startling her. Again she wondered why he'd called her out here.

"Here we go," Dylan said, even though she had no idea what he was talking about.

She nibbled a lip. "Are you sure you want me in on your meeting? Isn't this top-secret stuff, or something?"

Dylan flashed a grin. "We're U.S. Marshals, not CIA. Get back in the saddle and stay awhile."

Dylan leaned to the side so Rachel could get a good look at his tablet's small screen. A woman's face filled the screen. She didn't seem surprised to see Rachel seated behind Dylan.

"Stacy, have you checked into what Rachel told me?"

"I certainly have," she said. "Marco's still reaming our contact with the DEA, but he's fessed up. George Evans. Age fifty-two. He's a known high-end drug dealer but has never been caught. Rachel's friend is right. The DEA thinks he was present during the raid, but they didn't know it at the time. He got away. They never found the money that was supposed to be given to Jackson in exchange for the drugs. They acknowledge Evans might have taken it. They think the more likely scenario is that Jackson grabbed it, fled to the ranch and hid it before he was apprehended."

Dylan turned to Rachel. "When they picked up your brother, how long did the DEA agents stay on the ranch?"

"Hours."

"Did they search the entire place?"

"I don't know. They could have. I—I was so upset and focusing on Jax at the time, I didn't really pay attention."

He turned back to Stacy. "So they searched the place. Came up empty. But now that Kincaid has escaped and is heading back to the ranch for the money?"

"They figured they'd wait until you captured him, then try to talk to him again. Which they've tried doing several times in the past. All with poor results."

"And in the meantime, they didn't think we needed to know this? They didn't think the fact that Kincaid stands to gain not only his freedom but upwards of a million dollars was relevant to the danger he might pose to others in trying to get here?"

Rachel had been listening to Dylan's conversation with Stacy, but it took her several minutes for what Dylan was saying to sink in. Her first clue was that he was referring to her brother as "Kincaid" again. "Wait a minute," she said. "Are you—are you saying you *believe* Jax took the money and hid it on the ranch? That he's heading here because of that? Are you back to thinking he killed Josiah…for money?"

Dylan frowned. "I'm back to considering those are possibilities, of course."

"Of course? So nothing I've said about my brother, about him being good, about him not being capable of hurting Josiah, has sunk in?"

Dylan stared at her, deliberately reached out and turned off his tablet, then stood. "Rachel, I thought I explained that while I believe in the theory of being innocent until proven guilty, that can't stop me from considering the evidence as it stands, too. The evidence suggests your brother might have hidden a million dollars on this land. That's a huge motivation for him to come back here and to not get caught. Besides, even putting aside how I view the evidence, that's irrelevant to my job. I'm a marshal. My job is to bring your brother back into custody. It's not to interpret or gather the evidence. Even if I believed your brother was innocent, I'd still need to bring him in."

"But you don't *believe* he's innocent, do you?" She jumped off the saddle and began backing away from him and toward the open barn doors. "And I don't know why I believed *you* when you said you wanted to help me. The fact is you're too blinded by Jax's past mistakes to do that. Why aren't you considering that George Evans took the money?"

"Because if he did, there'd be no reason for him to hurt Josiah. Or to try and hurt you, and we both know…" A weird expression came over Dylan's face as his words trailed off.

Rachel wondered about it for a split second, but then all she could think about was escape. She felt as if everyone in the world was against her, and she was all that stood between herself and the total annihilation of everything she loved.

She'd forgotten that Dylan was her enemy for a short time.

She couldn't do it again.

She whirled and ran toward the house. Once inside, she flew up the stairs and locked herself in her bedroom. She knew she was fleeing. Hiding. But she didn't care.

Thank God she hadn't told Dylan about Jax's email.

Tomorrow would come soon enough. She'd take some time to hide and think of a way to help Jax.

And hope that as she did so, she purged every trace of the desire and building affection she'd started to feel for Dylan from her mind, body and soul.

Chapter 14

The next day, Rachel dealt with her frustration and anger with Dylan quite simply—she *didn't* deal with him. Instead, she kept a detached manner as she detailed the chores she wanted him to do, and she busied herself with her own chores, making sure to keep plenty of space between them. Any time she wanted to give in to her urge to see him or talk to him or daydream about the kisses they'd shared and how good the orgasm he'd given her had felt, she simply pushed herself harder.

She was a mother. She wasn't supposed to be running past third base and about to slide home with a man she barely knew. She was supposed to be making a living for her and her son. Most important, she was supposed to be considering what was best for Jax: continuing to keep his email from Dylan or trusting that despite his prejudices against her brother, he would do what he said, and treat him right.

By the time she'd finished her chores, it was evening and just starting to get dark. When she caught sight of Dylan dismounting from Row and walking the horse toward her, she said, "The alpaca herd has headed into the barn for the night," swinging off Anchor. "If you could take the tack off the horses and brush them down, I'll bring in the pregnant ones from the corral, then do one last count and make sure all alpacas are here. Put the horses in the far corral, then head on into the house. You get first dibs on the hot water—I'll whip up some dinner while you shower. After we eat, I need to spend time on the accounting, and I'll need you to pull nails out of old boards. There's a stack about shoulder-height in the barn."

Dylan reached for Anchor's reins. "Rachel, things don't have to be this way between us."

"What way?"

"Back to treating each other as enemies."

"You're here on my ranch, Dylan. Obviously I don't think of you as an enemy. But as we discussed yesterday, you plus me equals complication. I'm just playing things the way they need to be played. We keep our hands—and lips and bodies—and our opinions about my brother—to ourselves, no problem. That's all."

Without waiting for his rebuttal—and she was certain he'd come up with one—she turned tail and headed to the corral to bring in the pregnant alpacas.

Five minutes later, she returned, concern worming its way through her veins.

Dylan looked up from running a body brush over Row. He frowned. "What is it?"

She shook her head and nibbled her lip. "Two of the females are missing. There's a board missing on the corral—it looks like it was broken and dragged away. I brought the other three into the barn, but the rest of the herd seems nervous."

"Coyotes?"

"Alpacas are good at fighting off coyotes. I've lost crias to the varmints, but no adults. In fact, when I first got the herd, there were a few times when I actually watched as they fought off coyotes. The local pack knows to stay away from the adults now."

"Would they have run off?"

She nibbled her lip. "I don't think so. Alpacas are herd animals. They feel safest when they're together. It doesn't make sense that they would have gone off on their own, but I suppose it's possible."

He put down the brush and came over to her, the warmth of his body a comforting sensation. "I'll grab a flashlight and go look for them. Just tell me where to go."

"I wonder if they headed down the trail to the creek." Nerves twisted her belly. The two missing females were worth seven thousand dollars each, and both were carrying unborn crias that could fetch up to nine thousand dollars so long as their conformation and coats turned out perfect. She'd insured her herd, but not for the full value, the cost being prohibitive. She'd take a hard hit if anything happened to either of the females.

"I'll go," she said. "They're my responsibility. But if you want to come with me, I'd appreciate the company." And she would. Dylan was no Josiah, and he didn't have a clue about ranching, but he was a strong man and she was about to head out into the dark. Coyotes might not tangle with one of her adult alpacas, but that didn't mean she was without a healthy sense of fear of things that went bump in the night. As Dylan had pointed out, strange things were happening on the ranch, and while she didn't believe her brother was involved, she wasn't going to risk her life on her theory on coincidences, either.

She led the way, Dylan a step behind her, lighting the path with his flashlight. After reaching the trail, he swept the beam of light in cross sections as they moved forward until she heard a noise. She reached out and grabbed his hand to still the movement of the light.

"Listen," she breathed.

A rattling, bubbling sound came from not too far away.

"Is that the sound of alpacas?" Dylan whispered.

"No. At least, not a sound I've ever heard."

He twisted, breaking her contact on his wrist, then stepped in front of her. "Stay close, but be ready to run back to the barn."

She didn't argue. Sure, he'd be putting himself at risk if anything dangerous was out there, but she was a mother and that came first.

Slowly, Dylan swept his light in the same crosshatch pattern, but this time further ahead and off to the right. "There," he said. "What are we looking at?"

Squinting, Rachel looked to where the faint beam of light shone. There, lying on their sides, were the two missing alpacas. It took a moment for her to recognize that something wasn't right. Instead of lying still, both alpacas were writhing on the ground. Burbling, gasping sounds came from them.

"Oh, God!" she cried out. She moved to race forward, but Dylan grabbed her wrist and held her firm. "Let me go—something's wrong!" she shouted.

"Rachel, I know. I can see that. But I'm going first. Keep behind me." He pulled the handgun out from his boot holster and with one hand held the gun up and with the other held his flashlight against the gun as he stepped forward, slowly.

After sweeping the flashlight around, he beckoned for her to come closer. "It's not good, I'm afraid," he said as she stepped up to her stock. He focused the light on the two alpacas.

Both females still lay on the ground, but the one on the right had ceased writhing. As Rachel stood there, she could see it could barely breathe. Its eyes rolled in its head until they met hers, panicked. "Oh, no…" The words spilled from her mouth before she could stop them. A sob followed. Dylan placed a warm hand on her shoulder and instinctively, she leaned against him.

"No blood," he observed.

She swallowed several times, words sticking in her throat. The truth hurt. Ached. "No, they haven't been injured."

"They aren't giving birth, right?"

She shook her head. "No. Something's horribly wrong here."

"Do you know what it is?"

Her insides churned. She'd seen an animal look like this before when she was young—a neighbor's dog who'd gotten into some rat poison. She swallowed against the rising bile in her throat, then managed to get out, "I think they've been poisoned."

"We need to get them into the barn."

The alpaca on the right had grown too weak to do more than flick its ears at Rachel. Froth bubbled on its muzzle and a deep moan came from somewhere inside.

Pain scratched its way through Rachel's chest. "This one's too far gone," she murmured.

Stepping heavily, she made her way to the other alpaca, then bent down and lifted the hundred-plus-pound weight up in her arms. After staggering briefly, she turned and faced the barn, deliberately keeping her back to Dylan and the dying alpaca.

"Have any bullets left?" The words nearly choked her.

"Rachel?"

"This is a ranch, Dylan. Out here, we do what we have to. Shoot her."

The ache in Dylan's chest threatened to explode. Watching Rachel stumble to the barn, a poisoned and pregnant alpaca dangling limply in her arms, recalling the anguish on her face and the words she'd spoken—*shoot her*—had something inside him all twisted up and tangled. Getting turned on by the sexy widow he could handle. But this aching inside? This he could not handle. This emotion went well beyond what he expected of himself as a marshal. He needed to curb this connection he felt to Rachel Kincaid. Because no matter how many times he reminded himself she wasn't the type of woman that was good for him—no matter that she refused to let her brother take responsibility for his mistakes—he knew deep down that if push came to shove...

He'd be lost if somehow he ended up having to choose between her and his duty. He wasn't sure what that meant—if he'd actually let her brother go instead of taking him into custody. He hoped not. He prayed he'd still have the willpower to do the right thing. But he had to admit that the "right thing" was beginning to become less black-and-white to him.

He'd told Rachel that even if he believed her brother was innocent he'd still take him into custody. Would that really be right thing to do? Could he overlook his own gut feeling just to fulfill his job?

Wouldn't that be the opposite of justice? Of integrity?

And Rachel believed her brother was innocent. What if…just *what if*…she was right and the rest of them were wrong?

It took only a moment to put the soft, fuzzy creature out of its misery. After, he swept a hand over its face, shutting its eyes. He'd killed before—twice, actually. Both times in the line of duty. Both times someone else's life had been on the line and he'd had to take the shot. Both times he'd walked away from the shooting without regret. Left the bodies for the CSU team to photograph and dispatch. Now? His hands shook as he put his gun back in its holster. Something had edged its way under his wall of defense, and he needed to get a grip.

He followed the path Rachel had made in the dark, and entered the barn to see Rachel in a stall, the alpaca on a bed of sweet golden hay. "Will it make it?" he asked.

"This one seems better than the other, but only time will tell." Rachel kept her back to him as she spoke. She tucked more hay around the alpaca's heaving rib cage, then stood and pulled her phone out of her back pocket. "I'm going to call my vet. Not sure there's much we can do tonight, but I have to try everything."

He nodded, understanding. As he listened in on the conversation, it became clear the vet agreed with Rachel's assumption: the alpacas had been poisoned. The vet felt that the poison had probably entered the blood-stream and nothing could be done, but he'd promised to come over in the morning and gather blood samples to test for poison.

Phone conversation over, Rachel sank down to her knees in the hay. Without thought, Dylan came to her side and lowered himself down, next to her. She wrapped her arms around her knees and tucked her chin between her arms, hiding her face from him, but the sharp shakes of her shoulders told him all he needed to know: Rachel Kincaid was crying.

"Come inside," he murmured, stroking her hair off the back of her neck. Softly, he massaged the tight muscles there. "Soak in the bathtub while I make you something to eat. I think both the accounting and those nails can wait."

"I hate being such a crybaby," she said, the words sounding choked. "I hate falling apart."

"You've had a number of shocks over the last couple of days. And this isn't falling apart. This is a woman at the end of her rope, releasing some of the tension that's eating her up from the inside out." He realized he was stroking her skin, making small circles with the tips of his fingers along the line of her spine.

He rose, brushed hay off his rear and took a step back. "Let's go. There's nothing more you can do here tonight, but if you don't get some food and rest, you won't be good for any of your stock or business tomorrow. Bath, food and bed. In that order."

An hour later, he'd managed to get Rachel into a bath, fixed her a meal of soup and corn bread, made sure she spoke to her son and ensured that she was thoroughly tucked into bed. Only when her breathing settled into a deep rhythm, which he could hear from standing in the hall by her bedroom door, did he returned to his established headquarters in the barn and ping his team. One by one they all logged on until the faces of the entire team showed on the screen.

"Status update?" he asked.

"One of Eric's informants contacted him," Stacy responded, then frowned. When he tipped his head, she continued. "Said he heard a big-time American dealer is on the hunt for the guy who escaped prison transport."

"George Evans." The dealer present at the shoot-out in which Jax had been nabbed.

"We're pretty sure that's the one. And we're pretty sure he's after Jackson Kincaid. Eric's informant said the guy was headed to Texas. Maybe even put a hit out on the escapee."

"Not good." George Evans was out to get Jax.

It had to be because of the money.

Good news: if Evans wanted that money, he probably hadn't put a hit out on Jax. George Evans would want Jackson Kincaid alive to talk.

Bad news: once George Evans caught Jackson, her brother would be tortured into revealing the whereabouts of the money if he didn't do so readily. And then he'd be killed.

He also had to consider something that he'd only started to consider yesterday, when he was telling Rachel that if George Evans had taken the money, he wouldn't have a reason to mess with her or Josiah. That was true. But if George Evans suspected Jax had taken the money and knew where the money was and was now in a position to lead him to it, it could be that Evans was messing with Rachel and her ranch, hoping that news of it would reach Jax and be interpreted as a message: get Evans the money or watch your family die.

Now that they suspected Evans was after Jax, it made all the more sense.

"You know about the scares Rachel has had over the past few days," he said quickly, drawing the attention of Stacy, Marco and Eric back to him. "We found two of her stock poisoned earlier tonight."

"You think that's linked to George Evans rather than her brother now?" Stacy asked.

"It's possible," he said definitively. "It's also possible Jackson is trying to get his sister off the ranch just like I once thought. So he can get the money. The question is, does he want it for himself or to hand over to Evans?"

"You really think he'd put his sister in danger just so he can beat Evans to the money?"

"I have to consider the possibility."

"And the fact that his sister won't."

He twisted his mouth into a frown. Stacy was exactly right. Not only wouldn't she believe that about her brother, but if she knew Jax was being hunted by Evans, she'd do anything she could to protect him.

And in doing so, she'd be putting herself at even more risk.

That was why he was tempted to keep what he'd just found out from her.

The only thing that swayed him to a different course was Peter—and his belief that not even for her brother would she risk her son.

When she was young, Rachel would pretend to fall asleep in order to sneak on a flashlight under the covers and read her book. Her parents had been strict about bedtime—no reading after dark. So she'd steady her breath until she heard the creak of footsteps in the hall, then down the stairs, then the faint sound of the TV in the living room, and only then would pull out her flashlight and her book and tuck the covers securely around her.

Seemed the old falling-asleep trick had worked equally well with Dylan. She'd heard him creep away from her room and head outside to the barn a good fifteen minutes ago. She rose from her bed and padded across the room to unlock the double French doors leading to the balcony. Dylan had checked to make sure they were locked after sending her to bed. Now, if Jax came home in the dead of night, he'd at least have an open door to sneak into.

She returned to bed, sliding in between the cool, crisp pima-cotton sheets, and twisted her pillow under her head, staring into the darkness, willing the hot tears to stay in her eyes. Some alpaca owners named each and every one of their stock. Not her. She'd been raised to ranch the old-fashioned way: animals were stock, not pets. But even with a herd of thirty, the alpaca who'd died had been as familiar to Rachel as if she'd been given a name. The brown-and-cream five-year-old had been a good mother and a loyal member of the herd. She hadn't deserved to die.

To be murdered.

Because that was what had happened. The poisoning hadn't come from a wayward plant. Nothing grew in Rachel's fields or anywhere near that could have caused such a violent death. No, someone had deliberately poisoned at least two of her alpacas. But who? She gripped the soft coverlet in both fists.

Dylan would suspect Jax.

And God help her. For the first time, a flash of doubt sparked in her mind.

It was the information about the money that was causing her to doubt him.

She'd never thought Jax would have transported drugs for money, but he'd confessed to doing just that. She hadn't wanted to believe it, but what if she was wrong?

What if money could motivate her brother to do stupid things? Why couldn't it also motivate him to do even more horrible things?

Like cause a stampede? Kill alpacas? Kill Josiah?

Try to kill her?

She rolled over and buried her face in her sheets.

No, no, no.

This wasn't right. She was letting her feelings for Dylan mess with her head. And if she allowed herself to see Dylan as anything but her enemy, she'd open herself up to a world of hurt.

Chapter 15

Morning dawned bright and cheerful, a far cry from the dark mood that had settled over the house because of the poisoned alpacas. By the time Dylan had woken, stretched his aching back and taken a shower and dressed in faded jeans, cowboy boots and a white T-shirt, Rachel had already commandeered the kitchen, cooking up a hearty breakfast and brewing tar for coffee.

He'd half expected her to spend the morning in bed, grieving what had happened to her animals. The fact that she hadn't reminded him that while she might be felled low for a while by bad news, she never stayed down for long. In that way, she was very different from his mother. Watching her carefully, he poured a cup of coffee, swallowed, then grimaced.

Catching his expression, Rachel snorted. "Need

cream with that, city boy?" she asked, turning away from him and busying herself at the sink.

He snagged a strip of bacon from the fry pan and brushed past her, coffee mug still gripped in his other hand. "Nope. I promised to be your handyman. And I'm assuming Texan handymen drink their coffee black." He paused and gazed at the liquid sloshing in the cup. "Maybe I should get a fork, though," he added under his breath.

"It's not that bad. A little dark, maybe...."

"Rachel, if you think this coffee is a 'little' dark, you and I definitely don't see things the same way." As soon as the words left him, her face fell and he regretted what he'd said. Somehow a veiled reference to how she viewed her brother had wormed its way into what he'd thought was going to be a casual statement.

"I've checked on the sick alpaca several times. She's about the same. I'm not sure what time the vet will be coming by, but I'm thinking I'll take a drive and go see Peter afterward."

He cleared his throat. "Rachel, I'm not sure that's a good idea right now." Not when he and his team thought George Evans was after Jax and bent on using Rachel to get to him. "We need to talk."

Speaking around a clenched jaw, she said, "About my brother. You think he poisoned the alpacas. You're wrong." She kept her back to him even as she said, "But I want to thank you for what you did last night. Both for me and my alpacas. I—I was worried about the other one, or I would have taken care of it myself. I *should* have taken care of it myself."

God, he hated it when she blamed herself, considered herself weak, when she'd just been accepting help. He stepped up to her and laid a gentle hand on her shoulder. He frowned when he realized she was shaking, holding her spine straight, her shoulders stiff. The woman had been through a lot in her life—and even though sometimes she succumbed to tears, in no way did he see that as weakness.

No, Rachel Kincaid was one of the strongest women he knew. No matter what he threw at her, she'd keep her spine straight. Of that he was sure.

The house phone rang, and Rachel jerked, startled by the sound. She moved away from Dylan's touch and he let his hand drop away. After picking up the line, she listened for a moment, then handed the phone to him.

"It's the sheriff. He wants to speak with you," she said.

He took the handset. "U.S. Marshal Rooney."

"Good morning," the familiar sound of the sheriff's voice carried across the line. "I have news I figured you and your team might want to hear. Local police found the bodies of two men off the highway."

"And?"

"And…these men didn't die of natural circumstances. They've been murdered. Shot three times in the head, execution-style. But that happened after they'd been tortured."

Tortured. He pushed away from the kitchen counter and stiffened as tension crept up his spine. "Description of the vics?"

"Bodybuilder types. Mid-twenties. Shaved heads, multiple tattoos, with gang tats running along their necks. We don't have an ID, but we ran a trace on their tattoos, and we figure they're members of an exclusive gang from L.A.—one specializing in moving high-end drugs for the rich and famous."

Damn. Had to be the two men who'd tried to drive him and Rachel off the road. And if the sheriff suspected they were linked to an exclusive gang from L.A.—that had to mean they'd been working for George Evans.

He thanked the sheriff and hung up. Rachel watched him with a worried expression on her face.

"It's okay. Nothing's happened to Peter or your brother. They're fine."

Her expression and body relaxed substantially. "Then what is it? You look like something bad has happened."

"The two men who tried to run us off the road have been found dead. I have to check in with my team. I won't be able to get started on the chores right away, but I'll catch up, okay?"

She smirked, as if him asking her for permission for anything was the height of hilarity.

He went out into the barn and as soon as he had his team up on the monitors, he didn't waste time with pleasantries or bantering, but instead got right to the point, relaying the sheriff's information about the two gangbangers found tortured and dead.

"George Evans," Stacy said quickly. "Has to be. Hold on…" She focused on her keyboard and a second monitor by her right elbow for a few minutes. "Here," Stacy said. "I'm emailing you info. I got into the sheriff's database and found the photos of the victims' tats. Ran them through a couple of databases I have access to and came up with positive IDs. Both men were part of the Hurricane Gang—that's George Evans's crew.

And there's something else, Dylan. Something we just found out."

"What's that?"

"Those are also the two men we believe were responsible for busting Jax out of custody. Against his will."

What the hell? Not only was Jackson Kincaid busted out of prison but it wasn't his own doing? Dylan felt shock at the news, but he also felt a healthy bit of relief. Rachel had been right about this at least. If her brother hadn't tried to escape from prison, that meant...

"The second marshal that was shot? He just woke up from his coma last night. He's still weak, but he told us what he saw. Jax fought against two men who stopped the prison transport by force. They're the ones who shot the marshals, not Jax."

"So that can only mean, since word on the street is that Evans is hunting Jax..."

"Jax escaped from his own escape. He got away from Evans's two goons, and..."

Dylan closed his eyes as the worst possibilities filtered through his mind. "And Evans punished them for it." It made sense. "He killed and tortured them because they'd failed to bring him Jax. Failed to scare away me and Rachel. Probably failed to find the money after searching for it," he said, remembering the stampede and the cut wires of Rachel's fence.

George Evans wouldn't allow failures in his crew. Dylan knew the type. Evans wouldn't just fire a crew member. No, he'd make sure no one else on his crew ever screwed up by making him an example. And that meant torture and death.

Hell, forget death. Nothing kept a crew tighter than the threat of torture.

And if Evans found Jackson Kincaid, the same would happen to him. And anyone who tried to get in his way.

His team.

Him.

Rachel.

The image of her being hurt in any way made his stomach roil.

Dylan finished his talk with his team, then went inside, where he found Rachel still in the house. He fought against the urge to reach out and stroke a wayward strand of hair off her forehead. To rest the back of his fingers against her cheek. To wrap her up in his arms and hold her tight as he shared what he knew she needed to know. Instead, he kept his hands fisted at his sides. "Your brother is in trouble. We need to get him back into custody."

"That's why you and your team are here. Tell me something I don't know," she said, bitterness snapping the words out of her mouth.

"No, Rachel. He's in *trouble*. Jax is at risk of being killed. And tortured first, just like the two men who tried to run us off the road. This man we've been talking about, George Evans," he continued. "We have reliable information that he had two of his men, the same men the sheriff reported were killed, break your brother out of prison. The only reason that makes sense is that he wants the money your brother took from him. Only your brother must have escaped, and now Evans is hunting him. He's out to get your brother, Rachel. And when he catches Jax? He won't be satisfied until he tortures him and then kills him."

Damn her weak knees, wobbling underneath her like those of a just-born cria. Rachel reached behind her and grabbed the counter to steady herself. What the hell had Jax gotten himself into? Being an idiot and transporting drugs across state lines had been bad enough. Now her brother had a major drug dealer who tortured and murdered his crew members out looking for him. Dylan was right: Jax would die. But how could she help the U.S. Marshals? More to the point—*should* she?

Instead of pressing her for an answer, Dylan pulled out a chair from the kitchen table, then indicated she sit down. She did. He eased himself into a chair beside her. And sat. Waiting. Waiting for her to make a decision.

Because she needed to come to a hard realization. She needed to face the terrible reality.

Even though she disagreed with Dylan about Jax—in her heart, she knew her brother wasn't a criminal—she also knew at a deep level that Dylan was trustworthy. He cared. About her, about her son, about her livestock, even. And oddly, he seemed to maybe even come to care for Jax, who he'd been so derisive about when he first arrived. She might hate how Dylan had viewed her brother, but she knew without a doubt that he would do everything he could to protect the innocent.

Not that Dylan thought Jax was innocent, but he seemed to understand that her brother needed protection. Needed help.

"Can you guarantee he'll be placed in solitary when he gets back to prison? Not in the general population?" she asked.

Dylan nodded, holding her gaze with his.

She nibbled her lip. She wanted to talk to Julia, but she could almost hear her friend's voice in her head, telling her to get her brother back into custody. She didn't need to talk to a lawyer or a friend to know what her decision had to be. She was operating on mother instincts. And those instincts told her to protect her brother. The first child she'd ever raised.

"I'll help you," she said, straightening. "The way I see it, at this point, the best thing I can do for Jax is to make sure he goes back to prison alive. And the way I'm going to start is by confessing Jax sent me an email. He's on his way here to the ranch."

Surprise flickered along Dylan's expression and was swiftly followed by a myriad of emotions that Rachel wished she couldn't see—disappointment, anger, even betrayal. She tried telling herself that Dylan had no right to feel any of those things, that the only duty she'd had was to her brother and not to him, but it didn't matter. Guilt ate at her. And not just because she'd hurt Dylan by keeping such important news from him. Guilt that if she'd told him about the email right away, something might have been done to get Jax to safety sooner.

Instead, now he was out there. Scared and alone.

And with a madman after him.

Chapter 16

For the rest of the day, Rachel went about doing her ranch work as if she was in a daze. Dylan had stuck close to her, telling her he wanted to make sure she stayed safe, but his expression and body were distant and disapproving, suggesting the more likely reason he stayed close was that he no longer trusted her and wanted to make sure she didn't do something stupid like receive and hide another email from her brother. By quitting time, defeat had spread through Rachel's limbs like a thick miasma, rendering her almost immobile.

After cleaning up and calling Peter to say good-night, she headed to the stairs, intending to go up to her bedroom, but the trek seemed impossible. How had her life come to this? She'd always obeyed the rules—never bucked the system. Had given and given and given of herself—letting go of her dreams to provide for her orphaned brother. Putting her own grief for the death of their parents on hold for so long the pain had long ago faded without commemoration. Working above and beyond what she needed to in order to pay for Jax's legal fees.

And what had her brother given her for all her sacrifices?

Guilt swept over her. She didn't hate Jax. No, that wasn't the case at all. She loved her brother as both a sister and a mother. But she couldn't help acknowledging that had Jax not made such foolish, stupid choices, she wouldn't be in this situation.

And her brother wouldn't have a death threat hanging over his head.

In the kitchen, after telling Dylan about Jax's email, she'd confided that if Jax showed up in the dead of night, he'd most likely try to sneak into her bedroom. Dylan had asked if he could sleep in the room to be there to catch Jax when he slipped in. He'd asked her to sleep in her son's room for the night, but she'd refused. If she was going to help trap her brother, she wanted to be there and make sure Dylan handled the situation correctly. Figuring Dylan would argue, she'd been surprised when he hadn't, and instead simply told her he'd sleep on the floor in her room. Although she'd agreed, and although she knew getting Jax back into custody was the best thing for him, regret still stabbed at her.

Now, with one hand on the balustrade, she placed a foot on the first step, but her other foot seemed to refuse to move.

And suddenly Dylan was behind her. Sliding one arm around her rib cage. Sweeping another behind her knees. Lifting her. Carrying her. Cradling her. Seconds seemed to spread to minutes, as Rachel's senses took in Dylan's presence. His scent—fresh hay mixed with some sort of evergreen—filled her nostrils. His heat radiated, spreading across her skin. And his breath fell on her face, the sharp puffs of breath a reassurance.

How was it this man could reassure her? This man who thought her brother the scum of the earth because he was a criminal. This man who was about to send her brother back to prison.

But she knew. She knew in the core of her heart that this man, U.S. Marshal Dylan Rooney, was one of the good guys.

"You're angry with me," Rachel said.

Dylan shook his head. "No. Not angry. I know you did what you thought was right for your brother."

But not for us, she thought. Even though there was no him and her that she could speak of.

"Stay down," he said, gently laying her on her bed.

"Can't," she mumbled. "I need to shower and brush my teeth."

He backed away, then headed to the bathroom. Without looking at her, he called out over his shoulder, "I'll draw you a bath. You're staying down until your mind settles down. You're emotionally exhausted, Rachel. I've seen this before—stress can trigger a total collapse. And I won't have you collapsing on my watch."

She couldn't argue. Not that she didn't want to, just that she had no strength. A moment later, the sounds of rushing water out of the faucet came from the bathroom, followed by the sweet scent of blood orange and verbena. Warmth flooded her chest—how sweet. Dylan had found her secret stash of bubble bath.

As tough as the man acted, inside he was a marshmallow. Not that she'd tell him.

Just as she'd never tell him she was falling for him.

The bubble bath was a bit of heaven in the midst of a chaotic storm. Dylan let her alone to undress and ease herself into the suds. She just about fell asleep then, lulled by the gentle motion of the water and the warmth that sent her bones to liquid. She relaxed for a good quarter hour, then ducked under and got her hair wet. Five minutes later she'd shampooed and rinsed her hair and was realizing she had no desire to exit the bath and enter the real world again.

Dylan knocked at the bathroom door. "Rachel, I have food for you. Do you want to come out and eat in the kitchen or do you want me to bring it in?"

She stared at the door. Decorum and sense told her she should get out, dress and meet him in the kitchen. But she didn't want to. Maybe it was because she was so relaxed, but she was suddenly haunted by the memory of him cradling her in his arms and carrying her without effort up the stairs. That, of course, brought memories of his kisses. His touch. And the way he'd lit up her body, making her shudder as her first orgasm in years had coursed through her.

Unconsciously her hand strayed to her breast. Down her stomach. Between her thighs.

She gasped softly, then bit her lip.

On the other side of that door lay danger. Temptation. Pleasure.

For all his talk of duty, she knew Dylan felt the way she did.

That he wouldn't fight her if she asked him for what she wanted. What she needed.

But she couldn't. It wouldn't be right for either of them.

She knew it, but that didn't stop her from doing what she did next. She took a quick peek down to make sure the bubbles covered everything she thought needed covering. Ranching meant she kept her body in shape, but motherhood had caused stretch marks on her belly and her breasts no longer held their shape the way they had when she was a teenager.

Funny, how her thoughts had drifted from her worries over her life to stretch marks.

"You can—" She took a deep breath, then called, "You can come in."

Was it her imagination, but did it take him a few more seconds to open the door than he should have? He entered, bearing a tray with herbal tea and graham crackers. He paused after a few steps and stared at her, his eyes flashing darkly before his expression went blank. It didn't matter. She'd seen the desire he hadn't been able to hide. The man did something delicious to her very core even when her world was falling apart.

"You didn't have much in the form of comfort food," he said, setting the tray down next to the tub.

She reached for a graham cracker, trying to act cool. "Not exactly Ben and Jerry's Chocolate Therapy, but should do the job."

He turned toward the door. "You ready to get out yet? Because we should probably talk about…what's going on." He sounded a little desperate to get away from her.

She sighed. It was good he could be sensible, she told herself. One of them had to be. "In a minute. If you hand me the comb on the vanity, I'll get rid of my tangles before climbing out."

Dylan reached for the comb, then stood there, his back still to her. He didn't move and she could see the tension rippling through his body.

"Dylan?" she whispered.

He turned and she gasped yet again. This time, he didn't bother banking the heat in his eyes. He stepped closer until she was craning her neck to look up at him. Then he crouched down beside the tub. "Can I do it?"

Again, she told herself she should say no. But his question had been tinged with something...that same desperation she'd sensed earlier, but this time it was a desperation to touch her rather than to get away from her. Her heart was now beating so fast she was sure he must be able to see it causing ripples in the water.

Too shaken to speak, she simply nodded. He shifted closer, reached out and took the weight of her wet hair in one hand, then with the other began to work the comb through her wet tresses.

Oh, God. The man was combing her hair.

When had a man ever combed her hair before?

Never.

Tingles shot through her body—from the gentleness of his touch? From the way his breath brushed her wet shoulder? From the knowledge this honorable tough marshal was as tender and caring as a lover in a romantic movie?

"You...you don't have to do this, you know," she said, then bit her lip, mentally willing Dylan to continue.

"I know."

"This feels like a complication to me."

"It is."

"Then..."

"Then nothing, Rachel. We're in the realm of complicated now. No sense in denying it." He tugged gently, the action releasing a knot in her hair.

"But what about your job?"

"There are strict rules about getting involved with a suspect. That's a no-go zone. I'd never compromise my job or my responsibility to my country. But this? This thing between us? It's not a professional issue."

Just a personal one. She wondered who this man was—what made him tick. What his story was. The way he acted, how seriously he seemed to take his duties, gave her the sense Dylan Rooney wasn't the type to cheat on a woman. But still…

"You're not married, are you?"

His hand, the one holding the comb, stilled. "Not married. Not dating anyone, either. I wouldn't do that—see one woman and come on to another."

Was that what he was doing? Coming on to her?

She shifted, the movement sending the water into motion and washing away some of the bubbles covering her chest. A sudden sharp intake of breath from Dylan had her realizing one of her nipples was now exposed.

"Sorry," she whispered, sinking lower under the bubbles until her breasts no longer showed.

"I'm not. You're beautiful." The words had come out of his mouth tight, almost strangled. As if he were holding himself back from expressing emotion.

"Dylan…"

Behind her, he released her hair and stood, then came around the front of the tub to face her. "I'll get you a towel," he said gruffly. "Leave you alone for a bit. I'll go check emails, then will come back and make sure you got into bed okay."

"Okay," she said.

"Okay," he echoed.

But he didn't go.

And she didn't tell him to.

No. She was done denying to herself the fact that something existed between them. He'd been clear about the fact that he wanted her. Thought she was beautiful.

Heck. He'd even combed her hair.

She wanted him. Needed him. Even if only for a night. The lawman had somehow worked his way under her skin, and the drive to have him claimed her. Rode her. Drove her.

She stood, water and bubbles streaming down her body, and enjoyed the sensation of power and pure womanly joy that spread throughout her as Dylan gaped at her naked body. As he swallowed. As his heartbeat sent the pulsing vein in his neck into overdrive.

He wanted her.

As she wanted him.

"Dylan…"

This time, when she uttered his name, he didn't back off. Didn't turn and leave her alone. Instead, he reached behind him for the fluffy white towel hanging on the towel rack, still holding her gaze with his, then sucked in a deep breath.

"Are you sure?" he asked.

"I know what I want. And you know what I'm asking for. For tonight. It can't be for more than tonight, but…"

He nodded, then stepped closer. With both hands, he stroked the towel across her face. Then down her neck and against her body. By the time he was done, her body was dry, but she was still dripping between her legs for him.

After dropping the towel, he cupped her face in his

hands. "Fair warning, Rachel. If all we have is tonight, I'm not going to go easy on you. I'm going to sate myself on your body. I'm going to make sure you sate yourself on mine. I'm going to give you so much damn pleasure you're going to remember the feel of me inside you forever. I want that, because I know I'll never forget you. Or stop wanting you. Not in this lifetime. Maybe not even in the next. You okay with that?"

"More than okay," she whispered back.

Just as he'd done before, he lifted her into his arms. He carried her to her bedroom and laid her down on her bed as if she was precious. He stared at her, taking in her body with heated eyes that didn't miss a thing. She could feel herself blushing but refused to cower or cover up.

She wanted him to look at her. Want her. Pleasure her—just as he'd promised. But she hadn't forgotten his vow that she'd sate herself on him, as well.

So she lifted herself up on to her elbows. Waited until he bent, cupped the back of her head and kissed her for several long, wonderful minutes. When he reached down and caressed her breast, she almost forgot…almost lost sight of her goal because his touch felt so amazing. Somehow she managed to pull his wrist away.

He frowned. "What is it? Have you changed your mind?"

"Not at all. But you've looked at me. Before you touch me, before you make me lose my mind completely, I want to look at *you*. Take your clothes off, Dylan. Please?"

Dylan felt burned by the intensity of Rachel's gaze. Deaf to her pleas. Blinded by the sight of her naked body splayed out in front of him. Her endless curves and valleys made his mouth water as if he were a starving man presented with a buffet of the most decadent desserts imaginable. He wanted nothing more than to take her mouth again. Suck on her breasts. Plunge his fingers and tongue and more into the moist, tight cavern between her thighs. He wanted to ignore what she was asking so he could focus on *her,* but he'd promised this night would be a two-way street. With shaky hands, he unbuttoned his shirt. Before stripping it off, he removed his shoes. As he exposed more and more of his body, he watched her pupils dilate. Her breathing accelerate. Her nipples tighten. Her gaze roamed over him hungrily and she licked her lips more than once, urging him to move faster until he was practically ripping at his clothes. In under a minute, he was as naked as she. He stepped forward, but she shook her head again. "No. Wait. I want to look at you. Let me look at you."

She sat up and slid her legs over the side of the bed. Then she stood but didn't come closer. He wanted her to come closer.

Her gaze was a trail of fire that moved over his body, one that was almost painful as he anticipated her touch only to be denied. He wanted to preen and pose, flex his muscles and tempt her to touch him wherever she looked. His throat. His shoulders and chest. His abs. His...

His shaft jerked, growing harder and longer as she stared. Unable to help himself, he reached down and wrapped his fist around himself, making her gasp. "Come closer, Rachel. I'm dying for you." To give her added incentive, he began to stroke himself with slow, hard pulls. Without taking her eyes from his hand on his body, she moved closer. He released himself when she stopped within a foot of him.

"You're beautiful," she whispered. "So, so—" she raised her hands and rested her palms against his chest "—beautiful."

At that initial, gentle touch, he groaned. Clenched his fists. Trembled once more with the effort of remaining still. "Yes," he hissed out. "Touch me wherever you want. However you want. I want to give that to you. But in a minute, I'm going to take over, Rachel. And I don't know how long I'll be able to hold back."

Her hands smoothed over his chest to his shoulders, cupping and caressing. To his delight, wherever her hands went, her lips soon followed. The dual torture threatened to snap his control as she did exactly what he said. Touched and kissed him everywhere she wanted, however she wanted. It was a toss-up which he liked best. Her smooth hands or her soft lips and wet tongue. Thank God he didn't have to pick, because she gave him both. On his throat. Then his chest and shoulders. Then his abdomen. Soon she was kneeling in front of him, her hands on his butt, but her gaze, her focus, her *breath,* on his erection.

She looked up at him from beneath her lashes, a mischievous smile playing on her lips. "Is my minute just about done? Or can I continue without worrying that you'll take over?"

He loved her teasing even as it was killing him. "Why don't you come up here?" he suggested, moving to help her to her feet. "You'll like the way I—"

She resisted and he groaned as she circled her fingers around him. She pumped him once. Twice. Several more times. And it felt better than any woman's touch ever had. Unable to help himself, he buried his hands in her hair. Caressed the silken strands that reminded him of diamonds. Even though he wanted to, he didn't push her face closer. Didn't demand that she take him in her mouth. But then again, he didn't have to.

She'd been following up every caress with her mouth. And this was no different. He sighed in relief and utter pleasure when her lips brushed the sweetest of kisses against him. He groaned as she licked and nibbled at his shaft. Then yes, God, yes—he nearly shouted when she opened her mouth and took him in by degrees. Sucking him in before releasing him. Licking him before sucking him in again. Her hands stayed on his butt, pushing his hips closer as if she were afraid he was going to pull away at any moment, which was ridiculous. He was helpless against her. All he could do was moan. Encourage her. Call her baby. Plead with her to take him deeper inside her mouth. And she followed his instructions to a tee. Giving him pleasure as if she were born to do it. As if she'd been made just for him.

Before he knew it, his muscles were tightening all over and he could feel that familiar tingling at the base of his spine, warning him that he was close. That he'd let her take him further than he'd ever intended. That he was about to come and that was unacceptable because even as he relished the fact that part of him was inside her mouth, he knew he needed to be inside her in a different way altogether.

God, she was amazing. And he loved that she knew the power she held over him. He could see it in her eyes as she looked up at him. For once, they were clear of worry and shining with a single-minded determination to pleasure him.

Only he wanted to pleasure her first.

"Stop," he said.

She didn't listen. Gritting his teeth, he tightened his fingers in her hair and pulled until she reluctantly released him.

"I want you to come," she said.

"Not yet," he said. He helped her to her feet. "Not until I make you half as crazy as you make me."

The promise in Dylan's eyes and voice made her shiver. Before she could respond to his vow, he pulled her against his body and covered her mouth in a deep kiss. Her senses were immediately on overload. His tongue plunged into her mouth, robbing her of speech and breath and reason. Her breasts pressed into the hard muscles of his torso, stimulating her nipples to even greater tightness when she'd thought such a thing would be impossible. His shaft poked her belly and she arched her hips, trying to maneuver him to the V of her thighs so he could rub against her. Sensing what she needed, he cupped her rear and lifted her slightly even as he nudged his thigh between her legs, giving her not what she was aiming for but something fabulous nonetheless. She rocked against his thigh even as he broke their kiss.

"That's right, Rachel. Use me. Whatever part of me you need to make you feel good."

He kissed her neck, then trailed his lips down to her collarbone. As if she could lure him where she wanted him, she cupped her breasts, lifting them as an offering.

"You want me to kiss your pretty nipples, baby?"

"Yes," she moaned. "God, yes, Dylan."

"Shh," he said. "I'm going to give you my mouth,

baby, just like you need. But keep moving on me. Don't stop."

She didn't stop. In fact, when he sucked her nipple into his mouth, hard, then harder still, her hips jerked frantically before picking up speed. "B-bed," she managed to say. Then when he didn't move fast enough, she pushed, actually catching him off balance so he went down on his back on the mattress. Of course, he pulled her along with him.

She braced herself on her hand and knees until she was straddling him. His mouth was still playing with her breasts, and his hands smoothed over her hips, but not for long. One hand gently gripped her thigh and tugged her legs apart even farther. Then he touched her between her legs with his other hand.

She gasped, closed her eyes and threw back her head. His mouth briefly left her breasts so he could stare up at her. "God, I love that expression on your face. You look like you're dying with pleasure. Only I know I haven't even begun to pleasure you." His fingers, which had been gently sliding across her cleft, touched her with greater purpose. His thumb rubbed against her. His fingers probed. Spread. Then he slid one finger deep inside her. "Oh, yeah," he breathed when she cried out. "That's so hot. But I want more. I want to give you more."

He slid another finger inside her, making her feel almost too full, and she tensed for a second, remembering how big and hard he'd been in her hand. Trying to imagine how deep he'd go inside her body. She didn't know if she'd be able to take it. She already felt on the verge of insanity. How had he gotten her to this point? Past reason? Unable to think about…

For a moment reality intruded.

Control. She needed to stay in control, didn't she? As good as this felt, she had responsibilities. People who were counting on her. And Dylan, he was here to—

"Rachel."

Dylan's voice came to her from a distance, then seemed to grow louder as he continued to call her name. She blinked when she realized she was now on her back and he was hovering above her, frowning. "Baby, don't. Don't go there. Stay with me. Here and now. Give us tonight. I can't predict the future, but I'm here for you. I'm going to take care of you. You can count on me."

She stared up at him, at his beautiful face. She focused on the heat that still coursed through her body. She tightened her thighs, which were on either side of his hips, as he kneeled between her legs. He was braced above her, not touching her, yet she still felt him everywhere. In that moment, she knew it was too late. They hadn't had intercourse yet, but she'd already let him in. She didn't want to lose him now. Didn't want to trade the full experience of being in Dylan's arms for a control that she didn't need—not tonight, at least. Tomorrow would be different.

Tomorrow she'd focus on her responsibility to others.

But he was right. Tonight was hers.

It was theirs.

She reached down and caressed him between his legs. Then she guided his shaft between her thighs and rubbed him against her, covering him with her moisture even as she arched her hips in an unmistakable plea.

"Take me, Dylan. Now. Make me forget everything but tonight with your touch. With your kiss. With your co—"

His eyes flared a second before his mouth crashed

down on hers. His mouth was voracious. She tightened her arms around him, rejoicing in the fact that she seemed to have pushed him past *his* control. Because she'd be damned if she'd surrender control without him doing the same. When he lifted his head and moved away from her, she moaned in protest but then he said, "Protection."

She lay there, stunned, as he swiftly retrieved something from his pants pocket. A condom, which he slipped out of its wrapping and on himself so fast that he was back in position, crouched over her, before she'd have thought possible. "I didn't think—" she said.

"It's okay," he said. "I told you I'd take care of you and I meant it, Rachel." He cupped her face with his hands. "Now I want to watch your face as I take you. I want to see everything you're feeling."

She nodded, wanting that, too. She didn't take her eyes off him as he reached down and guided himself to her entrance. Then he pushed into her slowly. Steadily.

It had been seven years for her, something that her body wasn't hesitant to communicate. Her muscles resisted him at first. He was patient. Working himself in a bit at a time. Giving her a few inches, then sliding out before starting in again.

"You're so tight," he said. "You feel so good."

"You're so big," she responded. "And you feel so good. Keep going. Give me more. Give me everything you have, Dylan."

His eyes narrowed at her words and his hips thrust, planting himself to the hilt inside her. He rested his forehead against hers and they both groaned. She wiggled, trying to adjust to the overwhelming feeling of being filled to capacity and then some. Pleasure flared, mak-

ing her gasp. And wiggle even more. Soon she was arch-
ing, thrashing, rotating her hips, urging him to move,
not understanding why he remained still.

Then she looked at his face. His eyes were closed.
His expression one of agony. The muscles in his arms
bulged and his whole body trembled with the effort he
was making to hold back. He was waiting for her to get
used to him. Holding back to make sure she was ready.

True affection flooded her, combining with the respect she'd already grudgingly given him and the lust
she'd already surrendered to. He'd taken her, but he
wasn't taking *from* her. Just as he'd stood naked in front
of her, urging her to touch him, he was making her give
herself to him. And whether it was intentional or not
on his part, she was being moved to give him not just
her body, but her heart, too.

"Dylan," she said.

He opened his eyes and she saw what she both hoped
and feared she'd see. He was giving her more than his
body, as well. And right now, for tonight, she wanted it.

She arched her hips and this time he followed her
lead. Slowly, carefully at first, he thrust in and out of
her. Swiftly, his hips picked up speed so that her cries
of pleasure grew steadily louder and louder, and her
arms around him got tighter and tighter. He used his
mouth and hands, too, driving her closer and closer
toward climax with everything he had. And when he
pushed them both over the peak of pleasure, he didn't
say a word, but she still heard them. Words that could
have been just her imagination. But words that made
her feel loved nonetheless.

Afterward, they lay in bed, both recovering from
what had to have been the hottest sex Dylan Rooney

had ever experienced. He wanted more. More of Rachel. But more of what?

What they'd just shared had been more than sex. He'd felt emotionally connected to her in a way he'd never felt before in his life. And he knew she'd felt it, too.

Unsure of what to say or what to do, he held her close for a long time, stroking her hair and back, trying to tell her without words how much he liked her. Respected her. Wished things could be different for them.

Finally, when she said nothing, he pulled back. As he did, he saw the emotion flit over her face, changing from relaxation to wariness.

"I don't have meaningless sex, Rachel," Dylan said.

"Me, either," she said.

"Of course not. It's just…"

"What?"

"As clichéd as this sounds, I want to make sure you know where we stand. This thing between us isn't meaningless—at least, not to me—but I can't see it going anywhere. I don't want to set you up with false expectations."

A light laugh bubbled out of Rachel. She shifted, turning onto her belly and raising herself up to rest on her elbows to smile at him. "You're such a good guy, Dylan. No wonder you're a marshal. Such a sense of duty and responsibility." Her expression sobered. "But you're forgetting one thing. I said tonight, remember? Tonight only."

"Yeah, I know. But that was before."

"Before you gave me another orgasm, you mean? You expected me to be so dazzled by your sexual prowess that I immediately fantasized about riding off into the sunset together?"

He grimaced. "Something like that."

"Well, don't worry. No matter what happens, my brother is going to be in my life forever. That means things would never work out for the two of us. Right?"

"Right." An image of his mother's face, two black eyes welling with tears as she tried to justify his older brother's abusive actions, rolled into his mind. Following quickly was a more sickly image—him at fifteen, his mother in the bathtub, the water around her tinged red from the blood that dripped from her slit wrists. And finally his brother's pleas for understanding and forgiveness as he was taken away by the police that final time. Pleas for forgiveness that Dylan had never granted.

Oh, he knew his brother hadn't killed their mother. He wasn't technically responsible for her death any more than Dylan was. But technicalities didn't matter when emotion was involved. Their mother had failed them by taking his brother's abuse and making excuses for it. They'd both failed her in different ways—his brother by abusing her and failing to curb his lawless ways, and Dylan for not stopping his brother sooner or being able to make up for his brother's failings in time to convince his mother she had a life worth living.

Tension twisted his gut. Damn it—he didn't need to remember his past just now. But maybe remembering was what kept his heart safe.

Jackson Kincaid was between the two of them.

Rachel couldn't know in what way, but the fact remained that she, like his mother, instinctively took victimhood on as a shroud.

Dylan couldn't give his heart to her.

Doing so would only hurt them both.

Chapter 17

The next morning, after she headed downstairs to make breakfast and found an empty house, a surge of relief washed over Rachel when Julia walked into the kitchen a short time later. Sex with Dylan had been amazing, but now it was over. It had to be. For her brother's sake.

"You going to tell me what the text you sent me this morning meant?" Julia asked, plopping her purse on the wooden kitchen table. "I mean, cryptic much?"

"Sorry," Rachel said, ducking her head to let her hair hang in her face. "I wanted you here, but I didn't want to say too much in case anyone got a hold of your phone, or mine."

"Because 'J, come here now. Things U need 2 know' was way so descriptive," Julia scoffed.

Rachel peeked out at Julia, taking in her high heels, black pencil skirt and blush pink silk button-up blouse with lace insets. How could a country attorney look so pulled together? She glanced down at herself. Her jeans molded nicely to her form, but that was due to the years and years of wear and washing. Her white T-shirt had a stain on the right breast, which she'd conveniently covered with an old plaid flannel shirt of Jax's. She couldn't help thinking that if Dylan was here right now, he must see the differences between Julia and her. She had a feeling Julia was more like the women he dated than she was. But she also knew she was more than an easy lay to him. The fact that he was a marshal—he took that seriously, which meant his feelings for her had to be pretty strong for him to sleep with her in the first place. "Jax needs help. He needs protection," she said. She told Julia about George Evans and Dylan's certainty that Evans was after her brother.

Julia asked a few questions, which Rachel answered as best she could. Then she sighed and picked off a piece of fuzz from her brother's shirt. "You were right—I can't keep protecting my brother from everything. But this? Torture? I can protect him from that, at least. I only hope he'll see it that way when the marshals take him back into custody."

"He'll understand. I know he will. He loves you, Rachel. Don't forget that."

She would never forget. But until Dylan had come into her life, she never would have doubted how pure her brother's love was. Now? Now she had to wonder about that purity. How could he have not shared with her about this George Evans man, or the hidden money?

"How are things with the lawman?" Julia asked.

Unprepared for the sudden shift in conversation, Rachel felt heat rush up her neck and into her cheeks as memories from the night before swam into her mind's eye. "Um…"

"Oh, God," Julia said, clasping a hand over her chest, "you're blushing. What the heck, Rachel? I was curious about how the two of you are dealing with the fact that he's pretending to be your ranch hand while he's on the prowl for your brother. Looks like something else entirely is going on." She sat on one of the kitchen chairs, delicately placing one knee over the other. "Spill. You know you have to. I won't leave this alone."

And she wouldn't, as Rachel well knew. Huffing out a breath, she joined Julia at the table, then fiddled with a crumb she found there before speaking. "We had sex but it's over. He'll catch Jax, then will head back to L.A. or wherever he's from."

"But you like him. Despite everything you like him."

"It's not hard to like him. Dylan's a good guy—I know that. But he sees Jax as a criminal. Someone who is bad to the core. He lumps people like my brother—who was a stupid idiot but not a bad guy—in with all the other criminals. Even if he was interested in more with me— which he's not—I can't have someone in my life if that person views those who make mistakes with such contempt. We all make mistakes. I certainly have."

"What kind of mistakes are you talking about, Rachel?"

"I wasn't a good enough mother to him," she murmured, focusing on the multiple crumbs she'd created by crushing the original crumb.

"You're wrong. You can't blame yourself for Jax's mistakes. He's a grown man, responsible for his own actions. He made the decision to carry what he had to have known were drugs across state lines. You didn't make that call—he did. And he's to blame for everything, not you."

How easily the words seemed to come from Julia's mouth, Rachel thought bitterly. Julia hadn't been thrust into being a parent, or had her own dreams stolen from her. But instead of arguing, Rachel instead said, "You're right. I shouldn't have said that. I get it. I'm not responsible for Jax's dumb decisions."

"You're not responsible for Jax, period. It's time he accepts his responsibilities, to himself, to you and Peter and to society in general."

"But he didn't plan that escape, Julia. George Evans broke him out. He's not responsible for that—surely you can understand that."

"But according to what you've told me, he escaped George Evans's men. He had every opportunity to turn himself in to the law by now. But you're right, now you have to focus on keeping him safe. So what are you going to do?"

"I'm going to email him," she said simply. "Tell him to call me so we can set up a time to meet. That way, Dylan can be prepared to take Jax in safely." One simple email to her trusting brother and Jax would be back in jail. Jax would trust her to keep him safe, the way she always had. She had to hope and pray with everything she had inside that her decision to set him up to get taken into custody was the right one.

Or else she'd just signed her brother's death warrant.

Rachel's backbone had stayed stiff and strong while she drafted and sent the email to her brother. The decision hadn't been an easy one for her to make, nor had the actual email been an easy one to write. Dylan had to hand it to her—Rachel was one strong woman.

"Jax—I'm so glad you're coming home. Please call me so I know you're safe. I've been worried sick," was all the email had said.

It took several hours, but eventually Jax replied to Rachel's email. The response had been short—simply stating he was on his way but didn't have a phone to call her. Dylan's team had tracked the location of where the email had been sent from. Although they didn't have an exact location, Jax was in town—close by. Thinking he was communicating only with his sister, Jackson Kincaid had agreed to meet Rachel in the master bedroom at midnight. As Rachel had anticipated, Jackson planned to enter the house through the second-story French doors. Dylan prompted Stacy to pull in extra manpower, but made it clear that Jax wasn't to be detained until after he'd entered the house.

Now all they had to do was wait. In less than twelve hours, the team would have their charge in custody and would be headed back to California.

And he'd have to say goodbye to Rachel.

Rachel's phone rang, jerking her attention from the window she was staring blankly out of. She checked the caller ID, then clicked to take the call.

"Peter?"

Dylan couldn't hear what the kid had to say on the other end of the call, but whatever Peter was telling his mother wasn't sitting well with Rachel, whose face grew more pinched as she listened.

"It doesn't matter if Nonna and Papa are strict. It's their house, so you need to follow their rules," she said, then stood and paced the length of the kitchen and then back again. "Peter. I expect you to be respectful of your grandparents. I don't care if they won't let you play video games on a weeknight the way I do. Please listen to them. Please."

Irritation crept up Dylan's spine. The kid was upsetting Rachel. Her voice had gone from frustrated to pleading in a matter of seconds. She spoke with Peter a little longer, then ended with a quick "I love you, too" before hanging up.

When she was done, she wouldn't look at Dylan. "I'm going to check on the alpacas."

In the corral, alpacas nuzzled up against Rachel, who moved through the herd, picking up hooves to check for embedded rocks or the need to trim the one large nail the camellike creatures had, and plunging her hands into the soft fibers. In a few weeks she'd need to hire a shearer—her ranch hand had always shorn her herd, but with him gone, that would be an expense she'd have to figure out in her budget somehow.

After all, Dylan was going to be gone.

Jax was going to be in jail.

Peter was going to be back, butting heads with her.

She closed her eyes, so tired. Talking with Peter on the phone hadn't been a big deal. He was ten years old—of course he was going to complain that his grandparents were too strict. But as she talked on the phone with him with Dylan watching her, it had struck her how she wished she and Dylan had more than one night together. That they had night after night. That she had someone to share her life with. To share raising Peter with.

To share her bed with.

Dylan would be a wonderful life partner.

Sexy.

Sensual.

Excellent in bed.

Willing to do hard work and good with her kid.

Damn. The lawman checked all her boxes.

He just had a closed mind when it came to viewing flawed people as still worthy.

But she couldn't even fault him for that.

She struggled with the same thing when it came to herself.

She did blame herself for Jax's problems sometimes. But the truth was, she wasn't a bad mother. Sure, she'd made mistakes, both with Peter and with Jax, but she wasn't a failure. Parents who were failures beat their children. Starved their children. Abandoned their children. They did drugs and got drunk in front of their kids—they didn't get them to school on time or dress them or bathe them or show them any love.

That hadn't been her.

No, for the past ten years, she'd made sure the two boys she loved the most always had a roof over their heads, clean clothes on their backs, food in their bellies and were clean—except when catching frogs in the mud, of course. She'd read their favorite books to them, had helped them with their homework, had taught them how to ride horses, shoot, fish and even bake. She'd been on the PTA and a parent volunteer. Had stayed up all night with both when Jax brought home strep throat from high school and then gave it to Peter.

She'd been a good mother.

She only wished Jax and Peter could have had the benefit of a good father, too.

A good father would have raced down the ridge on a horse to rescue her son, the way Dylan had. A good father would have insisted she get her kid to safety, the way Dylan had. And a good father would have insisted his son act in a respectful manner...the way U.S. Marshal Dylan Rooney had with her son.

A strange sensation wormed its way up her body, a sensation full of tingles and accompanied by the sound of buzzing. She suspected what it was. It was a beautiful feeling—one that held both calm and excitement all at once.

A feeling she didn't want to experience. Not now. Not like this. Love.

"No!" she said, realizing after the alpaca herd scattered that she'd spoken the word out loud. "It's okay, babies," she crooned, but the herd was already reforming into its little group at the far side of the corral. The peace had been broken.

The way her heart would be if she kept down this path.

In her pocket, her cell buzzed. She pulled it out and noted an unfamiliar number. Climbing to the top of the corral to sit on the railing, she clicked the phone on and said hello.

"Sis?"

Her heart thumped against her chest and she sat straight. Jax. Sounding as if he were about to cry. Why was he calling now? He'd said he didn't have a phone— or had he just been worried she was trying to have someone track him? "What is it? What's wrong? Where are you?" she asked, the barrage of questions plummeting out of her mouth. "You said you didn't have a phone with you." In other words, he'd lied...

"I'm in town. Don't want to say exactly, but I'm nearby."

"You're still coming home tonight, right?" she asked.

"I have to. I don't have an option."

"You'll be safe," she promised. "I won't let anything bad happen to you." Like being caught by George Evans's men and tortured and killed.

"I didn't set up the jailbreak, sis. You have to believe me. There's this guy—a really bad guy. He hired people to break me out of the transport."

"I know," she said. "I knew you'd never arrange something like that. It's not in you. But why would he break you out, Jax?" She knew why, but she needed to hear it from her brother. Needed to hear the truth.

Jax choked out a few sobs before saying shakily, "Money. The money I was supposed to bring back to Texas after I delivered the drugs. I found it after the bust and hid it. But that Evans dude? He figured it out, and he had my cellmate killed when the guy couldn't get the info out of me. And he set up the jailbreak so he could get me to tell him where the money is."

"You could have told him, Jax. Just told him where you hid the money."

"No! It's my only leverage to keep you and Peter safe. He wants it. A lot of people do. So long as they don't have it, they won't kill me, and you and Peter will be safe."

"But we haven't been safe, Jax. Weird things have been happening on the ranch. Josiah is dead, and it seems suspicious. There was a stampede. Someone poisoned my alpacas. And someone tried to run me off the road. We think it was Evans's men."

There was tense silence on the phone before Jax asked, "Who's we, sis?"

Rachel cursed herself for her slip up. Now what did she say? She decided to tell the truth—at least partially. "The law sent some U.S. Marshals after you. They've been in touch with me, Jax." She quickly shared with him what she knew about the two murdered and tortured members of Evans's crew. When Jax started crying, loud, choked sounds, she wanted to comfort him. To tell him everything would be okay. But she couldn't. "Jax, I don't understand. Why don't you just tell Evans where the money is and be done with it? Peter and I won't be in danger if the guy gets his money back."

On the other end of the line, Jax's breathing grew more ragged, his voice rougher, as he said, "If only it were that easy. I'm doing this all for you, Rachel. I want to make sure that the money is there, where I hid it. And yeah, I hid it on the property. The only problem is that it was dark and I was freaked and I can't remember where the hell I buried it."

A gasp caught in her throat. "We don't have that big a property, Jax. How could you not know where you buried one million dollars?"

"I don't know, okay! I just know it's somewhere along the perimeter fence, the one that separates our property from Aaron Jacobson's. That's why I need to get onto the property without anyone knowing—so I can find where I buried the cash. Because there's no way I could tell anyone where to go—I need to get out to the fence line so I can figure out what's familiar."

"You have to remember, Jax! We have to get Evans the money."

Another moment of silence stretched between her

and her brother before he responded dully. "I—I'll try Rachel. All I can do is try. Maybe there's another way—"

"There's no other way, Jax," she began.

But the call had been cut off.

A few hours later, Rachel had finished most of her chores, including grooming the alpacas, and had turned the herd out into the far pasture to graze. She'd decided not to share the phone conversation with Dylan. After all, Jax hadn't told her anything new and what more could be done? Jax was in town, nearby, and would be at her place at midnight. All would be over at that point. Dylan would catch his fugitive, Jax would be safely tucked away in protective custody and they'd find the money hidden on her property and turn it over to the authorities.

George Evans would have to find another way to get his cash back.

She made her way back to the barn, where she checked on the poisoned alpaca, who seemed to be doing better but still struggled with breathing. Rachel could hear Dylan in the tack room—his makeshift office—speaking to his team members. Although his words were indiscernible, the low rumble of his voice somehow reassured her. Just having Dylan around as her world caved in on her gave her some semblance of strength.

Gathering up saddle soap, a bucket of warm water, a sea sponge and Anchor's and Row's bridles, she set to work cleaning the tack.

"Rachel?" Dylan's smooth, warm voice came from behind her.

She swung around, shoulders tensing at the frown on his face. Did he know Jax had called her?

"Rachel, I'm sorry, but your alpaca...she didn't make it."

"What?" she breathed out. "I just checked on her not only an hour ago. She was breathing then."

He shook his head gently. "I was just in there. She's gone, Rachel." With the pad of his thumb, he traced the path of a tear that ran down her cheek, his touch soft and cool and comforting.

God, she wanted so much to fall into his arms. To let him caress her, to take care of her. To comfort and care for her.

"I'm here for you," he said. "Let me hold you, Rachel. Please let me hold you."

How was it possible for her heart to ache in so many ways at the same time? For Jax. For Peter. For her alpaca. For this man.

He wanted to hold her. And suddenly she couldn't imagine anything that would feel better than being in his arms.

She placed her hands on his chest. "Please," she said. "Hold me, Dylan. Make love to me."

Chapter 18

"This isn't some fly-by-night hookup, Rachel," Dylan said, his words sending puffs of breath into her hair. It surprised him how content he was to hold her in his arms after their passionate lovemaking. He wasn't normally into cuddling.

How lovely she looked, covered by only the filtered light of the afternoon sun coming through the open window in the barn roof above. Lying on a bed of blond-colored straw and their clothes, her legs entwined with his and her fingers tracing a path across his chest, she'd never been more beautiful.

And Rachel was beautiful. Inside and out. From her slightly off-center nose to the fierce way she loved her son and brother, beauty radiated from her. If only their lives were different. If only they'd met under circumstances far removed from the ones they currently were living in. But life wasn't made up of "if onlys." Something he knew all too well.

"We've been over this before. I get it—you don't sleep around. But there's no future here," she said.

"Neither of us knows what will happen. But you need to know something. I care for you. Deeply. I—" Holy hell. The words *I love you* had been about to roll off his tongue with such ease it shocked him.

He'd imagined he was falling in love with her. Apparently there was no falling about it—he was there. That was what he'd been feeling when they made love in her room. He'd felt it again just moments before.

Against all reason, despite the fact that he'd wanted to keep his distance from her, a woman who couldn't accept the mistakes her brother had made, he loved her.

And he didn't want to let her go.

He blew out a breath. Talk about a complication.

She shifted, and the movement sent a shaft of light over her breasts. A few stretch marks gleamed silver on her tummy—marks of bravery.

Of life...

Of love.

Once again, the words swelled inside him, and this time he couldn't keep himself from saying them. "I love you, Rachel Kincaid," he murmured.

Shock rounded her eyes. Automatically she shook her head.

"Yes," he insisted. "I know it sounds crazy. That our situation is crazy. But I love you. I don't know if I can make things work out between us, but..."

"But what?" she said with a small smile.

"But I want to try. Do you?"

She twirled her fingertip around the copper circle

of his nipple, her smile fading. "I do. But with Jax...I don't know if it's possible."

Dylan was silent for several seconds before he said, "I have a brother, too, you know. A brother who made mistakes in his life."

At that, she sat up, coming up on one elbow to look down upon him. "You do?"

Dylan nodded. "He's older. A good ten years older than me."

"Is he alive?"

"Yeah. At least, I'm assuming he is. We lost touch when he started his fifteen-year sentence."

The warmth that had been in her face evaporated, and her expression grew cold. "Your brother's a convict?"

"He was arrested multiple times throughout his childhood. Was convicted as an adult five days after he turned twenty-five."

"What did he do?"

A wave of nausea built in his stomach. God, he hated the memories. Tried to shove them away any chance he got. But Rachel deserved to know. He swallowed, shoving the nausea back where it belonged. "When he was twelve, my dad took off. Brandon at first turned inward, but then he started acting out. In response, my mom tried to gain control of him."

"And?"

"And then he got bigger. Grew taller. And started beating her."

At Rachel's sudden intake of breath, he held up a hand. He needed to get through this. To tell her, to explain to her. So that she knew and understood him. "My mom took all the blame. She thought if she'd been a better wife, my father wouldn't have left. And she always said that if she'd been a better mother, my brother wouldn't have gone ballistic. According to her, it was her fault he hurt her."

Rachel shook her head. "Typical victim response, taking on the blame of the abuse. But not the truth. That's why you get frustrated with me when I shoulder the blame for Jax and Peter's actions," she said quietly.

He shrugged. Looked away. And she could tell there was more to his story.

"What happened to your mother, Dylan? Did he..."

He closed his eyes. "He didn't kill her. But he might as well have. She was so immersed in her guilt over everything, over what our father and my brother had done to her, that she killed herself. Slit her wrists in the bathtub. I'm the one who found her. I was fifteen years old."

"Oh, God," she cried out. Just like Jax, he'd found his parent dead. "I'm sorry, Dylan. So sorry."

He opened his eyes. "My brother...after my mother died, he just kept getting worse. He went on a downward spiral. Got drunk. Picked fights. Started using drugs. He beat a man so badly he put him into a coma for weeks. He was arrested, convicted and I haven't seen him since."

The story he was telling her was ugly, so ugly, yet part of her couldn't help herself—she couldn't believe that he'd abandoned his brother so totally. Yes, what his brother had done was horrible, but they were still blood. Didn't that matter to Dylan?

"Rachel, if I have any advice to share, it's this. Give Jax and Peter the freedom to make their own mistakes. Don't take on their actions as your own. You'll only end up creating monsters...and getting hurt."

* * *

Rachel sucked in a deep breath. Her mind spun—dizzy with all that had transpired in just a few moments. Dylan had confessed he loved her. Heady stuff. Was she ready to accept it as truth? Or did a part of her secretly wish he'd kept his heartfelt expression to himself? Complicated was an easy word at this point: convoluted, impossible…those were words that now came to mind. She almost wished they could go back to just "complicated."

And what he'd just shared? The story about his mother and his brother? How painful a past that must have been. He'd been ten years younger than his brother. Without a father, watching his mother being beaten by someone she loved…that had to have churned something up inside him that he'd never been able to settle. His suggestion to let her son and brother make their own decisions spoke to that. Dylan saw the situation as a wounded son, not as a mother.

"We've been over this before, Dylan. We won't ever see eye to eye. I appreciate all that you've shared with me, but my instincts tell me that when they get into trouble, I need to tighten the leash, not loosen it."

Dylan rolled away from her then, placing a hand over his eyes. "I think you're making a mistake."

"I know you do." She hesitated. Touched his arm. "I realize that I've been blind to Jax's faults. He confessed to transporting those drugs. He's never told me otherwise. I need to accept he made some bad decisions. But they're nothing we can't work past. I can't abandon him the way you did your brother. If that's a mistake…it's my mistake to make."

"I know. That's one thing that's become perfectly

clear over the last few days. You're strong. Independent. Willing to take risks. And I admire you for that."

She shifted, coming up onto her elbows, slightly buried in the fresh hay. The sunlight streamed through the window to cover Dylan in a swath of warm gold. Emboldened, she reached out a finger and traced a line down his chest, lower even, past his belly and followed the path lower still. When he groaned, she pulled her hand away. She wasn't quite yet ready to follow up on what they'd just experienced. And she had questions still.

"You admire me, even though I still believe in Jax. Even though I stick up for him the way your mother did your brother for so long?"

Dylan captured her hand and entwined her fingers with his, lightly stroking each of her fingers with the side of his thumb. "I admit…it's hard for me when you try to take responsibility that isn't yours. When you refuse to acknowledge the possibility that your brother has done wrong. But at the same time, you're not a victim. I see you as someone who loves fiercely, who protects with everything she has, and who makes tough choices. Between what the U.S. Marshals have brought to the table and what your brother has added into play, you haven't exactly been given many options. You've been doing the best with what you have."

"And so are you," she said softly. "I know you don't believe in Jax the way I do, but why would you? I'm his sister. You don't know him the way I do. And you're trying to do your job. So where does this leave us? I—I care about you, Dylan, but—"

Her phone buzzed. She thought of Jax. Hesitated. Then rooted through her clothes to find her phone. Even with Dylan here, she couldn't risk not answering. When she looked at the screen, she recognized the caller ID: Peter's grandparents.

She answered, "Hello?"

Maureen, her voice wobbly, said, "Peter's run off."

Shocked, Rachel looked sharply at Dylan. "When did he leave? Why did he leave?"

"He must have taken off sometime this morning, after he spoke to you. We're not sure why he left, but we assume it had something to do with the fact that we wouldn't let him play video games."

Disappointment tangled with worry in her gut.

"He's spoiled," Maureen said.

Spoiled? Maybe. Sure, she did allow Peter to play video games and watch TV, but only after he did his homework and finished his chores. And on a ranch, there were a lot of chores.

"And, Rachel," Maureen continued, "we're not pleased. This kind of behavior isn't acceptable. You need to get control over your child before he ends up like his uncle. You need to be a better mother."

Anger stabbed her in the gut. "I'm trying," she snapped out.

"Apparently not enough. Try harder. Or better yet—"

"Give me the phone, Rachel," Dylan said.

She stared at him, hesitated, then gave him the phone. He looked at her as he spoke into it. "This is Dylan Rooney. I'm a U.S. Marshal. Please tell me what you know about Peter." He looked at Rachel. "No, you can't talk to Rachel. Now tell me what you know."

As Dylan talked to Maureen, Rachel stood, swiped at the tears trickling down her cheeks, then swiftly dressed. As soon as Dylan disconnected, he dressed, as well. He hadn't gotten his shoes on yet when Rachel fell apart. Dropping to her knees in the hay, she covered her face with her hands and sobbed. "Oh, God. Now he's completely vulnerable."

She sensed Dylan drop down beside her. He held her shoulders, then pulled her close. "He's going to be okay, Rachel. He's done this before."

"This isn't a night out in the local woods—he'll be in towns, cities, crossing freeways. What if he tries to hitchhike? What if I lose him?" Her body wouldn't stop shaking. "This is my fault. I should have kept him with me. I could have kept him safe."

"Stop it," Dylan said roughly. "You know that's not true. You were protecting him."

"*Trying* to protect him. But now my son is out there, alone, and maybe afraid."

"He won't be for long. We're going to find him, Rachel." He gripped her chin and made her look at him. "Look into my eyes. Tell me you believe me."

She stared into his eyes. Saw the determination and truth there. He'd said he loved her. She hadn't said it back, but that didn't mean she didn't feel it, too. She loved this man. She'd trusted him with her body. Now she had to trust him to find her son.

She took a shaky breath, then nodded. "I do. I believe you. Find my son, Dylan. Bring him back to me."

Twenty minutes later, Dylan ended what was the latest in a number of telephone conversations and turned to her.

"Our sheriff will be coordinating the search since we think Peter's going to be headed here. We'll get all law enforcement officers on the lookout. The sheriff is calling a community meeting to help find Peter," he said. "There should be a number of people gathered in twenty to thirty minutes, including news crews."

"Where is the community meeting going to be held? Here?"

"No, they're gathering at the town square, according to what Stacy gleaned." He reached out and brushed a strand of hay from her hair. "Let's get you in the shower and changed into something more presentable. You're going on TV."

"On TV?" she said, her voice filled with trepidation. "But why? I understand why we need to gather volunteers to help look for him, but why go on TV?"

"It'll put more eyes and ears on the lookout for him. It's a basic press conference. You simply state that your son might be lost and headed home. Give a description, hold up a picture of his latest school photo and encourage people to keep an eye out and call the authorities if they see him."

Dylan's face had gone tight, the way it did when he didn't want to say something.

"What aren't you telling me?" she demanded.

"Nothing. Truly, I have nothing new to add. My team has great control of the perimeter of your ranch, but I can't forget that Evans it out there."

She should have thought of that, but she hadn't. Now the fear that rose inside her threatened to suffocate her. "Evans is out there. Putting Jax and now Peter at risk," she said, her voice flat.

"Putting you all at risk," he corrected.

The rest of the afternoon was rushed and hurried, with Rachel being so busy she felt she hardly had a moment to breathe. True to his word, the sheriff had organized a community gathering at the town square. There, a tearful Julia came up to Rachel and gave her a brief yet reassuring hug before Rachel had to step in front of the news cameras and microphones.

Before she made it to the media swarm, she heard a search party had been organized. Some of the ranchers planned to ride the range, where they figured Peter would head toward, and other townsfolk were calling friends and family members between here and Rachel's in-laws and sending out messages through Facebook and Twitter to keep an eye out for her son.

"Ready?" Dylan said. When she nodded, he pushed her forward to stand in front of the cameras, the microphones and the gathered crowd.

Her knees trembled as she looked at the multitude of faces—many familiar, but some strangers to these parts. The media, she figured. Peter would hate this, Rachel figured, but she had to protect him. She had to do her duty.

She cast a glance back at Dylan, who gave her a reassuring smile. Yes, she could do this. "My dear community," she began, and held up the picture of Peter. "Earlier today, we were notified my son had left his grandparents' home, and would most likely be trying to make it home." She continued speaking, laying out what Dylan had told her to say. After she gave her statement, some of the media asked questions, which she answered smoothly until she noticed Dylan had taken a call on his cell phone. She faltered in giving an answer, squinting to better take in Dylan's expression.

His pinched and tight expression.

No. That wasn't good. Oh, God. What had happened? "That's all," she said quickly into a microphone, then stepped down from the temporary dais and headed to Dylan, who ended the call just as she walked up to him.

"What is it?" she demanded. "Tell me."

He flicked his gaze at the crowd, then cupped her elbow and gently tugged. "Let's talk where no one can hear."

And she'd thought her knees had been shaking earlier. Now she could barely make them swing forward and hold up her weight at the same time. Something had happened to Peter; otherwise Dylan wouldn't look so concerned. At the alley between the bakery and the bookstore, he propped her up against the rough brick facing and braced his arms on either side of her shoulders.

"I have something to tell you, Rachel. Think you can remain standing, or should I find us somewhere to sit?"

"I want to stand. Whatever you have to say, I need to be strong enough to hear it if I'm to be strong enough to deal with it. Is Peter..." She choked on the words.

"No," he said quickly. "He's not dead. But it's bad, Rachel. Really bad."

His warmth and the scent coming off him and rolling over her brought her strength. Stability. Made her knees solid under her. "What is it, Dylan?" she whispered.

A muscle on the side of his jaw twitched as he switched his gaze from her eyes to her mouth, then back up to her eyes again. He swallowed, the action made visible by the long bob in his neck; then he spoke. "We believe Peter didn't run away. We believe he was kidnapped."

Her knees started their wobbling again. "No," she gasped out. "God, no." Thank God for the strong wall behind her. For Dylan's arms on either side of her. She wouldn't fall. She wouldn't allow herself to crumple.

"Rachel…"

She didn't have time for compassion. Or for herself to fall apart. She gathered her strength and willed her knees to keep supporting her. Her priority now was to find her son. Get him back from the kidnappers. Keep him safe. "Why do you think that? Was there a note? A phone call?"

"No. A witness saw Peter being taken from his grandparents' front yard by force."

"Why didn't this witness come forward sooner?"

"Remember, it's just been a few hours, and the guy was saying Peter had to come with him and go to school, so she didn't suspect anything. She just read about Peter being lost on a friend's Facebook and realized everyone had it wrong. He hadn't gotten lost—or even run away. He'd been taken. She contacted the police and they forwarded her to my team."

She looked at the media, most of whom still milled around the town square, some of whom were putting their equipment away in news vans. "We can use the media. Let them know about the kidnapping. They're out there looking for Peter—we can shift their focus to look for the kidnappers, right?"

"Wrong. We have to keep this quiet, at least for now."

"But why?" she argued, running a hand through her hair and coming up with tangles.

"Because we have to assume the person who has Peter is George Evans, who's proven himself to be a dangerous man. He seems to have a pattern of holding people who he thinks could be useful. He's using Peter as a pawn. Trying to draw out Jax."

The panic inside her increased, making it difficult to breathe. "And so long as we don't go after George Evans, Peter is safe."

"Right. We let Evans contact us first. Find out what he wants. We wait."

"Wrong!" All the logic Dylan was giving her wasn't sinking in. "My son is going to die!" Her heart flung itself against her rib cage, hatred making her strike out at Dylan and pound against his chest. "And your stupid 'let people make their own decisions' approach to life is going to kill Peter."

"That's not fair."

To his credit, even though Dylan had just about spat out the words, he hadn't backed away. In fact, he'd come in closer, almost touching his hips to hers. Reached out and grabbed her fisted hands. Held tight but stroked his thumbs over her clenched fingers. God, she wanted the comfort. The strength. She wanted to believe he was right. She wanted…she wanted him.

"At the risk of sounding like a wimpy female, would you…" She couldn't finish. Couldn't admit her weakness.

"Hold you?"

She swallowed back tears. "I feel so stupid. So weak."

Dylan wrapped his arms around her shoulders, supporting her weight with his strength, and kissed the top of her head. "Spine of steel. That's what you have. You're a mom, Rachel. Moms go into shock when their kids are threatened. You're just in shock, not weak."

The words were somehow reassuring. Released some of the tension cording around her chest. Brought her back to reality, back down to earth. She let out a shuddering breath, forcing herself to rationalize and not stay wallowed in the pain and drama of the moment. "I'll bet your knees have never threatened to dump you in an alley," she joked halfheartedly.

"I peed my pants when the neighbor kid sicced his dog on me."

She gave a hollow laugh. "Yeah, but you were probably like, eight. I'm a grown-up."

"Grown-ups get scared, too." He kissed her forehead, then bent a bit to give her a light kiss on the lips. "And if you weren't scared, you wouldn't be a good parent. You care, Rachel. You just take too much responsibility for the actions of others."

"You're right. I do," she said quietly. "Sometimes I get mixed about what's mine to feel guilty about and what's not."

"Why?"

She shrugged. "You have your past…I have mine."

He raised his head and gazed down at her, his expression full of tenderness and care. "Want to tell me about it?"

"I'd gone away to college," she began, then hesitated. "Shouldn't we be talking about how to get Peter back?"

"My team's contacting the FBI and setting up a plan. For right now, I need you to get calm. In control. Maybe telling me about your past might help ground you."

She nodded, understanding what Dylan was trying to do. By putting her attention on her past, she could get those damn knees to stop wobbling under her. Then she'd be able to be rational and could deal with the fact that her son had been stolen by the very man out to kill her brother.

The thought made deep shudders rack her body. Damn. She needed the focus. She started again. "My parents wanted me to go to a local community college for two years so I could help on the ranch. They'd just transitioned from sheep to the alpacas, and the herd needed constant care. They were exhausted but couldn't yet afford to hire a ranch hand."

"But you say you went away...."

She stared vacantly at the empty alleyway, barely seeing the hundred-year-old brick of the building facing her. Empty. That was how she felt. Empty. Depleted. Sucked dry. Her son was in the hands of a killer. How could she survive?

But her knees were still holding her up. Dylan's arms were still braced on either side of her. The rough texture of the brick wall was a reassuring strength behind her back. She'd get through this. She had to. There was no other option.

"Rachel?" Dylan prompted.

Struggling, she worked to bring her focus back to his face. What was it he was asking? Oh, that's right. They'd been talking about her brother. How they'd ended up in this situation because of one stupid, idiotic choice made in her youth. A choice she'd made.

"If you don't want to continue," he said, "that's fine. I'm just glad to see you still standing."

She shook her head. "I want you to know. I want you to understand how it is we came to be in this place— or at least, how I came to be in this place. It's my fault Peter was kidnapped. My fault Jax made bad mistakes and ended up tangled with a drug lord. My fault my parents—" The words wouldn't come, lodged in the back of her throat. Casting her eyes upward, she caught Dylan's reassuring gaze with hers.

"Your parents wanted you to help on the farm. You wanted to go out and live your life," he prompted.

She could do this. Tell him the full story. Then he'd understand. He might not like her much after, but he'd at least understand what made her. What kept her driven to help her brother. "Yeah. I refused to stick around. Fought with my mom and dad about it, then got a scholarship to my dream college back East. For the first semester, things were great. I rarely called my family. Just partied, had fun, enjoyed learning and college life."

"Sounds normal."

"If you're not a rancher, maybe. But this ranch goes back to just after the Civil War. Peter's the sixth generation to work this land. We don't just take off...not when the ranch needs us. But I did. And because I did—" Tears pricked her eyes as they did every time she thought of that day. That horrible, horrible day.

"You don't have to tell me. Or you can wait until another time. Sometime when you're not so vulnerable over your kidnapped child."

"I need to get this out." To her relief, he didn't argue with her, but instead stayed silent, rubbing his thumbs in little circles against her back. She cleared her throat, then managed to speak. "Because they were overworked and had no cash, they didn't remember to get the house heater checked, even though they knew it needed maintenance. Jax came home from school and found our mom and dad dead in their bed."

"Carbon monoxide poisoning?"

She nodded. "There was a warning alarm, but the coroner thought they were so exhausted from working the ranch that both were sleeping too soundly to have been woken by the sound. They died. Jackson became an orphan at age ten. He lost his childhood. And it's all my fault."

Dylan swore inwardly. No way was the death of Rachel's parents her fault. How could she even think that? But she'd been young when they died—just eighteen. Still almost a child herself. She'd probably see the situation through a child's eyes, rather than the eyes of an adult. Of someone with balanced reason and capacity of logic. He knew too well what it was like to create a belief system as a child and to fight to get away from that belief system when it was no longer working.

Rachel's belief system had been broken for some time now, but she hadn't been able to pull away from it. Not yet. And as much as he wanted to tell her she was wrong—dead wrong—now wasn't the time. She wouldn't be open to shifting the paradigm of her beliefs. Not when her son was kidnapped and her brother had a death threat hanging over his head. Not when she was so very vulnerable. Now was the time for him to be supportive, no matter how much he disagreed with this beautiful, amazing woman in his arms.

A sudden shout off in the distance caught his attention. Pulling away from the exterior wall, he lightly stroked Rachel's arm as he craned his neck to see what had caused the ruckus.

One of the TV newscast vans had backed into a bench, was all. But he noted how many newscasters remained next to his truck, presumably waiting to get an exclusive with her. Damn. There was no way he could get her out of town and back home without her encountering microphones shoved in her face. So far the kidnappers weren't aware anyone knew Peter had been kidnapped. And if the reporters had included him in any of their coverage? As far as anyone knew, he was just Rachel's ranch hand, albeit one that acted more like a lover than an employee. Nothing too surprising there. So he was a man comforting a mother worried about her son. It worked with the message they wanted to send. Keeping the ruse that Peter had run away would be of benefit to his team. With the kidnappers thinking the public believed Peter had run away, they could become lax in their actions.

And he knew all about being lax—that's when people can take advantage. And he'd take any advantage he could to get Rachel's son back.

Chapter 19

"Need help getting out of the truck?"

Dylan's voice cut through her mental fog, and she looked about. They were back at her ranch. The late afternoon sun had lowered even more, casting a wide, dark shadow when it filtered through the willow tree.

"No," she murmured. "I can walk on my own."

"Ready to meet with the team?" Dylan asked. "I have a meeting set up—it'll start as soon as we're in the headquarters in the barn."

On the drive, she'd overheard him on the phone with Stacy, filling her in on the latest turn of events. She was invited to the meeting? "Isn't helping find a kidnapped kid completely outside a marshal's job description?" she asked.

Before answering, Dylan hopped out of the truck and came around to her side just as she opened the door. He held out a hand in a silent offer of assistance, which she took, welcoming the warmth of his touch.

"Officially, we're treating this as part of getting Jackson Kincaid back into custody. The FBI handles kidnapping cases—we're here as support. According to Stacy, the FBI has asked us to continue working on the issue until they can show up here."

They walked the few yards to the barn, then entered. Diffused light filtered through the windows, and a few streaks of light illustrated the need to repair holes in the roof. So much work, so little time.

"What do you want from me now?" she asked.

Dylan held open the door to the tack room and gestured for her to sit on the saddle—her makeshift chair. "Just listen. Stacy will fill you in on what we're going to do."

He went to the computer and flicked it on, as well as the monitors. Stacy's face appeared on one, and the other monitors slowly filled up with faces of the other team members. Rachel sat on the saddle and placed her hands on the pommel, the warm leather soothing to the touch. She'd listen, if that was what would get her baby back.

"How are you doing, Rachel?" Stacy asked, compassion in her voice and expression.

Rachel cleared her throat. "This is a nightmare. Tell me you have a plan to get my boy back."

Stacy nodded. "At the moment we're keeping the information that Peter has really been kidnapped to just us and the FBI, in case there are any leaks at the sheriff's office. Everyone is still out looking for Peter, and we're tracking down the leads. We figure George Evans will get one of his underlings to call you with a ransom demand, and we're assuming that ransom demand will be the missing money your brother made off with."

Rachel choked. "But I don't know where the money is. Jax is the only one who knows where the cash is hidden, and he's not even sure where he put it on the property. We won't be able to trade the cash for my son."

Even as she said the words, she saw the confused look Dylan shot her. His confused expression quickly turned into one of laser-eyed focus. And suspicion.

"How do you know that, Rachel?"

"Earlier," she whispered. "He called me on my cell. He told me about the money. Confirmed he escaped from Evans. But he said he didn't know where the money was. Just that he needed to get back to find it so he could keep Peter and me safe."

"And you didn't tell me this because— Damn!" he clipped out. "Never mind." He turned back to Stacy and snapped, "Go on."

Rachel wanted to whimper at the anger on Dylan's face.

But damn it, she was going through hell here. How dare he judge her?

"The FBI has assured us that the money isn't important," Stacy said. "Finding Peter is—and we're going to find Peter before we have to do any kind of exchange. So again, don't worry."

But she would. Not having the money when the ransom call came went against every grain in her body. This didn't feel right. She had started to voice her concerns when Stacy interrupted her.

"I've already got a tap on your phone and can trace the call when it comes in. You've watched TV and movies—you know the drill. Keep whoever calls on the line for as long as you can. We'll track the call and get a location. Ask to speak to your son. We have a program where we can tell if he's there at the actual site of the phone call, or if he's been patched in to the call. If he's been patched in, we can track that location, too. Remember, ask for proof of life."

Proof of life? Rachel's mind spun and the room seemed to float around her. Her stomach heaved and she fought to hold back the rising need to vomit. Oh, God. No. She reached out and placed her hand on the wall next to her, trying to connect back to the earth. Peter couldn't be dead. Not her sweet, spunky little boy. Dylan's firm hand on her shoulder brought her back to reality. She looked up to catch his gaze with hers.

"My team will do everything we can to get your boy back," he said. "I won't rest until he's in your arms, safe and sound."

The reassurance of his words and tone helped calm her system. He might be angry she didn't tell him about Jax's call, but he was still going to be here for her. She breathed in through her nose, controlling her intake, settling down the carbon dioxide overload that threatened to make her faint.

"Rachel." Stacy's voice interrupted her thoughts. "Keep your phone on you. We expect a call at any time. But we do want you to rest. Dylan, can you get her to take a nap or something?"

"Will do," Dylan said.

Rachel grew aware of the gentle caress he was giving her shoulder. His hand moved up to stroke the back of her neck. She shuddered, leaning back into the warmth of his hand. God, how she wanted his touch.

But she wanted her son back even more.

And to get Peter home safe, she needed to be stronger than she'd ever been before.

Rachel sat on the edge of her bed, wondering how she'd make it through the next few hours. After the meeting with Dylan's team, he'd brought her up to her room and told her to rest while he made her a snack to keep up her strength. She'd kicked off her shoes and propped the pillows up against the headboard so she could look out the French doors to the verdant land below. Nerves had her stomach knotted up. So far she hadn't received a ransom call from George Evans, nor had she heard from Jax. So she had to wait. And wish. Wish that her son was safe. Wish that this all would be over soon, and her life would get back to normal.

But she knew nothing would be normal again. Her life would never be the same.

"Rachel?" Dylan's soft voice came from her doorway.

She looked up to see him leaning on a hip against the doorjamb, one foot hooked over the other, one hand shoved deep in his pocket and the other holding a plate of cheese, crackers and grapes. A deep frown marred his handsome face.

"You okay?" he asked.

"I'm not sure how to answer that," she whispered, glancing away. She fingered the patchwork quilt that lay under her on the bed, tracing a line of hand stitching. Stitching her great-grandmother had made eighty years ago, back in a time when the Dust Bowl was the greatest thing to fear, not murdering, torturing drug dealers who wouldn't hesitate to hold a child in captivity to get what they wanted.

And yet the thick thread of the stitches under her fingertips somehow reassured her. Her great-grandmother Betsy had survived the terrors of seeing her family's ranch decimated by the drought and subsequent dust blizzards and had sewn this quilt by hand as the family had packed up and driven off to a new home in the hill country. Betsy had made it through the death of their entire herd of cattle and the plow horses. Rachel could do the same. She could make it through this day.

She had to.

Dylan entered her room and placed the cheese tray on the dresser, then came to stand before her. This close, his scent penetrated her senses, his body heat caressed her skin. Desire curled around her insides, making her quiver deep in her core. Wetness dampened her panties. Guilt suffused her. Her son was being held by a kidnapper, and here she was, wanting sex. Was it the distraction she needed? Or the strength Dylan exuded?

"Would you like to eat anything?" he asked.

Shaking her head, she patted the quilt, indicating for him to sit next to her. "I know I need to keep up my strength, but I'm not hungry. At least, not for food." She caught her breath in the back of her throat and let the words hang in the air, wondering what Dylan would do with what she'd said. Had she been too brazen? Inappropriate?

He sat next to her, his weight causing the bed to squeak, then took her hand in his, turning it so he could trace the lines of her palm with the tip of his index finger. "That was suggestive, Rachel," he said, not skirting the issue. "Are you sure it's what you want?"

"I can barely breathe, can hardly keep my mind focused on one topic for longer than a few seconds. I think maybe I need the distraction." She waited, hoping her blunt answer hadn't been taken as rude. Or crude.

Dylan let go of her hand and traced his finger up the underside of her arm, curving the arc of the path when he reached her biceps and circled her breast. She caught her breath in her throat, aware of the sudden increase in her heart rate. Without looking at her, he palmed her breast, then leaned down and placed his mouth on her other breast, sucking gently through the thin fabric of her T-shirt and lace bra. Her nipple pebbled under his tongue and a groan fell from her lips.

Soon those groans turned to screams as Dylan gave her exactly what she needed.

Pleasure and a few blessed moments of forgetfulness.

Rachel sucked in deep gulps of air. Enjoying sex had never been an issue for her. She never had problems coming to climax, had never found the act to be a chore. Had always enjoyed herself. But this? This thing that she'd experienced with Dylan? Could she even consider the heady sensation to be sex? No. Just like the past two times, this hadn't been about sex. It was about passion but so much more than that.

"You okay?" Dylan whispered, pulling her to him in spoon fashion. He kissed her spine and she shuddered.

Okay? That was hardly the word to describe how she felt. A quivering had started inside her belly and had moved upward to her chest, filling her, stretching her, making her feel lighter than air. She was floating. Untethered. Ethereal.

In love.

But she didn't want to be in love with this man. They

were like two puzzle pieces from completely different puzzles—they'd never fit together. Ever.

The sun shifted, a shadow falling across the bed and illuminating her phone on the bedstead. As great as sex had been, it still hadn't completely distracted her from the horrendous situation they all were in. She'd been aware even as Dylan stroked her from the inside that her phone remained silent. When would George Evans call and arrange a ransom?

She shifted, pulling away from Dylan's naked body, and checked her cell phone again. Yes, the ringer was on and turned up to the highest volume. Yes, she had all four bars. Yes, the battery was fully charged. And no, she'd not received a ransom call.

How had this happened? How had she gone from being a plain old single mother struggling to make ends meet to a woman whose son had been kidnapped? Tears pricked the back of her eyes, the sensation gritty and painful. How had she failed?

"I just wish I'd done better by Jax and Peter," she said, choking back the unshed tears. "Maybe neither would be in this situation if I'd known what I was doing."

"Growing up is tough. And parenting is tougher. I get it. But you have to let Peter and Jax make their own mistakes and learn from them."

Irritation crept up her spine. "No. I refuse to believe that. I need to teach them how to not make mistakes. And to do that, I need to guide them."

"What you're talking about is controlling them, Rachel. Not guiding. If your brother or your son is never allowed to make mistakes and suffer the fallout for what they've done, they'll never get that understanding of what works and what doesn't. Don't you get it? You've been so busy protecting them from life and all its pain, and justifying reasons for their failures, that you haven't been teaching them about how to actually live."

"That's not true," she said harshly. "Don't think that just because you have a particular way of looking at the world, that way would work for anyone else's life."

"I don't think you're really hearing me." Frustration laced Dylan's voice. He pulled away and sat up, the bed squeaking loudly in protest at the sudden movement.

The bedsprings, which minutes before had squeaked in response to their passionate lovemaking, now grated in her ears. "I do, though," she responded. "You think I should have just let Jax and Dylan make their own decisions so they could learn through their mistakes. But that's stupid. It was Jax's decision to transport drugs across state lines. I didn't make that decision for him. And it's not like Peter chose to get kidnapped."

"That's interpreting my words literally. I'm trying to point out that if you hadn't taken the blame for the mistakes your brother made as a youth, he'd have learned his lesson by now. Instead, the minute he gets free from Evans's men, instead of going to the police, he heads for this ranch, bringing danger to his sister and nephew for stolen money and giving some story that he doesn't know where he buried it."

Bastard. Rachel barely kept the word from slipping out between her lips. He was blaming her, saying that it was her poor parenting that had resulted in this situation. Shaking, she reached out and grabbed her shirt from where it had ended up stuffed between the slats in her bed's headboard and flung it on.

Eyes narrowed, Dylan watched her cover herself up.

"I guess this is your way of telling me you don't want to continue the conversation," he said, standing up and snagging his boxer briefs from off the floor.

"I think maybe you've been angry at your mother for taking the blame for your brother's actions for too long. And I think you're projecting that onto me. And that's not fair."

"My mother accepted blame when it should have been put on my brother's shoulders. Because of that, my brother never learned from his mistakes. She always made excuses for him, always made his actions her responsibility. He never grew up learning how to be a man. So yeah," he said, anger tingeing his voice, "I guess I am projecting that onto you. Because I see you doing the very thing my mother did. The therapists called it enabling, and—"

She laughed harshly, without humor. "Now you're giving me a lecture and therapy? All this, while my brother is out there under a death threat and the very monster capable of killing him is holding my son God knows where? And you're lecturing me on parenting?"

Bile rose in her throat. She fought the building nausea, swallowing hard to keep the acid down. Not long ago, she'd accepted that she was in love with this man. Now she wanted him out of her sight.

Yet the truth was, she *wanted* him in her life. *Needed* him. But they were too different. She couldn't open herself up to being with someone who thought the way Dylan did. In his eyes, Jax would always be a criminal. Peter would always be a recalcitrant kid. She'd always be a poor parent. And she'd never believe the way he did. She refused.

"Rachel, I don't want to fight," Dylan said, his expression fading from anger to compassion. "I'm sorry I said all that. Whether it's true or not doesn't matter at this moment. What matters is that you remain steady and stable and we get your son back. And your brother back into custody, safe and sound."

"I think you need to leave," she said, her voice hollow. She dropped her gaze from his and stared out the window, noting the gentle sway of the willow tree down at the creek. God, what she'd do to see Peter climbing that tree right now. Pain scratched the back of her throat. Yes, she needed to be steady and stable. And to get there, she needed nothing to do with the U.S. Marshal who stood before her, holding her bleeding heart in his hands.

"Are you sure?" he asked quietly.

As an answer, she bent and scooped his pants and shirt up off her floor, then handed the articles of clothing to him. He took the offered clothing with stiff arms, then put them on as she wrapped herself up in a sheet and sat back down on the bed.

"This 'complication' of ours has had its moments, Dylan. I appreciate you helping me get through this by distracting me. But it's time we both admitted it's nothing more than a physical need. I'm done. It's over."

Dylan's chest tightened, a vise squeezing the air out. He shoved his legs into his jeans, then zipped the fly, keeping his gaze fixed on Rachel. She wouldn't look at him, but by the way she held her jaw clenched and her eyes glittered with unshed tears, he knew what she'd said hadn't been easy.

And it hadn't been what was in her heart.

But the complication had increased to the point of

being unmanageable. She was a woman determined
to control her environment in a misguided attempt at
protection. He was a U.S. Marshal—a man assigned to
bring in escaped criminals. And one of those criminals
was her brother. Rachel was right. Their complication
had been fantastic while it lasted, but it was over.

He'd get over it. He'd get over her.

He had to.

Buttoning his shirt, he cleared his throat, catching
her attention, although she still wouldn't look at him.
"Fine. No more complication. Now it's time to get back
to work."

"That's what you call this? You consider this work?"
Rachel asked, gesturing to the phone.

The phone that still remained silent. Why hadn't
Evans or one of his crew called Rachel yet to demand
the money in exchange for her son? He plowed a hand
through his hair and said, "It is for me. This is my job."

"It may be your 'job,' but it's my life," she said.

He couldn't argue. "It's about five-thirty. You said
your brother will show up around midnight, in about six
hours. We have to figure George Evans has people scattered around, looking for your brother. I doubt Evans
or his crew know for sure when Jax will turn up, so in
that we have an advantage. But I do believe they want
your brother—even if they get the money."

"Oh, God," she murmured. "So even if we get Peter
back, Jax will still be at risk?"

Her brother was as good as dead, he thought, but
kept the words inside his head. Instead, he said, "Eat the
cheese and crackers. You need to keep up your energy.
I'm going to go downstairs and do some digging online. I have your phone calls doubled to my cell phone,

so if you get a call, I'll immediately be on it, even if we aren't in the same room." He knew she needed space— needed to be alone for a while.

"Thank you," she said quietly. The tears that had made her eyes glitter suddenly spilled over, and she made no movement to stop their flow, but instead let them trail down her cheeks.

He fought the urge to kiss the tears away. To cradle Rachel in his arms. To croon that everything would be okay.

He couldn't. He just had to do his job, and hope that he did it well enough to bring her boy back to her. There were no other options.

Chapter 20

With Dylan downstairs in her kitchen, tapping away at his laptop, Rachel had the freedom to act on a plan she'd formed. Stacy had said that the money wouldn't be an issue, but Rachel wasn't counting on that. Money always mattered. And she'd make sure she had as much as she possibly could when the call came.

She'd take control. She'd get her son back.

Within twenty minutes, she'd texted Julia and had set up a quick liquidation plan, thanks to her neighbor Aaron Jacobson. Julia hadn't told Aaron why Rachel needed money, just that she might need quick cash, and soon. Aaron had agreed, and if needed, he'd purchase her entire ranch and all the stock.

With each alpaca worth up to ten thousand dollars and a herd of fifty, that meant a quick five hundred thousand available. Her land—about a thousand acres—

was worth an easy million. All it would take was a few quick pushes of the button and Aaron would put one million and a half into her account. She had to hope it wouldn't come to that—hoped that Stacy was right and the money would never come into play—but she felt better about taking control and arranging the contingency plan.

Downstairs, Dylan's deep and smooth voice sounded. Rachel picked up the nearly empty platter—she'd managed to choke down the cheese and grapes but hadn't been able to swallow the dry crackers—and headed to join Dylan. No need for him to know of her plan to sell off her land—which was why she'd texted instead of talking on the phone. She supposed he'd be angry with her for not informing him of her plans, but at this point, she couldn't see how the action would compromise her son's safety. A contingency plan was just that, right?

She caught Dylan's attention when she entered the kitchen. He was sitting at the kitchen table, his computer tablet in front of him and a half-eaten sandwich on a plate off to the side. He quickly clicked off the tablet, then stood and took the platter from her hands. Turning to the sink, he asked, "How are you holding up?"

"Wobbly," she answered honestly. She placed her cell phone down on the table and stared at it, willing the damn thing to ring.

It was several minutes later that the phone rang, and a wave of pain made its way up her spine. She looked quickly at Dylan. "Do I answer it now?" she asked, almost breathless.

He nodded, then quickly pulled out his own phone from his front pocket and placed it to his ear. "Give it two more rings. I'm already connected—he'll never know I'm on the line. Remember, pretend you don't know your son has been kidnapped, pretend law enforcement isn't involved and, above all, keep the person on the line as long as you can."

And ask for proof of life, she mentally added, sitting down on the kitchen chair as her knees threatened to buckle under her. Goose bumps raised the hairs on her arms—as if the kitchen had suddenly gone cold. But that wasn't it—fear for her son was sending her into shock. *Keep it under control,* she reminded herself. She focused on the cracked tile Jax had promised to repair so long ago. How convoluted she'd thought life was back then, back before her brother had made his huge mistake. She never could have imagined this scenario, though. Never could have anticipated how horribly worse things could have become.

The phone rang again and she brought her attention back to Dylan, who nodded. Time to act. She pressed the button to connect the call, then as cheerfully as she could muster, answered the phone with a breezy hello.

"Rachel Kincaid?" a man's hoarse voice sounded across the line. When she acknowledged her name, he continued. "We have your kid."

Delay, Dylan mouthed to her from across the table.

"Oh!" she exclaimed, forcing brightness into her tone. "You must be one of the volunteers! Thank you so much!" Across the table, Dylan was making a drawn-out signal with his hands. She continued jabbering, working to fill the time with inane words. Anything to keep the call going and help Dylan's team track the call. "He's not really a bad kid, you know, just a bit rambunctious, and impetuous. Doesn't really think before taking action. I suppose it's the ADHD—or maybe it's just being a boy. Where is he? Can I meet you somewhere?"

"Shut up," the man said harshly.

"Excuse me?" she said loudly, pretending affront. "Listen, you might want to get on your high horse and think I'm a bad mother for raising a kid who would run away and get an entire community upset, but that doesn't mean you get to tell me to shut up. Just put my son on the line and I'll figure out a way to get him back home." She glanced at Dylan, who smiled with lips pressed firmly together and held up two fingers. She'd done fine, but he needed two more minutes to get a trace on the phone.

"Your brat didn't run away," the man said. "He's been kidnapped."

A gasp tore its way out of her throat, and her heartbeat thundered in her head, blocking out sound. She struggled to remain upright. She no longer had to pretend—now she could be the panicked mother she truly was. "What do you mean? Is this some kind of joke? Why would you kidnap Peter, of all kids?"

"You have something we want, Ms. Kincaid. We'll give you your kid in exchange."

The money Jax had stolen. One million dollars.

"How much do you want?" she asked dully.

"Oh, we don't want money," the man said, with a sneer in his voice.

She frowned. They didn't want money? Wasn't this what everything had been about—chasing her off her land, trying to run her off the road, kidnapping Peter? Hadn't all this been put into place so George Evans could get his money back? "I don't understand," she said quietly.

"Your brother stole from me, Ms. Kincaid."

The man had used the word *me*. That meant she was speaking directly to George Evans—not even one of his flunkeys. "What did Jax steal from you? And how can I get something my brother stole back to you? Why don't you want money?"

"Stop asking questions. I don't just want the money your brother stole from me. I want the money and your brother. And you have twenty-four hours to get him and the money to me, or something very bad will happen to your kid."

"Peter!" she cried out. Sobs formed in the back of her throat. "Please don't hurt my son," she managed to choke out.

"Call the cops and the kid's dead."

An empty threat? Or the truth? Those members of this man's gang had already been tortured to death—an order made by the very man who held her son. Dylan made a violent gesture, catching her attention.

Oh, yes, proof of life. She needed to get herself under control and keep George Evans on the line—she needed proof that Peter was safe. She shoved the painful sobs down, deep, and willed her voice to work. "I won't go to the cops. But put Peter on the line. I'm not talking to you any more until I hear my son's voice."

But all she heard was empty space. George Evans had ended the call.

Without allowing her to hear her son's voice.

After the call from George Evans, Dylan managed to convince a shaky Rachel that they needed to act normal—whatever that might be. Evans might have members of his crew spying on Rachel's ranch, so he continued to play the part of Rachel's ranch hand and went outside to dig a grave for the two alpacas.

Rachel went with him.

"You don't have to be here, you know," he said to a quiet Rachel, who sat on a boulder next to where he was digging a large hole in the earth. They were about two hundred yards from the barn—in view of almost any angle of the surrounding area. He'd made sure both their cell phones had the full number of bars, and he'd tucked his computer tablet into a cloth bag Rachel had brought along.

"I know," she said, quietly. "But I want to be here when you bury them. They were my responsibility, and I failed them somehow. Just like I failed Josiah."

"Don't go there, Rachel. Their deaths were not your fault."

She closed her eyes and shook her head. "With everything going on, Josiah's funeral has been put off too long. It isn't right. I need to make sure the services are held in the next few days. I just hope..." Her face crumpled as she no doubt imagined other funerals she might have to attend if their plan to get Peter back safely didn't work.

"Rachel," he said, about to throw down the shovel and go to her, but she shook her head and blinked her tears away."

"No. No! You have to finish what you're doing. And I have to be strong. We're going to get through this okay. We all are."

As they stared at each other, Rachel gave him a trembling smile. He nodded. "Believe it, Rachel." Then he got back to digging.

Soon the day had faded and evening was almost upon

them. The sound of crickets surrounded them, and in the distance, frogs croaked out a sonorous song.

Under any other circumstances, the setting would be considered bucolic…beautiful. Romantic, even.

But not now. Not when the woman he loved was faced with the fact that she might never see her son again. His heart twisted up inside his chest, the ache he felt for Rachel making it almost impossible for him to breathe all of a sudden. Angrily, he shoved his foot down hard on the shovel, then lifted and flung the load of dirt up out of the pit and onto the pile nearby. He continued to work and had just finished burying the alpacas when Rachel's cell phone rang.

"Jax?" Rachel fought to keep her voice from trembling.

"I saw you on television, Rachel. Oh, God, is it true? Did they find him?" Her brother's voice sounded ravaged by fear and grief.

Nausea tore at her gut. Knowing George Evans had her son was one thing, telling her brother his nephew—her son—had been kidnapped was another. She wasn't sure she could make her throat work. Next to her, Dylan gave her a reassuring look. "Peter's been kidnapped."

"Oh, God! No!"

"Those people you got involved with?" she continued, "They know he's your nephew. They grabbed him at his grandparents' place and called me just a little while ago."

"They want the money," Jax said dully.

She hesitated before plowing forward. "They want you and the money, Jax. They want to trade Peter for you."

Silence met her statement. Worry added its unwanted presence to the nerves that were twisting her innards in knots. Why wasn't Jax saying anything? "Jax?" Her voice came out shaky. Uncertain.

"I'm so sorry," he finally said in a whisper. "I'd never have knowingly done anything to put you and Peter in danger. These people are bad, Rachel. Really bad. Once I get them the hidden cash, this will be all over. I'll trade myself for Peter, don't worry."

"But how?" George Evans hadn't told her how to exchange her brother for her son. And even though Dylan's team had a fix on the general location of the call Evans had made, no one knew for certain yet if the man was still at that location or if he'd moved on already. No one knew where Peter was.

She couldn't let Jax know about Dylan or the other marshals currently spying on the property. As much as she hated admitting it to herself, there was a part of her that didn't quite trust her brother fully.

"They'll find me. I promise, Rachel, that I won't tell them where I hid the money until Peter is safely back with you."

Wait—what did Jax mean, "tell them"? Didn't he have to go out to the property line and figure out where he'd buried the cash?

Realization hit. Her brother had known the location of the money all along.

"Oh, God," she breathed out, then clapped a hand over her own mouth. Her brother had lied to her. Had he actually run from Evans's men because he was afraid for his life, or had he run because he wanted to get to the money before George Evans could pry the location out of him? Anger spread through her, setting her limbs on fire. Jax wasn't the innocent victim she'd made him out to be. Dylan, with his caustic comments and jaded opinion of criminals, had pegged her brother more accurately than she.

What a fool she'd been.

All that money and time wasted on Julia's attempts to get Jax out on appeal. All that anguish Rachel had spent on thinking she'd not protected her brother enough. All the heartbreak thinking her brother was an innocent dupe—it had all been based on a lie.

Because her brother sure as hell knew what he'd been getting himself into when he took those drugs across state lines. And he sure as hell knew what he wanted when he ran from George Evans's men.

Jax wanted the money—for himself.

"Rachel?" her brother's voice sounded over the line, the same fear and worry apparent now as had been in his voice the day he called her at college to tell her their mom and dad were dead in their bed.

The sound of childlike fear in Jax's voice, reminding her of his innocent youth, just about broke her. Yes, Dylan was right—her brother was a criminal, and needed to pay his debt to society. But she was also right—Jax, as flawed as he was, was still her brother. Still a good person inside.

The fact that he was willing to sacrifice himself for her son proved the point. If he spoke the truth.

"Rachel, can you hear me?" Jax asked again.

"I'm here," she managed to get out.

"There's something else I need to ask you. I was hiding out behind the feed store just before you called and overheard Aaron Jacobson talking to someone on the phone. He was joking about loaning out Ginger to a city slicker—a guy pretending to be a bird-watcher. Aaron said that the man was really a U.S. Marshal. He figured the dude was out looking for me."

Rachel held her breath and looked frantically at Dylan, whose expression had gone grim. If her brother knew he'd go back to prison after the exchange, would he come back to the property? Would he risk his freedom for the life of her son?

"You aren't saying anything," Jax continued, his voice small. "I'm guessing that's the case, then, and the marshals are there, scoping out the place, waiting for me to come home."

"Jax," she whispered, anguish tearing at her chest. If her brother knew the feds were there, he'd run, and then her son— No! She couldn't think that. Couldn't bear to think of what could happen to Peter if her brother didn't cooperate.

"Sis, I'll do it," Jax said quickly. "I'll trade myself for Peter. But if the marshals are there, let me talk to them. I need to make sure they won't put me in custody until after you get Peter back, okay? I promise—I won't let anything happen to your boy. I—I—I—" He sputtered to a stop, then with a ragged breath, said, "I love him, too."

Dylan shifted, coming closer. He reached out a hand in a silent gesture for her to give him the phone.

Her stomach knotted and she began breathing in and out rapidly. Dare she trust him?

"Rachel," Dylan said, his voice a low murmur. "Trust me. I can help. This is what your brother wants, after all."

She looked up and held his gaze with hers. His eyes were soft, glistening, warm. Inside her mind, a sense of calm began to overtake the panic. Her heartbeat slowed and her breath came out in even puffs. She'd trusted this man with her son's life. Had trusted Dylan with her body, even. Had been prepared to trust him to bring her brother back into custody safely. What was different about now?

Nothing, really, she realized. Dylan was still the honorable man she'd fallen for. A man who did his duty, no matter what. He wasn't out to do her brother wrong—he was out to save the boys she loved. Peter. Jackson. A sob caught in the back of her throat. She trusted Dylan with Peter's life—she could trust him with the life of her brother. Silently she handed him the phone.

"Jackson, this is U.S. Marshal Dylan Rooney," he said, his voice even but a flashing pulse of tension shooting rhythmically through his jaw. "First, I want to commend you for doing right by your nephew. Second, I want you to know that your sister loves you very much. She's done everything she can to protect you from going back to prison, and she recognizes what a huge sacrifice you're making."

Rachel couldn't hear what her brother was saying to Dylan, but she could see Dylan's gaze flicker, his focus shifting from one point of the room to the other.

"We need to work together to come up with a plan, Jax," Dylan continued, his calm voice soothing. He cast his gaze at Rachel. "Hold on a second, Jax. I want to keep your sister out of this. This is between you and me."

"No!" Rachel exclaimed. "This is about my son. I have to be involved. Don't kick me out!" Her pulse pounded in her ears. How dare Dylan tell her he didn't want her involved? Didn't he understand what this meant to her?

"Rachel, you need to trust me. This is my job—getting Jax in custody, yes, but doing so in a way that there's no harm done to anyone is my priority. And I need to feel free to make whatever decisions need to be made without you here. God," he swore, wiping a hand across his face, "I can't think when you're around, Rachel. And I will not, I repeat, I will not compromise your son or your brother. You need to let me work with Jax alone."

Emotions made the inside of her chest swell. He couldn't concentrate with her around? The way he'd said it, with the mouthpiece covered so Jax couldn't hear, told her it was because of how he felt in his heart, and not because she was an irritation. He loved her—he'd told her so.

If only she could allow herself to love him back.

If only there wasn't a chasm the size of the Texas Panhandle between them.

But if giving him room to breathe, to think, was what it took to get her son back, she'd give him all of Texas if that was what he needed. Yes, she trusted him. Trusted the lawman. And it wasn't because she had to—because he was her only hope in finding her boy again. It was because she believed in him. Believed he'd get her boy home safe...even as he slapped cuffs on her brother.

She leaned in close so her brother could hear her voice over Dylan's phone. "I trust Marshal Rooney, Jax," she said. "You need to, too. Do what he says." She pulled back and looked full-on at Dylan. "He's in your hands now," she whispered, then fled.

Chapter 21

Dylan found Rachel down at the creek, sitting cross-legged on the wooden footbridge that went over the shallow depths. She was skipping stones across the lightly burbling surface. Nearby, a bullfrog sounded a mating call—a sound impossibly deep for something that small. Dylan found himself suddenly experiencing a tug inside himself, from a place in his heart he didn't even know existed.

God, he'd miss this place when he returned to California.

He'd miss the hill country in Texas, with its impossibly brilliantly painted bluebonnets, with its chirruping crickets and frogs. He'd miss the scent of the creek and the sound the rushes made as the breeze tickled down the creek bed. Miss the dappled patterns the willow branches made in the new green grass as they swayed in time. He'd miss the fluff ball alpacas, with their big dark eyes so full of innocence and wisdom. He'd miss Peter and his smart-ass ways.

Most of all, he'd miss Rachel.

How was it the widow had slid under his skin when he wasn't watching? How was it she practically lived inside him? How could he bear to cuff her brother, put him in the transport vehicle and drive off into the sunset…without Rachel?

They'd been at odds throughout all this. He realized, though, that when it got down to it, he'd been obstinate in how he viewed her. In controlling the lives of her brother and son, in not allowing them to make their own decisions and ultimately their own mistakes, she hadn't been acting as his mother had all those years ago with his brother. No, that had been his own interpretation of Rachel's actions. Yes, she probably could have used a less tight leash with both Jax and Peter. Could have let them make their way into the world. And maybe, just maybe, if she had, none of them would be in this position.

But he couldn't fault her. It had been Jackson's choice to get involved in drug dealing—that wasn't Rachel's fault. In trying to protect her boys, she'd been acting as a mama bear—furious and protective and full of courage.

In no way had she acted like his mother—passive and fearful.

Hell, he'd pegged her wrong since the beginning. Had set up a barbed-wire fence between the two of them from the start. And now it was too late for them to make anything of the passion that existed between them. He could apologize, sure, but that wouldn't be enough. Would never be enough. Rachel would always see him as the big bad U.S. Marshal who sent her brother back to prison.

And even if she didn't see him that way, that was how he'd see himself. He'd let his past interfere with his present. There was no way out now.

He stepped closer and Rachel tipped her head up, glancing at him. She paused midchuck, then turned her head away and resumed skipping stones.

"Can I ask if you and Jax came up with a plan?" she said.

Dylan sat down beside her, letting his feet dangle from the footbridge. He leaned forward until he could see their reflections in the water—him, tight and corded, and Rachel grim-faced and with a determined set to her jaw. He fought the temptation to reach out and stroke her hair and instead tucked his hands under his thighs, sitting on them. "You can ask..."

"But you can't tell me," she said, continuing his unspoken statement.

"It's better that way, Rachel. The team has a plan in place, and we don't want you in on it. We may need to do things that..." He couldn't finish the sentence. Couldn't so much as hint as to the plan he, Jax and his team had come up with. Had to trust that Jax would do the right thing.

And he did.

Trust Jax, that is. Strange, how he'd come to this remote ranch out in Texas seeing him only as a criminal, and now? Now he knew Jax to be a loving brother. A self-sacrificing uncle. A man of compassion and intelligence. Yes, Jackson had done wrong, and no, he wasn't the paragon of virtue the way Rachel thought, but he wasn't a bad seed, either.

"I understand," she said quietly, then dropped a stone down into the water instead of skipping it across the surface. They both watched as ripples radiated outward, each one strong and forceful at the apex, then softening and finally fading away the farther away they moved from the point of contact.

With evening fast approaching, Dylan could barely make out the ripples, could barely see his and Rachel's reflections in the water. In the distance, an owl hooted, the sound startling Rachel, who jumped.

"Time to go inside," he said, standing.

When he reached down to offer his hand to her, she looked at it for a moment, as if contemplating the meaning of placing her hand in his. Of touching him. Of allowing him to get close. Then, deliberately, she placed her hand in his.

The moment their hands made contact, electricity bolted from his hand through his arm, straight through to his heart. He pulled her up suddenly, before she could back away, and then held her there, pressed up close against his body, her heat blending with his, her breath on his face.

Oh, God. He knew better. Knew he shouldn't be getting this close. Shouldn't be about to kiss Rachel Kincaid. But he did, anyway. He kissed her. Long and slow and sweet, the sound of her mewling in the back of her throat carrying him along a river of desire. Sweeping him along in a current of heat and want and need and—

Rachel's phone rang. She pulled back, dazed, then fumbled with the pocket of her jeans, working her phone out of the tight constraints. By the time she held her phone in the palm of her hand, he already had his out and was ready to hit the button to connect his phone to hers.

"I don't recognize the number," she said, her voice shaky. "What do I do?"

"Answer it. Could be George Evans on a burner. Pick up the call on the next ring. I'll be on the line with you, okay?"

She swallowed, the long column of her neck going tight with worry, but clicked on the call on the next ring. He did so as well, and placed the phone to his ear. Stacy would be listening in, too, and that reassured him.

"Mom?" a small voice came over the line.

"Oh, God! Peter!" Rachel cried out. Her body shook violently. Dylan put an arm around her and held her steady. "Where are you? Are you safe? Does the bad man still have you?"

"Mom, I'm fine. I mean, yeah, I've been kidnapped and the guy's a jerk. He gave me a peanut butter and jelly sandwich on whole wheat bread, the kind with those stupid nuts. And he doesn't even have any video games. Um…hey, is Dylan there?"

Odd. The boy's voice had gone from tight but a bit laconic to high pitched when he asked for Dylan. What was that about?

"I'm here," Dylan said. "Peter, are you alone? Can you tell us where you are?"

"The jerk is right here with me. He wants me to tell you something really, really important, but I told him I only would if I— Ow!"

"Peter!" Rachel screamed into the phone, her face going white at the sound of her son in pain.

"I'm fine," Peter said, his voice tight. "I promised I'd

tell you his message but only if I got to thank Dylan for teaching me to shoot the BB gun the other day."

Rachel frowned. "Peter, when did you—"

Instantly Dylan reached out and pulled her phone away. She gasped, staring at his violent actions.

"What are you doing?" she ground out. "That's my son!"

He shook his head, narrowing his eyes at her and trying to convey the intensity of the moment through his eyes. She hadn't understood her kid's message. Peter had just given them two clues and Rachel was about to blow it. He brought his own phone back up to his mouth and said as calmly as he could, "Happy to teach you anytime, kid."

"Yeah, maybe next time we can do it in the dark."

Another clue.

"You got it. I appreciate you being a man. And for thinking the way you do." He could only hope Peter understood his cryptic way of conveying that he'd understood the boy's message. "Now, what was it the man wanted you to tell me?" He could hear murmuring in the background, and hoped to all that was holy that Stacy was getting a trace on the call.

"He says you know what he wants. Uncle Jax. You have until midnight tonight, or—"

The call cut off.

And Rachel fell apart.

"Oh, God, no!" Rachel heard herself screaming and realized she was pounding Dylan's hard chest with her fists as the tears streaming down her face blinded her. "What kind of sick bastard would do this? Kidnap a child and threaten to…to…" The rest of the words wouldn't come out of her mouth. But Dylan had to know what she was saying—he had to. How he could stand there, calm, rubbing his hands in circles on her back, seemed almost illogical when her own hands were shaking no matter how tightly she clenched them and her knees threatened to give way under her like the banks of a flooded creek.

And yet even as she didn't understand Dylan's emotionless state, she craved his strength. Craved his comfort. Slowly the sobs racking her body subsided, until she was left emotionally drained, sniffling against Dylan's warm chest. She fought to gain her senses, to make her mind work. She had to figure out what to do now—but no plan came forward no matter how hard she scrabbled her mind.

"Why didn't you let me talk to him?" she asked, her voice hitching.

"Rachel, there are parts of my job I can't share with you. And I know this is tough. Awful. Horrible, even. But I need your strength now. I know you have it— I've watched you over the last few days. You're strong."

"It's here," she said, knowing she needed to stand on her own two feet but not yet backing away from his warm embrace. "I'm here. I can function. Just tell me what you need to save my son." She paused, then added, "But I'm not sure my legs are working right."

Suddenly he swept her up in his arms, apparently uncaring of the fact that they'd essentially ended any possibility of happiness together hours earlier. There might be no future there, but she needed him, and he'd responded.

Within minutes he'd followed the path from the creek back up to the house, and settled her down on the ancient leather couch in the living room. There, she curled her feet under her as he wrapped her up in a faded and frayed quilt, made by one of her pioneer ancestors. He squatted and sat on his heels in front of her. She noted he seemed careful not to touch her. She'd gone stiff when he scooped her up but hadn't resisted him carrying her. He'd gotten the message she was trying to send him, though—it was okay for him to touch her if she needed the help, but not in any romantic way. That was over and done, and she needed to put it behind her in order to get her son.

But there seemed to be nothing she could do to get Peter. Nothing. She felt helpless—without any control.

"You okay?" he asked.

She nodded but kept her gaze fixed to the floor in front of her, unable to look at him. No, of course she wasn't okay. She was powerless—the sensation ate at her. Clawed around inside her, twisting up her insides. She'd already set up the sale of her land and assets, but money wasn't what George Evans wanted. There was nothing else for her to do.

But wait.

"Stacy was patched into that call, too, and she's probably already doing her thing, trying to trace the call, but I should go into the tack room and connect with the team, anyway."

"I understand."

"You okay here on your own? Want me to get someone to take you to stay with your friend Julia while we...wait?"

"No." The fewer people involved the better. "You should go," she said abruptly. "I'm counting on you. We all are. Fix this, Dylan." The harshness of her voice surprised her, but when she cast a glance at Dylan, he seemed unfazed. How many times had he experienced something like this? she had to wonder. As a marshal, he was tasked to apprehend fugitives, not placate panicking mothers of kidnap victims. But he seemed to take everything in stride—even this.

A muscle on the side of his face flickered, and he stood. "I'll be in the barn. And, Rachel? You can do this. I know waiting must be incredibly hard for you right now, but that's the best thing you can do for your son. Wait, and let us handle this."

She watched him leave, a sense of calm settling down the urgency that had been churning inside her. Dylan was right. It wasn't that she had nothing to do—it was that what she must do was nothing. The sensation was foreign. Alien. After years of being the sole provider, the decision maker, the one holding the reins of her brother and son's lives, she now had to let go and trust others.

Her breath caught in her throat, and her heart fluttered in her chest—not from panic over the situation, but over knowing she trusted Dylan Rooney completely.

"Listen up," Dylan said to the several screens in the makeshift office in the tack room. All of his team members were on one of the screens, anxious faces gazing back at him. "We can't blow this. This comes down to trusting two people who haven't proven to be very trustworthy in the past, who have issues with law enforcement. Plus one of those people is a ten-year-old kid. The other person is the escaped fugitive we've been tasked to bring back into custody. And he knows we're after him. But this is all we've got, and that kid's life hangs in the balance."

"You sure we can trust these two?" Eric asked, worry etching his forehead. "Especially Jackson Kincaid—he's probably aware Evans is out to kill him. We already know George Evans is fully capable of killing a kid—after all, he'd had his own crew members tortured and killed when they couldn't deliver."

Dylan grimaced. Hell. He'd been in tough situations before, but this? Trying to rescue Peter—a boy he'd grown to admire in just a few days, a boy whose mother he loved? This bordered on impossible. He shoved the panic churning about in his stomach down low, forcing it away. No time for panic. No room for error.

"Uh, Dylan?" Stacy said.

He refocused, cleared his throat and said, "Thankfully Evans had the kid call with the ransom demand. From what I understood the kid was saying, he can escape once it gets dark, and he wants us to find him. I already know where—at the spring where we found the ranch hand's murdered body."

"You got that from the kid while Evans was right next to him?" Stacy asked, her skepticism clear by how she cocked one eyebrow.

"Kid's smart," he responded. "Really smart. Even his own mother didn't hear what he was really saying. He said I taught him how to shoot a BB gun—a clear indication that what he was saying was a message to me. I never taught him how to shoot. But I did see him shooting it by the spring. Now we just have to wait until dark."

"He's got to be close by," Stacy said, "if he's going to make it to the spring."

"That's what's so great about the kid's message—we can implement the plan we set up with Jax more securely once we know Peter is safe. I figure Evans probably has him stashed on the neighboring property, but we have no clue where. This is Texas—properties are thousands of acres. We have to wait for the kid to come to us before we get Jax involved. There's no way I trust Evans to turn over Peter after he gets Jax." Dylan turned to look at the computer screen with Eric's face on it. "You got men in the trees out at the spring yet?" At Eric's nod, he added, "And what about the bullet-proof vest—you put that in the cache site where Jax can pick it up?"

"Vest is at the site, along with a burner phone with our numbers plugged in, and vice versa. The intel Jax passed on to you was right—there's an underground tunnel from during the Mexican-American war days that leads from the cliffs down under the field and comes out just near the house. He'll pick up the vest and phone and gun at the start of the tunnel, then will come out at the base and wait for our call. He assures us the tunnel is traversable—guess we'll have to take his word for it."

There was a lot of trust going on for a man who'd spent time behind bars. Dylan shoved his hand in his hair and blew out a breath. "No other options. We need Jax as close to the house as we can get, and we need him in cell range."

"Sir, are you sure you don't want to let Rachel Kincaid know what's going on? After all, it's her son we're in the middle of rescuing. And we're not, you know, the FBI. This isn't what we're trained for." Stacy's voice held respect but came out tight and worried.

Damn FBI. The team they'd sent had been waylaid when their private jet blew a tire partway down the runway. Because of the strewn rubber and steel mesh scattered about the tarmac, the runway had been closed. Although the FBI had been in constant contact with Stacy once they'd all learned of the kidnapping, their "help" hadn't been all that helpful.

"We can't involve Rachel," he said. "Not in this, at least. She has a habit of controlling the situation out of an attempt to help. We can't have that— We need to trust our training, our judgment and our instincts. Also, it's possible that she could react the wrong way, and if Evans is watching when we 'give' him Jackson, she might give the game away. She needs to stay in the dark."

"I just hope you're right about what you say the kid was trying to tell you," Stacy said. "And I hope you're right about Jackson Kincaid."

So did he. Everything that mattered in the world now rested on the shoulders of a criminal.

Chapter 22

Rachel busied herself in the house, doing nothing, besides tidying up a few dishes, answering emails about her alpacas and tallying receipts for her recent wool sales. Three hours had passed slowly, punctuated by the solemn ticktock of the hall clock. Night had fallen hours ago, and yet Dylan remained in the barn, presumably making arrangements to get her son back. And to save her brother.

Now, all the puttering she could force herself to do thoroughly completed, she sat on the bench at the kitchen table and sipped a cup of Earl Grey tea. The warm drink wasn't enough to keep her from shuddering, even though the house was warm. Two nights ago the temperatures had been nippy. That was springtime in Texas's hill country, though. Once the sun warmed the land, the land retained the heat at night. The cattle and alpacas would be comfortable from now on until autumn dropped the temperatures back down. No need for a barn for Aaron Jacobson's pregnant cattle. She wondered what he'd done with those who'd been close to calving since he'd lost the use of the pasture with the larger barn because of the vandalism.

Oh, God. She sat upright, worried excitement shooting adrenaline through her body. She knew where Peter was being kept. No wonder Dylan had pulled her off the call when Peter appeared to be lying. Her son wasn't fabricating some story. No, he'd been giving them clues. Clues where he was, what he'd be doing. Dylan had recognized her son's attempts, even when she hadn't.

She ran through Peter's words in her mind. If she had the clues Peter had given pieced together correctly, he was being held in a location close enough to get to the spring where they'd found Josiah's body. Somehow he had information that made her believe he could get away sometime in the dark. He'd surreptitiously informed Dylan where the marshals could find him after he escaped.

And she knew where that location was. Where he was being held.

But the question was, did Dylan know, too?

Dylan entered the house and was almost bowled over by a wide-eyed Rachel. "Steady," he said, holding her by the shoulders when she stumbled after charging into him. "Don't go outside now. We have everything in place."

"I know where they're keeping Peter!" she exclaimed.

He propelled her backward and kicked the door shut with his foot. His team assumed Evans and his crew were now on the property, watching their every move. The last thing they needed was a panicked Rachel trying to take control and blowing the whole operation.

"What do you mean you know where they're keeping him?" he asked.

"You thought Jax caused that stampede, to get me off the property so he could get the money without being seen by even me."

He didn't deny it.

"But it was George Evans, I'm sure of it. You marshals all knew where Jax was headed and set up your own sting operation. Why wouldn't Evans have done the same? And I know where he would have hid out— or where he would have stationed people. Aaron Jacobson's barn, the one in the pasture that had the fence line cut."

He froze. "Are you sure?"

"It's where Peter used to hide out, before I figured out it was his go-to place. Peter knows the place inside and out— If Evans and his crew are holding him there, he knows how to escape. He told you he was going to escape, right? That's what he was saying when you tore the phone from my hand. Don't deny it—I know it's true."

Instead of responding to Rachel, he pulled out his phone from his pocket. Instantly Stacy's face appeared on his screen. "You get that?" he asked.

"Got it and on it already," she said, her gaze focused on her own computer screen and the sound of her fingers hitting the keyboard coming through clearly. "Eric's routing a few marshals out there—don't worry, they'll be in silent mode. These guys are good. You and the farm girl make a great team, by the way."

He cast a quick glance back at Rachel. Yes, they did make a great team.

He clicked off the call with Stacy.

"You wired my place?" Rachel asked.

He nodded. "The day before. The whole house, actually. Stacy and the rest of the team have full access."

"You didn't need a warrant?"

Probably. Maybe. He'd been invited onto the property, though, and Rachel knew he was out to apprehend her brother. When bad things kept happening, he'd added the extra safety features.

"Rachel, things are going to happen suddenly now. I need you to trust that I'm doing the right thing, okay?"

"You're not going to tell me the plan?"

"No. After, I'll explain why."

"Just get my son back safe and make sure that bastard doesn't torture and kill my brother. That's all I ask."

"You know I can't promise anything. I won't lie to you and give you false hope. All I can do is tell you my team is good. Solid. We know what we're doing. Trust me with this plan."

A sudden rustling outside told him the plan already started.

Rachel turned and gaped at the figure outside on the porch. "Jax!" The word came out hollow, almost silent.

Dylan reached out and grabbed her arms again, holding her in place. "You can't go to him, Rachel. Do you understand?"

"No!" she cried, twisting to get out of his grip. "I don't understand. Where's my son? Jax can't trade himself without Peter being present. Are your people out at the barn yet? Are they?" The last sentence had been ripped from her lungs and thrown in his face.

He hated himself for doing what he was about to do but forced the word from his mouth. "No."

"Jax! Jax!" she screamed again.

Her brother turned to look at her but remained where he was on the porch, at the very tip where it jutted out and was visible from the north, west and east. Jax, his face so very young, his stance so vulnerable that Dylan could see why his sister had fought to protect him for so long, gave Rachel a soft, sweet smile and tipped his head to the side.

As if he were saying he was sorry.

As if he were saying goodbye.

Rachel sobbed, her mouth going wide but no sound coming out. Dylan's phone rang, and he let go of her, whispering, "Stay still" even as he clicked the call on.

On the other end of the line, Stacy confirmed what he'd hoped to hear. Had needed to hear. It was time.

"Go!" he shouted, and hoped that in time, Rachel would forgive him for what he'd just done.

Chapter 23

Rachel couldn't seem to move, and instead watched helplessly, her gaze firmly fixed to that of her brother, as marshals swarmed the porch. Men and women in tactical gear had materialized from the shadows around the house and were now training their weapons on her brother.

Who stood stock-still, still smiling at her. She knew that smile. It was the sweet one, the smile he used only when looking at her or Peter. It was the same smile he used to have when their mother gave him a snuggly hug, or their father patted him on the back and told him job well done. It was Jax's smile. And she loved him for it.

"Get behind me!" Dylan shouted, grabbing her by the arm and propelling her backward to block her with his body.

She lost visual contact with Jax as she stumbled and

almost came to her knees. Gaining her balance, she peered from behind Dylan's wide shoulders, visually searching for her brother again. There. He still stood on the edge of the porch the way he had just a moment before, but now there was something in his hands. Something small and shiny and black.

Oh, God, no.

Jax had a gun.

And was raising it. Pointing it. Squeezing the trigger.

A percussive boom rent the air and suddenly her brother was jerking in time and space and her world was falling apart.

She collapsed, hitting the tile hard, a sharp edge gouging into her knee. The tile Jax had promised to fix the day before he'd taken off for California to transport heroin. On hands and knees, she shook, sobbing, aware of the blood trickling from her knee and blooming, coating the broken tile red.

No. Her brother had so much to live for. Why would he have chosen to die—to shoot at law enforcement? He had to have known he'd be shot dead if he so much as raised a gun at one of the marshals. Didn't he know what pain he'd be leaving behind by making that choice? Had he felt so trapped he thought death was his only escape?

And what about Peter?

Jax could not possibly have given up on his nephew. She couldn't believe that.

She reached up and grabbed the kitchen table, the worn wood warm under her cold fingers. With effort, she pulled herself to standing, then tried to push past a silent Dylan.

"I can't let you go out there," he said quietly.

Outside, marshals buzzed around, placing Jax's limp

form in a black body bag. Rachel gagged. What kind of sick bastards brought a body bag to a kidnap exchange?

"Why did you have to shoot him?" she railed at him. "That was suicide by cop. He felt cornered. Trapped. As if he had no way out. Why didn't you convince him he'd be safe?"

"You'll understand soon," he said. "My task was to apprehend your brother. But my first priority was making sure your son came home safe."

"Right," she spat out. "And how'd that turn out? Peter is still in the clutches of a torturer, and my brother's dead!"

"Rooney!" a male voice called from outside on the porch. Eric. "You're needed—now!"

Rachel couldn't believe Dylan was walking away from her. He pulled open the door and shouldered his way past a couple of marshals in field jackets to join a marshal on the corner of the porch. She recognized the man as Eric, one of Dylan's team. His stupid team. His incompetent team. Why had she trusted them? They'd killed her brother. Their actions might even kill her son, if Peter wasn't dead already.

Somehow she made her feet move. Made her legs work. And followed Dylan out to the porch. Why? She didn't know. She simply couldn't believe this was over. Couldn't fathom her brother was dead and her son was God knows where. Didn't know if Peter was alive or dead.

"We found him," Eric said to Dylan in a hushed voice. "He was right where you said he'd be."

Rachel crept closer, her heartbeat so hard and pounding it echoed in her ears, but she knew what she'd heard—they'd found Peter. But alive?

"In the barn on the neighboring property?" Dylan asked.

"Yep. The team's bringing him here now." Eric nodded at the SUV that had just arrived.

Oh, God, he had to be alive. Rachel hugged the side of the house, trying to stay out of sight, but headlights swept the area, illuminating her. Dylan noticed she had come outside and was standing next to him.

"Rachel, go back inside," he demanded.

"No," she managed to get out. "I want to see Peter."

"You don't understand, that's not—"

But Rachel had torn from his grasp and was running down the length of the porch, toward the SUV. Alive? Would she find him alive, or…God, she couldn't even think the word. Couldn't bear it.

"Rachel!" Dylan yelled.

The car door opened, and a figure exited the vehicle. A man. Rachel halted. He was tall, well dressed and in handcuffs. A marshal followed him out, then slammed the door shut. Not Peter, then. Where was her son?

Rachel turned back to face Dylan. "Who is that, and where is my son?"

"The little punk-assed kid?" the man behind her said.

She whipped back around. Realization hit her hard. Made her stagger. She knew who this had to be. "Oh, God. You're George Evans. You took my son. Where is he?" she asked, her voice low and throaty.

"You'll never find the kid." He sneered. "And I'll never tell where he is. He'll die, only unlike his uncle—" George Eliot nodded to the inert body wrapped in black vinyl at the edge of the porch "—he'll die slowly. Know how horrible it is to die from lack of water?"

Bile rose in her throat and for a moment her stomach heaved, but she managed to remain upright. "You bastard."

"You and your idiot brother screwed with the wrong man."

Dylan stepped between her and the man, Eric beside him. "Rachel, go with Eric and get back in the house. I'll explain everything in a minute, but not here."

"Yes, widow Rachel, go back inside," George Evans mimicked. "There's nothing for you here, anyway. No brother, no son…"

No! Rage filled her. Consumed her. Set her on fire and stopped her from thinking. The world in front of her blurred…all but one object. A black, shiny object on Eric's hip. As if the world had stopped spinning and time had frozen in place, Rachel saw her hand reach out. Felt the cold metal under her fingers. Hefted the weight and raised the gun.

Aimed at George Evans and placed her finger on the trigger.

Dimly, she could hear the ringing of a phone over the roar of anger in her head. In the back pocket of her jeans, her phone vibrated. And over the sound of the ring was Dylan's voice, shouting at her to put down the gun. To answer her phone.

Why should she take a damn call when all she wanted to do was shoot the man who'd caused the death of her brother and maybe the death of her son?

"Rachel! Listen to me. You are a good mother. You were right to believe in your brother. Believe in him and your son."

The world still whirled around her, but she could make out Dylan's words. Why, though, was he talking about her parenting?

"You're not a killer, Rachel. No more than your brother is. Answer the phone, Rachel. Grab hold of that control that keeps you so strong and put the gun down. Take the call."

Dylan thought she was a good mother? That she'd done right by her brother and son? That her brother wasn't all bad, the way he'd originally thought?

Still holding the gun pointed at George Evans, she reached behind her and slid her phone out of her pocket. The man wasn't going anywhere. But the call was important to Dylan. And Dylan was important to Rachel.

She was better with him.

She trusted him.

She believed him.

She let him take control.

Pressing the accept key, she held the phone up to her ear.

"Mom?"

The gun tumbled to the ground and Rachel followed it, going to her knees for the second time in the day. She couldn't speak. Could only rock back and forth, silently crying as she cradled the phone to her ear and heard the excited, happy voice of her son.

Vaguely, she was aware that Evans was stuffed back into his car and driven off. Then Dylan was there.

"Rachel, look." Dylan had bent to his knees and had wrapped his arms around her. His strong, warm arms. He pointed back to the house, to the porch.

She twisted, still holding the phone firmly to her

ear, and watched as the second miracle of the night occurred.

Jax stepped out of the body bag.

Alive.

Chapter 24

Back inside the house, seated on the couch in the living room, Rachel sat between Dylan and her brother as they talked through the wild events that had just occurred.

"So you were shot with blanks?" she asked, seeking clarification.

Jax nodded. "I had what are called squabs inside my shirt. Someone else pressed a remote control button when the guns were fired, and the squabs went off, squirting out red gel." He grinned. "Pretty cool, huh?"

She shuddered. "Why pretend to die, though? I mean, Jax, they put you in a body bag!"

"So I can enter Witness Protection. The marshal here—" he nodded to Dylan "—said they'd capture George Evans alive. But the dude's one sick jerk, and he has connections everywhere. I wouldn't be safe unless he thought I was dead."

Rachel turned to Dylan. "So you had a plan to capture Evans but made sure it would keep Jax safe, not just in the present but in the future."

Dylan cleared his throat. "Of course, Rachel. I told you I'd do whatever it took to keep you safe. That included keeping your son and brother safe, too. Because they mean everything to you. You'd never be safe unless they were. And none of you would be safe if Evans thought he could still get to Jax through you or Peter. I'm just grateful Jax was willing to take the risks he did and help us. Thank you."

The last words he spoke directly to Jax, and Rachel was pleased to see her brother duck his chin and give the shy smile she used to see on his face when their father paid him a compliment. Yes, her brother was flawed. Wasn't perfect. But in the end, her parents—and she— had raised him right.

"And no one thought of informing me about this dramatic plan?" she asked.

Dylan shifted, settling her more firmly against his chest. "We needed Evans to be convinced your brother was dead. Your reactions needed to be sincere. Believable. And they were. Even though Evans wasn't on the property, he had someone videotaping it and transmitting it live. He was convinced enough to walk outside the barn to make his escape—and walked right into the arms of the marshals who were thronging the place."

"Had you figured out where he was hiding before I told you?" she asked, tipping her head up so she could see Dylan's face.

"Nope. You gave us the key information we needed. And we were able to surround the barn and take out a

few of his crew before he walked outside. Easy capture."
He smiled, his eyes crinkling at the edges.

"But I thought you weren't going to exchange Jax
until Peter was safe," she said, worrying the corner of
her lip with her teeth.

"We held off on having Jax show himself until after
we had Peter safe. That's the call I got—my team had
found him at the spring. Once we knew your son was
safe, I gave the order for the fake suicide by cop."

"You did great," she murmured to her brother. "I'll
forever be thankful for what you did to save Peter."

"Speaking of," Jax said, looking around, "where is
the little squirt?"

"About five minutes away," Dylan said. "A few of
the marshals are bringing him here. Apparently he's a
bit wet and muddy. Thanks to Peter's cunning, he escaped the storage cabinet in the barn where Evans had
stashed him. And thanks to his quick thinking, we knew
where to go to find him."

"At the spring," Rachel said quietly.

"Yes. At the spring. Which, by the way…" Dylan
cleared his throat and looked hard at Jax.

"You find the money there?" Jax asked, his eyes
wide and innocent.

"The briefcase was there, all right," Dylan said.
"Money's a bit soggy from being stashed in a spring,
of all places, but we have it in custody now. Thanks for
turning it over to the authorities."

"It's all there. I didn't take any of it. Not even a C-
note. When the guns went blasting during the raid, I
ducked and hid. I saw the briefcase. Knew it had the
money, so I grabbed it and slid out of the building
through a ground-level vent."

"And came home to hide the money on our property." Rachel couldn't help the stern tone in her voice. Yes, she'd thought her brother had been killed and was relieved beyond measure to see him alive, but he never should have subjected her or Peter to drug money.

Jax dropped his gaze and lowered his head. "Yeah, I know. You taught me better, sis. But I was still being stupid. I—I wanted that money. Wanted us all to have a better life. I've had a year to contemplate my stupidity in prison. Believe me, I've learned my lesson."

"I want to believe you," Rachel said, "but one thing I don't understand. Why didn't you ever just tell me all of this, Jax? About the money? Why didn't you ever tell the cops? I mean, if you'd truly learned your lesson and the money didn't matter anymore...why did you lie and tell me you couldn't remember where you'd buried it?"

Rachel hated the confusion and mistrust she heard in her voice, hated the shadow of guilt that crept over her brother's face, but Dylan had been right. She couldn't take responsibility for everything. If she and her brother were ever going to have any type of relationship again, she had to confront him about his mistakes and make sure he was willing to do right by her.

"Rachel," he began, but then they heard the thumping of footsteps on the porch just as the door flew open.

"Mom! Uncle Jax!"

Peter flew at them like a missile, throwing his arms around her and Jax. Rachel wrapped her arms around her son and sobbed with relief. She sprinkled kisses on his face, telling him over and over again how happy she was that he was safe. It was only when she pulled back and swiped at the tears running down her face that she realized that her son was crying, too. That Dylan and

Jax were crying. And that Peter was even including Dylan in his embrace.

Rachel's tears started flowing again when she saw that Dylan was hugging her son back just as fiercely.

"You did great, kid. I'm glad you're safe," he said.

"Thanks," Peter said. With a grin, but without letting go of Dylan or Rachel, he turned to Jax. "So, how many songs have you written since you've been gone?"

They all laughed.

Dylan rose and whispered to Rachel that he was going to give her and Jax some alone time with Peter but that he'd be close by. After squeezing her hand, he let go and walked to the other side of the room, where he began to talk to his teammate Eric.

They gave them almost an hour, enough time for Rachel and Jax to put Peter to bed before returning downstairs. Then, his eyes shadowed with regret, Dylan explained it was time for Jax to go. Eric would be taking Jax back into federal custody. Jax hugged Rachel and told her he loved her.

Before he left, however, he gave them one more bit of shocking news.

He explained that he had lied to Rachel about not knowing where the money was buried. The only reason he'd done so, however, was that he hadn't been sure whether her phone had been wired. Or who'd be listening.

As it turned out, Jax had had good reason to think not just Rachel's phone, but her computer and her entire house might have been wired, which was why he'd refused to speak to her at all after he was sent to prison. After Evans's men broke Jax out of prison, Jax had been running from Evans and his men, but they weren't the only people he feared might try to hurt Rachel and Peter. While it was Evans's money that Jax had stolen and Evans who'd broken Jax out of prison, there was another threat that had been lurking near Rachel all along—Sheriff Ryan, the man who'd hired Jax to deliver the drugs to Evans in the first place. Right before he took Jax into custody and handed him over to the DEA, he'd warned Jax not to say anything to anyone about his involvement, saying he had eyes and ears on Rachel and Peter and would make sure they died if Jax didn't listen to him.

To be safe, Jax hadn't uttered a single word about the sheriff's involvement. And in the likely event the man knew Jax had escaped and was headed to the ranch to retrieve Evans's money, Jax had sent Rachel that first email, worded so strangely because he'd wanted to deliver a message in case the sheriff was tracking her messages.

As Jax had explained himself, Rachel had retrieved the email and shown it to Dylan.

I ran. I swear I didn't shoot those men. As long as you and Peter are safe on the ranch, I'm coming. We can work out a deal. I'm coming home, but promise on the memory of Mom and Dad you won't tell anyone. Love, Jax.

As she reread the email, Rachel saw the message Jax had intended to send the sheriff—that someone else had shot the marshals, that he was coming home but wasn't planning on ratting the sheriff out, and that they could make a deal—so long as Peter and Rachel remained safe. In Jax's mind, his best bet for making any kind of deal, whether it was with Evans, Ryan or the cops, was by staying free and getting hold of Evans's money. But at the same time, he couldn't let Rachel know any of that in case Sheriff Ryan was listening.

"It turns out the sheriff was lying," Dylan explained after Jax left and just minutes after he made a call to have Sheriff Ryan brought in for questioning. "We found no evidence that your house had been wired before we got here. But the fact that Jax took such care with you, and that email message he sent you, shows how much he loves and cares for you. Yes, he made mistakes, but you're right, Rachel, there's nothing that you can't all work through so you can be a family again."

When he said the words, there was both happiness for her and sadness for himself in his eyes. She knew what that meant. That he didn't think the same thing applied to himself. What his brother had done wasn't something that Dylan was ready to forgive and move beyond…yet.

"You and your brother haven't seen each other in a long time, Dylan. I'm not saying you can forgive him, but maybe someday, you'll be able to see him. Talk to him."

He smiled and smoothed his thumb across her cheek. "Maybe. I could see you being strong enough to do that. To hope it might make a difference. But I'm not sure I'll be able to."

She reached out and took his free hand. "What are you talking about? You're a U.S. Marshal. You're braver than any man I know. *Better* than any man I've ever met. Plus…"

She hesitated and he squeezed her hand tighter. "What?"

"Well, if you think it would help, I could always go with you. To see him, I mean. If you ever wanted that."

"You'd do that for me?"

"Of course. I love you, remember?"

When he didn't reply right away, fear began to creep in. Had she misread him? Much had happened between them from the time when he'd first voiced his feelings. Had he changed his mind about her? Or was he worrying about other things? Struggling to imagine their lives intertwining? He lived in California, and as willing as she'd been to exchange all her livestock for her son's safety, she couldn't imagine not tending to the land that had been in her family for six generations.

"Rachel," he said, his voice serious.

Scared, she interrupted him. "My life is a mess. I have issues. My brother and Peter have issues. We're flawed and we're going to continue to make mistakes. But we can make things work, Dylan. I know we can."

Dylan frowned. "Of course we can."

"But…why are you frowning? Why haven't you said…" She bit her lip.

He pulled her in for a hug. "God, I'm sorry. I was just thinking about my brother. What you said about visiting him. I can't promise that will ever happen, Rachel, even knowing how important family is to you. But you have to know how much I love you. That will never change."

Relief flooded through her.

So there it was. That easily, he'd reassured her. Her doubts floated away. Because Dylan Rooney was a good man. A good man who kept his word and had promised to keep Rachel and her family safe.

Her love wasn't dependent on him reuniting with his brother. That was his decision and always would be. He'd kept her safe, and she'd spend her whole life proving to him that she intended to do the same for him. She'd be a safe harbor for his heart.

Always.

"So are you saying I might not need to hire a handsome stud to muck out my stalls anytime soon?"

He gave a mock growl as he swept her up in his arms. "I'm saying that as a marshal, I can work out of Texas just as easily as California. I'll travel, and be gone for a few days at a time, but I'll always come back to you. And it will make our reunions all the more exciting. I'm also saying you can hire anyone you want to muck out your stalls so long as you only have eyes for me."

She laughed. "Well, that's no problem. But be warned. I'm not just going to have my eyes all over you."

"Is that right?"

"That's right. Because I love you, too, Dylan Rooney. I might not have known it when you came riding up on your horse, but you're better than any knight in shining armor. You're a U.S. Marshal and I'm just so happy that not only did you get your man this time, you got your woman, too."

* * * * *

Tamara Owens is supposed to be finding the person stealing from her father. But when she meets prime suspect Flint Collins—and his new charge, Diamond— she can't bear to pull away, despite her tragic past. Will Flint be able to look past her lies to make them a family by Christmas?

Read on for a sneak preview of the next book in The Daycare Chronicles,
An Unexpected Christmas Baby
by USA TODAY bestselling author Tara Taylor Quinn.

How hadn't he heard her first knock?

And then she saw the carrier on the chair next to him. He'd been rocking it.

"What on earth are you doing to that baby?" she exclaimed, nothing in mind but to rescue the child in obvious distress.

"Damned if I know," he said loudly enough to be heard over the noise. "I fed her, burped her, changed her. I've done everything they said to do, but she won't stop crying."

Tamara was already unbuckling the strap that held the crying infant in her seat. She was so tiny! Couldn't have been more than a few days old. There were no tears on her cheeks.

"There's nothing poking her. I checked," Collins said, not interfering as she lifted the baby from the seat, careful to support the little head.

It wasn't until that warm weight settled against her that Tamara realized what she'd done. She was holding a baby. Something she couldn't do.

She was going to pay. With a hellacious nightmare at the very least.

The baby's cries had stopped as soon as Tamara picked her up.

"What did you do?" Collins was there, practically touching her, he was standing so close.

"Nothing. I picked her up."

"There must've been some problem with the seat, after all…" He'd tossed the infant head support on the desk and was removing the washable cover.

"I'm guessing she just wanted to be held," Tamara said. What the hell was she doing?

Tearless crying generally meant anger, not physical distress. And why did Flint Collins have a baby in his office?

She had to put the child down. But couldn't until he put the seat back together. The newborn's eyes were closed and she hiccuped and then sighed.

Clenching her lips for a second, Tamara looked away. "Babies need to be held almost as much as they need to be fed," she told him while she tried to understand what was going on.

He was checking the foam beneath the seat cover and the straps, too. He was fairly distraught himself.

Not what she would've predicted from a hard-core businessman possibly stealing from her father.

"Who is she?" she asked, figuring it was best to start at the bottom and work her way up to exposing him for the thief he probably was.

He straightened. Stared at the baby in her arms, his brown eyes softening and yet giving away a hint of what looked like fear at the same time. In that second she wished like hell that her father was wrong and Collins wouldn't turn out to be the one who was stealing from Owens Investments.

Don't miss
An Unexpected Christmas Baby *by Tara Taylor Quinn,*
available November 2018 wherever
Harlequin® Special Edition books and ebooks are sold.

www.Harlequin.com

⊞ HARLEQUIN®

SPECIAL EDITION

Life, Love and Family

Save **$1.00**

on the purchase of ANY
Harlequin® Special Edition book.

Available wherever books are sold,
including most bookstores, supermarkets,
drugstores and discount stores.

Save $1.00

on the purchase of any Harlequin® Special Edition book.

Coupon valid until December 31, 2018.
Redeemable at participating outlets in the U.S. and Canada only.
Limit one coupon per customer.

52615971

Canadian Retailers: Harlequin Enterprises Limited will pay the face value of this coupon plus 10.25¢ if submitted by customer for this product only. Any other use constitutes fraud. Coupon is nonassignable. Void if taxed, prohibited or restricted by law. Consumer must pay any government taxes. Void if copied. Inmar Promotional Services ("IPS") customers submit coupons and proof of sales to Harlequin Enterprises Limited, P.O. Box 31000, Scarborough, ON M1R 0E7, Canada. Non-IPS retailer—for reimbursement submit coupons and proof of sales directly to Harlequin Enterprises Limited, Retail Marketing Department, Bay Adelaide Centre, East Tower, 22 Adelaide Street West, 40th Floor, Toronto, Ontario M5H 4E3, Canada.

U.S. Retailers: Harlequin Enterprises Limited will pay the face value of this coupon plus 8¢ if submitted by customer for this product only. Any other use constitutes fraud. Coupon is nonassignable. Void if taxed, prohibited or restricted by law. Consumer must pay any government taxes. Void if copied. For reimbursement submit coupons and proof of sales directly to Harlequin Enterprises, Ltd 482, NCH Marketing Services, P.O. Box 880001, El Paso, TX 88588-0001, U.S.A. Cash value 1/100 cents.

HSECOUP04505